Critical acclaim for award winning author
T.L. Williams debut novel, Cooper's Revenge

T. L. Williams's debut novel, Cooper's Revenge,
is 2013 President's Book Awards Winner.
Florida Authors and Publishers Association

"T.L. Williams shows himself a master at detailing
Special Forces stealth operations."
Florida Weekly

"With more than 30 years in intelligence operations,
Williams knows the stuff."
Florida Times Union

"Cooper's Revenge examines the impact that Iran's Islamic Revolutionary Guard Corps has had through its ultra secret Qods Force as it trains
terrorists in Iranian camps and abroad.
NBC 12 Jacksonville

"No one writes pulse pounding military thrillers quite like a man who
knows the ropes."
NBC Radio

"Cooper's Revenge grabs the reader's attention from the first page and
keeps up the electrifying pace all the way to the explosive ending.
Broadway World

T. L. WILLIAMS

First Coast Publishers

www.unit400.com

Acknowledgements

The author and publisher wish to acknowledge the work of Emily Carmain, whose expert editing contributed immeasurably to this novel. Many thanks go to the staff of the Central Intelligence Agency's Publications Review Board, whose helpful suggestions and favorable responses facilitated timely coordination of the review process. A special thanks to the CIA's Map Library for permission to include their map, Iran Physiography. Finally, a big thank-you to you, the readers, who have been generous with your reviews and comments on my work.

T. L. Williams
Ponte Vedra Beach, Florida

For MARY & ED

To my father,

Charles William Williams (USAF Retired)
World War II and Korean War Veteran

1922-2004

With love

All the Best,

Jerry

Printed in the United States of America

Publisher's Note
This is a work of fiction. The people, events, circumstances,
and institutions depicted are fictitious and the product of the
author's imagination. Any resemblance of any character to any
actual person, whether living or dead, is purely coincidental.

The publisher is not responsible for websites (or their content)
that are not owned by the publisher.

Library of Congress Cataloging-in-Publication Data

Williams, Terrence L.
Unit 400 : the assassins / T.L. Williams.
p. cm.
ISBN: 978-0-9884400-3-6 (pbk.)
1. United States. Navy. SEALs—Fiction. 2.Terrorism investigation—Fiction. 3. United States. Central
Intelligence Agency—Fiction. I. Title.
PS3623.I5641 U96 2014
813—dc23
2013943666

Epigraph

I watched as the Lamb broke open the first of the seven seals, and I heard one of the four living creatures cry out in a voice like thunder "Come forward!" I looked, and there was a white horse, and its rider held a bow. He was given a crown, and he rode forth victorious to further his victories.

When he broke open the second seal, I heard the second living creature say, "Come forward!" Another horse came out, a red one. Its rider was given power to take peace from the earth so that men would slaughter one another. And he was given a large sword.

When he broke open the third seal, I heard the third living creature cry out, "Come forward!" I looked, and there was a black horse, and its rider held a scale in his hand. I heard what seemed to be a voice in the midst of the four living creatures. It said, "A ration of wheat costs a day's pay, and three rations of barley cost a day's pay. But do not damage the olive oil or the wine!"

When he broke open the fourth seal, I heard the voice of the fourth living creature cry out, "Come forward!" I looked and there was a pale green horse! Its rider was named Death, and Hades accompanied him. They were given authority over a quarter of the earth to kill with sword, famine, and plague, and by means of the beasts of the earth.

The Book of Revelation

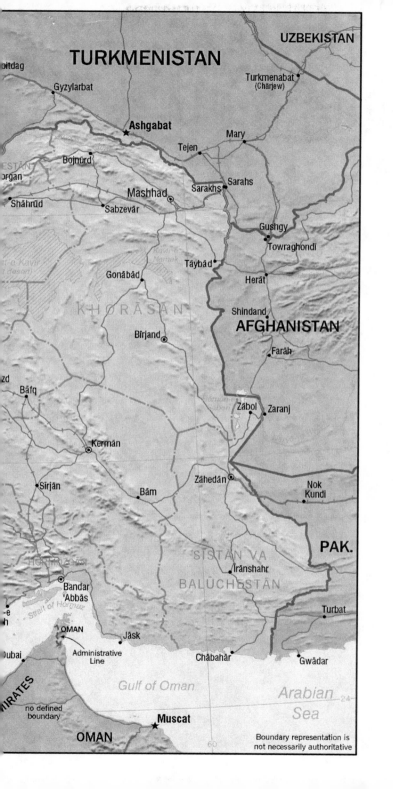

Chapter 1

Logan Alexander breezed into the main foyer of One Marina Park Drive at Fan Pier, and strode toward the elevator bank in the center of the lobby. The slight Hispanic concierge seated behind the reception desk on the right glanced up and smiled as Logan crossed the expansive marble floor.

"How 'bout them Red Sox, Mr. A?"

Logan paused before the smiling face. "They were hot, Miguel. Anytime Boston whops the Yankees is a good day. Fifteen to two." He shook his head in wonder. "Hennie actually went seven innings before he retired. He had it all working: fastball, curveball, change-up, cutter."

"Yeah, Sammy was good. I thought Fuentes was going to be in the rotation for Saturday, but Hennie got the nod. Good thing. There aren't that many southpaws that can do what he's doing this season."

"Let's hope he stays healthy. They've got a shot at the Division series next month."

"Oh yeah. They're in it to win it." Miguel gave Logan a thumbs-up and a broad smile.

Logan waved and continued over to the elevator bank. He punched number 16 and rode the lift up to his harbor view office. Miguel was an interesting character, he thought to himself as he opened the door to the two-room suite. He was a new breed of Southie, from that influx of Latino and Asian immigrants who were changing the historically vanilla flavor of the Hub. Miguel's parents had immigrated from Central America during the war in Nicaragua, settling in what used to be Dorchester Neck. They were hard working, religious and family oriented. Miguel had earned a Golden Gloves welterweight

1

championship title in high school, and except for a four-year stint in the Marine Corps, had never strayed far from his adopted hometown.

Before sitting down at his desk, Logan walked to the window and looked out over the Dorchester Heights cityscape. He'd learned the area's history long ago — including how George Washington's troops had stood their ground here in 1776 and chased the British out of Boston. A century later Dorchester and South Boston had been annexed by the city. Washington wouldn't recognize the place today, Logan mused as he caught sight of a water taxi in the inner harbor on its run from the Aquarium to Logan International Airport. The Boston Redevelopment Authority had spent billions on the waterfront redevelopment project. Over twenty-one acres covering nine city blocks had been developed into prime real estate.

Logan had been drawn to the South Boston Waterfront area in January when he'd opened Alexander Maritime Consulting, following his medical discharge from the Navy.

"Morning, Logan. How's my favorite SEAL this morning?" Alicia Gomez got up from her desk and followed Logan into his office.

Logan flashed Alicia a smile. She was raven-haired, with soft brown eyes. Her bubbly personality and zest for life were infectious. He could see in Alicia's face an uncanny resemblance to her older brother, John, who'd been killed in a tragic accident in London almost a year ago. John had been part of a ten-man team of former Army Rangers and Navy SEALs led by Logan on a sensitive mission to destroy an improvised explosive device (IED) research and training facility in Iran.

That operation, which had been funded by the family of a Kuwaiti billionaire, Nayef Al Subaie, had resulted in the complete destruction of the IED facility and the death of its commander, Colonel Barzin Ghabel. An added bonus had been the discovery there of renowned Al Qaeda bomber Mustafa Al Adel, who only weeks before the raid had been released from house arrest in Iran. Ed "Blackjack" Wozolski had shot Al Adel in the head during the raid as the terrorist raced for his firearm.

Logan glanced at the framed copy of the *Wall Street Journal* hanging behind his desk. It was the first of a four-part series under the byline of Beth Stoner, exposing Iran's IED program. Her exposé had rocked the world when it was first published in January. Stoner had been awarded the Pulitzer Prize for her in-depth reporting.

Few people knew that the revelations were the result of the Special Forces operation that Logan had led into Iran, and he wanted to keep it that way. For him, it had been enough to avenge the death of his brother, Cooper, an Army Ranger who had been killed a year before in an Iranian-backed IED attack in Ramadi, Iraq.

"Hey, Alicia. How was your weekend?"

Alicia smiled, and followed his gaze out to the water. "It rocked! Millie told me about some lawyer friends of her husband's that needed help crewing their sailboat, and I hooked up with them on Saturday."

"I didn't know you were a sailor!" Logan smiled.

"When I was in high school I used to babysit for this family that belonged to the Chico Yacht Club. They kept a thirty-six-foot sailboat over on Lake Oroville, and a lot of times they took me along to look after the kids while they were sailing. Sometimes they let me help crew. I learned a lot from them. Then, when I went to UC Santa Cruz, we had a community boating center and I got into racing. Eventually I got onto the UCSC sailing team."

"Oh yeah? What did you guys race?"

"Mostly thirteen-foot dinghies. We initially sailed in Santa Cruz Harbor, but then after we were more experienced we'd race in Monterey Bay. We used to compete against Stanford, USC and UCLA. We were pretty good."

"Cool." He gave her an admiring look. "So anything on the calendar this morning?"

"Your nine o'clock with Mr. Willoughby from Portsmouth Naval Shipyard has been cancelled, or I should say postponed."

"What happened?" Logan sighed in disappointment as he sat down at his desk and turned on his computer.

"Some kind of family emergency. I think one of his kids broke an arm playing paintball. He called me on my cell last night from the emergency room."

"That's too bad. Let me know when he can reschedule. We've been talking about some consulting work I might do for them. Anything else?"

"You're having lunch with Hamid Al Subaie at twelve-thirty at Macello on Washington Street."

Logan smiled at the thought of seeing his Kuwaiti friend again. Hamid had been working undercover for the Kuwaiti Intelligence and Security Service, and had been the first person to identify the secret Qods Force facility in Iran when he had infiltrated a Kuwaiti foreign fighter group going there for training.

Later, he had traveled into Iran with Logan. During the raid, Hamid had saved Logan's life by shooting an Iranian commander who was threatening to kill him.

"I wasn't sure Hamid would be able to get away for lunch. Harvard's MBA program is pretty intense."

"He didn't seem too worried about it. It sounded as though he was anxious to see you."

"I haven't seen him since we left Kuwait last year. I think his father convinced him that joining the family business was safer than risking his life going after bad guys. The one stipulation he made was that Hamid had to get an MBA. Nayef wanted him to go to Princeton, but I think living in Boston appealed to him more than New Jersey."

Logan worked through the morning and then decided to walk to Macello for his rendezvous with Hamid. The restaurant was only two miles from his office and the cool temperatures typical of Boston in September made it ideal for a stroll. Logan waved to Miguel as he exited the building and walked down A Street in the direction of West 4th. It was still early and the noon hour traffic was just beginning to pick up. Crossing West Dedham Street, Logan's attention was diverted by a homeless person sitting on the steps of the Salvation Army Building. She was panhandling, and as he walked past, she mumbled something about money for food. Logan paused to drop a few coins into her plastic cup and then continued walking up the street.

Logan spotted Hamid, half a block ahead of him sliding out of a Mercedes SLK 350 in front of Macello. Nice wheels, he thought, and made a mental note to razz him about being a struggling graduate student. He watched as Hamid locked the car and turned toward the restaurant.

A young Middle Eastern male was exiting the restaurant as Hamid approached the door. They came together for a moment and then the stranger turned and darted away in the direction of West Brookline Street, hurrying into the park at Blackstone Square. Logan shifted his attention back to Hamid and was alarmed to see that his friend had stumbled and was leaning against one of the gold and green wood columns framing the door.

"Hamid!" Logan rushed to his friend's side. The little Kuwaiti was tugging at something and Logan was horrified to see a knife protruding from his chest.

Hamid slid down to the pavement and began to shake as he tugged at the blade and, as it came out, blood gushed from the wound. Logan clamped his hand down on Hamid's chest, and the warm blood spurted against his palm.

"Help!" With his free hand he pulled out his cell phone and punched in 911.

"This is the 911 operator. What is the nature of your emergency?"

"There's been a stabbing. My friend's hurt."

"Is he still breathing? Can you tell if it's a life-threatening injury?"

"Yes, right now he's breathing, but it doesn't look good."

"Sir, could you please give me your current location?"

"We're outside the Macello Restaurant. 1527 Washington Street. It's at the intersection of Washington and East Brookline. Hurry! Can you get somebody here fast?"

Hamid clutched at his hand and his body shuddered as he began to convulse. He tried to speak, but blood was foaming at his lips as he struggled to mouth something. Logan asked the operator to wait a second as he pulled a handkerchief from his pants pocket and wiped the blood from Hamid's mouth.

"Hang in there, buddy. Help's on the way."

"Sir, an officer is three minutes out from your location. An ambulance is en route, with an ETA of less than five minutes. Could you give me your phone number in the event we're disconnected?"

"Yeah. 617-177-9482." Logan hung up and looked around. A crowd had gathered around them and they stood there gawking and speculating about what had happened to the little foreigner lying on the sidewalk.

Logan's mind was racing as he tried to reconstruct what had just happened. That Middle Eastern guy that had come out of the restaurant must have been the one who stabbed Hamid, but why? He glanced at his watch and saw that less than five minutes had passed. He heard the intermittent shriek of a siren growing closer and a few seconds later out of the corner of his eye saw a blue and white Boston Police Department Crown Victoria cruiser screech to a halt at the curb.

Hamid's eyes were going glassy, and he struggled to speak. Logan leaned in close and spoke into his ear. "Easy. Settle down. The police are here and an ambulance is on its way. Hold on. I know you can do it."

Hamid clutched Logan's wrist and his eyes cleared for a moment as he whispered something. Logan bent over so that his ear was almost brushing Hamid's mouth. "Be careful, Logan. Unit 400." And then he was still. Logan felt for a pulse but couldn't find one.

"All right, everybody clear the way. Make room so the EMTs can get in here. This is a crime scene. Stand back, but don't any of you leave. We'll be looking for witness statements." The cop was young. Late twenties, maybe early thirties, but he was taking charge. He knelt down to check on Hamid, and then looked up at Logan. "You the one that made the 911 call?"

"Yeah. He's a friend of mine."

"You see what happened?"

"We were supposed to meet here at Macello for lunch. I was about a half a block away on Washington Street when I saw him pull up in front of the restaurant and park his car. That's it over there, the Mercedes. He didn't see me when he got out of his car, but I could see him walk up to the restaurant."

"What happened then?"

"This guy came out of the restaurant just as Hamid was getting ready to go in. He must have been the one that stabbed him, but I didn't see any kind of altercation because the way he was walking, Hamid's body blocked my view. It happened so fast. It looked like they just passed each other. One second he was getting out of his car and the next he's stabbed and lying on the sidewalk."

"What did this guy look like?"

Logan described the Middle Eastern male, down to the black leather Frye boots he was wearing. It was an uncanny skill that he possessed. He was always observing, cataloging. When he walked into a bar his brain took a snapshot of everyone in there. Where were the threats? What were the escape routes? Who did he need to worry about?

The young cop pulled out his radio and called in the description that Logan had just given him. "Get somebody over to the area of Blackstone Square. Suspect was seen less than ten minutes ago heading in that direction."

They were interrupted by the EMTs, who wheeled a stretcher over to where Hamid was lying on his back. They started working on him right away. One of them checked his airway while the other removed his jacket and shirt to expose the wound. He whistled and shook his head when he saw where the knife had gone in and the amount of blood that Hamid had already lost.

"There's no pulse," one of them said as he held Hamid's wrist. He placed a sterile dressing on the wound. "Keep your hand on that," he instructed Logan. "Peter, get him on oxygen. I'm going to start chest compressions."

The EMT placed his hands on the lower half of Hamid's sternum, avoiding the chest wound. He began doing rapid chest compressions, a hundred a minute, in an effort to revive the stricken Kuwaiti. He broke into a sweat as the minutes went by and got no response. He swapped out with the other EMT, Peter, and the compressions continued uninterrupted. They continued like that every five minutes for twenty minutes and then Peter called it. Twelve-fifty-five.

Logan stumbled as he stood up. His head ached and his hands and clothing were soaked in Hamid's blood. He felt lightheaded. He caught one last glimpse of Hamid's face as the EMTs placed his body on the stretcher and wheeled it over to the ambulance. They pulled the white sheet, now a shroud, over his face and closed the door.

Logan looked around, and for the first time noticed that additional police had arrived and were busy preserving the crime scene and talking to witnesses. The young cop who had first arrived and spoken with Logan, came over and stood next to him.

"You all right, mister?"

"Yeah, it's just the shock. One minute he's going into a restaurant for lunch and the next he's dead."

"You did everything you could. You stayed with him. He probably would have bled out sooner if you hadn't jumped in there the way you did. Look, we're going to need some more information from you. If this is a good time I'd like you to come down to the station with me."

"That's fine. I need to make a couple of calls first though." Logan punched in Alicia's number, and after she picked up, told her that something had come up, and that he probably wouldn't make it back that afternoon. Then he called his wife, Zahir. He didn't want to tell her about Hamid over the phone. Zahir had been a former interpreter with the U.S. Army in Iraq, and later had accompanied Logan's team into Iran to take out the Qods Force IED facility. She, Logan, and Hamid had all become pretty close last year, and she deserved to hear this from him in person.

"Hey, sweetheart. How's it going?"

"Logan! I just put Cooper down. He was so tired and cranky."

Normally Logan would love to talk about his son's antics, but Hamid's brutal murder had stolen the light from the day, leaving him drained and sober. He struggled to keep his tone light.

"I just called to let you know I may be a little late for dinner. Something came up." He strained to keep his voice even, but Zahir was nothing if not perceptive.

"Logan, is everything all right?"

Logan hesitated, undecided as to whether he should tell her about what had happened over the phone. "I'll tell you about it when I get home. See you tonight, sweetheart."

After he had hung up, he shielded his eyes from the sun and caught sight of the young cop studying him. He held up one finger and, and then catching his breath, searched his address book. He dreaded making this call, but there was no other choice. Highlighting the name of Nayef Al Subaie, he punched the call button.

"Hello?"

"Nayef? Hi, it's Logan."

"Logan, how are you? I spoke with Hamid earlier today and he told me that you two were going to have lunch. I'm actually in New York on business and was going to come up to Boston to see him before I fly back to Kuwait. Perhaps we can have a drink together."

"Nayef." Logan's voice cracked and he let out a heavy sigh.

"Is everything all right? What's the matter?"

"It's Hamid." He paused before continuing. "He's been killed."

There was a moment of stunned silence on the other end. "But… are you sure? I just spoke with him a few hours ago!"

Without going into all the details, Logan explained that Hamid had been stabbed and pronounced dead at the scene. He tried to console his friend, but, under the circumstances, what could he say?

"I'm so sorry, Nayef. They just took him away, and I'm on my way to the station house right now."

"I'm catching the first flight I can get to Boston. Will you be able to meet me when I get there?"

"Of course. I don't know how long this is going to take, but I want to do everything I can to find out who did this to Hamid." After he hung up, he walked over to the cruiser and got in. As they drove past Blackstone Square, Logan stared in the direction the killer had taken. Who are you, he seethed, and what the fuck is Unit 400?

Chapter 2

Logan's throat constricted as he stared at the bloody SOG-S37 SEAL knife wrapped in the plastic evidence bag lying on Detective Breen's desk. It had somehow escaped his attention in the horror of the brutal attack on Hamid and his gory death. The killer's weapon must have fallen to the ground as Hamid strained to wrench it from his chest. It might be a coincidence, but Logan had learned long ago not to trust in coincidences. That was his knife, the knife he had plunged into Colonel Barzin Ghabel's gut on that fateful night in Bandar Deylam almost a year ago.

Logan's mind raced as he tried to digest the meaning of this bizarre twist of events. How had his knife survived the explosion when they'd blown up the IED headquarters building where Ghabel had been killed, and more importantly, how had it ended up here in Boston as a murder weapon?

"You all right, Mr. Alexander?" Detective Peter Breen took a long draw on his cigarette and stubbed it out in the vintage ceramic ashtray on his desk.

"Yeah, I'm fine. Hamid's father's in the States on business and he's flying up here this afternoon. I'm going to take him over to the morgue so he can identify the body. Do you know how long it'll take before the coroner will release it? They're Muslims, and for them, burying their dead as soon as possible is important."

Breen stared at a distant wall, and then rubbed his forehead. "They'll release the body as soon as they can. The forensics work can take some time. They'll want to see if they can collect any evidence from the body that'll help us in our investigation. Like, did the murderer leave any DNA at the crime scene? For instance, did your friend fight this guy off, and maybe get some skin under his fingernails while he was grappling with him? That kind of thing."

"The murderer was pretty smooth. He timed his attack just right. When he came out of the restaurant it's almost as though he didn't even pause when he stabbed Hamid."

"There's a strong possibility he knew your friend, or at least was able to positively identify him when he arrived at the restaurant. Do you know if Mr. Al Subaie had any enemies, people that would want him dead?"

"He comes from one of the wealthiest families in Kuwait. I don't suppose you get to be that powerful without making some enemies. But he hasn't been in the States that long. He just got here last month to start an MBA program at Harvard."

"How'd you get to know him, Mr. Alexander?" Detective Breen scrutinized his face in a way that made Logan realize Breen had not ruled him out as a suspect.

"His father's a client of my sister's law firm. Theirs is mostly a foreign clientele and a big part of what they do is international arbitration, trade disputes and that sort of thing. Anyway, I met Hamid's father, Nayef, at my sister Millie's apartment last year and we became friends. When he told me that Hamid was going to be coming over here to study, I offered to help him get settled in."

Take it slow, he thought to himself. No way he could reveal the true extent of his relationship with Hamid and the Al Subaie family. That whole business in Iran had to remain strictly under the radar. That was the agreement he'd made with the Kuwaitis. There was no way Breen, or anyone else involved in the murder investigation, would be able to figure out their covert connection given all the precautions they'd taken.

But obviously somebody had, somebody from Iran, by the looks of it.

The young cop from the crime scene knocked on the door and poked his head into the room. "Hey, Detective, we were able to pull the surveillance video from the restaurant and get some still shots from it. This guy was good. It's almost as if he knew where the security cameras were because he did a damn good job of hiding his face from them."

Breen took the DVD from the cop's outstretched hand. "Thanks, Murray. You guys do awesome work."

"Only the best for you, Breensie. You know that. Oh yeah, here are some witness statements too. The one on top is from the hostess at Macello who actually talked to the guy. A sketch artist is working with her right now to get a description."

"Great. Maybe we'll catch a break." Breen took the sheaf of papers from Murray and shoved the DVD into his computer. He invited Logan to come around his desk to view the surveillance tape with him.

The footage was clear. There was about ten minutes of coverage, showing customers entering and exiting the restaurant. The Middle Eastern male suspect strolled into Macello at twelve-twenty-two. He was a cool customer; went right up to the hostess and spoke with her. Breen paused the computer, but all he had was a side profile of the man who appeared to be about five feet eight inches tall, 150 pounds, muscular, with short curly hair and a faint beard.

Breen stopped the DVD after the suspect exited the restaurant. Motioning Logan to sit down, he shuffled through the transcript of the interview with the hostess.

"Listen to this. This guy told the hostess that he was joining a friend for lunch. When she offered to seat him he said no, he would rather wait. She says that he just milled around near the window looking out onto the street and then went out the door at twelve-twenty-five. She didn't think anything of it. She was busy seating other patrons."

"Twelve-twenty-five? That's when Hamid got there. I remember looking at my watch. We were supposed to meet at the restaurant at twelve-thirty. I just can't believe that he's dead."

"Please give my regrets to the father when you see him and let him know that we're doing everything we can to find the suspect. We may want to talk to him if he's going to be in town for a few days. He may know something that will trigger a lead in our investigation."

Breen stood up and handed Logan his card. "Thanks for your cooperation, Mr. Alexander. My cell phone number is written on the back. Give me a call if anything comes to mind. Will you be available if we need to talk to you again?"

"Sure, anything." Logan withdrew a name card from his coat pocket and gave it to the detective. He looked at his watch. It was almost four o'clock.

"Murray will give you a ride, if you like. You probably don't want to be out walking around like that."

Logan looked down at his suit. His clothes were ruined, drenched in Hamid's blood. "That would be helpful. I appreciate it."

Twenty minutes later Murray dropped Logan off at his East Boston loft on Porter Street. Zahir had bought the duplex penthouse a year ago, just before she started teaching Arabic at Boston University. They both loved the location, with its diverse ethnic neighborhoods, and waterfront views of Boston's skyline. And with three bedrooms, the condo provided ample space for their young family to grow.

Logan let himself into the apartment, making certain to be quiet in the event Cooper was napping. He caught sight of Zahir working at her desk in the study. Her initial warm smile turned to horror as she saw Logan's blood-drenched clothing. She raised her hand to her mouth in shock.

"Oh, my God, Logan. What happened?" She leapt out of her chair and rushed to his side, anxiety etched across her face.

"Let me clean up first, and I'll explain everything. I don't want to get blood all over you."

Zahir followed him into the bathroom and watched him with apprehensive eyes as he stripped off his suit. She picked up the soiled clothes and took them out of the room as Logan turned on the shower and stepped in, welcoming the scalding needles of water as they penetrated his skin. Ten minutes later he was toweling off. He put on a pair of sweatpants and a tee shirt before walking into the kitchen, where Zahir had put on a pot of coffee. Logan walked over to her and they embraced. He rested his chin on her head and stared into the distance.

"So...?" She raised her face with a questioning look in her eyes.

He looked down into her probing eyes. "It's Hamid. He's dead."

Zahir pulled back from him with a shocked expression on her face. "But—what happened? Weren't you supposed to meet him for lunch today?"

Logan pulled her to him and kissed the top of her head. "He never made it."

He shook his head and grimaced as he recounted the events of the last several hours. How he'd arrived at the restaurant just as the mysterious Middle Eastern killer had escaped from the murder scene; how he had held Hamid in his dying moments, trying to stem the flow of blood from his body; and how Hamid had uttered a final warning about the mysterious Unit 400.

Zahir blanched when Logan uttered the words Unit 400. "I can't believe that!"

"What? Do you know what it means?"

"I remember a few months ago there was a report out of Europe on Sky News about Unit 400. It's supposed to be a super-secret special operations unit inside the Qods Force. Apparently it's a network of Iranian assassins that Iran's Supreme Leader can task to attack the country's enemies. They seem to be going after U.S. and Israeli targets."

"How come we never heard of them before?"

"I don't know. This may be a new development, or maybe they've just managed to stay out of the limelight in the past. These are the same people that supposedly tried to assassinate the Saudi Ambassador to Washington in 2011. But why would they kill Hamid?" She moved away from him, pacing back and forth, clenching and unclenching her hands.

"I remember when that happened. But I thought the Mexican drug cartels were behind that attack in DC."

She turned to face him. "I'm sure that's what Iran wanted everybody to think, but later it came out that Unit 400 was the group working behind the scenes. They've also been involved in attacks against the Israelis in Turkey, going back to 2009.

"You know," she said slowly, "since the government in Ankara has become more pro-Islamist, there's this feeling that the Turks will just look the other way if extremist groups like this Unit 400 plan attacks on Turkish soil. Do you think they're behind this attack on Hamid? That's pretty bold."

"I don't know. From what Hamid said it seems plausible that this Unit 400 was targeting him. I mean, based on what you just said, and the fact that he warned me about Unit 400 before he died, I think we have to assume that Tehran is behind this."

Zahir looked troubled. "This has to be in retaliation for Bandar Deylam." As the meaning of what she had just said dawned on her, Zahir trembled. "What if they come after us, Logan?"

He looked grim as he moved to her side and gave her a reassuring hug. "It doesn't make me feel warm and fuzzy, but it does make me wonder how they could've found out about Hamid's involvement. There weren't any survivors from the attack on the base, so if the Qods Force found out about it, my bet is that they have a penetration inside the Kuwaiti Intelligence and Security Service." Logan went on to tell her about his knife in the evidence bag in Detective Breen's office.

There was a loud squawk from the baby monitor. "Cooper's up," Zahir said. "We'll have to talk about this later."

"I'll get him." Logan went into the nursery and picked up the baby. "Hey big guy. You ready for some dinner?" He sniffed Cooper's diaper and made a beeline for the changing table. Despite his sorrow he couldn't help smiling down at his son as he changed his diaper.

The child bore a strong resemblance to his biological father and namesake, Logan's younger brother, Cooper. Zahir had been working as an interpreter with Cooper's unit in

Iraq and when Cooper was killed, she had been pregnant with his baby. Returning to the States, she met the Alexander family at Cooper's funeral. Later, when she found out that Logan planned to mount a covert operation to avenge his brother's death, she wanted to help him. She joined his team as interpreter for the secret mission into Iran, where she and Logan almost lost their lives. Despite a rocky beginning, the two had fallen in love and married in the Spring. Their son, Cooper, had been born in June.

When he finished changing the baby, Logan picked him up and cooed into his ear as he carried him into the living room where Zahir was waiting. Cooper smiled and waved his tiny fists as Zahir unfastened her blouse and offered him her breast.

Logan watched the baby nurse for a moment but then remembered that he had another call to make. He reached for his cell phone. "I have to let Millie know about Hamid. She'll want to see Nayef while he's in town. Maybe her firm can lean on the State Department so the coroner's office expedites release of the body. Also, I told Nayef I'd meet him and take him over to the morgue. He's due in from New York at six-thirty."

Logan punched in Millie's number and waited for her to pick up.

"Hey, big brother, how's it going?"

"Hi, Mills. Look, I'm sorry to tell you this over the phone, but I have some bad news."

He sensed Millie tensing up as she took a deep breath, and he knew she was preparing for the worst. Cooper's death last year had been a big blow to the Alexander family and Millie seemed to have taken it harder than the rest. She and Cooper had been closest in age and she was still struggling to come to terms with his death. She had confided to Logan last month that her grief counselor had recommended that she seek professional help.

"It's Hamid. He was killed today, outside Macello."

Millie's voice trembled. "What! What happened? Was it an accident?"

17

"No, Mills. Hamid was murdered." Logan went on to give her an abbreviated run-down of the afternoon's events.

"Look, Nayef is coming down from New York and I promised to meet him and take him over to the morgue. I don't know what he's going to want to do, but I imagine he'd prefer to take the body back to Kuwait as soon as possible. The detective I spoke with said that the coroner's office will try to release it as soon as they can, but they have to complete their forensics investigation."

Millie was silent for a moment. "Nayef must be devastated. Hamid was his only son. And they were very close."

"Oh, I know. You should have seen the look of pride on his face when the crew on the *Ocean Dreamer* pulled us out of the water in the Persian Gulf last year. He was there. Remember how the Kuwaitis had held off telling us that Hamid was really an Al Subaie, and we didn't find out until Hamid told us, on the yacht heading back to Kuwait? I thought Nayef was going to burst with pride."

Millie was silent for a minute and then said that she would look into having the State Department contact the Boston coroner's office if it appeared there was going to be a delay. They made plans to meet at Logan and Zahir's later that evening.

Logan changed into gray slacks and a button-down shirt. He kissed Zahir and Cooper goodbye and headed for the parking garage in the basement. It was just minutes from his apartment to the airport, and as he was pulling into the arrivals area, he received a text message from Nayef telling him that he had landed. Ten minutes later Logan spotted the anguished Kuwaiti billionaire walking towards him. He got out of the car and took Nayef's outstretched hand.

"Logan, thank you for meeting me." His voice trembled with emotion.

"It's good to see you again. I'm just sorry it had to be under these circumstances." Logan's voice caught as he uttered these words. He and Zahir had developed a real friendship with Hamid. They owed the little Kuwaiti their lives. Logan put Nayef's carry-on in the cargo area of the BMW and closed the door.

The two men got into the SUV and Logan pulled out into traffic. "Where is he?" Nayef's voice was grim.

"Boston Medical Center. We should be there in about fifteen minutes at this time of day." He exited the airport and merged into the Ted Williams Tunnel. Nayef was silent as they drove through rush hour traffic. Logan took the off-ramp at Exit 18 and eased onto Massachusetts Avenue. Moments later he pulled into the visitors' parking at the medical center.

A Red Cross volunteer at the admissions desk directed them to the morgue in the basement. When they arrived a few minutes later, a doctor from the office of the Chief Medical Examiner came out to the waiting room to meet them.

"Mr. Al Subaie? I'm Doctor Hodges. I'm very sorry about your son. Please come this way."

Nayef fell in step with the medical examiner while Logan decided to remain in the waiting room. When Nayef noticed that Logan had stayed behind, he turned back and looked at him with raised eyebrows.

"Logan, if you are able, I would like for you to come with me."

"Of course, Nayef. I didn't want to intrude."

"Not at all. You were Hamid's friend. And you are mine."

When they entered the morgue, the doctor took them over to a row of refrigerated compartments. Opening one, he slid the tray containing Hamid's body out and folded down the sheet to expose his face. Nayef struggled to breathe as he looked down at his son. He nodded to the doctor and then reached out to stroke Hamid's brow. He bowed his head and stayed like that for several minutes before turning and trudging out of the room.

In the waiting room, the doctor turned to Nayef. "Mr. Al Subaie, we're prepared to release your son's remains to you tomorrow morning. There is no need to perform an autopsy.

Cause of death was a severe trauma to the chest; a knife wound which penetrated your son's aorta."

He turned to Logan. "Mr. Alexander, I understand that you were with the deceased immediately following the stabbing and that you tried to save him. You did everything you could, but I'm afraid the wound was so severe that there was no chance for him to survive. I just wanted to tell you that, so that you don't blame yourself."

Logan swallowed hard, struggling to keep his emotions in check. "Thanks, Doc. That helps."

Nayef gave the doctor his card, and said that he would make arrangements with a local funeral home to have Hamid's remains moved as soon as possible. As he and Logan walked out of the hospital Nayef gave Logan a sidewise glance. "I didn't know that you were with Hamid when this all happened. I thought you got there afterwards."

"No, I got there literally seconds before this guy stabbed him. I actually saw the man coming out of the restaurant, but it happened so fast, and he was so smooth that he was gone before I was even aware that there was a problem. When I got to Hamid, I tried to stop the bleeding and called 911."

"Was he able to talk? Did he say anything?"

"He was struggling to speak. The last thing he said was to be careful, it's Unit 400."

Nayef appeared startled at the mention of Unit 400. "You must be careful, Logan. You're in danger!"

Chapter 3

Nayef leaned forward in the leather armchair and accepted a scotch, neat, from Zahir. He sipped the twenty-year-old Balvenie single malt, and then sat back in his seat, one hand tapping his leg as he surveyed the sorrowful faces before him.

"A week before he left for the States, Hamid went in to see the director of operations of our Intel Service, Thamir Alghanim. Hamid told Thamir that he suspected that there was a penetration of the service. He didn't have a smoking gun, but things were not going well with their Iranian program."

"Did he give you any idea what was happening?" Logan rose from where he was sitting to refresh Nayef's drink.

"Hamid said that about four months after the raid on the IED camp last year, they lost the first of their top two Iranian agents. He said it's normal for agents to come and go, but these were long-term, productive agents. Never in his wildest dreams would he have picked them to just vanish off the face of the earth. He confessed that sometimes even the best agents dry up. Things like their access to information or their motivation can affect their productivity. But that wasn't the case with these two."

"Did Hamid feel there was something unusual about how they disappeared?"

"Yes. They just dropped out of sight within a couple of months of each other. The pattern was the same in both cases. The agent failed to make a scheduled meeting, and then didn't show up for the alternate meeting time. Not only that, neither of them activated their emergency communications plans either. They haven't been heard from in over six months. They simply vanished."

"So what did Hamid think happened to them?"

"He said that it's not unheard of, and it doesn't necessarily mean that they've been wrapped up. He told me a story about going to Greece once to try and track down an agent who had disappeared and he decided to go to the agent's neighborhood and poke around. When he was walking down the street he spotted an obituary plastered to a telephone pole and it had a picture of his agent. He had died!"

"What are the chances of seeing something like that? I've heard the Greeks do that, post obituaries on walls and things in the neighborhood where the person lived." Zahir's consternation was evident on her face.

"Anyway, Hamid thought the service should do a counterintelligence investigation or at least begin a damage assessment to see if there were any clues to their disappearance. He said it was tricky though. They would have to be circumspect because they couldn't risk having the Iranians discover our interest in the missing agents. If they did find out, and the agents were under investigation, it would confirm their suspicions. It would be a death sentence."

"Did Thamir take Hamid's concerns seriously?"

"Oh, yes. Over the past year he's been looking for any indication that the Iranians suspect Kuwait's role in the whole Bandar Deylam affair. He felt that if they had found out about it, they wouldn't necessarily go public with it, but they wouldn't just let it slide. It was too big a deal. The regime was humiliated by those *Wall Street Journal* articles that brought to light, with irrefutable proof, Iran's support for terrorism, not to mention the complete destruction of their IED facility."

"I can tell you right now that, not only do they suspect it, they know it."

"What do you mean?"

Logan had a grim look on his face. "The knife that was used to kill Hamid, is the same knife I used to kill Barzin Ghabel. It was the knife I carried when I was a SEAL."

Nayef sat dumbfounded looking at Logan. "I don't understand. How did the killer get your knife?"

"That's a good question. The last time I saw it, it was sticking out of Ghabel's chest. In all the confusion that day I forgot to take it with me and just assumed that it was destroyed in the explosion."

"Could you be mistaken?"

"No. It had the date I entered on duty as a Navy SEAL etched on the blade – October 17, 2001."

Nayef leaned back with a stunned look on his face. "That changes everything, but it still doesn't explain why they would go after our Intel program. You know our service is small. It's not like the CIA, with its global presence. We have to be selective about where we put our resources. Iran is our single most important target."

Nayef's eyes narrowed. "I think once Thamir's people started looking into it, he became convinced that the Qods Force wrapped up those two agents as a way of sending us a warning. But now, with what happened to Hamid..." Nayef's voice cracked and he paused to regain his composure before continuing. "It's obvious the Qods Force was involved in his murder."

There was a moment of stunned silence around the room. "You mean because of what he said about Unit 400?" Logan glanced sideways at Zahir, who had turned to give him a worried look.

"What other explanation can there be? I need to talk to Thamir to find out if there's a Unit 400 component to their investigation and if so, how the Qods Force could have learned Hamid's identity."

"When he went into Iran the first time with that Kuwaiti foreign fighter group, he was there under the alias Jaber Behbehani, right?"

"Yes, I believe so."

Zahir spoke up. "We know that when Hamid was confronted by Colonel Ghabel in Bandar Deylam he was tortured. Is it possible that he revealed his true identity to them then?"

"No, he was very clear about that. I remember asking him about it when he got back to Kuwait. They could not get him to reveal his true identity."

"What about those missing Iranian agents?" Zahir persisted. "Did Hamid have any contact with them?"

"He may have debriefed them at some time or other. But he was not their principal handler. He would have used an alias when dealing with them, so they wouldn't have known his true name."

"It sounds as though Hamid's concerns about a penetration could be true." Logan walked over to the expansive window overlooking Boston Harbor and gazed at the city's sparkling skyline in the distance. His heart was heavy with grief as he recalled the image of Hamid lying on the sidewalk with his life's blood draining out.

The chiming of the doorbell jarred him from his thoughts, and he turned from the window as Zahir opened the door to admit Millie and Ryan. Without saying a word, Millie walked over to where Nayef was sitting. As he rose to greet her, she enveloped him in a warm embrace.

"I'm so sorry, Nayef." Logan could see the pain on his sister's face as she pulled back to study her client and friend. Although she had barely known Hamid, she had handled the Al Subaie account for her law firm for the past two years, and had spent a lot of time with Nayef. "Is there anything we can do for you?"

"Thank you for asking, Millie." Nayef took Ryan's outstretched hand as he joined them to offer his regrets. "You've all been so kind. The medical examiner has agreed to release Hamid's body in the morning, and Logan recommended Thompson and Sons to handle the arrangements. They'll be at Boston Medical Center first thing in the morning to pick him up. My people in Kuwait are handling the transportation details; we're chartering a private jet for the trip home."

"How is Nisreen handling everything?"

Nisreen, Nayef's wife, had accompanied him on a number of business trips to the U.S. and Millie had enjoyed entertaining the vibrant beauty. Nisreen was a respected writer throughout the Arab world, having published three collections of contemporary prose. She was also a strong voice for Arab women's issues and used her social position and popularity as a Kuwaiti author to advance women's causes in the Middle East.

"As you can imagine. It was a tremendous shock. Actually I contacted my uncle, so that he and his wife would be there with her when I called. Hamid was our only son, and Nisreen doted on him. She never liked it that he was involved in intelligence work. She would have much preferred that he follow my path in business. She was over-joyed when he decided to attend Harvard, and was already planning a trip to see him this winter."

"If there's anything I can do for you, Nayef, don't hesitate to ask. I'm not saying this as your lawyer, but as a friend."

"Thank you, Millie. I will. Tomorrow morning I'm meeting with the detective who is handling the investigation – Detective Breen. Obviously I won't get into this whole Unit 400 business with him or even bring up Iran. But I am going to put him in touch with Thamir, who will know best how to deal with the police."

"I'm sorry, but what's Unit 400, and what does Iran have to do with Hamid's murder?" Millie searched Nayef's face as she waited for an explanation."

"Millie, I'm sorry, since you just got here, but I need to get going," he said. "I have to make some phone calls and cancel meetings I had planned for the rest of this week. I think Logan can fill you in on the Iran connection. Thank you all for everything."

"Where are you staying? Let me give you a ride." Logan stood up and reached for his keys.

"No, please. You've done enough already. I'll just catch a cab outside. I'm staying at the Taj on Arlington Street.

"Well, then, let me take you to the police station tomorrow morning. What time are you meeting Detective Breen?"

"Nine o'clock. Actually that's a good idea. If I get a chance to speak with Thamir tonight, I can fill you in on anything he's found out."

"He won't be able to tell you much on an open phone line. I don't know what kind of SIGINT capabilities the

Iranians have, but I'll bet you anything that they are capable of targeting your phones."

"Ah, you underestimate me, my friend. Don't forget that the Al Subaie family manages a pretty substantial telecommunications franchise. We did over $20 million in the last two years alone selling cell phone encryption software in our Middle East market."

"And it's good enough to make you confident about your phone security?"

"Oh, yes. This has become a big business, particularly because of privacy concerns in the financial sector. With this software you can enable your phone to encrypt and decipher speech."

"That's pretty impressive. All right, I'll pick you up at the Taj at eight-thirty. And look, if you're ready to go after that, I can give you a ride to the airport. Is your plane flying out of Logan or Hanscom Field?"

"Where's Hanscom Field?"

"It's in Bedford. About twenty miles northwest of here."

"No, it's definitely Logan. We're flying out of the executive terminal there."

"OK. Do you need any more help coordinating with Thompsons?"

"No. They told me that they would have their mortician prepare Hamid for the trip first thing in the morning, and they have a proper shipping container there at the funeral home. One of their administrative assistants was called in tonight to handle the paperwork. Massachusetts requires a Burial/Transport Permit, a Communicable Diseases Affidavit, certified copies of the death certificate and his passport. So much paperwork." Hamid struck his head. "Damn, I forgot about the passport!"

"Nayef, why don't you let me handle the passport," Millie said. "I can draw up a limited power of attorney right now, and if you like, Ryan and I can go over to Hamid's place and pick it up. Also if you want me to take care of his affairs here, we can go through his things for you. We can arrange to sell his car and send his personal effects to you."

"He didn't bring very much with him, Millie. Mostly clothing. That could be donated. But if there are any photos or personal papers..." Nayef's voice trailed off as the finality of these preparations hit him.

After Millie had executed the notarized power of attorney, Nayef left for the Taj and she and Ryan left for Cambridge to pick up Hamid's passport. Zahir sat down next to Logan and leaned her head against his broad chest.

"This is all so depressing, Logan."

He stroked her long hair and kissed the top of her head. "I know. I feel bad for Nayef. He's usually so sharp and funny, but you can tell this has hit him really hard."

"Can you imagine flying all the way back to Kuwait with your son's body lying in a casket in the cargo hold?"

About thirty minutes later Logan's cell phone rang and he sat up straight as he listened to Millie's taut voice. Zahir gave him a questioning look and he lifted his finger to his lips.

"Millie, calm down. Just tell me what happened."

"When Ryan and I got to Hamid's apartment, there was this guy trying to get in the door. When Ryan asked him what he was doing, he attacked Ryan. He did this crazy karate move and all of a sudden Ryan was lying on the ground. I yelled at the guy but he just pushed me away and then walked out of the building."

"Are you all right? How's Ryan?"

"I'm fine, just mad. I think he knocked the wind out of Ryan, but it looks like he'll be OK."

"Did this guy say anything? What did he look like?"

"No, that was the eerie thing. He just stared at me. He was pretty young – late twenties to early thirties. He had short, dark, curly hair and a wisp of a beard. Thin. Oh, and he looked Middle Eastern."

Logan's pulse raced as he put two and two together. "That's the guy from Macello. That's the guy who killed Hamid! You need to get out of there!"

After Millie reassured him that the man had left and that they would leave as soon as they found Hamid's passport,

Logan hung up. He turned to Zahir, who had sat up and covered her mouth with her hand.

"Did you catch all of that?"

"Yes. My God, Logan, Millie and Ryan could have been hurt!"

"If that was the same guy, we know he's a killer. Even so, that's pretty brazen, showing up at Hamid's apartment. What was he looking for? Millie needs to see if she can ID him from those surveillance videos they got at the restaurant."

At eight-thirty the next morning Logan picked Nayef up at the Taj Hotel. He was subdued on the ride to the District D-4 police station on Harrison Avenue. Inside, a receptionist asked them to take a seat because Detective Breen had been called into a meeting with his commander, Captain Givens.

Logan was fidgety, and walked over to look at the announcements on the community bulletin board in the lobby. One poster declared that Operation Hoodsie Cups had been a big success that summer. Officers from the community service office's Safe Street Team had visited neighborhoods, handing out ice cream and coloring books, while maintaining a nonthreatening presence in the community.

His attention shifted to a photo of a recent police academy class that had just completed a 10-K run in honor of fallen officers. Logan's gaze slid over the young faces, some smiling and some grimacing from their exertion. He leaned forward and honed in on one face that he thought he recognized, and then he gasped in shock. He was staring into the eyes of Hamid's killer.

At that moment Millie walked into the station. She and Ryan had decided to go right home after their altercation at Hamid's apartment, although they had called in the incident on the Crimestopper's hotline. She walked over to where Nayef was seated and fished Hamid's passport out of her bag.

"Morning. Were you able to get any sleep last night?" She handed the passport to him and gave his shoulder a sympathetic squeeze.

"I was on the phone until after midnight. I took something to help me sleep, but it didn't do much good. A troubled mind is a hard thing to calm."

"Oh, Nayef. Did Logan tell you about our incident at the apartment?"

"No. What happened?"

Millie described their encounter with the Middle Eastern man, how he had attacked Ryan and then fled the apartment building before they could do anything.

"Is Ryan all right?" Nayef's brow was furrowed and his eyes darkened.

"Yes. His pride and his ribs are hurt, but other than that I think he'll be OK. The scariest part though is that Logan thinks his description matches Hamid's killer."

They both looked up at the strained sound of Logan's voice. "Millie, come look at this and tell me if you notice anything unusual."

She walked over to where Logan was standing and scanned the picture that he was pointing to. She clasped her hand to her mouth. "Oh my God, Logan. That's him." She jabbed her finger at the likeness of the young Middle Eastern police academy graduate staring out from the photo. "That's the guy from the apartment last night."

Nayef rose from his seat and walked over to stand next to them. "What's this all about?" he demanded.

Logan looked at him, and then shifted his gaze back to the photo. He pointed to the person in question. "That's the guy. That's the guy who killed Hamid."

Shock registered on Nayef's face as he grappled with the meaning of Logan's words. "But, that doesn't make any sense. Are you certain? Why would a police officer murder my son?"

"I don't know, Nayef. But we're going to find out."

Moments later Detective Breen ambled down the hall from Captain Given's office. "Morning, everyone. Come on in."

"Wait a second, Detective. You need to check this out." Breen walked over to where they were standing and Logan pointed to the picture. "This is the guy who was at Macello yesterday. He's the one who killed Hamid."

Breen looked at Logan as though he had lost his mind. "Wait a minute. You're telling me that police officer is the one who killed your friend?"

"He was the one who was at the apartment last night, too," Millie spoke up.

"Now, how do you know about that, and who are you? I just got out of a meeting with the commander about a tip we got on the Crimestopper's hotline last night, reporting an assault at Mr. Al Subaie's apartment."

"I called that in. I'm Logan's sister, Millie Cook."

Breen pulled the photo off the bulletin board and walked over to his office. He handed the photo to his receptionist. "Karen, drop whatever you're doing and get me the name of this officer." He pointed to the officer Logan and Millie had identified. "Also, get me the Superintendent's office at the Academy ASAP. They probably have a copy of this picture in their files and can ID him over the phone."

"Yes, sir."

Breen sighed, and turned towards Nayef. "You must be Mr. Al Subaie. I'm sorry for your loss, sir. I hate to trouble you at a time like this. I'll try to make it quick. I understand you're flying your son's remains back to Kuwait later today. I have to tell you, though, this development is way out there. There has to be some explanation." Breen led them into his office. He moved a stack of files from one of the chairs and deposited them on his already cluttered desk. As he took a seat his phone rang.

"It's the Superintendent for you, sir."

"Thank you, Karen. Mark, thank you for taking my call. How're Marsha and the boys?" Marsha was Mark O'Reilly's wife of thirty years, and his two boys, his pride and joy, had followed in their father's footsteps. One was a state trooper and the other was a police officer working out of District E-13 in Jamaica Plain.

"Look, Mark, I know this is going to sound crazy, but I have two witnesses here who identified one of your recent academy graduates as the person who killed that Kuwaiti fellow over in the South End yesterday afternoon."

"Yeah, that's right. The one outside the Macello restaurant." Breen stared at the photograph in his hand. "OK, if you're looking at the same picture I am, it's the guy in the third row, second over from the left. Looks like he's ethnic Middle Eastern.

"Armeen Khorasani? Do you know where he was yesterday afternoon?" Breen listened to O'Reilly for a minute without comment. "All right. Thanks for your help, Mark. I'll call over there and see if we can figure out what this is all about. Give my best to Marsha." He hung up the phone and looked up at the expectant faces.

"O'Reilly says that officer is a new academy graduate by the name of Armeen Khorasani. He was just assigned to the South End. That's here. According to O'Reilly, Khorasani was supposed to be in a new officer orientation program here all day yesterday. I usually speak at those new officer orientations, but obviously we got busy yesterday afternoon, so someone else filled in for me."

"So, if he didn't show up for his orientation program yesterday, that pretty much confirms it, right?" Logan gestured towards the photo.

"Hold on. I think we can get an answer to that question pretty fast." Breen picked up his phone and punched in Captain Given's number. His secretary picked up on the first ring.

"I'll put you right through, Detective."

Breen drummed his fingers on the desk as he waited for his boss to pick up. "Captain, Breen here. I've got Mr. Al Subaie and the witness to yesterday's murder here in my office. Mr. Alexander. Yeah, he's the one who was at the restaurant; plus his sister. She's the one that called in the incident at the apartment last night. Anyway, bizarre as it sounds, they saw a picture on the bulletin board when they came in and identified one of our new recruits as the murder suspect."

Breen listened to the Captain's tirade on the other end and then interrupted. "Yeah, I know it sounds off the wall, but they both identified him separately. It was Khorasani, Armeen Khorasani." Breen listened to the Captain for another minute, and then hung up.

He turned to the waiting group. "Khorasani has an ironclad alibi. He was in orientation here all day. In fact, the three new officers we got from this batch of academy graduates, Khorasani included, were having lunch with the captain when Mr. Al Subaie was murdered. Khorasani is on his way over here right now to put this to rest."

Five minutes later there was a knock at Breen's door and Armeen Khorasani walked in. Except for the brand-new police uniform, Khorasani was a dead ringer for the killer. Logan searched his face and Millie edged away from him, despite the revelation that he could not have been the murderer. They both looked baffled.

Khorasani looked around at the expectant faces. "I'm Armeen Khorasani. Captain Givens just told me what happened yesterday, and just now with the picture from our 10-K run. I wanted to come see you myself because I think I can explain what you saw in that photo."

Millie and Logan looked at him as though he was crazy. "But Captain Givens said that you were here when Hamid was killed," Millie murmured.

"I was. But five years ago a guy named Nouri left his family home in Massachusetts, and was never seen again. There were rumors over the years that he had gone to Iran. Last year a relative in Iran confirmed that Nouri was living in Tehran. Nouri Khorasani is my twin brother!"

Chapter 4

Logan and Millie embraced Nayef as he prepared to board the corporate jet carrying him back to Kuwait. Zahir had also joined them at the airport to say goodbye. The ground crew, assisted by Thompson's funeral director, had just finished loading Hamid's casket into the hold. It was encased in a special transportation container packed with dry ice to preserve the remains. The crew handling the casket had worked without the customary banter on flight lines. They went about their duties in a solemn and respectful manner as Nayef and the others looked on.

"Thank you all for everything. Logan, I'll let you know if I find out more on Unit 400 once I get home. I also want to find out if Thamir's people know anything about Khorasani. If he went to Iran five years ago, maybe the Qods Force recruited him. Millie, I'm not sure when I'll be back in the States on business. I want to stay close to home in case Nisreen needs me. And, Zahir, your son is beautiful. Watch over him. He's precious." Nayef had poked his head into Cooper's nursery the night before to have a peek at the sleeping baby.

Zahir gave him an appreciative smile but appeared perplexed at the mention of Khorasani. "I'll explain it after," Logan whispered in her ear.

"Please give your family our regrets, Nayef." Millie clutched his hand one last time before he turned and mounted the boarding ladder of the sleek Gulfstream jet. He paused at the door and waved to them once more before ducking his head and going inside. Almost immediately the steward secured the ladder and the pilot began taxiing to their designated runway. The roar of the twin jet engines was deafening as the plane accelerated and then climbed into the late morning sky.

"It's going to be a long flight for Nayef. They'll fly all the way to Kuwait City from here without refueling." Logan gave the jet an appreciative look as it banked and gained altitude. In seconds it had turned east and was over Boston Harbor heading out over the Atlantic.

Millie shielded her eyes from the glaring sun as she gazed upward. "Poor Nayef," she sighed.

As they turned to walk back to Logan's car, they were subdued. Once they were in traffic, Logan and Millie filled Zahir in on their meeting with Detective Breen.

"It was so strange, Zahir. If Logan hadn't spotted that picture of Armeen Khorasani, we never would've even known about his twin brother."

"It's unusual for pro-Shah Iranians who left Iran in the '80s to go back, given the political climate," Zahir said.

She was related to the deposed Iranian leader through her mother, one of the Shah's nieces. Although he had died in 1980 of non-Hodgkin lymphoma, just before Zahir was born, she felt a deep affinity for that side of her family.

"Think about it," she continued. "Most of the Iranians who left in 1980 were pro-monarchists. A bunch of them went to Europe, and many of them ended up in the States. They gravitated to three big cities — LA, Washington, and New York. Most of them saw themselves as exiles, and believed they would return to Iran, under the right conditions. So, I think it's credible that someone who grew up in a family immersed in Persian language and traditions would be curious about Iran and would want to check it out."

"But if that's the case, what's he doing back here, and why would he murder Hamid?" Logan said. "The strange thing is that once Nouri disappeared, he never tried to get back in touch with his family.

"According to Armeen, the first clue they had that he was alive and in Iran came from an uncle who still lives there. He works in a government office that deals with immigration issues. Armeen's father reached out to him to see if he could help them find Nouri. It took a little while, but about a year ago they got a very cryptic note back from the uncle saying that Nouri was alive and living in Tehran."

"That's very strange. There must have been some kind of falling out between the father and son. Iranian families are traditionally very close."

Logan almost rolled his eyes. He was tempted to comment on the cold treatment Zahir's family had given her when they found out that she was pregnant. This had all come out right after Cooper was killed in Iraq and Zahir had been sent home when the battalion commander found out she was expecting.

Although there had been a reconciliation of sorts between Zahir and her parents after she and Logan were married, her brother still refused to have anything to do with her. From his warped perspective, Zahir was damaged goods and her indiscretions had disgraced the family name.

Logan dropped Millie off at her office and then gave Zahir a ride to Boston University, where she was teaching an advanced Arabic language course. "Will you be home by six o'clock?" she asked. "I told the sitter one of us would be there by then."

"That should be fine. I need to check with Alicia to see what's on the schedule, but I think I'm good to go." He leaned over to kiss her goodbye, and held the kiss for a moment as he brushed her face. "Don't worry about this, sweetheart. I'm sure we'll find this guy." He gave her a reassuring hug and then waited as she reached into the back for her briefcase and purse.

When he reached his office a short time later, Alicia was on the phone. She waved to him as he came through the door.

"Yes, Mr. Willoughby. He just got in. Please hold for a moment while I check his calendar." Alicia put him on hold and smiled at Logan.

"Hi. It's Mr. Willoughby from Portsmouth Naval Yard. He's in Boston today, and wants to know if you're available to meet at three o'clock."

Logan looked at his watch. It was just one o'clock, so there would be plenty of time to grab a sandwich and get caught up with his email. "Tell him yes. If we can meet here that would be great."

"OK." Alicia turned back to the desk and hit the hold button on her phone. "Thanks for holding, Mr. Willoughby. Yes, Mr. Alexander is available to meet with you at three o'clock." She gave him directions to the office and then hung up.

"He seems like a nice man. He was telling me about his son's visit to the emergency room the other day. I guess it was a compound fracture."

"Ouch. Hey, changing the subject, have you had lunch yet?"

"No, I wasn't sure when you were getting in."

"All right. How do you feel about take-out – maybe a deli sandwich from Sammy's place across the street? You fly, I'll buy?"

"Deal!"

Twenty minutes later Logan was tucking into pastrami on rye while Alicia munched on a tabouli salad and hummus dip. Logan had just finished filling her in on the events of the last two days.

"God, I can't believe your friend was murdered in plain daylight right in front of you! How awful for his family." Alicia gathered up the remnants from their lunch and dropped them into the trashcan next to her desk. "So what are you going to do?"

"Just sit tight until we hear back from the Kuwaitis and Detective Breen. Nayef is going to ask Hamid's former boss, Thamir, to coordinate with the Boston Police. He'll know how to handle them in terms of keeping the Iran operation secret. If that gets out, there could be hell to pay on a number of levels."

Logan had revealed the details of the Bandar Deylam operation to Alicia when she had come to work for him. He wanted her to know that her brother had been working on something important when he was tragically killed in a traffic accident in London when they were on their way to Iran.

"I don't think there's any way the Qods Force could've found out who the Americans on the team were," he said. "Everyone we dealt with, except for Nayef and Thamir, knew us in our alias Canadian identities."

"How do you think they figured out who Hamid was?"

"His situation was different. If the Iranians had penetrated Kuwait's Intel service and had come into contact with Hamid, they probably could've figured out who he was. Besides, when they caught him at Bandar Deylam that first time, we can assume they checked out his cover story. If he had any holes in it, that might have been all they needed."

"But how can they just show up here and kill somebody? That's what I don't understand."

"We don't know very much about Unit 400. I do know that there's a history of secret societies in Iran involved in assassination. As far back as the 11th century, the Hashshashin were involved in political assassinations."

"What's the Hashshashin?"

"Historians always thought the word literally translated into 'The Assassins' but it has more to do with the name of their leader, Hassan. They were a bunch of radical Ismailis, a branch of Shia Islam, who followed this Nizari missionary by the name of Hassan I Sabbah. His goal was to get rid of the Turks and the Sunni Muslims who controlled Persia in those days."

"How did he do that?'

"Well, he started by taking over a castle at Alamut, which is in this mountainous area between Tehran and the Caspian Sea. He wanted his base of operations to be in a place that was remote and hard to get to."

"How do you know so much about this?" Alicia looked at her boss in admiration.

"I did some research on the internet early this morning. Cooper was up at five o'clock. Anyway, this guy, Hassan, used the castle as his headquarters and gradually set up a bunch of other fortresses in out-of-the-way places. The

Hashshashin's M.O. was to go under cover and get close to their targets. They were ruthless. They would bide their time, and when the situation presented itself they'd attack. They didn't care if they got killed in the process. Their goal was to eliminate their enemies at all costs."

Alicia shuddered. "That sounds creepy. Almost like suicide bombers."

"Something like that. They were very powerful. By the middle of the 13th century they probably had over 100 fortresses, but then they made a big mistake."

"What happened?"

"One of their leaders at the time lived in what today would be Uzbekistan. He picked a fight with a really nasty dude – Ghengis Khan. Anyway, this guy arranged to have a bunch of Mongol traders in Uzbekistan killed and when Ghengis Khan found out about it he declared war on them. The guy had enough sense not to go to war with the Mongols. Eventually there was a truce because he pledged allegiance to Ghengis Khan."

"These are the same people that were trying to get rid of the Turks and the Sunnis, right?"

"Yes."

"So, why would they tolerate the Mongols? Wasn't Ghengis Khan trying to conquer the world?"

"I doubt they were really loyal to Khan. They just knew they couldn't openly challenge him. Anyway, years later the Hashshashin tried to kill Mongke Khan, Ghengis Khan's grandson. After that they were doomed."

"What happened to them?"

"The Mongols attacked their headquarters at Alamut and then lured the Hashshashin leader to their capital by offering him clemency. When he and his guys showed up, Mongke Khan's brother took them out and killed them."

Alicia shuddered. "That's just way too much killing as far as I'm concerned. Those guys needed to chill out." She looked at her watch. "Hey, changing the subject; it's two-thirty. Mr. Willoughby will be here in half an hour. Do you need to review anything before your meeting?"

"Thanks for reminding me." Logan stood up and stretched. "Could you bring me the notes from my trip up to Portsmouth last month?"

Logan had visited Portsmouth at the invitation of Willoughby, who was running a small project for the SEAL and Special Warfare Combatant Craft (SWCC) people in the Navy. Willoughby had been an SWCC crewman in Vietnam, and although they had never worked together, Logan had found his name on the SEAL and SWCC Special Warfare website, where Willoughby had posted a message about his program. One thing had led to another and he had invited Logan to come up and check out their program at the Naval shipyard.

The shipyard at Portsmouth had been in continuous operation for over two centuries. In recent years their bread-and-butter program had been servicing Los Angeles-class submarines. The naval yard had been awarded the contract to overhaul and modernize the aging fleet of fast attack subs that were first commissioned in 1976. Forty-two of the original sixty-two LA-class subs were still on active duty.

But constant pressure from Congress to reduce defense spending, $500 billion this year alone, regularly threatened to close Portsmouth's historic gates. The bipartisan Base Closure and Realignment Commission (BRAC) was all set to shut the shipyard down in 2005 and again just this year, but special interest groups and Portsmouth's new contract to overhaul the Navy's newest fast attack submarine, the Virginia class, had bought them a reprieve. Their motto, "From Sails to Atoms," must have resonated with someone, Logan thought, as Alicia deposited his notes on the desk.

"Do you think Mr. Willoughby is going to offer you something?"

"We'll see. He's running a small program that's been working on the Mark V special operations craft. It's been around for a while, but the Navy's had some problems with it."

Fifteen minutes later Gordon Willoughby (USN Retired) breezed into the office. At sixty-two, the former Navy SEAL was distinguished by his close-cropped white hair and slate-blue eyes. He oozed the kind of confidence and vitality evident on the handsome profiles of sailors on Navy recruiting posters. His friends said that after his first wife unexpectedly passed away from breast cancer, he had gone into a downward spiral, but then, three years later, had met and then married Gabby Hughes, a vivacious local TV news anchor twenty years his junior.

"Hi, Logan."

Logan gave an involuntary wince as his hand was enveloped in Gordon's vice-like grip.

"Sorry I had to cancel the other day. Did Alicia fill you in on the paintball accident?"

"Yeah, she told me. How's your son doing?"

"He'll be all right. At eighteen they think they're invincible. It was his left arm. It seems that falling twenty feet out of a tree onto hard ground isn't good for the body." He grinned, and then took the seat that Logan offered.

Willoughby pulled some notes from his briefcase. "So, last time we talked, we were going over the Navy's special boat teams. Now, this little program they've seen fit to give me involves some of the craft being used by Special Boat Team 20."

"The SBT 20s are the units doing maritime and coastal operations over in Europe and the Mediterranean, right?"

"And South America. Each of those commands has detachments on board amphibious ships and then there are a couple of units in Stuttgart, Germany, and Rota, Spain."

"Aren't those units mainly using the Mark V?" The Mark V had been manufactured in Gulfport, Mississippi, back in 1995, but had seen its share of problems over the years.

"That and some rigid-hull inflatable craft." Willoughby paused before continuing. "It's the Mark V that I'm working on. You know the history of the Mark V, right?"

Logan nodded.

"After it went into service in 1995 our crews began complaining that the aluminum hulls vibrated too much. They'd open them up full throttle and the whole boat would vibrate like nobody's business. No one thought that was going to be a big deal until we started to see an increase in crew injuries. Everything from serious neck trauma to cracked ribs." Willoughby shook his head and exhaled in exasperation as he looked down at his notes.

"Right, and then the Navy contracted with a company up in Maine to modify the Mark V to get rid of that. They came up with some kind of a new hull design that's supposed to be stronger and vibrate less. I was reading something the other day that said the Navy's optimistic their new design will solve the problem." Logan pointed to an article on the bookshelf next to his desk.

"It's still too early to tell while it's being tested. That's where I could use your expertise. It's not that I don't trust the people up in Maine. They're a respected design and build outfit. What I'd like to do is give you all their design data, their test results, etc. I want you to crunch their numbers and give me an independent assessment. The deliverable would be a written report and briefing to my command in six months."

"You want me to *red-team* their results? Do they know you've approached me?"

Willoughby pulled some additional paperwork and computer discs out of his briefcase and looked up at Logan. "No, and I want to keep it that way. It shouldn't come as a big surprise to them. They know how the DOD operates. But to preserve the integrity of what I'm asking you to do, I'd rather they not know who's doing the *red-team* exercise. I think that way, when you present your report, there will be no question about whether or not they influenced your findings."

"All right. Will I get a chance to go over any of their modified boats?"

"That won't be a problem. We're supposed to get one in next month. You can take a look at it before it's delivered to them. Meanwhile, take a look at this contract and nondisclosure agreement. If you agree to the terms you can get started right away.

"Your clearances should still be valid; it's only been a year since your discharge. I'll have our security people transfer them over to us. Once you're on board we'll give you access to our database at Portsmouth. You can get into it from home or your office using an encryption program. It has all of the current Mark V documentation, and there's also an archive in there with all kinds of historical background on the program."

Logan looked over the contract and secrecy agreement. He resisted the urge to gulp when he saw how much they were offering him for his assessment. Six figures was a lot more than he had ever made as a Navy SEAL.

"Looks good."

After they had both signed the contract, Logan walked Willoughby down to the lobby.

"I'm looking forward to working with you, Gordon." They shook hands and after Willoughby had disappeared through the glass doors, Logan danced into the elevator and rode it back up to the 16th floor.

Alicia was just hanging up the phone as he walked into the office. She finished scribbling on her notepad and arched an eyebrow as her boss did a little jig and gave her a smile and a big thumbs-up as he headed into his office.

"That was Thamir Alghanim. He's coming to Boston next week and wants to meet with you. He said it was important. Here's his contact information." Alicia handed the note to Logan, and looked as though she was going to say something, but thought better of it.

"What?" Logan sat down in the chair opposite her desk. "Did Thamir say where he was going to be staying?"

"At the Hyatt Harborside."

Alicia looked down at her desk, and Logan was surprised to see that she was on the verge of tears.

"Hey, Alicia, what's going on? What's wrong?" He got up and walked around the desk to stand next to her.

She sniffled and then burst into tears, looking up at him. Her voice cracked as she spoke. "It's just that with Hamid getting killed and all this talk about Iran, and now

Mr. Alghanim coming here, I couldn't help thinking about John."

She plucked a tissue out of the box on her desk and blew her nose. Removing a compact from her purse, Alicia examined her face to see how much damage she had done. "Darn, my mascara's all over the place." She dabbed at the splotches on her cheeks, and then sighed.

"Hey, I know what you're going through. After Cooper was killed, I was a wreck. I think the only thing that kept me from losing my mind was the thought of getting back at those bastards. I don't think you ever really get over it, though."

Logan stared out at the boat traffic on the harbor. He could barely make out the ferryboats maneuvering into their moorings near the Aquarium, white foam from the prop backwash churning the water. The haunting sound of the foghorns wafted all the way up through the double-plated windows.

Turning back to Alicia, he took the note with Thamir's contact information and then folded it, putting it into his pocket. "Thanks. Why don't you take off? It's been a long day. We can talk more about the Portsmouth project tomorrow."

After she left, Logan returned to his office. His mood was deflated as he ran through yesterday's events in his mind. Thamir must be coming to Boston to coordinate with Breen on Hamid's murder investigation, he reasoned. The Kuwaitis were moving fast on this. Maybe they had dug up something on Nouri Khorasani. And maybe Thamir could fill him in on what they knew about the mysterious Unit 400.

Chapter 5

Nouri Khorasani hurried away from the Cambridge apartment building. His assignment had been to eliminate Hamid Al Subaie, and he had accomplished that with surprising ease. It had taken almost a year for the Qods Force to piece together the story of what had happened at Bandar Deylam, culminating in his successful attack against Al Subaie. But the Kuwaiti's death wasn't enough. Sure, the little bastard had played an important role in destroying the IED facility, embarrassing the Republic beyond repair. But he hadn't been acting alone. There had to be other accomplices and it was Nouri's job to find and punish them.

It was risky for him to operate in Boston. Even with his authentic Spanish passport and cover legend, he was concerned that someone might recognize him. Still, it had been five years since he had boarded the plane for Dubai at Logan International Airport, eventually making his way to Tehran.

It had been an easy decision for him to leave Massachusetts. His brother, Armeen, had always been the favorite child in their family. And although Nouri and Armeen were physically identical twins, their similarities ended there. Armeen had been a star in high school – honor student, class president, drama club, and popular with everyone. After graduation he went on to Northeastern to major in criminal justice.

Nouri, on the other hand, had been flunking most of his classes, was sullen and a loner. It hadn't helped that in his senior year, his parents, desperate to get to the bottom of his dissolution, in a series of psychological tests, discovered that he had a rare condition producing a chemical imbalance in his brain.

Nouri's condition could be treated with drugs, but his years of loneliness, deep feelings of inadequacy and nearly universal estrangement had become a kind of shield, buffeting any attempt to steady his badly damaged psyche. After high school Nouri tried setting up a home business as a reseller on E-Bay, and he showed some entrepreneurial talent. He valued the solitude of working by himself at his computer.

Nouri glanced back over his shoulder and saw that he was alone. He slackened his pace and contemplated his next move. Going to Al Subaie's apartment had been a calculated risk. The police might have had the place under surveillance, and nothing he could have said would have explained his presence there. It was bad luck that that couple had stopped in front of Al Subaie's door just as he was trying to jimmy the lock. But he was desperate to find out if there were any clues in the apartment that would lead him to the others who had been working with Al Subaie.

Nouri found his rental car and threaded his way through Boston traffic to the Ted Williams Tunnel and connecting arteries feeding into the Boston Turnpike. He was catching a flight out of Hartford's Bradley International Airport for Madrid via Toronto at eleven o'clock. He planned to take a train to Burgos that same afternoon.

Two hours later Nouri dropped off his Buick Regal in the Enterprise lot at the airport. His flight boarded on time and he settled into his business class seat.

"Going to Toronto on business?"

Nouri appraised the paunchy, balding man sitting beside him. "No, actually. Pleasure. I have a friend from college who's getting married and we're all meeting up there for a bachelor party." No sense revealing his actual destination to this clown. You never knew when a careless remark might come back to haunt you.

"First time to Toronto? You'll enjoy it. I live in Mississauga – a Toronto suburb."

Nouri didn't want to encourage conversation with his seatmate so he just nodded, closed his eyes and pretended to sleep. In less than an hour the captain was announcing their imminent arrival in Toronto.

Nouri transited the airport without incident and departed on his Iberia flight to Madrid on time. Driving to Hartford and going through Toronto had been a hassle, but he had learned that in the long run it paid to be cautious. He was setting up smokescreens, covering his tracks. His Claudio Diez Perea identity was authentic. It had been carefully pieced together over time, beginning shortly after his uncle had introduced him to the Qods Force colonel who would change his life forever. It was highly improbable that anyone would make the connection between Spanish businessman, Diez Perea, and the troubled dropout, Nouri Khorasani.

He thought back to that conversation five years ago. He had met the colonel at his uncle's apartment in south Tehran. Nouri had arrived there only two weeks before, but he had been restless, uncertain of what the future held for him. One certainty was that he did not want to go back to his life in Boston.

His uncle had introduced him to Colonel Kashani and then had left the two of them alone in the den. Nouri was grateful that his parents had insisted on teaching the twins Farsi when they were growing up and using it with them at home. They were both fluent.

"Nouri, your uncle tells me that you've recently arrived from the United States, no?"

He had felt uneasy under the colonel's intense scrutiny, but managed to mask his discomfort. "Yes, I wanted to check out the place. My parents left Iran in the late '70s and have never been back. They always talk about how great it was here, and how they wish they could visit."

"What's preventing their return?"

"You know. They left because of the change in government. I mean, they're religious but they're not fanatics. From what they've told me, I doubt they'd fit in."

The colonel had merely given him a tight-lipped smile. They had talked for a half-hour on a wide range of subjects, and then Kashani had bid him goodbye. They had met several other times over the next month, and one day Kashani had invited Nouri to the Laleh Hotel for a meeting with a colleague of his. He had been surprised when the man introduced to him, Hans Fitzer, turned out to be a German businessman from Frankfurt.

Over a lunch of *chelo kebab* in the hotel's thirteenth-floor restaurant, Nouri had become increasingly puzzled over the purpose of his meeting with Fitzer. Colonel Kashani had disappeared right after the introductions were made and had not returned.

After their meal, over coffee, Fitzer had folded his hands together under his chin and studied Nouri. "Nouri, would it surprise you if I were to tell you that I am not really German, that my birthplace is Mashad, and that I am an officer in the Qods Force?"

Nouri sat back in surprise. Fitzer admittedly did not have traditional Germanic features, but his accent, mannerisms and dress all bespoke a northern European background. "What do you mean? Why are you telling me this?"

Fitzer paused before responding. "What I am going to tell you is very sensitive. The reason I'm talking with you is that Colonel Kashani feels that you have the background and qualities to become one of us."

Nouri took a sharp breath and his mind began to race.

"Several years ago Iran's leaders recognized that we needed certain capabilities if we were going to be capable of operating effectively abroad. The Islamic Revolutionary Guard Corps was aware of MI-5's and CIA's use of non-official cover officers to conduct their most sensitive clandestine operations. Our group, Unit 400, has a very narrow mission, one which will be shared with you only after you are deemed a suitable candidate." Fitzer withdrew a card from his pocket and handed it to Nouri. "Come to this address tomorrow morning at eight-thirty if you're interested in finding out more."

Fitzer paid the bill, shook his hand and said goodbye. "Think about it, Nouri. I haven't regretted one day since

I said yes to the same question you are being asked to consider."

That had been five years ago. Despite some trepidation, and perhaps more out of curiosity, Nouri had shown up at the nondescript address opposite a park in the northwest suburb of Shahara early the next morning. He was admitted to the building, and over the course of the day had been subjected to a battery of written and physical tests. He also had several one-on-one interviews. At the end he was told that he would be contacted if there was interest in following up.

Nouri snapped out of his reverie.

"Excuse me, sir. Would you like the filet mignon or the salmon?" The Spanish flight attendant was pure eye candy, with her long jet-black hair and expressive brown eyes, and her pert breasts stretching the fabric of her red jacket.

"I'll have the filet mignon, please. Oh, and could I have a glass of the Rioja?" Nouri had to admit that he enjoyed this aspect of his life under cover in Spain – taking delight in the wide variety of Spanish wines, something he could never do in Iran. After the flight attendant brought his meal, he continued to reminisce about his transition from misfit to elite Qods Force killer.

For that is what he had become. Over the course of three years he had learned his craft. At a secret Qods Force training facility just outside Tehran, Nouri had been transformed into a killing machine. He had become proficient in the use of an arsenal of weapons — handguns, assassin's dagger and garrote — and had earned a black belt in *wushu*. Unit 400 was a team of assassins.

While in training, Nouri had also begun to hone his skills as a computer security consultant, working several afternoons a week in a Qods Force front company in Tehran. He had spent so much time around computers growing up that he soon mastered the intricacies of the work.

Building his Spanish identity had been complex, but not insurmountable. Nouri had accessed several databases of online immigration records to identify a deceased Spanish immigrant to the United States with no living kin. Using this man's records, Nouri had applied to the Spanish government for Spanish citizenship, claiming to be the deceased immigrant's grandson. He had used a Qods Force-manufactured alias U.S. passport and the actual immigration records of the purported relative to support his application.

Backstopping the story had been labor-intensive but well worth the effort. The Spanish government had changed its immigration code in 2003 to permit the children and grandchildren of Spanish citizens who had immigrated abroad, to become Spanish citizens themselves. Accordingly, the petitioner only had to reside in Spain for one year and then apply to the head of the civil registry where he was living for permanent immigration status. That office would submit the application to the Ministry of Justice to adjudicate.

Because his fictional grandfather had maintained dual citizenship, and because there were no living relatives to throw a monkey wrench into his application, the immigration petition had sailed through the ministry without a glitch.

The Qods Force had decided that Nouri should attend the University of Salamanca to further bolster his cover story and to satisfy the one-year residency requirement. He had moved to Salamanca, just west of Madrid, two years before to enroll in the university's world-renowned Spanish language school. Nouri spent a year in the intensive language program, and the following year moved to Burgos, where he had set up a small computer security consulting company.

He dozed off and on and before he knew it the pilot was announcing their imminent arrival at Madrid Barajas Airport. He took the metro to Madrid Chamartin train station, just four miles from the airport. It was still early and with any luck he'd be able to make the two-thirty Renfe express to Burgos. That would put him in just a little after five.

After he'd purchased his ticket at the Renfe kiosk, he browsed the shops in the huge hall. He was looking for something to read, something in English. It would help him pass the time until he got home. After selecting a recent John Grisham novel, Nouri boarded his train, found his seat and placed his bag in the overhead rack.

What he'd love to do, but couldn't risk with so many people around, was to log onto his computer and check the website his Unit 400 handlers used to get messages to him, to see if there was a message from Tehran. He imagined that news of his exploits would have reached them by now. They would be pleased with him. They always were when he killed. He settled back into his seat with a self-satisfied smile and a sense of anticipation. Perhaps there would be news of his next assignment.

Chapter 6

Thamir Alghanim emerged from Customs and Immigration towing a carry-on bag and nothing else. He caught sight of Logan in the Arrivals area and waved to him as he jostled through the crowd. As director of operations for Kuwait's Intelligence and Security Service, Thamir sometimes traveled in alias, but because he had official business with the Boston PD, Logan was pretty sure that he would be entering the U.S. in true name on his diplomatic passport.

Logan recalled the first time that he had met the Kuwaiti Intel chief. It had been at the Crowne Plaza Hotel in Kuwait City about a year ago. Nayef had arranged for Logan to meet him and his uncle, billionaire financier Ali Al Subaie, doyen of the Al Subaie family, to discuss plans to destroy Iran's IED research and training camp at Bandar Deylam.

That initial meeting had been cordial, but Thamir had struck Logan as something of a cold fish. His handshake had been limp and he had a tendency to let his gaze wander around the room rather than making direct eye contact. Over the past year though, Logan had come to respect Thamir's judgment and decisiveness. Logan had concluded that while he might not be comfortable around his fellow man, Thamir was an honorable professional who could be trusted to keep his word.

"Logan, it's good to see you again!" He reached for Logan's outstretched hand, and, true to form, gave it a limp squeeze.

"I'm sorry it had to be under these circumstances, Thamir. I know that Hamid was one of your best officers." Logan offered to take his bag but the slender Kuwaiti demurred as they walked towards Logan's car in short-term parking. The air outside was bracing, and Thamir instinctively buttoned up his overcoat.

"No, it's not just that. Hamid had already moved on and I had accepted his decision. With his father wanting him to get into the family business, I knew there was little chance that I could convince him to stay on with us. No, I have known Hamid since he was an infant. I was even at his *Aqiqah* ceremony."

"What's that?"

"It's a naming ceremony. According to traditional Islamic practice, when a child is seven days old his head is shaved and he's given his name. I can still see Nayef holding Hamid up for all of us to see and shouting out, Hamid Al Subaie! After that the family typically sacrifices an animal to celebrate the occasion. In Hamid's case, two goats were offered that day."

"So, is it like being a godfather?"

"No, that's a Christian custom. Muslim families are typically multi-generational so usually there are many family members around. As you know, men and women are, for the most part, segregated, and for a boy, those male relationships matter the most. I was a close friend of the family. I suppose my relationship with Hamid could best be described as that of an uncle."

Once they were in the car, Logan looked at the clock on the dashboard and saw that it was already eleven-thirty. Thamir had a one p.m. meeting with Detective Breen at the District Station on Harrison Avenue.

"What do you say I get you over to the Hyatt? Did you request early check-in?"

"Thanks, that would be perfect. Yes, my secretary took care of it. They said it wouldn't be a problem. I'd like to take a shower and change before I meet with the police. Logan, I don't know what your thoughts are, but I think it would be best for me to see the police alone. I don't want to arouse any suspicions over how we know each other. They would certainly be interested if you were to show up there with me."

"Not a bad idea. I think it pays to be careful. When I first met with Breen last week, he was curious about how I knew Hamid. I told him that I had met Nayef through my sister, Millie, and that he had asked me to help Hamid if he ran into any problems getting settled in here. But there's really no logical explanation for how you and I would know each other. I suppose if it comes up, you could just tell him that Nayef asked me to help you out in Boston. Will we have time to get together after your meeting?"

"Yes, I'd like that. I'm flying to Washington tomorrow to meet with my people at our Embassy. They have also arranged a meeting for me with some of the CIA's Iran analysts. They are very good in some areas, but I want to see if they have anything on this Unit 400 that they can share with us. Anyway, perhaps we can meet later this afternoon. I have discovered some things that you will find interesting. I also have a letter in my bag for you from Nayef."

"Why don't you come over to our place for dinner? I'm sure Zahir would like to see you again."

"That's very nice of you. What time is best?"

"How about seven?"

"That's perfect. I'll see you then."

Logan pulled up to the Hyatt and helped Thamir get his bag out of the back. They shook hands and Logan watched as the Kuwaiti Intel chief disappeared inside.

Later that evening Logan had just put Cooper down for the night and walked back into the kitchen, where Zahir was putting the finishing touches on dinner. He wrapped his arms around her and breathed in the mint smell of her shampoo.

Zahir leaned back as he buried his face in her hair. "What do you think Thamir found out today?"

Logan pulled back and walked over to the wine cooler to select a bottle of red for dinner. "It's hard to say. Breen hasn't re-contacted me since that meeting I went to with Nayef."

"The one where you spotted the picture with Armeen Khorasani on their bulletin board?"

Logan was looking in the drawer for a corkscrew. He found one and began opening the bottle of Cabernet Sauvignon. "Yeah. I think Breen thought I was a nut case when I told him that Armeen was the killer."

"But then it turns out that Millie recognized the same guy as the one who attacked them at Hamid's apartment."

"Millie and Ryan were lucky he didn't do anything more violent. It's a good thing Ryan didn't try to be a hero. Nouri's already proven himself to be a ruthless killer. I didn't see his face when he stabbed Hamid, but he strolled away from that as cool as a cucumber. He could have killed Millie and Ryan and just walked away."

Zahir shuddered. She walked over to the stove to check on the *tah-dig,* a golden-crust rice dish that her mother had taught her to make. The hardest part with *tah-dig* is getting the crust on the rice just right. She liked to use basmati rice with just a hint of saffron. The trick was to cook the rice on low, and use a dish towel wrapped around the lid to absorb the liquid.

Logan lifted the foil covering the rack of Persian chicken and sniffed. He had never eaten much Persian food before he'd met Zahir but since then had become a fan. He unconsciously patted his stomach. This recipe was simple – garlic, lemon, cracked pepper and salt mixed into yoghurt and slathered over boneless chicken breasts.

"Are you sure Thamir won't be offended if we have wine at dinner?" Zahir moved into the dining room to survey the place settings.

"I don't think so. I mean, I know he doesn't drink, but in his job he travels a lot and is entertained by foreigners who serve alcohol at meals. I'm sure he'll ask for tea but won't mind that we're having wine."

The doorbell chimed, and Zahir walked over to welcome their guest.

"Zahir, how nice to see you again. Thank you for inviting me." He handed her a bouquet of purple asters and walked into the room where he caught sight of Logan lighting the gas fireplace.

"Hi, Thamir. Thought I'd start a fire to take the chill off."

"Logan." He walked over to where Logan was standing and clasped his hand. Looking at the photos on the mantelpiece, he did a double-take, and then looked over at Zahir.

"So, rumors that you are related to the Pahlavis are true? But this picture of you and the Shah. It's not possible. You can't be that old." Thamir looked perplexed as he gazed at the photo of the former Shah of Iran and a young woman in her twenties.

"Actually, you're right. That's not me. That's a picture of my mother. She was the Shah's favorite niece, and that picture was taken in 1975, so she would have been twenty-five years old. Everyone tells me that I look just like her when she was my age."

"Do you stay in touch with that side of the family?"

"My parents' generation was always pretty close. I grew up in Virginia, and a lot of my mother's family gravitated to D.C. after they left Iran, so there was a fair amount of interaction with my cousins while I was growing up."

Thamir looked thoughtful. "I always felt that what happened to the Shah was a shame. It was certainly a lesson for others in the region whose power was being challenged by conservative Islamist theocrats."

"I think a lot of Iranians who supported the Shah's removal from power rue the day they handed the government over to the Ayatollahs. It hasn't turned out quite as they had hoped." Zahir sighed and gave Thamir a wistful look.

"Would you like a cup of tea? Why don't you and Logan talk, and I'll finish putting dinner together. Is black tea all right?"

"That's perfect, Zahir."

Logan led their guest over to an armchair in front of the floor-to-ceiling windows overlooking Boston Harbor. Zahir returned with Thamir's tea and a glass of wine for Logan. Thamir leaned back in his chair and sipped his tea appreciatively as he gazed out at the lights on the harbor before speaking.

"Hamid was right."

"About what?"

"About the service being penetrated by the Iranians."

Logan sat up straight. "How did you find that out?"

"After Hamid raised his concerns about a penetration, we went back and scrubbed our entire Iranian program." Thamir set his cup down. He leaned forward and fixed his gaze on Logan. "Do you remember that fellow, Simon, who was at the safe house when you first met Hamid?"

"Yes." Logan had debriefed Hamid in Kuwait City almost a year ago. Hamid had been masquerading as Jaber Behbehani, and had just returned from an undercover operation in Iran, where he had suffered a brutal beating at the hands of the Qods Force base commander.

"Well, it turns out that Simon was recruited by the Qods Force, almost three years ago."

Logan let out a low whistle. "But how did that happen? Wouldn't your internal security procedures have picked up on something like that?"

"It's not that cut and dry. Simon had been in the service for over ten years. There was nothing in his background to indicate that he was capable of a deception of this magnitude. He came from a good family and there were no red flags in his personnel file.

"When we started looking into this, though, we discovered that Simon had taken a number of trips outside of Kuwait over the past several years which he could not explain. Normally our officers have to report all of their private foreign travel, but he had failed to do so. Oh, he tried to tell us that his trips were for tourism, but that story didn't hold up under questioning."

"Don't your officers have to take polygraph exams or get their clearances updated? It seems like that would have come out then."

"No, we don't use the polygraph. We find it too unreliable. A good liar can manipulate the results. But we do conduct periodic background checks. Normally these take place every five years or so. Simon was about due for one when all of this came to light.

"But I digress. Aside from the unauthorized travel, when our investigators began to dig they discovered that there were occasional deposits into Simon's bank account from an unknown source."

"Have you confronted him with this?" Logan knew that in the U.S. the FBI would sometimes allow an espionage suspect to continue operating while they built their case against him. This is a risky business because the Feds don't want to tip off their target by taking away his access to sensitive information, but on the other hand they can't risk having highly classified information being passed to the enemy.

Typically they'll arrange to transfer the individual to a position requiring a lower level security clearance in order to minimize the damage the person can do as the investigation plays out. This tactic also helps to allay any concerns the suspect might have that he's under investigation.

Thamir paused before responding. "Yes. It turns out that his handlers were not as careful as they should have been. While they were mindful not to meet Simon in Kuwait for fear of being discovered, they were less discreet about his financial affairs. The suspicious deposits and lifestyle changes are what tipped us off."

"What was he doing?" Logan asked, just as Zahir walked into the living room to tell them that dinner was being served.

"Oh, he bought a Mercedes and bragged to some of his colleagues about an expensive piece of jewelry that he had purchased for his wife."

Thamir sniffed appreciatively as they arranged themselves around the dining room table. "What are we having?" he asked as he took his seat.

"Persian food. *Tah-dig,* which is a kind of golden crusty rice, and a Persian chicken dish my mother makes."

As they ate, Thamir continued the discussion from before. "Simon was exposed to most of our Iranian program. He was working with our non-official cover officers like Hamid, who conduct sensitive operations inside Iran. He had access to nearly everything we were doing."

"Did he know about our operation at Bandar Deylam?" Logan poured another glass of wine for himself and refilled Zahir's glass. "Thamir, more tea?"

"No, thanks." Thamir helped himself to a piece of chicken. "Simon knew that we were interested in the base, and obviously was aware of what had happened to Hamid there. Also, he was one of the few people in the service who knew Hamid's true identity. Despite the fact that he had met you and interpreted for you when you debriefed Hamid, he didn't put two and two together.

"Of course, he must have suspected that something was going on but probably assumed that you were just collecting intelligence, not plotting a covert attack. I don't believe Simon had an opportunity to meet with his handlers before he died."

Logan looked up, startled by Thamir's words. "What? He's dead?"

"Yes. About four months ago, he went into the hospital for a medical exam. He had been experiencing some sharp pains in his stomach and back and had lost an unusual amount of weight. He was diagnosed with pancreatic cancer, and his condition deteriorated rapidly. He never returned to his home."

"I can't say I feel very sorry for him based upon what you just told me. It's probably because of him that Hamid is dead." Logan pushed his rice around his plate, and winced at the thought of his friend's murder.

"Simon made a deathbed confession of sorts regarding Hamid. Apparently he had no means of contacting his handlers except through pre-arranged out-of-country meetings. Obviously he knew that we were sending Hamid into Bandar Deylam with that group of Kuwaiti foreign fighters, but he had no way of letting his handlers know that before they left."

"But how could you believe him after what he did?" Zahir looked at Thamir with an expression of disbelief on her face.

Thamir held up his hand. "Let me finish. Believe me, it was not easy. After Hamid returned to Kuwait, Simon wanted to set the record straight with the Iranians. Remember,

Colonel Ghabel thought he was dealing with some low-level Jihadi named Jaber Behbehani, when in reality he had one of Kuwait's elites in his hands."

"So, do you think this was all about Simon trying to preserve his relationship with the Iranians?" Logan wondered if Ghabel would have handled Hamid differently if he had known his true identity.

"It's hard to say for certain. He may have been concerned that Hamid's family connections would come to light once the Iranians started looking into it, and he was afraid they would think that he had purposefully withheld this information from them. Worst case, he feared that the Qods Force would conclude that he had been doubled back against them by our service and that he was responsible for running Hamid into Iran to collect intelligence."

"Shall we have coffee and dessert in the living room?" Zahir asked. "I have some baklava."

"That would be nice, Zahir," Thamir replied.

Logan helped her clear as Thamir returned to the living room. He was inspecting family photos on one of the bookshelves when Logan returned bearing a tray with coffee and an assortment of baklava.

"Logan, who is this other couple?" He pointed to their wedding picture, which had been taken earlier that year in Montpelier.

"That's my sister, Millie, and her husband, Ryan. We had a double wedding up at my folks place in Vermont in April."

"Ah, yes. Nayef has mentioned her before. She's a big help to him in his work."

As they sat down and helped themselves to coffee and dessert, Logan returned to the subject of Simon's espionage for the Qods Force.

"So how did Simon get word to the Iranians?" he asked.

"He went to the one person he felt he could trust," Thamir replied. "One who would not betray him. Simon recruited his son."

Chapter 7

Logan stared at Thamir in disbelief. "Are you telling me that Simon lured his own son into this mess just so he could save his relationship with the Qods Force?"

"Don't be so shocked, Logan. The annals of espionage are replete with cases of fathers who have ruined the lives of their children by recruiting them to spy for them. Look at that U.S. Navy communications specialist, John Anthony Walker. His whole family became part of a spy ring for the Soviet Union."

"You're right. That case was a black mark on the Navy. Walker started spying for the Russians way back in the '60s. If I remember correctly, Walker first got his wife to help him, but later on he recruited his brother and his children, too. The Walkers gave the Soviets so much sensitive information on our naval capabilities that at one time they knew where the entire U.S. submarine fleet was. If the balloon had gone up during those years that Walker was working for them, we would have been hosed."

"Do you remember the case of that CIA Operations officer, Jim Nicholson? He also worked for the Russians. After he was convicted and serving time in prison, he recruited his son, Nathan, to meet with his handlers so that he could collect money they had promised his father. I don't believe Nathan was convicted of espionage when this came out, but he was charged with conspiracy after he met with the Russians abroad and at the Russian Consulate in San Francisco."

"Anyway, it seems that Simon and his ilk had plenty of company."

Zahir brought in a sugar bowl and creamer. As they helped themselves to the baklava, Logan recapped what Thamir had said for her.

She shook her head in disbelief. "So, what's Kuwait going to do about Simon's son? Are you pressing charges?"

"He was cooperative with our agency and the investigators, so we will go easy on him. He won't go to jail, but this will be a black mark on his record forever. Personally, I think Simon knew that he was dying and he told his son to save himself. We know from our investigation, that the son met with the Qods Force one time in Kuwait City. It was at that meeting that he passed the Iranians a message revealing Hamid's true identity.

"When we tried to demarche their station chief, he was suddenly unavailable and supposedly had to travel back to Tehran. He hasn't returned to Kuwait. We know from the description that Simon's son gave us that he was the one at that meeting."

"How was your meeting with Detective Breen this afternoon?" Logan reached over to refresh Thamir's coffee.

"Not entirely satisfactory. The police are using facial recognition technology to see if they can identify Khorasani transiting any of the regional airports around Boston. They also have an APB out with a picture of him, and they're running name checks through state and local databases to see if they get a hit. But nothing has come up so far.

"What I didn't tell them," he went on, "but what has become increasingly clear to me, is that Nouri Khorasani is somehow linked to the Qods Force."

There was a moment of stunned silence as the others took this in. Zahir was the first to speak. "So, you've confirmed that he's working in this Unit 400? But how does an Iranian kid from Boston end up in Iran working for the Qods Force?"

"Obviously we don't have irrefutable proof yet, but it looks more and more to be the case. We've been trying to get a handle on Unit 400, which we have confirmed is a Qods Force operational unit, and while there is much that we don't know, we have uncovered some facts."

Thamir took a sip of his coffee before continuing. "It seems that about five years ago, just about the same time that Khorasani disappeared, there was a push within the Qods Force leadership to augment Unit 400 with foreign recruits. Essentially, Iran's Supreme Leader wanted to develop a capability to conduct political assassinations while maintaining plausible deniability."

"So you're saying that this program had the backing of the Iranian regime's leadership?" Logan shook his head in amazement.

"It isn't a question of the leadership backing it. They were the drivers behind the program. Anyway, we now understand that the Qods Force had some success recruiting first-generation Iranian immigrants in Europe, South America and the United States. Their thinking seems to have been that amongst this group, they would be able to identify young men who had not adapted to their adopted countries and, therefore, felt no particular loyalty to them."

"In a way it reminds me of my brother's situation," Zahir interrupted. "He never fit in here. And it seems that with all the U.S. involvement in the Middle East since 9/11 he's become increasingly conservative and hostile in his attitude towards the government."

"He sounds like the disaffected Kuwaiti youth that we were tracking when Hamid went into Iran the first time with those foreign fighters. The Iranians are recruiting from the same pool for this program. Their spotters are out there, and when they identify someone with the background and qualities they're looking for, they bump him."

"I haven't heard that term before. What do you mean, bump?"

Logan spoke up. "It's like physically bumping into someone. They'll find an innocuous way to meet their target so that they can assess him in person. If he looks like a good fit they might approach him then and there, but if they think he won't be receptive to their approach, they'll find a way to introduce him to somebody else. If they like what they see, they'll try to recruit him."

"We think that's what happened to Khorasani," Thamir said. "His uncle may have been a spotter for the Qods Force.

I understand that he was working in Iran's Department of Immigration and Citizenship, so he would have been in a perfect place to pass leads on to his buddies in the Qods Force."

"So you think the Qods Force recruited Khorasani and then set him up in this Unit 400?"

"We're still working on it, and I'll let you know as soon as I find out anything definitive. One thing we do know is that after they're trained, Unit 400 personnel deploy as singletons around the world. They get set up in their cover businesses and wait for orders from Tehran.

"They're mostly autonomous as far as their cover jobs go, but Tehran gives them their operational marching orders and funding. Ali Al Subaie is trying to help me figure out what we need to look for in order to grasp how their funding mechanisms work. Understanding that may give us some leads."

Logan knew that the elder Al Subaie fully understood the intricacies of financial transactions in the Middle East. He had set up a funding mechanism for Logan to use when they were planning the raid on Bandar Deylam. It had involved what amounted to cut-outs and money laundering in order to de-link Kuwait and the Al Subaies from Logan's special operations team.

"Well, I have to be going. I have an early flight to Washington tomorrow. Thank you both for dinner. Oh, before I forget, Nayef asked me to give this to you personally." Thamir withdrew an envelope from his pocket and handed it to Logan. "I have a feeling I know what that is about. Let's stay in touch."

After Thamir had left, Logan and Zahir sat down in the living room. Logan slit the envelope and unfolded the single sheet of paper.

"Dear Logan and Zahir,

"We buried Hamid last week. It was the cruelest moment of my life. To put him in the ground before his time was heart-wrenching. He was my hero. Naturally, Nisreen is devastated by his death. He was our only son, and she worshipped him.

"By now, Thamir has told you what we know about Unit 400. It is precious little, but, Logan, we must stop them before they kill again! If we can find the person that did this to Hamid, he must pay for what he has done to our family.

"I will be in Boston in ten days on business. If you have the time, I would like to meet with you to see what might be done.

"Sincerely,

"Nayef Al Subaie"

Logan stared at the letter for a moment and then looked up at Zahir. "Nayef wants to go after Unit 400. He's asking me to take out Nouri Khorasani!"

Chapter 8

Logan had to drive up to Portsmouth the next morning to meet with Gordon Willoughby, who had arranged for him to get some time on one of the Mark V special operations craft that had just been delivered to the shipyard. He'd left Boston at six o'clock, but Willoughby had been called into a meeting at the last minute so Logan and one of his sailors, Seaman First Class Cyle Hockaday, were having breakfast before heading over to the shipyard.

Hockaday had recommended Ruth's Diner, a greasy spoon perched on Daniel Street, a quiet passage in historic downtown Portsmouth near St. John's Episcopal Church. It wasn't much to look at, but people traveled far and wide to eat at the local landmark. Ruth's Down East Special, with bacon, eggs, home fries, French toast, and coffee, was a gut-buster.

Hockaday was a scrawny kid from Biloxi, Mississippi. He had the pinched look of one chronically underfed, and indeed the seriousness of purpose with which he tucked into the Down East Special caused Logan to wonder if the Navy wasn't feeding its own as well as it might.

Logan had ordered coffee and Irish eggs — eggs Benedict atop a mouthwatering helping of corned beef hash.

"So, Hockaday, how long have you been in the Navy?" Logan could tell from the red stripes on the sleeves of Seaman Hockaday's Navy whites that he was a fireman, meaning that he specialized in ship's engineering and hull maintenance.

Hockaday finished chewing a mouthful of French toast before responding. "Three years, sir. Signed up in Biloxi and shipped out to Great Lakes Recruit Training Command. After that I went to tech school in San Diego. Spent two years out there and took some correspondence courses. Got my E-3 last year and was transferred up here to work on Mr. Willoughby's program." He took a tentative sip from his steaming mug of black coffee and relaxed.

"Portsmouth's a long way from Biloxi."

"Yes, sir, but I've always been on the water. Our family ran shrimp boats in Biloxi. Seems like that's what we've always done. We shrimped just off the Gulf of Mexico in Mississippi Sound. We was on the water pretty much from June to December every year. I worked on one of our boats all summer, and then when school started, just weekends and holidays."

"So you're no stranger to the water. How do you like working on this project with Mr. Willoughby? The Mark V's?"

"It's pretty good. Ain't nobody going to make a career out of working on the Mark V, though. The Navy's spent a whole lot of money fixing something they should've got right the first time."

"How's that?"

"I think they rushed 'em into production back in the '90s without working out all the kinks. The first ones came out in 1995, and right off they started having problems. Them things would just jitterbug like all get out if you cranked 'em up over thirty knots in rough seas."

"Right. And then a lot of the crews were getting injured because of the excessive vibrations. I remember reading an article about it in the *Journal of Ship Production and Design*." Logan shook his head and picked up his coffee cup.

Just then Gordon Willoughby walked into the diner. He slid into the booth next to Logan and ordered a cup of coffee. "Damn bureaucrats," he griped.

"What's going on?" Logan gave Willoughby a questioning look.

"Oh, the usual. You don't want to hear about it. You guys solving the problems of the world?"

"Seaman Hockaday's been filling me in on some of the historical problems with the Mark V."

Willoughby gave Hockaday an appreciative look. "Hockaday's good on the Mark V. Don't let his youthful looks fool you. He's sharp as a razor."

Hockaday appeared embarrassed by his boss's praise, but continued, "Thank you, sir. The Navy knew they had a big problem on their hands and they had to do something about it, so in 1998 they started looking for a fix. The issue was that they weren't really focused on the hull problem. They came up with what turned out to be a short-term fix, although at the time I think they figured they were good to go. It did help, but in reality it didn't cut down on the number of injuries SEALs were reporting."

"What was their solution? I hadn't read about any modifications to the boat that early." Logan looked a little perplexed as the waitress came by and refilled their coffee mugs.

"Well, a couple of guys thought that if they could reduce the vibrations in the seats, that would solve the problem. So they designed a new seat with shock absorbers and then got the Navy to buy off on retrofitting all of the Mark V's in their inventory."

Logan looked at Seaman Hockaday with newfound respect. "How'd you get so smart on the Mark V?"

"When I found out I was coming up here to work with Mr. Willoughby I read everything I could on it. But, getting back to your question. There was twenty Mark V's in operation in 1998 and each one of them had twenty-one seats, so the Navy figured it was going to have to replace over 400 seats altogether.

"So they did it, and I think it did smooth things out a bit. There was one problem though. If you cranked that sucker up to forty-five or fifty knots in rough seas it would still shimmy like a belly dancer. I think that made the Navy brass more nervous than a long-tail cat in a room full of rocking chairs." Hockaday sat back in his seat and nodded his head.

Logan chuckled at Hockaday's colloquialism.

"The design people had just spent all this money retrofitting the seats, and they still had a problem. The Navy's still throwing money at the Mark V, but I'm not sure that at the end of the day we're going to get there." Hockaday glanced over at Willoughby as if to seek reassurance that he hadn't spoken out of turn.

Willoughby just grimaced and shook his head. "Well, if you guys are done jawing, why don't we go on over to the shipyard and have a look-see for ourselves?" He grabbed the check and handed the waitress a twenty. "Keep the change, sweetheart."

Fifteen minutes later they drove onto the base. As Willoughby edged through morning traffic towards the drydock where the Mark V was moored, Logan could see the bridge and conning tower of an old submarine on display in a grassy area off to the right. He hadn't noticed it the last time he had visited the base.

"What's that?" he asked, pointing to the beached sub.

Willoughby pulled over next to the curb in front of the sub. "Come on. I want you to see this."

As they piled out of the car and walked up to the display, Logan could see from the brass plate affixed to the sub that the aging hulk was a memorial to the *USS Squalus*.

Walking around the bridge, Willoughby explained the significance of the memorial. "The *Squalus* was built at this shipyard in the late '30s. She was conducting sea trials just off the Isle of Shoals in the spring of 1939 when she went down."

"What happened?"

"If memory serves, the main induction valve failed, causing massive flooding below decks. I think it started in the aft torpedo room and then spread to the engine compartments and the crew quarters. The *Squalus* sank in over 200 feet of water. Twenty-six sailors drowned that day."

Logan shuddered as he thought of the sailors stranded beneath the surface, water gushing in and nowhere to go. They were trapped and knew they were going to drown. "It must have been terrifying for them."

Willoughby continued. "The Navy brought in a submarine rescue ship. We didn't have a whole lot of experience with that kind of operation in those days. They used the ship as a diving platform, deploying a diving bell, which was a fairly new piece of gear for the Navy then. It took them awhile but they managed to save the remaining crew members. Thirty-three of them had found airtight compartments on the sub where they could hunker down.

"After the rescue the Navy salvaged the *Squalus* and brought it back here to the shipyard. It was refurbished and then re-commissioned as the *Sailfish*. I believe the *Sailfish* went on to make a significant contribution to the naval effort in the Pacific during World War II and was eventually decommissioned in 1948."

They piled back into Willoughby's car and drove over to the drydock facility. Inside, the *Seahorse* was out of the water, suspended like a beached whale. Despite its problems, the Mark V was an amazing weapons system, Logan thought as he ran his hand over the port side of the ship. He'd been operational in the Mark V on a couple of missions and recalled the excitement of yanking and banking, that feeling of flying and turning through the water as the helmsman approached their insertion point.

The Mark V could rip, that was for sure. He climbed aboard and, going below decks, poked his head into the engine compartment. "Hockaday, what are the specs on these engines?"

Hockaday joined him below decks. "What you're looking at there are twin MTU 12-cylinder Diesel engines. There's also two K5OS water jets. That's what gives the Mark V that sudden acceleration when you need it.

"Lookit here," he said pointing to the fuel tank. "This thing will hold 2,600 gallons of diesel fuel. That's almost 500 nautical miles range if you're operating at maximum speed."

As they moved about below decks, Logan had a feeling of déjà vu. He'd been on a Mark V SOC detachment that had deployed from Norfolk to Southeast Asia to conduct a hostage rescue mission. Their entire mobile unit had been deployed aboard two U.S. Air Force C-5 Galaxies within forty-eight hours of notification.

The unit had consisted of two boats, each with five crew members plus sixteen SEAL operators. It had been tight quarters over the course of two days, but they were too focused on the mission to worry about their own comfort.

A group of American missionaries who had been running an orphanage in Jakarta, had been kidnapped by the terrorist group Jemaah Islamiyah, or JI. The terrorists had moved the hostages from Jakarta to the western part of Java, and were reported to be holding them in the vicinity of Ujong Kulong National Park.

The SEAL detachment had liaised with a CIA paramilitary officer with contacts inside the Indonesian National Police. One of the INP's counterterrorism experts from Detachment 88 came down to work with them and to provide intelligence support.

They'd gone in under cover of darkness from the Sunda Strait, deploying off the tail end of the Mark V's in combat rubber raiding craft. That had been a good night. Eight dead JI and five live hostages. As Logan was reminiscing, Willoughby peered down at them.

"You water jockeys going to keep jawing down there?" He grinned as he climbed down to join them.

"Nah. I was just thinking about the last time I was on one of these babies."

"It gets the job done, no doubt about it. It packs in a whole lot of capacity in a relatively small package. Eighty-two feet long, 17.5-foot beam and about fifty-seven tons when it's fully loaded.

"Let's go back topside and take a look at the hull." Willoughby turned to lead the way out. The three men climbed back up the ladder and dropped down to the dock.

"You know the Navy originally had three different hull designs they was considering when the Mark V proposal was first bid out," Hockaday said.

Logan looked surprised. "I knew there was talk about using Kevlar for the hull, but I didn't think they were serious. I thought the two most competitive design teams came up with a couple of different concepts for an aluminum hull. One was for a catamaran design and then this one, the monohull. What else were they looking at?"

"One of the teams came up with a Kevlar composite monohull. I don't know what the Navy thought of it at the time but the aluminum monohull obviously won out over the other two." Hockaday scratched his head.

"Pork."

Logan and Hockaday both looked at Willoughby in surprise. "Pork?" They both echoed the question at the same time.

"Yeah, pork. Some fat-ass senator from Mississippi was probably sitting on the Senate Appropriations Committee and worked the deal so that company back home would win the bid."

Logan recalled then that the Mark V had originally been built in Biloxi. He and Hockaday shook their heads in disgust.

"Hey, it must be nice to have friends in high places. Those politicians in Washington are always looking to work the system so that it benefits their constituents back home. This may have been a good deal for Mississippi, but it sure as hell ended up being a bad deal for the Navy." Willoughby tapped the aluminum hull with his fist, producing a dull thud.

"Each of these babies came in at about $3.5 million each. There were twenty built, so that's around $70 million. Not exactly chump change in those days."

"It's ironic that the modification this company in Maine put forward is in fact a composite hull." Logan gave a rueful shake of his head and walked along the side of the *Seahorse*, running his hand along the hull. "It's not going to be Kevlar, though, right?"

"No, sir. Not just Kevlar. They're planning to use Kevlar on the outside, but inside they're going to alternate layers of carbon fiber and a foam core. It's surprising, but this boat's going to be lighter than the original design and a whole lot sturdier."

"These guys were smart," Willoughby interjected. "Their design team got together with some folks at the

University of Maine who were working on advanced composite materials. They collaborated and came up with what looks like a winner.

"But that remains to be seen. The Navy wants to get it right this time, Logan. With sequestration being a near certainty in Washington, our pot is about to get a whole lot smaller than it has been over the past ten years.

"That's where I'm counting on you. With you bird-dogging this thing for us, I'll feel a whole lot more comfortable making a decision when it comes time to fish or cut bait." Willoughby appraised the former SEAL with unblinking candor.

"You can count on me, Gordon. Just make sure you keep me in the loop as this thing moves forward." Logan gestured towards the Mark V. "The last thing we want is any surprises."

Chapter 9

"Get up, Pedro!" Nouri, now in his Claudio persona, circled his sparring partner at the *wushu dojo* on Calle de San Juan, like a caged animal. It had been a week since his return to Burgos, and he was still feeling the jet lag from his trip to the U.S. Still, he was pleased with how easy it had just been to take Pedro down.

"You're too good for me, Claudio," Pedro grumbled as he got to his feet.

Nouri's preferred style of the *wushu* martial art was *kung fu* and his favorite form had been developed centuries before by the monks at the Shaolin Temple in China's Henan Province. The Five Animal Form was based upon special attributes ascribed to the dragon, snake, tiger, leopard and crane. The dragon form was Nouri's favorite.

Pedro had come at him with an aggressive right punch, and he had countered by using his left hand to fend off the attack while thrusting his right to execute a dragon claw to Pedro's throat. After inflicting the dragon claw, Nouri delivered a two-finger strike to Pedro's eyes with his right hand.

Blinded, Pedro didn't see the sweep kick to his front leg coming, followed by a right knife-edge kick to his left leg. He had gone down hard. Nouri took perverse pleasure in seeing the *dojo* master writhe in pain.

They sparred for another fifteen minutes before calling it a day. Nouri showered and left the martial arts studio. He had a meeting later that night with a Qods Force courier from Tehran. Normal protocol was to meet in a third country; they didn't like to meet him in Spain, and frequent travel to Iran was too risky for him. But there were times when Tehran needed to get something to their man and the only way to do it was through a personal meeting.

73

Nouri passed in front of the monument to El Cid and reflected on the irony of El Cid's life. Rodrigo Diaz de Vivar, more commonly known as El Cid Campeador, had been a nobleman born just a short distance from where this monument stood. Although he was regarded as Spain's national hero, few people remembered that he had actually served the Muslim rulers of Zaragoza for almost a decade after a falling out with King Alfonso of Leon and his subsequent exile.

In 1086 El Cid had been offered an opportunity to reconcile with the king, when Alfonso was defeated by Almoravids from North Africa. But he did not join Alfonso in his bid to regain the contested territory, choosing instead to turn his attention to Moorish-controlled Valencia. There he spent the next several years wresting control of the city away from its Muslim occupiers, eventually going to war with them.

Nouri turned to cross a small footbridge spanning the Arlanzon River. It was still early, and nearly deserted. Midway across, two men turned onto the trestle from the opposite side, and began walking in his direction.

Nouri watched as they approached him. Burgos had a very low crime rate, but with Spain's economic problems, thefts and burglaries were on the rise. He tensed as the two pedestrians drew abreast, but relaxed as they passed him without saying anything.

"You!"

Alarmed, he turned to look back and saw that the two men had reversed direction and were approaching him. One had withdrawn a knife from his waistband and the other was brandishing a flexible metal baton.

They stopped a few feet from him. "All right, asshole. Just give us your wallet and you won't get hurt." The one with the knife had spoken. He licked his lips and made a menacing gesture with the knife.

"You want my wallet? Fuck you. Come and get it."

The one with the baton rushed him, snapping the baton open and lashing out as he approached. Nouri watched him coming and at the last second, moving with lightning speed, sidestepped and executed a kick to his assailant's groin. The man went down hard, dropping the baton and curling up in a fetal position. As he lay there moaning, Nouri faced the knife-wielding attacker and waited.

The man circled him and then lunged forward, thrusting the knife in a downward motion towards his chest. Nouri came in under the thrust, pivoted and turned the knife on his foe, driving it into his heart. The man's eyes went wide as the knife entered his body. He shuddered and his body slackened, flailing against the bridge railing.

Nouri stooped and flipped his assailant over the guard-rail, watching coldly as the corpse plunged into the river below. He then turned back and looked at the crumpled shape on the bridge. Walking over to the now motionless figure he stared into his antagonist's eyes. "Who's the asshole now, asshole?" He delivered another well-aimed kick to the man's head. "Don't come near me again or I'll kill your ass." The limp figure shuddered and then was motionless.

Nouri briefly considered just getting it over with then and there. Then he wouldn't have to worry about whether or not his victim would come looking for him later. He was feeling magnanimous, though. Let the poor bastard live. Once he got his balls dislodged from wherever they'd landed he'd be spending the rest of his days looking over his shoulder.

Brushing off his clothes, Nouri continued across the bridge and turned down Calle San Pablo. He entered a non-descript café and ordered a *café cortado,* espresso with just a drop of milk, and a chocolate croissant.

After the waiter had brought his order, Nouri let his mind wander. Selecting Burgos as his base of operations had been a calculated decision. The incident on the bridge was the first time he had experienced a problem here. With a population of just under 200,000, crime had not been a major concern. He'd have to be more careful, though. As unemployment edged upwards of twenty-five percent across Spain, people were becoming desperate.

Burgos offered all the amenities of a small city and pro-
vincial capital. There were good transportation links in and
out of the city, and despite the heavy Christian emphasis,
with medieval churches, palaces and other landmarks, it
was not an unpleasant place to live. Besides, who would
think to search for the elite Unit 400 assassin in a city whose
streets were lined with gothic cathedrals, monasteries and
ancient universities?

Nouri finished his breakfast and wandered outside. It
was cool and he buttoned his leather jacket to ward off the
chill as he began his surveillance detection route. His meeting with the Qods Force courier was not until eight-fifteen
p.m. at site *Lobo*, a pedestrian underpass northeast of Burgos
Cathedral. He would spend the next twelve hours cleansing
himself, making certain that he didn't have any company
when he met his contact.

He flagged a taxi and got in. "Take me to the Monasterio
de las Huelgas," he instructed the driver.

"Yes, sir."

Fifteen minutes later, the driver let him out in front of
the monastery, located on the western outskirts of Burgos.
Nouri stood in front of the twelfth-century royal retreat and
marveled at the extravagance that generations of Spanish
royalty and their pope in Rome had lavished on these clois-
tered halls.

He spent forty-five minutes wandering through columns and arches, pausing to read the inscription in front of
Alfonso the VIII's sepulcher. He looked at the gothic memorial with a mixture of respect and repugnance. Alfonso had
been the one responsible for reestablishing Christian control
on the Iberian Peninsula. Nouri continued to search for any
signs that he was being followed, but could see nothing out
of the ordinary.

Although the Berbers had defeated Alfonso's army,
the king had rallied a coalition of Christian sovereigns and
knights from all over Europe to take on the entrenched occupiers. The Christians had prevailed at the famous Battle of
Al Uqab, which in turn had set in motion events that would

ultimately dislodge the Moors from Europe. Nouri liked visiting the royal retreat to remind himself that there was still much work to be done to reinstate Islam and wipe the self- satisfied smiles off the faces of these Christian devils.

After leaving the monastery, Nouri crossed to the north bank of the Arlanzon at the Malatos Bridge. Descending to the path, he walked southeast on the Paseo de la Isla, a tree-lined pedestrian and bicycle path paralleling the river. He stopped to purchase a lottery ticket from an old man, and then turned north, cutting through a nameless alley before stopping at a hole-in-the-wall café with outdoor seating.

Nouri ordered a café con leche and sat back, appearing relaxed. His easy appearance belied a mind at work. He was observing, cataloging, and filing away for reference any anomalies that he had seen on the street. Did anyone seem to have more than casual interest in him? Were there people out there whose movements tracked with his own? Had he noticed any vehicles multiple times over the course of the morning?

He paid for his café and walked over to a nearby *bicibur* station. The *bicibur* was Burgos' public bicycle rental system. The bicycles were staged at more than twenty locations around the city and were available to both residents and tourists alike. Burgos had over sixty miles of bicycle lanes throughout the city and Nouri liked incorporating them into his surveillance detection runs to make it more difficult for anyone who might be following him in a vehicle.

Nouri navigated the bicycle onto a path, following the yellow scallop shell that marked El Camino (the Way of St. James). El Camino was a Christian pilgrim route through Spain to Santiago de Compostela. For centuries, Christians had been making the trek to Santiago to pay homage to the martyr St. James, the only apostle whose remains were alleged to be buried in Europe.

Nouri smirked inwardly. The Camino was known worldwide to be a Christian pilgrimage, but he had noticed that, of the thousands of pilgrims from all over the world trekking through Burgos every year, many didn't seem particularly religious. They were there for the food, the wine, and the scenery. And for some there *was* a spiritual component, but it wasn't necessarily religious.

Nouri, like any healthy young male, had a strong sex drive, but, given his work, he couldn't afford to be seriously involved with anyone. Thus he had found it relatively easy to prey upon many of the young women making the pilgrimage alone to satisfy his cravings. A casual encounter over wine often led to dinner, and then an invitation to his apartment. There was no illusion that these liaisons were about anything other than uninhibited sex.

He was an experienced lover, but he was a taker, not a giver. The women he brought to his apartment never wanted to spend the night, sensing his detachment or perhaps the danger that lurked just beneath the surface. They always made an excuse about needing to get back to their hostels. He could envision them, shouldering their backpacks at daybreak, flocking out of the city like lemmings in the direction he himself was now headed.

After about forty minutes on The Camino, in the direction of Fromista, Nouri got off the trail and doubled back towards Burgos on the highway. He hadn't seen anything suspicious, but then again his ability to detect surveillance under these conditions was limited because the path was not unlike a channel. A capable surveillant could remain out of sight, lingering behind, knowing that Nouri was somewhere up ahead.

He ditched the bicycle at a *bicibur* station in a northwest suburb of the city. The exercise had made him hungry and he decided to find some place to grab a *bocadillo*, those tasty sandwiches made from baguettes filled with razor-thin slices of *jamon serrano*, the dry-cured Spanish ham. He had long ago given up any pretense about not eating pork.

After lunch, Nouri left the tavern in search of a taxi. He flagged down a white Mercedes and told the driver to take him to Parque del Castillo, a hilly area in the north section of Burgos, offering a panoramic view of the city. Nouri positioned himself in the rear seat so that he could covertly check the mirror to see if they were being followed, but he saw nothing untoward.

Later, walking through the terraced gardens below the ruins of the castle, he cast a hasty glance over his shoulder. His pulse quickened as he thought he recognized a middle-aged man in a green windbreaker from his stop at the monastery, but upon closer scrutiny this proved to be a false alarm.

And so his day continued. The monotony of the exercise was undeniable, but the benefit of having the level of certainty he required in order to preserve the fiction that he was nothing more than a computer security consultant with a day off was invaluable. It's what made him an effective instrument for the Regime, an anonymous killer.

As the time of his meeting approached, Nouri's pace involuntarily picked up. He caught himself rushing, and forced himself to slow down. It wouldn't do to get to site Lobo too early. At eight-ten he committed to going to the meeting. Except for the fellow in the windbreaker at the Parque del Castillo, Nouri had seen no anomalies all day. He was confident that he was alone.

As he entered the dim pedestrian walkway he was on high alert. He was uncertain whom he would be meeting; it was never the same person. His contact would be wearing a yellow sweater vest and would use the word *soup* in a sentence. He was to reply with a sentence using the word *shelter*.

A street person was walking towards him and Nouri grew anxious that the beggar would see him meeting his contact. Nouri kept a wary eye on the panhandler as he approached, and was surprised when the latter adjusted his raggedy jacket to reveal a yellow sweater vest beneath.

"Excuse me, sir, do you know if there is some place I might get a cup of soup around here?"

Nouri looked at the bum, and wondered if it was just a coincidence that he was looking for something to eat. But, no, he was wearing the visual signal. Well, he'd use his verbal paroles and find out. Then it would be the bum's move.

"I'm sorry, friend. There's nothing close by, but there is a rescue shelter only five blocks from here. Perhaps you can get something there."

The bum relaxed and, after looking around to make certain that they were alone, withdrew a bulky envelope from within his jacket. "Tehran's come out with new COVCOM software for everyone." Nouri nodded. He was familiar with having to learn new covert communications software, as it was frequently updated.

"The program is on the thumb drive in the envelope and it will walk you through the download and installation. Here's your mid-year funding, 100,000 in clean euros, and finally an operational note from the boss."

"General Salehi?" Nouri took the envelope from the courier and stuffed it into an interior pocket in his leather jacket.

But the bum was already moving away from him, shuffling and hitching up his pants. He looked back. "Yes," was all he said and then he was gone.

Nouri continued moving in the opposite direction. It was imperative to clear the area, just in case anyone had been following the courier or had observed their brief meeting. He spent another hour walking, and when he was certain that he had no surveillance he took the stairs up to his fourth floor apartment on San Juan, in the city center. He was tired, but he was anxious to see what the general had to say. Maybe Tehran had found out what he had not. Who had been working with that little Kuwaiti bastard, Hamid Al Subaie?

Chapter 10

"Thanks for coming in, Mr. Alexander." Detective Peter Breen gestured towards the empty seat next to his desk. It was Thursday afternoon, a week after Logan's encounter with Thamir Alghanim. He had been surprised by the unexpected call from the detective, and had readily agreed to meet with him.

The afternoon shift change at the station was in full swing and the hallway outside Breen's office was crowded with blue suits. As Logan took his seat he was startled to catch a momentary glimpse of newly-minted rookie, Armeen Khorasani walking by Breen's office. He made eye contact with Logan and nodded in recognition.

Logan inclined his head and then turned back towards Breen. Armeen was a carbon copy of his brother, Nouri. This was only the second time Logan had come into contact with the young police officer since Hamid's murder, and he still found the likeness somewhat unnerving.

Breen got up to close the door. "They're all coming in for their pre-shift briefing," he explained.

BPD was one of the oldest police departments in the nation, second only to Philadelphia, Logan reflected. The Hub had its share of violent crimes, but with over 2,000 police officers and half as many civilian employees, Boston's streets for the most part felt safe. Unless you were an innocent victim like Hamid, he mused.

Breen returned to his desk, shuffling through several reports in a file folder marked Hamid Al Subaie. He pulled one out, sat back in his chair and looked at Logan. "We got a hit on Nouri Khoransani."

Logan sat up straight in his chair. "Where'd you find him? Is he in custody?" His mind rejoiced at the prospect that Hamid's murderer would soon be brought to justice.

"Not so fast. We're not exactly sure where he is. What we were able to do, though, is figure out where he went the night that Mr. Al Subaie was murdered, but for now that trail's gone cold."

"What do you mean?"

"After our last meeting, when you identified Khorasani, we decided to use Armeen's photo on the APB we put out. We couldn't very well use a still shot of Nouri from the surveillance footage at Macello because there wasn't a good image of his face. Anyway, we had several initial false sightings, people who had actually spotted Armeen and called it in, but nothing on Nouri.

"We had no idea what Khorasani was doing. Did he decide to lay low? Was he on the run? If so, how was he traveling? Our premise was that he was probably on the move, thinking it would be too dangerous to stay around here."

"Was there any record of Khorasani entering the U.S.?"

"That's the strange thing. Nothing. Oh, we were able to dig up an old ICE record of his departure five years ago. Flew to Dubai out of Logan. But that was of no help in this instance.

"We have a good relationship with TSA, so we were able to watchlist Khorasani's passport right after you identified him. For some reason that was never done when his parents filed their missing person's report five years ago. But like I said, no hits on the passport so far." Breen pulled a pack of gum out of his desk drawer and offered Logan a stick.

"You know anything about biometrics, Mr. Alexander?"

"No more than the next guy. I know it's been a big part of Homeland Security's push to improve airport and border security under the Patriot Act. They've supposedly spent billions of dollars doing research and installing equipment in airports."

Breen nodded in agreement. "There were pilot programs in our regional airports beginning as early as ten years ago. I think pretty much everybody does fingerprints nowadays, but they've also experimented with other capabilities. A number of airports are trying out retinal scanners and facial recognition technology. Logan Airport and Hartford International both got in on the ground floor and they're using facial recognition technology to screen incoming and outgoing passengers on international flights.

"Nouri Khorasani went through security at Hartford International Airport the night Mr. Al Subaie was murdered."

Logan stared at Breen in disbelief. "I don't understand."

Breen looked grim. "The Feds have been working since 2005 with other federal, state, local and international law enforcement agencies on something they call their Next Generation Identification program, a biometrics program on steroids. A key component of NGI is its archival capabilities and computer systems running algorithms only a grad student at MIT would understand.

"When our request hit TSA, they ran it through their system and got a hit. Khorasani went through airport security at ten-thirteen p.m. September 17th."

Logan's mind raced at the implications of what Breen had just said. "So let me get this straight. Khorasani passed through security, but he wasn't flagged as a person of interest because your APB hadn't hit yet, right?"

"Bingo. The reason it hit the next day is because TSA ran the photo we gave them against its archived database and identified Nouri as having gone through the previous evening. The interesting thing though is that there is no record of a Nouri Khorasani boarding a flight out of Hartford on September 17th."

"That's because he's probably using a fake identity. He must be traveling on an alias passport." Logan looked glum. "Is there any way to check the security cameras in the airport to track which way he went after he got through security?"

"We're already on it. But I think we've got something better."

"What's that?"

"There was only one flight scheduled to depart Hartford that night between the time Nouri transited security and the time flight operations closed down at midnight."

"Where was it going?"

"Toronto. We're already working with Air Canada to get a flight manifest. Once we have that in hand we can get TSA to run the names against the passport information in NGI. The facial recognition program will flag the passport and that should tell us what identity Khorasani's using."

The phone on Breen's desk rang. "Breen here. Hi, Sheila. That was quick." He mouthed the letters TSA to Logan. Logan leaned forward in his seat in anticipation.

"Any luck with the Khorasani file?"

"What?"

Logan could not hear the other end of the conversation, but he could tell from the exasperated sound of Breen's voice that he was unhappy.

"But how can that happen? All right. Let me know as soon as you hear something." He hung up the phone and shook his head in disbelief.

"You're not going to believe this. That was my TSA contact in Hartford, Sheila Kennedy. According to her, there's no way to identify Khorasani's alias identity from the information we have.

"She says that under current procedures, Khorasani was able to check in, go through security and board his flight without scanning his passport. At each of those points, standard protocol is to perform a visual inspection of the travel document."

"So you're saying there's a flaw in the system?"

"It would seem so. Someone who hasn't been flagged in the NGI system as being a person of interest can go through security in an alias persona, and TSA wouldn't be any wiser. As long as their documents didn't raise a red flag and the photo on the passport matched their face, the inspectors wouldn't have a reason to question them.

"The only way TSA might catch someone at that point would be if the traveler was acting suspicious in line and they pulled him into secondary for questioning. You know they have people whose job it is to just study the passengers for any unusual behavior, evasive actions, that sort of thing."

"So what's your next play?"

"I'm not sure. We're going to have to work this out with the Canadians. We don't know if Khorasani's destination was Toronto, somewhere else in Canada or if he was just transiting Canada to get to a third country."

"How's your relationship with the Canadians?"

"We've actually got an officer doing liaison work up there. He's in Montreal, working on a counterterrorism project with the Royal Canadian Mounted Police — you know, the RCMP. He gets along with them, cop-to-cop kind of thing. But their bureaucracy is ten times worse than ours."

"Why's that?" Logan felt a mounting sense of frustration as he listened to Breen's explanation.

"They go way overboard on what they call their charter rights. I think the full name of it is the Canadian Charter of Rights and Freedoms. It's essentially Canada's bill of rights. You know — their political, social and legal rights. Things like habeas corpus, right to privacy, and due process.

"Anyway, in many cases their charter guarantees all these rights, not only to Canadian citizens, but to anyone, regardless of citizenship, who is physically present in Canada."

"Why is that bad?"

"It makes it almost impossible to get any information out of the Canadians. Used to be that despite the charter, their law enforcement would share information with us. That all changed a few years ago because of a high profile Al Qaeda terrorism case that blew up in their faces. The Canadians felt like we pulled a fast one when one of their citizens, a dual Canadian-Syrian national that we'd been investigating, traveled to the U.S. right after 9/11. He was detained by the Feds, and subsequently deported to Syria, where he later claimed he was tortured. Trouble is we didn't tell the Canadians we were planning to send him to Syria, even though we have a bilateral consular agreement with Canada and should have given their people consular access to this guy while he was in U.S. custody."

"Who made that decision?" Logan shook his head in disbelief.

"I think it was some hotshot lawyer at the Department of Justice. Anyway, flash-forward a couple of years and this guy gets out of prison in Syria and gets repatriated to Canada. He goes public with his story, and a bunch of bleeding heart liberals in Parliament decided to call for a special investigation. They established a government commission to look into the matter, the head of the RCMP got the axe, and the government tied itself up in knots answering the commission's questions. The cops up there called it Judicial Jihad. The RCMP, Canada's Security Intelligence Service, and everybody else involved in the thing had to stop doing their regular police work because they had all their people culling through files for the commission. At the end of the day, the Canadian government awarded this guy millions of dollars in damages and extended an official apology from the prime minister.

"So now, whenever we ask the Canadians for information we just get stonewalled. If it's about a Canadian citizen or someone in Canada, you might just as well forget about it."

Logan felt his heart sink at the prospect that Khorasani might just get away with Hamid's murder. "So where does it stand now?"

"We'll keep pushing this request with the Canadians to see if they'll tell us anything. At the same time we'll still go through the passenger manifest to see if we can track him down that way. We're also going to alert INTERPOL to our investigation and get Khorasani on their watchlist.

"Don't get discouraged. Sometimes these things take awhile. There's a lot of moving pieces, but it's going to become increasingly difficult for Mr. Khorasani to move around."

Logan stood up and thanked Detective Breen for his time. He was disheartened by what he had just heard. If the detective was right, Khorasani could be anywhere by now.

Traffic was light as Logan left the station house. It was three o'clock, and Boston's heavy rush hour had not yet begun. He wheeled away from the curb in the direction of Fan Pier. Fifteen minutes later he pulled into his underground parking spot, locked the car and took the stairs to the main lobby.

Miguel wasn't at his usual spot behind the reception desk. An elderly African-American male whom Logan didn't recognize rose to greet him as he paused in front of the desk.

"Good afternoon, sir. May I help you?"

"I'm Logan Alexander. Alexander Maritime Consulting. And you are?" Logan peered at the concierge's name tag.

"Sam Cleveland, Mr. Alexander."

"Are you filling in for Miguel?"

"Miguel's going to be off for a couple of days. His wife went into labor early this morning and had to be rushed to the hospital."

Logan recalled then that Miguel had told him that he and his wife were expecting their first child in October.

"Hope everything's going to be all right. Seems a little early. You don't happen to know where they took her, do you?"

"I think Miguel said something about Mass General."

"Thanks."

Logan continued moving towards the elevator, lost in thought. He'd have Alicia call over there to see if she could find out anything. If Miguel's wife had gone into labor this morning, she might have already delivered. Or worse yet she could still be in labor.

Seconds later the elevator doors whished open and Logan walked the short distance down the hallway to his office. Alicia was on the phone, and waved to him as he entered the suite.

"Yes, Mr. Willoughby. I'll tell him. I'll let you know as soon as we get the file." She hung up the phone and smiled at Logan.

"That was Mr. Willoughby."

"So I gather. What's up?" He plopped down in the armchair next to Alicia's desk.

"Two things. He's sending over a compressed file of test data from that company that's refurbishing the Mark V. He'd like you to take a look at it and give him your initial impressions. Oh, and he wants you to go to Rota."

"Rota? As in Rota, Spain?"

"That's what he said. The SEALS have a unit over there."

"I know. But I thought the Navy was talking about closing it down. Not Rota, but Special Warfare Unit 10, the SEAL special boat team based there."

"He didn't say anything about that. Just that their special boat team is scheduled to do some training in the two Mark V's they have there."

"Yeah, those Mark V's belong to Special Boat Team 20 out of Little Creek, Virginia. I wonder what Gordon's up to, sending me to Spain?"

"He said you'd probably ask that question. The big thing is that he wants to keep our role in the project under the radar. He said that the contractor that's refurbishing the Mark V's has somebody working with Special Boat Team 12 in Coronado and another guy working with Special Boat Team 22 at the John C. Stennis Space Center in Mississippi. If they saw you poking around asking a bunch of questions they'd be suspicious."

Logan stood up and stretched. "Did he say when he wants me to go?"

"The training is scheduled for Monday and Tuesday next week. If you were to leave tomorrow that would get you there in time for briefings over the weekend and to observe the exercise."

"OK. Did Gordon mention a point of contact?"

"Yes. A Lieutenant Belcher will be expecting you."

"Can you make a reservation for me? First flight out tomorrow, returning Wednesday. I hope Zahir can get some help with Cooper on short notice. I don't know what her teaching schedule is like next week."

"I can help her out if she's in a bind."

"Thanks, Alicia. I'll let her know. I better get home. I've got to pack. Oh, can you also book me into some place near the base. Now that I'm no longer active duty I don't think I'm eligible to stay in transit quarters."

"OK. I'll let you know what I come up with."

"Oh, before I forget. You know Miguel, our concierge?" Alicia gave him a questioning look. "Yes."

"His wife's having a baby. Looks like it's early. She was due in October, but today they rushed her over to Mass General. Could you call over there and see how she's doing? Her name is Paula. Paula Hernandez de Colon."

"Anything else? You want me to send flowers?"

"Oh. Yeah. Flowers would be nice."

"OK. I'll call you as soon as I get your reservations taken care of. Let me know about Cooper."

"Thanks, Alicia. Talk to you later."

When Logan opened the door to his apartment fifteen minutes later a strong floral scent greeted him. He sniffed and then noticed the vase of lilies, he guessed, in the foyer. Zahir had a passion for fresh-cut flowers and ordered them from the Flower Market in the south end once a week.

He paused in the entryway. Zahir was feeding Cooper and reading him a story about a big yellow dump truck. She paused and flashed a smile at Logan when she noticed him standing there.

He walked over to where they were sitting and bent down to kiss Zahir. Cooper turned his head to look at his father and then nuzzled back into Zahir's breast, making greedy sucking sounds as he smacked his lips.

"How's it going?" Zahir shifted the baby in her arms and smiled as he tugged on an extended finger with his pudgy little hand.

"Just got back from a meeting with Detective Breen down at the station house." He brought her up to date on the BPD's investigation into Hamid's murder.

"They don't have much to go on right now. They know Khorasani left the country the night Hamid was murdered, but other than the fact that he flew into Toronto on some unknown alias travel document, they don't have a clue where he is."

"But now at least he's in the system, right? I mean, from what you said, they didn't have a record of him before in this, what did you call it, NGI?"

"Right, they've got his true name information and all the details from his real U.S. passport, even if it is dated. And, they've matched that to a photo they have of him going through security in Hartford. But, they still have no idea what his alias persona is. Is it U.S., or some foreign passport? We know he's not using his real name, so it's anybody's guess what name he's using.

"I don't know if he realizes how risky it's going to be for him to travel here again. Obviously I didn't mention this to Breen, but if Khorasani is working for the Qods Force, that changes things because the Islamic Revolutionary Guard Corps has access to resources a private person wouldn't have."

"Logan, do you think we're at risk? I mean, look how these people were able to track down Hamid. I can understand how they penetrated the Kuwaiti service and learned his identity, but how were they able to track him to Boston, find out where he lived and know that he was going to be in that restaurant?"

"I don't know. It shows a level of sophistication and dedication of resources that makes me think they're very serious. They probably have other assets in Kuwait and maybe even here who can do stuff like putting a listening device in Hamid's apartment, tapping his residential phone, following him around.

"They must be pretty sure of themselves too. I mean, if they were able to track Hamid around Boston, why didn't they just wait until he was going into his apartment to kill him? It would have been less dangerous for them because it wouldn't be out in the open. We know Khorasani knew where Hamid lived because that's where he was going when he confronted Millie and Ryan. Why would Khorasani do this in a public place? It just doesn't make sense."

Cooper had fallen asleep, and Zahir got up to put him down. When she came back into the living room, Logan told her about his trip to Spain. "I'll be gone for less than a week. Alicia offered to help you out with Cooper if you're in a bind."

"I should be all right. Later next week though things are going to get a little hectic with my PhD course work beginning. I met with my adviser today and registered for two courses – 'Women in the Qur'an' and 'Islamic Thought on the Eve of Modernity.' But the university is really good about letting instructors work their teaching hours around their graduate work."

They moved into the kitchen to work on dinner. Logan opened a bottle of Rioja in a nod to his upcoming trip and sat down on a barstool. Zahir moved over to accept a glass of wine from him. She dipped her finger into the wine and traced it along Logan's lips. He pulled her to him as she lightly ran her tongue along his lips.

His cell phone rang, and he groaned in frustration. Glancing at the caller ID he saw that it was Alicia.

"I have to take this," he whispered.

"Hey, boss. I just sent you two emails – your itinerary and your hotel reservation. There wasn't anything direct out of Boston. You'll be flying into Madrid and then Madrid to Rota. It's Jerez de la Frontera Airport in Rota. You need to be at the airport at ten o'clock tomorrow morning."

"How about my hotel?"

"You're staying at Duque de Najera on Calle Gravina in Rota. It's only four miles to the naval station. That should do it. Have a safe trip and let me know if you need anything."

"Thanks. Call my cell if anything comes up."

He disconnected and looked up. Zahir had moved away and was walking in the direction of their bedroom. She looked over her shoulder and gave him an inviting smile. Dinner can wait, Logan thought, as he grabbed the bottle of wine and hurried after her.

Chapter 11

Although he was fatigued from the lengthy surveillance detection run, Nouri decided to clean up and go trolling. He felt stronger after a hot shower and was relishing the prospect of getting laid. Before going out he scanned General Salehi's note, warming to his praise for the successful Boston operation but noting with a twinge of irritation that he was being directed to travel within days, this time to South America. There was little he could do about it at the moment, so he stashed the note and went out into the night.

He cut through Plaza Mayor, heading to an outdoor tapas bar along the banks of the Arlazon River that he often frequented. After he was seated Nouri spotted an attractive foreigner sitting by herself and invited her to join him. Her name was Pam Stoner. She was a middle-school teacher from upstate New York in Spain to walk El Camino and catch a little action. He asked her if she was enjoying the sites in Burgos, especially the famous cathedral, and she replied that she wasn't really on the cathedral circuit.

She loosened up over a bottle of Casar de Burbia and tapas and did not hesitate, after finishing most of a second bottle, to accept Nouri's invitation to his apartment. She was hornier than hell, reaching for him in the darkened stairwell even before they got inside. He was jarred by her ardor and fumbled with the key as she pressed against him. Once inside, they ripped at each other's clothes and collapsed on the floor, writhing with a desperate, almost primal intensity. Later they fell into a sated slumber on Nouri's bed.

Now it was morning, and Nouri groaned as he tentatively opened his eyes, straining against the glare of the morning sun streaming in through gauzy curtains. He rolled over and contemplated the figure sprawled beneath the covers next to him. The sheet had slipped down below one breast, tattooed with a mini-constellation of blue stars sweeping under her left armpit and up over her shoulder. Little satisfied sighs emanated from her parted lips as she slept undisturbed. Nouri groaned as he slipped out of bed and walked over to his desk, fumbling for a pack of the Ducado *rubio* cigarettes that he preferred. He found the distinctive blue-and-white pack and withdrew one. He was not a big smoker; in fact, the only time he craved the little cancer sticks was after sex.

Pam stirred and opened her eyes. She sat up, stretched her arms wide and yawned. Slipping out of the bed she glided over to where he was sitting and perched on his knee. She removed the Ducado from his lips and took a long drag before returning it to him. She exhaled and cocked her head to one side, examining his face through the spiraling smoke as he fixed his gaze on her.

"That was good, Claudio. Very good."

She reached down to fondle him, and finding him responsive, repositioned herself so that she straddled him in the chair. Their lovemaking was unhinged, and Nouri chuckled to himself as the nursery rhyme "Twinkle Twinkle Little Star" came into his mind as he watched the stars on Pam's breast rise and fall with their movement. She climaxed and then slumped against him until her breathing normalized.

He hoped that she wouldn't be clingy. That didn't usually happen when he brought women here. Besides, he was anxious for her to go so that he could re-read General Salehi's letter.

"I should go." Pam looked at him to see if he would protest, but when he remained silent, she stood and walked over to retrieve her clothes from the floor. "Do you mind if I take a shower? I'm staying at the new municipal hostel near the center of town, and by the time I get over there it'll be time to check out."

Nouri knew that she was right. The hostels ran a tight ship. Lights out by ten p.m. and checkout was usually no later than eight a.m. "Feel free," he said. "There are clean towels over there." He pointed to a linen closet next to the bathroom.

While Pam was showering, Nouri put on a pair of running shorts and went into the kitchen to make a pot of coffee. He could hear the woman singing to herself in the shower. Hitting on the female travelers was genius, he thought. They weren't looking for complicated, long-term relationships. A little action and they were ready to move on. It was perfect for him.

Pam came out of the bathroom, patting her blond hair dry. She walked over to where Nouri was seated.

"Buen Camino," he said, with as much sincerity as he could muster. It was the constant refrain from pilgrims walking, not only through Burgos, but all over Spain. Literally it meant "good walk" but what the words conveyed in Spanish was, "Have a good pilgrimage."

"Do you want some coffee or breakfast before you go?"

She shook her head. "Bye," she whispered. She squeezed his arm and then she was gone.

As he listened to her receding footsteps, he walked into the bedroom and pulled back the wool Persian carpet in front of his bed. One of the floorboards had been modified so that when pressed just so, it popped open on a spring action hinge to reveal a spacious cavity beneath. Within this concealment Nouri kept his operational funds, communications plan, and crypto gear. It was an ingenious device. If anyone were to search his apartment while he was away, they would have to rip the place apart to find his cache.

Reaching down into the hollow space he withdrew the operational note from General Salehi, the Qods Force commander. Nouri had met him only once before. That was when he had graduated from his unit's training class two years ago. Salehi had come out to the school and had given the graduates their marching orders. He was a legend in the Islamic Revolutionary Guard Corps, and, despite his mundane appearance and the flecks of white in his beard, his presence commanded respect. You could almost feel the power pulsating from him, like an old lion. He might be past his prime, but he was still a force to be reckoned with. The general interacted on a daily basis with the Republic's leaders and was a favorite of the Supreme Ruler, Ayatollah Khamenei.

Withdrawing the note, Nouri walked over to his desk and sat down.

"Greetings, Comrade,

"Word of your exploits has reached us, and you find favor at the highest levels of the leadership. In fact, the Supreme Leader himself asked me to pass along his accolades for your brave actions. With this deed we have struck fear into the hearts of those who themselves sought to strike a blow at the Republic with their ill-conceived attack in Bandar Deylam last year.

"That said, we remain convinced that the Kuwaiti aggressors did not act alone. I have said from the outset that this operation has the mark of the Great Satan, the United States, on it, and our people will continue to pursue every lead so that we might identify the perpetrators."

Nouri paused and his chest swelled with pride as he basked again in the general's praise. Salehi himself had said it. None less than the Supreme Leader had commended his actions. He returned to the letter.

"I have appointed a new commander of Unit 400. He is a young colonel, who previously served as the chief of operations at Bandar Deylam. His name is Tahmouress Samadi. You will have a chance to meet him soon. I have asked Colonel Samadi to convene a meeting in Caracas, Venezuela, of our European-based cadre so that he can get to know all of you. The meeting will be next week. Colonel Samadi will reach out to each of you in other channels with specific instructions. Do not make your travel arrangements until you hear from him, but for general planning purposes you should plan to arrive in Caracas over the weekend before the 27th."

Nouri searched the calendar on his smart phone. This unexpected trip only left him a couple of days to take care of some cover business in Burgos that had been awaiting his attention. He shuffled into the kitchen and holding the letter over the sink, set fire to it with his cigarette lighter. As the flame obliterated the general's words, Nouri made a mental checklist of things he needed to do before his trip.

The next morning he took a cab to the Science and Technology Park's Research, Development and Innovation Center, which was affiliated with the University of Burgos. The university had contacted Nouri last year after they had discovered that hackers had breached their system and were stealing proprietary information.

He had put together a security plan that the university had accepted and agreed to implement with some alacrity. Today's meeting was mostly about customer relations, seeing if the university was happy with the results they had achieved. This aspect of his cover job was the least appealing to him. He could be charming when it was called for, but it ran counter to his natural instincts.

He took the stairs to the second floor and saw his contact at the center, Rolando Garcia Lopez, standing outside his office flirting with an attractive brunette. Rolando was the chief information officer for the center.

"Ah, Claudio. Good to see you. How long has it been? Eight weeks?"

"Something like that. It's been awhile." Nouri gave the brunette an appreciative look, but Rolando didn't bother to introduce her.

"Come in, and we can talk about where we are. Dora, let me know about Saturday." He winked, touching her arm in a familiar manner as she turned to go.

Nouri entered Rolando's office. Like the man himself, it had an unkempt look to it. Computer literature was stacked haphazardly around the room, a smudged whiteboard graphically depicted the security infrastructure he and Rolando had first talked about several months before and another chart had a timeline for phases of implementation.

Rolando cleared a chair for him and gestured for him to sit down. He smoothed his beard and tugged restlessly at his mustache. "Would you care for a coffee?"

"No, thank you. I had a cup before I left home."

Looking at Rolando's timeline, Nouri could see that the center had made little progress since their last meeting. He squinted to read his scrawl and was surprised to see that the line addressing equipment purchases remained unchecked. "Didn't the university approve the security upgrades to the system?"

"Well, yes, in principle. The problem is that they don't have the means to fund them at this time. The university has taken an unprecedented cut in its operating budget due to the financial crisis. Our enrollment remains high, over 10,000 students, but the percentage of funding that we normally get from the government has been slashed by twenty-five percent over the last two years. Unfortunately the university does not view computer security upgrades with the same level of urgency that I do."

"Did you explain to them that if these security enhancements aren't implemented, the center is likely to continue bleeding proprietary information to the hackers? That will have its own cost down the road. The last time we met you told me that one of your labs was on the verge of a breakthrough in the biotechnology area. Think of what it would mean if the Chinese or Russians were to get hold of that information."

Rolando shrugged and made a futile gesture with his hands. "Yes, I understand the risks. But it can't be helped. For now my hands are tied."

Nouri shook his head in disgust. It was of no concern to him if the fools making these decisions failed to understand the long-term consequences of their inaction. China and Russia would continue to undercut everyone in the international marketplace because they had turned legions of hackers loose on the world and were siphoning off proprietary information at a breathtaking clip — everything from jet engines to pharmaceuticals.

"Well, there is nothing to do then. When you're ready let me know and we can move forward."

They chatted for a few minutes about the prospects for Real Madrid and Barcelona (Real and Barca) in upcoming league play. Nouri had found that Spaniards were feverish about soccer. The nation was still smarting from its men's team's loss to Honduras in the last Olympics. The Spanish team had been one of the favorites to win a gold and had fallen short, failing to make even one goal in the two matches.

Nouri took a cab back into the city center. He called his contact at Caja de Ahorros Municipal de Burgos to see if his ten-thirty appointment at the bank was still on. The bank had been experiencing anomalies in cash disbursements from its ATMs. As one of Spain's smaller banks, it did not have a very robust information security department in Burgos, and after exhausting all avenues internally to solve the problem, the bank had reached out to him. The person answering the phone told him that there had been a death in his contact's family, and he was unavailable to meet with Nouri until the following week.

Nouri had his driver drop him off in the Villimar neighborhood and walked into Burgos-Rosa de Lima train station. Checking the schedule, he booked a reservation on a mid-morning train to Madrid for the 25th. The route wasn't direct, passing through Aranda de Duero to the south. He was looking forward to the day when the high-speed rail line would link Madrid and Burgos, cutting the travel time to just eighty-four minutes.

Departing the station, Nouri caught sight of his assailant from the week before walking in his direction. He had almost forgotten about the altercation. There had been an article in the local newspaper, *Diario de Burgos,* reporting the murder/drowning of the knife-wielding attacker, but there had been no further leads in the case, according to police investigating the crime.

Meanwhile the survivor of the attack was shuffling towards Nouri, hunched over, hands in his pockets. He glanced up as he drew abreast, and then looked away. Nouri thought for a moment that he would pass by unrecognized but suddenly, realization set in and the would-be thief's head swiveled back to stare at his tormenter in horror. "You!" he stuttered.

He visibly paled and lunged away from Nouri, clawing to get past other pedestrians, looking back over his shoulder as he shoved his way through the crowd. He soon disappeared from sight.

Nouri smirked inwardly. It was gratifying to see the look of panic on the inept thief's face as recognition set in. He frowned at the thought that his attacker could pose a risk to his security if he were to identify him to the police. But he dismissed the worry almost as quickly as it came into his mind. From all appearances the highwayman looked like a drug addict and the last thing he would want to do is draw attention to himself by approaching the police.

Burgos was a small enough city that it was not unlikely they would cross paths again. He would not take any action now, but if he felt that his security might be compromised he would eliminate the threat. He didn't like the idea of killing in his own backyard. It posed a risk to the cover persona he had so carefully crafted.

On the 25th, Nouri arrived at the railway station thirty minutes before departure. He normally traveled in and out of Spain on his Claudio Diez Perea identity. It wasn't worth risking the possibility that Spanish authorities would connect "Claudio" to Nouri or any of the other alias personas that he maintained. He had safe deposit boxes stashed around Europe – Bern, Brussels, and Paris – with half a dozen identities that he could draw upon, depending upon the mission.

But for the trip to Venezuela, Colonel Samadi had ordered him to travel on a new Costa Rican passport in the name of Claudio Frontera. He'd been directed to an unscheduled meeting the night before with a contact who had passed him the Costa Rican passport with a Spanish entry stamp dated September 20 and a handful of credit cards and pocket litter. Tehran was going to great lengths to de-link this trip to Caracas from his Spanish identity.

He had a direct flight from Madrid and was not worried about going through customs and immigration in the Venezuelan capital. Ever since Hugo Chavez had come into power in 1998, the South American petroleum juggernaut had been like a thorn in the side of many, especially the U.S. Chavez had even tested Venezuela's relationship with Spain, but relations there were more cordial than with most nations.

Nouri wondered what had prompted Colonel Samadi to choose Caracas for this conference. He knew from what he had read in the papers that Iran and Venezuela considered themselves allies against U.S. imperialism.

He'd also read somewhere that Chavez was looking for a new world order, one that was multi-polar rather than one dominated by the superpower to the north. He had aligned himself with Fidel Castro, the ailing Cuban revolutionary, a relationship that served Chavez well when his health began to deteriorate, necessitating several trips to the island for cancer treatments.

Nouri found his seat on the *Renfe* and settled in for the two-and-a-half-hour trip. Mentally he reviewed the note that he had received from Colonel Samadi yesterday on his COVCOM system. He would be staying at the Hotel Alba, just off Central Park in downtown Caracas. Unit 400's European cadre would be meeting on the 27th at the Gran Meliá Hotel on Sabana Grande Boulevard, a short cab ride away from his hotel. Nouri presumed the others would be dispersed to different hotels around the city for security purposes.

Their group was meeting under the auspices of a European front company that the Qods Force had set up for just such purposes. It wasn't a bricks and mortar enterprise, but had a virtual presence on the Internet, backstopped by a European asset living in Belgium. The company ostensibly represented a consortium of European investors looking for investment opportunities in South America.

After a while, Nouri got up from his seat to purchase a *café corto* in the dining car. He could tell from the view outside that they were still about an hour from Madrid. When he returned to his seat he sipped his beverage and stared at the passing countryside, wondering if Samadi would have any updates for him. In his note he had said that he wanted to set aside one-on-one time with each of the attendees to discuss their specific assignments.

Arriving at Chamartin Madrid Station. Nouri followed signs for the subway. He caught a train to the Nuevos Ministerios station, where he switched lines, boarding the next car for Madrid Barajas Airport.

He had forty-five minutes before his flight was scheduled to depart. He passed through customs and immigration without incident and began walking in the direction of his gate. Just beyond the security point, on the other side of a glass barrier, he could see transit passengers disembarking from an international flight. They were on their way over to another terminal handling domestic connections.

Nouri became aware of a tall, athletic-looking male in his early thirties on the other side of the barrier staring at him. The man had reversed himself and was tracking Nouri with an attentive look on his face. There was something vaguely familiar about him, but Nouri could not put his finger on it. He looked like the popular toy figure, G.I. Joe.

Nouri continued walking towards his gate. He felt a tingling sensation, that sixth sense ability he had developed to detect danger just before it struck. He glanced back over his shoulder and could see the stranger staring at him intently. He had his cell phone in his hand and appeared to be searching his address book for a number.

Nouri shrugged and kept moving, racking his memory for a clue to the stranger's identity. It wasn't until several hours later, midway over the Atlantic, that he connected the dots. That guy had been outside the Macello Restaurant in Boston, when he had taken out Hamid Al Subaie. He felt a chill ripple across his chest. Who was he? And, more importantly, what was he doing in Madrid?

Chapter 12

L ogan fixed his gaze on Nouri Khorasani's receding back with mounting frustration. He had just arrived at Madrid Barajas Airport's international arrivals area, Terminal 4, and was making his way to the transit shuttle that would take him to domestic Terminal 1, where he would catch his connecting flight to Rota. It was Saturday, September 25, and he was scheduled to observe Special Warfare Unit 10 in action using the Mark V's on Monday.

As he had exited the gate into the terminal he was funneled into a transit line leading to customs and immigration and the shuttle for outlying terminals. Glancing around, he had been startled to see a face that he thought he recognized, on the other side of the glass, walking towards the international departures area.

Shouldering his way through the other passengers, Logan had positioned himself next to the glass barrier and stared in disbelief at Nouri Khorasani. The killer must have sensed his presence, because he turned and with a quick cast of the eyes, looked directly at Logan, but gave no sign of recognition. He paused for just a second, and then resumed his leisurely walk through the airport terminal.

Logan's mind raced as he considered his options. There was no way for him to gain access to the international departure area. He yanked his cell phone out of his pocket and waited impatiently for it to power up. It was eleven a.m., meaning that it was about five a.m. on the East Coast. He didn't have Detective Breen's phone number in his address book so decided to call his sister instead.

"Millie!"

"Logan. What time is it?" Her voice sounded sleepy.

"I'm at the airport in Madrid, and you won't believe who I just saw."

"Who?"

"Nouri Khorasani!"

There was a moment of stunned silence on the other end as Millie digested the words. "Are you sure? I mean, what are the chances?"

"I'm absolutely certain. It was him." Logan explained the circumstances leading to his sighting of Hamid's attacker.

"I wonder what he's doing in Madrid?"

"I don't know, but we need to find out. Look, can you give Breen a call? Tell him Khorasani's in Madrid, getting ready to board an international flight. I have no idea where he's headed, but if Breen's buddies at INTERPOL can move on this fast enough, maybe they can contact the Spanish police and detain him before he gets away."

"All right. I'll call him right now. Is there anything you can do there?"

"I'm headed over to security to see if I can talk my way into the departure terminal. I doubt they'll let me in, but it's worth a try."

"OK. Good luck. I'll call you back after I talk to Breen."

Logan disconnected and hurried over to the security area. He got the attention of one of the uniformed officers and spoke to him in English. The man shrugged his shoulders indicating that he did not understand. He held up his hand, advising Logan to wait, and walked over to another officer and spoke briefly with him. The latter glanced over at Logan, appraising him with dark, brooding eyes. He changed places with the first officer Logan had spoken to, and sauntered over to where Logan stood fidgeting.

"Yes? May I help you?"

"I need to go into the terminal departure area."

"Why? Do you have a ticket?

"No. I just got off a flight from the U.S. and while I was on my way to the shuttle, I spotted a man in there who is wanted for murder by the police in Boston."

"Are you certain? What makes you so sure?"

Logan was agitated. With each passing second the odds were that Khorasani would board his flight and disappear. Breathe, he told himself. He exhaled slowly and explained the circumstances of Hamid Al Subaie's murder. How he had seen the killer on the street that day, and later, under the most improbable circumstances, had identified him to the Boston police. And now this unlikely chance encounter.

"Look, INTERPOL is working with the Boston Police Department. Perhaps if you have some contacts there, they can verify what I have told you." Logan's pulse was racing, and it was all he could do to refrain from jumping the line and racing after the fugitive.

"Wait here. Let me have your passport, Mr...."

"Alexander. Logan Alexander."

"Let me see what I can do."

The policeman walked back to where his colleague stood and conferred with him. He then picked up the phone and dialed a number. He spoke in rapid fire Spanish and kept turning his head to look at Logan. He opened the passport and read the particulars to the person on the other end. A few moments later he hung up and returned to where Logan was standing.

"No one in that office has any information about this case, but they are going to contact INTERPOL and see if they can find out anything. I can't allow you to go into the departure area by yourself, and we can't spare anyone from here right this minute to accompany you, but I have asked for three men to come here and escort you into the terminal to see if you can find Mr., what's his name again?"

"Khorasani. Nouri Khorasani."

"Ah, yes. Please wait here until my men arrive." The officer scribbled the name in his notebook and then returned to his station.

The wait was interminable. With each passing minute Logan's frustrations grew. His phone rang and he saw from the caller ID that it was Millie.

"What's up?" He held his hand over his left ear and turned away from the loudspeaker announcing flight departures. When the noise subsided, he repeated himself. "I'm sorry, I missed what you said. It's noisy in here."

"I just got off the phone with Breen. As soon as we hung up he was going to call his contact at the INTERPOL Washington Operations and Command Center. He told me that their Violent Crimes Division has the lead on Hamid's case. They'll have to bring the Spanish National Bureau into it. They're based in Madrid. Maybe they have someone out at the airport."

Logan filled her in on his attempt to get into the departure area. He was heartened by Millie's call. Breen had told him that INTERPOL was a great organization for police organizations around the globe to share information and expertise.

Unlike many other countries, the U.S. doesn't have a national police force. There are over 18,000 federal, state, local and tribal law enforcement agencies with disparate missions, jurisdictions and capabilities just in the U.S. alone. INTERPOL has 190 member nations, each with a National Bureau that fields requests from and cooperates with other members.

After disconnecting, Logan saw three uniformed officials walking together in his direction. They conversed with the officer holding Logan's passport and then beckoned to him to accompany them inside the terminal. He looked at his watch and realized that nearly forty-five minutes had passed since he first spotted Khorasani. He sighed in frustration. In all likelihood the elusive killer had once again slipped through his fingers.

Logan provided the three officers a physical description of Khorasani and described what he had been wearing. The four men fanned out and began walking through the departure terminal, scanning passengers in lines, walking through crowded departure lounges and investigating restrooms, restaurants and duty free shops. It took them two hours to scour the entire terminal, and with each passing minute, Logan's hopes diminished.

It was nearly two o'clock when they called off the search. Khorasani had evaded capture again. He had been within their grasp, but like a phantom, he had managed to slip away. When Logan returned to the security area, a representative from Spain's INTERPOL National Bureau was there to speak with him. The detective, who introduced himself as Julio Montoya, ushered him into secondary, a cramped cubicle behind the security checkpoint. An assistant brought in two cups of tepid coffee and then left them alone. After a couple of minutes an INTERPOL interpreter arrived to translate Logan's statement.

As Logan answered Detective Montoya's questions, his mind was racing. Never one to let a momentary setback rule his emotions, he put away his sense of dejection and focused on what the detective was saying. At one point Montoya confided that Spanish airports lag behind the U.S. in terms of security infrastructure. They had no facial recognition technology installed at Madrid Barajas, and if Khorasani was traveling on alias documents, it was highly unlikely they would be able to trace his movements.

"He could be going anywhere. Madrid Barajas has over 50 million passengers a year. It's one of the busiest airports in Europe and ranks as the 10th busiest in the world." Detective Montoya made a futile gesture with his hands.

"Still, we are not without some recourse. Our General Secretariat has already issued a Red Notice on Mr. Khorasani."

"I'm sorry. What does that mean?"

"INTERPOL issues notices by color. Red Notices refer to cases that are active within certain jurisdictions where the goal is arrest and detention. INTERPOL will arrest these individuals and facilitate their extradition to the jurisdiction claiming interest."

"But does INTERPOL take an active role in pursuing these criminals?"

"Yes. We have global communications and a Command and Coordination Center that operates twenty-four hours a day. We also have Incident Response Teams whose personnel have forensics and analytic capabilities. If any INTERPOL member country requests our assistance, we can deploy a team to support or assist them anywhere in the world within twenty-four hours."

A lot of good that does, Logan thought to himself. Khorasani had been right here in Montoya's own back yard and he had been powerless to prevent his escape. He kept his mounting frustration to himself. Despite his disappointment, he knew that he could not give up. He was determined to do whatever it took to track down the killer. He owed that much to Hamid. He concentrated on the rest of the detective's questions.

An hour later Montoya signaled that he was through. He returned Logan's passport and escorted him through security to the area where he could catch the shuttle to Terminal 1.

"Do not lose hope, Mr. Alexander. Mr. Khorasani is bound to slip up. And when he does, we will be there waiting for him."

"I just hope it happens before he kills again." He bid the Spanish detective goodbye and walked the short distance to his shuttle.

Logan was pensive as he traveled the short distance to Terminal 1. Staring out the shuttle window, his resolve hardened. He had to find Khorasani and get to the bottom of this. But how? So far all the breaks had gone the killer's way. At some point he was bound to slip up. Now, especially with INTERPOL, Homeland Security and local police joining the hunt, Khorasani would have to sense the noose tightening. His ability to freely move around would be sorely compromised. He'd have to be out of his mind to attempt travel to the U.S. again. But, what if there were others out there working with him? If the Qods Force had turned a group of assassins loose to go after Hamid, who else was Unit 400 targeting?

At the customer service desk for Iberia, the agent was efficient and soon had him re-ticketed for a flight departing at four p.m.

An hour later Logan arrived at Jerez de la Frontera airport. He found the Europcar desk, got directions to Rota and set off. Bypassing the historic center of Jerez de la Frontera, famous for its wines, horses and flamenco, Logan merged onto the A-4 west. He followed signs for the E-5 to Cádiz, AP-4 and Sevilla. Logan toyed with the radio but could not find an English-language station. He switched off the radio and settled in for the drive. Traffic moved at a quick clip and he soon found himself on the outskirts of Rota. Directions to his hotel were straightforward, and ten minutes later he wheeled the BMW sedan onto Calle Gravina and pulled into parking for the Duque de Najera Hotel.

Despite his preoccupation with the whole Khorasani fiasco, he found himself admiring his surroundings. The hotel was situated on Cádiz Bay, right next to Rota's beach and nearby marina. After checking in, Logan decided he needed a workout to soothe his pent-up frustrations. Lieutenant Belcher wasn't expecting to see him until Sunday, so he decided to wait until after he exercised to give him a call.

He spent an hour in the fitness center. They had a pretty good set-up for circuit training and more free weights than the average hotel fitness center had. He started with the free weights, jumping into a forty-minute aerobic routine that focused on multiple reps with minimal rest for recovery. He liked the effect this produced, and ten minutes into his workout began to feel the burn. He was soaked by the time he was through, but felt reinvigorated. He decided to finish off with a mile-long swim in the bay.

After changing into his swim trunks in his room, he took the stairs to the lobby level and found the path to the beach. The early evening temperature was comfortable at seventy-three degrees. Surveying the small inlet off the Gulf of Cádiz, Logan could see the Isle of Leon to the south, home to the Port of Cádiz . Plunging into the waves, he gasped at the initial jolt of the cool water temperature, but shook it off as he began swimming with strong, decisive strokes parallel to the shore.

When he was done, he toweled off and walked back to his room. He was feeling energized by the workout, and before jumping into the shower, gave Belcher a call to let him know that he had arrived.

"Lieutenant Belcher? Logan Alexander here. Just wanted to let you know that I got in OK, and see what time you wanted to get together tomorrow?"

"Hey, Mr. Alexander! Good to hear from you. We don't stand on formality around here. Please call me Tim."

"All right. Tim it is. You can call me Logan. Look, if you don't have any plans, maybe we could grab a couple of beers. The hotel looks like it has a pretty good bar."

"Where're you staying?"

"The Duque de Najera on Calle Gravina."

"That's pretty nice. I know the bartender there, Luis. What time were you thinking?"

Logan looked at the clock on the bedside table and saw that it was already seven-thirty. "Eight? Eight-thirty?"

"Let's make it eight-thirty."

After hanging up, Logan climbed into the shower. He turned it on full blast and let the scalding spray pelt his body.

Refreshed, he donned a pair of khakis and a polo shirt and walked down to the bar. It wasn't very busy for a Saturday night. Looking around he spotted the young Navy SEAL seated at a back table.

"Tim?"

"How'd you guess?" Belcher stood up to greet him.

"Must have been the haircut." Logan grinned and stuck out his hand.

Belcher grasped it in a paw the size of a catcher's mitt and flashed a toothy smile. "Good to meet you."

They ordered a couple of San Miguels and settled back in their chairs.

"Willoughby sent me your bio in an email. I don't think we crossed paths when you were active duty but I bet we know some of the same people," Tim began.

"When'd you go through BUDS?" Basic Underwater Demolition/SEAL training was an essential part of becoming a SEAL.

"I was at Coronado in 2005, and finished SEAL Qualification Training in November 2005."

"Where'd you go from SQT?"

"I got DEVGRU." The term referred to the Naval Special Warfare Development Group.

"Seal Team Six." Logan looked at Belcher with new-found appreciation. "Did you guys see much action?"

"You remember that Somali piracy op in 2009, the one where the captain of the Maersk *Alabama* was taken hostage?"

"Yeah. I remember that. In fact I have a friend, Norm Stoddard, who was one of the shooters on that op."

"Norm, from Burnt Cabins, Pennsylvania?"

"Yeah. Do you know him?"

"You bet. I was standing between Norm and Ricky Preston when we took out the three pirates holding the *Alabama's* captain."

Logan gave a low whistle. "You were one of the shooters?

Belcher drained his San Miguel but didn't say anything. Logan could tell by the glint in his eye that he was one of the three snipers who had tagged the three Somalis with si-multaneous shots to the head from the *USS Bainbridge* from about 100 yards distance.

"Norm never told me he was part of that operation. He's a hell of a shooter, though. I remember once he was telling me about all the factors that go into setting up a shot – range to the target, wind speed and direction, air density and the shooter's position relative to the target."

"It's true. It's a lot more complicated than people think. But a lot of the gear that we have today gives you more confidence that you're going to get it done. I mean, back in the day shooters just had to wing it. But you know what kind of gear we have access to now — laser rangefinders, computers, even mobile weather stations to help us set up the shot. At the end of the day, though, it comes down to the skill of the shooter, the quality of his weapon and the ammunition."

"What's your favorite weapon?"

"I like the McMillan Tac-338. Takes a .338 Lapua Magnum. McMillan hand-builds those weapons. Some

components, like the barrels, are manufactured by specialist barrel makers, but McMillan's gunsmiths assemble the
final product. They do all of the cutting and fitting by hand.
That's why one of those babies goes for $10K a pop."

"What kind of range do they have?"

"They're capable of making a shot up to 3,000 yards.
Think about it. That's over a mile and a half! That's about the
longest confirmed combat kill I know of. Some Australian
sniper did that in Afghanistan. He was part of the Australian
2nd Commandos. He wasn't using a McMillan though. I
think he took that shot with a Barrett M8A21."

"They American made?"

"Yeah. Been around since the early '80s. The Marine
Corps bought a bunch of them when they first came out. I
haven't fired one, though."

They ordered two more San Miguels and when the waiter brought them he set down a plate of green olives and a
dish of piping hot *pulpo gallego,* the Galician-inspired tapa
made from cooked octopus and potatoes, drizzled with olive oil and sprinkled with paprika.

Belcher polished off his beer. He plucked a piece of the
octopus off the plate and chewed on it before speaking.
"We're kicking off at zero-dark-thirty Monday morning.
We'll be taking out the two Mark V's. The scenario will be
an anti-piracy hostage rescue. We'll fast-rope a team onto
the Mark V's, insert them at a notional location where the
hostages are being detained and then extract them after
they've cleared the area."

"Sounds familiar." Logan grinned as he recalled the
hostage rescue mission in Indonesia that he had recounted
to Gordon Willoughby in Portsmouth.

Belcher gave him contact instructions for Monday morning. They chatted for a few more minutes and parted ways.
As Logan headed up to his room he savored the sense of
anticipation he felt over being out on a mission again, even
if it was only training.

Chapter 13

Logan yawned as he pulled out of his parking spot into pre-dawn darkness. He felt a little groggy as he navigated the short distance to Rota Naval Station. He had spent Sunday sightseeing around Cádiz. The city had always held a special allure for him because of its rich naval tradition.

He had first learned about Cádiz in a European Naval History elective he'd taken at the Academy. Its prominence dated back to the Roman Empire, when a number of notable Romans lived in the outpost and the Roman military maintained a naval base there. Cádiz was later destroyed when the Visigoths defeated the Romans and the city languished until the mid-13th century, when Alfonso X routed later occupiers, the Moors.

Cádiz began to flourish again in the 15th century. Columbus sailed out of here and for years much of the Spanish booty from the New World passed through the port. This did not go unnoticed by Spain's enemies and there ensued years of fighting over this wealth. Both the British and the French made forays into Cádiz over the next 200 years, but somehow the city prevailed.

The Spanish Navy has called Cádiz its home port for over three centuries and the U.S. Navy has considered Cádiz its gateway to the Mediterranean since the naval station was built in the 1950s during the Eisenhower administration.

As Logan pulled up to the access point for the base, a Spanish naval security official requested his identification. Logan handed him his passport, and the guard checked it against that day's visitor access roster. Finding Logan's name, he handed him his visitor's ID and gave him directions to Special Warfare Unit 10's area of the base.

Pulling into the lot beside the wharf, he saw a smatter-ing of vehicles and a couple of motorcycles. He walked over to the pier, zipping up his jacket against the morning chill. The two Mark V's were tied up to the dock, and the distinct sound of water lapping at their bows brought back nostal-gic memories of the years he had spent as a SEAL.

As he turned away from the craft, he caught sight of Tim Belcher standing in the doorway of a squat building set back a hundred feet from the water. Steam was rising from a mug of coffee he cradled in his hands, and he smiled a welcome as Logan walked up.

"How'd it go yesterday? Do anything interesting?"

"Yeah, spent some time walking around Cádiz. I went over to Castillo de San Marcos, and poked around the his-toric part of town, you know, Plaza de España, near where the watchtowers are."

"Right. The locals used those watchtowers as lookouts for ship traffic coming into the port."

"Pirates and such?"

"The British were famous for pillaging Cádiz. Guys like Sir Francis Drake and the Earl of Essex, although they were here earlier. Drake kicked ass. He took out so many of the Spanish Navy's ships that it took Spain a year before they could launch the Armada."

"Yeah, and I read somewhere yesterday that Essex was ruthless. He burned the city to the ground!"

"Rotten bastards."

They both grinned. Spain had plundered the New World with unabashed enthusiasm, using its raw military might, and unparalleled military and naval technology to defeat the Americas. Of course, killing off large numbers of the indigenous population with smallpox and other diseas-es hadn't hindered their advance. Spain had made its bed, and by hoarding all that new-found wealth, the Spanish monarchs had opened themselves up to English and French aggression.

"Come on in. Let's get you suited up. We won't be doing any live fire drills out here today, so I'm just going to issue you the basics." Belcher handed Logan a bag containing boots and BDUs and pointed him towards the men's locker room. Ten minutes later Logan joined the team, standing before a map of the coast.

"All right, everybody, listen up. This here is Mr. Alexander. He's with us today in an observer role, but you should know that he wore the SEAL trident for many years before he got out. He's got more experience than most of you water jockeys, so pay him some respect."

Logan noticed a few of the SEALs stealing glances his way with newfound recognition. He was a little uncomfortable with the praise, but sanguine with the fact they knew he was one of them.

"You all know the drill today. We're simulating a hostage rescue over here." Belcher pointed to a spot on the map outside the Gulf of Cádiz on the Atlantic Ocean. "We're going to practice fast-roping half a dozen of you off a Blackhawk onto the Mark V's once we get out of the gulf. Then we'll do a high-speed insertion, and finish with a recovery. We'll also practice evasive measures on our egress out of the area to simulate pursuit by hostiles. Any questions? All right. Saddle up."

There was a lot of chatter as the men filed out of the room. Logan could feel the adrenaline as they grabbed their gear and headed for the door. A bus was waiting outside the building to transport six of the men to the flight line. Everyone else loaded onto the Mark V's.

As the twin twelve-cylinder diesel engines roared to life, the pilots, who were more like jet fighter pilots than boat captains, edged away from the pier, and headed out to sea. Once they had cleared the no wake zone, they opened the Mark V's up to about twenty-five knots. It was choppy on the water, and the waves buffeted the boat. Logan could feel the vibrations reverberating through the hull, and he knew that once they really cranked them up the vibrations would be more pronounced.

Belcher did a comms check and looked at his watch as they cleared the gulf and turned north into open seas. There was a flurry of activity, and Logan could tell from the muted sound of a helicopter that a Blackhawk was approaching them from the south. Craning his neck he looked toward the stern of the Mark V and could just make out the bird as it lined itself in a hover about sixty feet above them. Spray kicked up from the rotor action doused the men, as the boat and helicopter synchronized speeds. When they were moving in unison, the crew chief on the Blackhawk lowered a line to the deck of the Mark V.

A figure appeared in the doorway of the helicopter. He clipped on his carabiner and an instant later dropped off the skid in a fast rope maneuver that had him on the deck in seconds. He released and moved forward, making room for the two remaining SEALS, who repeated the maneuver.

Once they were secure, the crew chief hauled in the line and the Blackhawk repositioned itself to repeat the maneuver with the other Mark V, 200 feet off their port side. Just as the first man out was about to land on deck, a strong wave buffeted the boat, sending it into a trough and leaving him dangling like a slippery fish on a hook. When the boat rose up to meet him he slammed into the deck hard. He seemed momentarily shaken, but shook it off and moved forward.

When all three were safely aboard, the Blackhawk sped past them, banked, and headed back to base.

With everyone on board, the pilots of the two boats advanced their throttles and they began to pick up speed. Logan estimated that they were doing about thirty-five knots. He could feel the vibrations from the boat racing up his spine.

Twenty minutes later the two Mark V's began their approach to the insertion point. Once they were about a mile offshore, the pilots slowed the boats to ten knots and two invading parties of eight SEALS each launched their sixteen-foot combat rubber raiding craft, or CRRC, from the sterns of the two boats.

Logan made his way over to where Belcher was standing. He was listening to communications between the two platoon leaders as they made a heading for their insertion point.

"We did a scenario like this a couple of months ago, but the objective wasn't a hostage rescue. The task was to take out an enemy facility."

Logan gave Belcher a sideways look. There's no way Belcher could have known about his role in taking down the IED facility in Iran almost a year ago. There had been no leaks, although the *Wall Street Journal* and *Al Jazeera* coverage of the incident had been extensive. He kept a neutral expression on his face as Belcher continued.

"Most of the men had explosives on them with magnetic limpets for attaching the packages to the target. Anyway, our helmsman was a rookie and didn't realize that his compass was giving him a false reading because of the magnets. That sucker was headed straight out to sea and would have kept going 'til he ran out of fuel."

They both chuckled at the young SEAL's discomfiture upon realizing his error. "That's why we train," Logan commiserated. "You wouldn't want to be doing any of this stuff for real the first time out. Too many ways for things to go south in a hurry. Murphy has a way of showing up at the worst times.

"Changing the subject, have you guys had any injuries on the Mark V that you can attribute to the boat itself? You know the history on injuries in the Mark V, and how the Navy came out with a new design for the seats to solve the vibration issue. Now they're looking at a whole new hull design using composite materials. The idea is to create a stronger hull and reduce vibrations."

Belcher screwed up his face and thought for a moment. "It's hard to point to any one thing and blame it on the Mark V. Everyone talks about the vibrations, and most of us are pretty sore after one of these ops. But think about it. We all work hard and play hard. There aren't any couch potatoes in the SEALs, although Galloway over there probably spends way too much time playing Guitar Hero." He gestured toward a lanky youngster manning an M-60 machine gun from a gun mount on the starboard side.

"I just think soldiers, especially special ops types, are more likely to have injuries than the general population.

Who's to say that some SEAL yanking and banking out here all night, didn't knock his spine out of alignment mountain-biking in his free time?"

"You're right. It's a hard thing to quantify, but I think the evidence is still pretty strong that the way this boat is designed has put a lot of guys in sick bay."

There was a rustling sound and Belcher's radio came to life. The muted voice of one of the platoon leaders could be heard over the sound of waves crashing on the beach.

"Base, this is Team Alpha. Comms check. Over."

"Alpha, this is Base. Read you loud and clear. How you me? Over." Belcher moved closer to Logan so that he could hear the exchange.

"Team Alpha is approaching the target area. No sign of hostiles. We're going in. Over."

"Roger that, Team Alpha. Over."

There was a similar exchange from the Bravo Team.

Unbeknownst to the two assault teams, Belcher had positioned an observer on the beach to report on the teams' approach and egress. There were no actual hostage role-players or hostile forces at the insertion point. Once they had secured their position, the teams' objective was to retrieve a flag at the target site as proof that they had successfully located the target.

Thirty minutes later the teams had successfully retrieved the flag and were egressing on a heading perpendicular to the shore. The two Mark V helmsmen gunned their engines, swooping in close to shore, their water jets propelling the boats forward in shallow water without fear of damaging them because there were no propellers to contend with.

Logan could feel the adrenaline as the CRRCs came into view. He stood to one side and held on to the gunwale where he had a view of the action. The Mark V's slowed to ten knots and the CRRCs ran right up the stern and onto the aft deck.

The two Mark V's immediately picked up speed and set a course for the base. The CRRC crews secured the rubber boats and assumed defensive combat positions around the combat craft. The helmsman opened up the throttle, and moments later the boat was slicing through the water at fifty knots, almost sixty miles per hour.

Simulating hot pursuit, the helmsmen began yanking and banking to avoid enemy fire. Logan lurched as he clutched the gunwale in response to a tight turn as the Mark V raced towards the gulf entrance. Standing there, he grimaced as shock waves from the beating the boat was taking raced up his leg to his bad knee. He'd had knee replacement surgery on that leg almost three years ago after being hit by machine gun fire during a Taliban ambush in Afghanistan. His recovery had been pretty good after months of physical therapy, but the damage was severe enough to end his career as a SEAL.

Once they were inside the gulf, the helmsmen backed off the throttle, cruising at twenty-five knots and then slowing to just ten knots as they approached the dock.

Logan sat in on the hotwash, an informal after-action review. These AARs are invaluable for capturing the lessons learned during training exercises so that there can be continuous improvement. Everybody's encouraged to participate, from the lowliest seaman to the senior officers.

After about an hour, they broke up. Logan thanked Belcher and the other SEALS for allowing him to observe the exercise.

As he was leaving the building, Belcher gave him a Unit Ten challenge coin as a keepsake. Logan was touched. He'd been on the giving end of this military tradition for years. He fingered the metal coin with the unit's insignia on one side and a Spanish navy emblem on the other, and reminisced about how many times the simple gesture had served to boost morale and camaraderie amongst service members.

"Hoorah!" Logan fist-bumped Belcher, held up the coin in appreciation and walked to his rental car.

The trip had been interesting, not the least his incidental encounter with Nouri Khorasani. He was looking forward to discussing the Mark V exercise with Gordon Willoughby. But most of all, he smiled to himself; he was looking forward to seeing Zahir and Cooper.

Chapter 14

Nouri gave Colonel Samadi a skeptical look when the latter offered him a scotch from the mini-bar. Was this a test? He decided that it was not, and accepted the drink. Samadi guided him over to two leather armchairs and gestured for him to take a seat. They were meeting in the colonel's suite at the Gran Meliá Hotel in downtown Caracas.

The last of the other Unit 400 team members from Europe had just left the room after a day of group meetings. They could not be seen together in public, so they had departed the hotel room separately. Samadi was now holding one-on-one sessions with each of them in order to compartment their respective operations.

Nouri had only recognized one of the other six men. Hans Fitzer, the ersatz German businessman that Colonel Kashani had first introduced him to in Tehran — when Fitzer had revealed that he worked for an elite unit in the Qods Force. Nouri had not seen him again until today.

The day had been strange, Nouri reflected as he sipped his drink. They were, because of the nature of their work, lone wolves. Putting seven of them into the same room was akin to putting seven alpha males together and expecting everyone to behave. But they had been mostly in receive mode today as Samadi introduced himself, gave them updates from Tehran and talked about General Salehi's strategic goals for the coming year.

Samadi toyed with his drink before speaking. "Before we talk about your situation, I wanted to thank you personally for your work in Boston. You know, what the Kuwaitis did in Bandar Deylam is personal for me. I was the chief of operations there. But for the grace of God, I would have been killed that night." He shook his head and pursed his lips before speaking.

"As it was, I lost my boss and mentor, Colonel Ghabel, as well as a couple of our men who were killed in the attack."

"I remember seeing the *Al Jazeera* reports of the incident last year. But they gave no clue as to who was behind it. How did we figure out it was the Kuwaitis?"

"We had a source inside Kuwaiti intelligence. Unfortunately, he became ill shortly after fingering Hamid Al Subaie. He died a few weeks later and we were never able to figure out who else was involved.

"It has the mark of the Great Satan." Samadi paused to take a sip from his drink. "I was the one who found the knife in the administration building near Colonel Ghabel's body. The same knife that you later used to kill Al Subaie. It was scorched but still lethal. I thought using it on Al Subaie was a nice touch. Let them know that we know." He gave a mirthless laugh.

"Is that the end of it then?" Nouri searched Samadi's face for a clue to his thinking.

"Oh, far from it. You see, both General Salehi and the Supreme Leader are determined to get to the bottom of this. We will never give up." He slammed his fist down on the side table, rattling the lamp and knocking some papers to the floor. "Whoever was behind this thought they would bring the Republic to its knees, but they underestimated us. We will find them out!"

Nouri was not surprised by Samadi's fury. The attack on Bandar Deylam, and the resulting international exposè, had embarrassed the regime almost beyond repair, although it had not brought the country to its knees. U.S.-led sanctions against Iran, on the other hand, nearly had.

"I have something to report. It may be nothing, but I don't believe in coincidences." Nouri went on to describe his encounter with the suspicious American at the airport in Madrid.

"This guy was looking at me like he'd seen a ghost, and he got on his cell phone right away. I couldn't figure out where I knew him from, but afterwards I realized that he'd been on the street in Boston the day I took out Al Subaie. He probably saw me coming out of the restaurant, but I was gone before he realized what had happened."

"This is troubling. It may be something or nothing, but I agree with you that it's unlikely you would run into the same person thousands of miles away." He put his fingertips together and tapped his chin. Let me think about this. He took out a notebook and wrote a cryptic note to himself.

"I know you're careful, but take extra time to make certain you're clean when you do your surveillance detection runs. If, as unlikely as it seems, the Americans are looking for you in Spain, the new initiative I am going to brief to you comes at the perfect time."

"What new initiative?"

"We want you to set up an operational cell here in Caracas."

Nouri sat back, too stunned for words. His mind raced as he thought through the possibilities.

"We believe that for some time Europe has been heating up. Most of the EU members are well disposed towards the Americans, although the French are often a thorn in their side. But still, there is unprecedented cooperation between their police forces. There may come a time when we can't operate there, and we need to have infrastructure in place for that possibility."

"But why me? There must be others out there who are much more qualified than I am."

"Don't sell yourself short, Nouri. Your superiors have had nothing but praise for you. You get results.

"Now, as for the specifics, you'll have to find a way to put your cover office in Spain on ice. I don't think we need to pull the plug on what you have set up there, but you will need to be here for several months to get this cell up and running.

"Also, if it turns out that there is something to this encounter you had at the airport, there are obvious security ramifications. Could it be a coincidence? Is there a linkage between Al Subaie and this man you saw? If so, that would tend to confirm our suspicions about America's role in all of this. We need to get to the bottom of this before you go back."

Nouri looked thoughtful as he thought through the possibilities. He'd never spent any time in Latin America, but from what little he'd seen of Caracas it could be interesting. "It shouldn't be that difficult. Most of my consulting business in Spain is in a slump because of the economy. Maybe I could say that I've taken a temporary position with a non-governmental organization in some emerging market country."

"Yes, I like that. Make it some place like Africa. We don't want any linkage between your Claudio Perea persona and what you set up here. But keep your apartment in Spain. How do you handle your bills?"

"I use online banking. It helps maintain my cover profile."

"That's fine. You know how to route your emails to confuse anyone who's looking at your online activity. Do you need to return to Spain to wrap up your affairs?"

"I can manage for now. Will I have any inside support here? I entered the country on this Costa Rican passport. At some point I may have to exit Venezuela and come back in to renew my visa."

"We'll see. For now you are good for three months. If you need longer you can do a border crossing between Colombia and Venezuela at Cúcuta. You just walk across the Simon Bolivar Bridge, enter Colombia, and then turn around and come back into Venezuela. It will take a day, but it's the easiest way we've found."

"All right. You also mentioned a cell. This is something new for me. I thought we always worked alone."

"We prefer it that way. It minimizes collateral damage if the balloon goes up. No one else's operations are tainted if there's a flap involving one person. But we are under orders by the Supreme Leader to beef up our foreign presence. One way we can do that is to shorten the learning curve for our new officers by getting them into the field earlier, working with proven winners. People like you."

Nouri looked thoughtful. He had heard that there was a push to beef up the ranks of Unit 400, and this was a sign that Tehran was serious about it. "How many people do you plan on having here?"

"Just two initially. We want to see how it goes. Your initial activities will involve setting up a cover operation here, and developing an understanding of the security environment. We don't expect to give you any special assignments during this period, but eventually we'll want you to launch from here into the U.S.

"I think you'll find your new colleague a quick study. She's very motivated."

"She?" Nouri had thought the unit was all male. This was the first he had heard that women were being recruited.

"Yes, as much as it pains many of us, just think of it as another tool in your toolbox. Our enemies won't expect us to come after them with a woman." Samadi smiled.

"You'll be meeting her tomorrow. Her name is Azar. Azar Ghabel."

"Ghabel. You mean...?"

"Yes. She's Colonel Ghabel's widow."

Chapter 15

"Hey, buddy." Logan plucked Cooper out of his crib and walked him into the kitchen. He balanced the baby on one arm as he looked at the confounding array of dairy products on the refrigerator shelf in front of him. There were cartons of organic whole milk, two percent, one percent, fat-free and the heart-busting dairy creamer he liked, all lined up in a row.

Zahir had decided that it was time to wean Cooper from breast-feeding, but he had not gone quietly. As Logan measured out a portion of whole milk, Cooper's face scrunched up, all contorted at the sight of the bottle. Still, hunger got the best of him, and after the milk had warmed he latched onto the nipple and began to suck in greedy little gulps.

Zahir wandered into the kitchen and walked over to the two of them, bending to kiss the baby, who nuzzled her in return but latched back onto his bottle. She put her arms around Logan and brushed her cheek against his. "I missed you."

"Me too." He lifted his head for her kiss.

"What time did you get in?" She pulled her hair into a ponytail and walked over to the coffee pot to put on a pot of the dark French roast they both liked.

"It was after midnight. Our flight was delayed out of Rota because of a big storm in the Med. It must have been raining sideways. You were both sound asleep when I got in."

"Cooper's been fussy. He's teething and it's taken him awhile to get used to the bottle. I think last night was the first time he's slept through all week."

"Boob man to the bitter end."

"Logan!" Zahir moved over to where he was seated and gave him a playful punch on the arm.

124

"Have you talked to Millie?"

"Not since last week. We were supposed to have dinner at their place Saturday, but something came up at work and she was crashing so we postponed. Why? What's going on?"

Logan picked Cooper up to pat his back and the baby produced a satisfied burp. "I saw Khorasani in Madrid. At the airport."

Zahir almost dropped the coffee pot. "What! Are you sure?"

"Oh, it was Khorasani all right."

"What happened?"

Logan relayed the events of that afternoon. How he'd been unable to get out of the transit area into the main terminal after spotting the killer. His frantic call to Millie. The frustrating wait for airport security to help him search for the fugitive. His hour-long interview with Julio Montoya, the INTERPOL detective.

He shook his head in discouragement. "I mean he was right there. Not more than twenty feet away from me, and all I could do was watch him walk away."

"Do you think he saw you?"

"He looked right at me, but I don't think it registered. He had to know that I was keyed in on him, because he looked back at me, and saw me staring at him and fumbling around with my phone."

"Maybe he didn't see you at the restaurant that day."

"I don't know, Zahir." Cooper had fallen asleep, and Logan walked back to the nursery and tucked him in. When he returned to the kitchen he topped off their coffee and joined her at the counter.

"That day Khorasani made eye contact with me, just as he came together with Hamid. Unless he's inhuman, his adrenaline was pumping 100 miles an hour. When you're in the thick of it, you don't always see the big picture. Everything just telescopes down to you and the other guy. It's possible he didn't see me, but if he's a trained assassin, he knows every detail of what went down on the street."

"What do you think it means? What was Khorasani doing in Madrid?"

"Your guess is as good as mine. Did he have business there? Was he going back to Iran? Does he live in Madrid? The problem is unless we can tie his face to whatever identity he's using we're hosed." Logan exhaled in exasperation.

Zahir stared at him in sympathy. "What's your day look like?" She gave his knee a consoling pat.

"I had an email from Alicia saying that Willoughby's in town and wants to have lunch with me to talk about my trip. Oh, and I need to give Millie a call to find out when Nayef is due in. I thought it was supposed to be this week. How about you?"

"I had some good news at school. You know most PhD language programs have a second language requirement, and there was some question about whether or not BU would accept my Farsi scores, but they did so I'm all set."

"That is good news. But what's it do to your course load?"

"I can use that time to learn another Arabic dialect."

"Which one? I know there are several but how many are there altogether?"

"Let's see. Close to a dozen major dialects and then within those there are tons of sub-dialects. I've already got modern standard Arabic, but BU offers a survey of regional dialects, which might be interesting. One other thing I've always wanted to do was learn Andalusi Arabic. It's no longer spoken, but there's a lot of important classical literature written in Andalusi.

"Anyway, I have class this afternoon, and am teaching two classes tonight. I should be home by seven-thirty."

"All right. What time does the sitter need to leave?"

"Can you be home at six?"

"Got it covered." Logan walked over to the sink to rinse their coffee cups and then left to get ready for work.

An hour later he walked into One Marina Park. Miguel was back in his place behind the concierge desk, wearing a smile that spread from one side of his face to the other.

"Hey there, Mr. A. How you been?"

"Morning, Miguel. Welcome back. How's Paula doing?"

Miguel stepped around from behind the marble counter, reaching for his breast pocket. "She's good. But have a look at this!"

The young man was beaming as he withdrew a picture of his newborn, cradled in its mama's arms.

"Nice looking kid, Miguel. What's his name?"

"We decided to call him Dennis, after Dennis Martinez."

Logan did not recognize the name. "Who's that?"

"You don't know Dennis Martinez?" Miguel looked at him with a hint of disbelief. Logan shrugged and raised an eyebrow.

"Dennis Martinez was the first Nicaraguan to pitch in the majors. He's from Granada, my parents' hometown. When he was with the Expos he pitched a perfect game against the Dodgers. Only twelve other pitchers in history had done that, " he said.

"Oh. My wife says thanks for the flowers. That was very thoughtful."

"Now that you mention it, he does kind of look like a ballplayer." Logan grinned and handed the picture back to him. "You only have your first son one time, Miguel. Congratulations! Are we going to get a chance to meet the little guy?"

"Yes, sir. Maybe in a week or two we'll bring him in to meet everybody."

"All right. Looking forward to it." Logan waved and continued up to his office.

Alicia was standing before the door to their suite as he rounded the corner. She was juggling a vase of flowers and a cardboard tray from Starbucks with two venti lattes as she jiggled the key in the lock.

"Darn." Looking up at the sound of his footsteps, her face broke into a smile. "Hey, boss. Welcome back!"

"Here. Let me help you with that." He reached for the key, and opened the door.

"So how was your trip?" Alicia set the vase down on a side table, handed him his latte and then followed him into his office.

"It was good. I'd forgotten a lot about how the Mark V handles on the water; it's been a few years since I've been out on one, so that was useful. I made some notes, so if you could type them up for me, it'll help when I'm meeting with Willoughby. What time am I meeting him?"

"Twelve-thirty at a Vietnamese Pho restaurant on Commonwealth. He said if you don't like Vietnamese food, to suggest something different."

"No, that's good." He gave Alicia his notes to organize and then worked through the morning catching up on his email and reviewing a couple of draft consulting propos- als that had come in while he was traveling. Checking his voicemail, he saw that he had a message from Detective Breen.

"Mr. Alexander? Breen here. I talked to your sister the other day after you called her. If you get a chance, could you stop in and see me when you get back? I have some time Wednesday afternoon if that's convenient. Look forward to hearing from you."

Logan replaced the phone and called out through the open door. "Alicia, would you call Detective Breen's of- fice and tell him that I'll stop by there after my lunch with Willoughby, say three o'clock?"

"I'm on it. Any new developments in that?"

"Oh, I forgot to tell you."

"What?" She walked into his office and leaned against the door.

Logan filled her in on the whole Khorasani debacle in Madrid.

Alicia shook her head in disbelief. "That guy's scary. I hope somebody catches him soon."

"You and me both."

A little after twelve Logan left for his lunch date with Willoughby. He found the Asian Bistro Pho on Commonwealth Avenue and spotted the former Navy SEAL seated in a booth on the right-hand side. The restaurant was beginning to fill up with diners, many of them young Asian professionals, and Logan could hear the dissonant sounds of Chinese, Vietnamese and Thai languages being spoken at the tables he passed.

Willoughby stood and gripped his hand in greeting. "Logan, glad you could make it on short notice. I had to come down to Boston for a meeting and decided to check with your office to see if you were back.

"I had an email from Belcher, who said you guys had fun out there. He wasn't sure if you were going to get out because the weather had turned to crap, but he hadn't heard from you so he figured you had."

"Hey, Gordon. Yeah, we were delayed for a couple of hours, but there was a window and we were able to take off. Good thing that storm didn't hit earlier. We would've had to cancel the exercise, or at a minimum postpone it."

At their waiter's suggestion they both ordered the house special, *pho dac bie,* which was a meat eaters' dream – noodle soup with steak, brisket, and meatballs. Tendons and tripe were also featured but they both opted out of those.

The two men made small talk until the waiter returned with their soup. Logan heaped a couple of spoonfuls of Vietnamese hot chili sauce into his bowl and his eyes began to tear up from the spicy peppers.

"So, how'd the exercise go?"

"Like I told Tim, I hadn't been operational on a Mark V for several years, so it was a rush being out there with those guys. The scenario was pretty straightforward and realistic for today's operations with all the piracy and terrorist attacks we're seeing. I think it's going to continue to be a critical special ops platform for the foreseeable future."

"How'd it perform in those conditions?" Willoughby signaled the waiter to refill their water glasses.

"It was perfect when we first went out. The bay's protected from big swells, but once we got out into the open ocean, and picked up speed in those conditions, the vibrations coming through the hull were much more obvious

I didn't think it was going to be a problem until we were doing the extraction, and the pilot began executing evasive maneuvers."

"Oh, to simulate hot pursuit?"

"Yeah. Did you ever watch a guy using a jackhammer? You know how it looks like he's just barely hanging on? Well, that's what this felt like."

Logan handed Willoughby a manila envelope. "These are some general observations. Also, talking to Belcher and the other guys I get the sense that their injury rate in the Mark V corresponds to what's been documented by other SEAL units using the boat."

Willoughby took the envelope. "Thanks. I'm expecting a big data dump from the boys up in Maine next week. They think they've cracked the code with this new hull design, and plan to have a prototype retrofit ready to test in a couple of weeks."

"Where are they going to test it?"

"Norfolk. I'm planning to go down for that test, and I'll take Hockaday with me. I'd like you to be there too."

"Sure. Just let me know when."

They chatted for a few more minutes, paid the bill and got up to go.

"You need a ride anywhere, Gordon?"

"No, thanks. I've got wheels. I drove down this morning. Stay in touch."

They shook hands and as Logan got into his SUV he glanced at the dashboard clock. Two-thirty. Just enough time to get over to the station house on Harrison before his meeting with Detective Breen.

Chapter 16

Logan walked into Peter Breen's office just before three o'clock. Approaching his desk, he could see that the detective was reading what appeared to be a report from the Spanish INTERPOL office. After greeting Breen and taking a seat, Logan gestured towards the report.

"Anything new from the Spanish?"

"Not really. This is their write-up of your meeting at the airport," he grumbled. He leaned back in his chair, clasping his hands behind his head as he swiveled back and forth.

"I still can't believe what that must have been like. Standing there with Khorasani right in front of you and nothing you could do." He leaned forward and rubbed his hand across his chin. "How was it dealing with, what's his name?" He searched his notes. "Montoya. Detective Montoya?"

"We talked through an interpreter, so you're not always sure you're getting your point across. I don't know. He seemed to know what he was doing and it sounds like the Spanish are with it."

"Yeah, but they couldn't get off the dime when they had Khorasani right there." Breen let out an exasperated sigh. "I mean, if that had happened in Boston we would have shut the frigging airport down until we found him!

"We need a break. I went back to Montoya and asked him if they had developed any new information they could share. He told me they're not using any biometrics at Barajas, so even if we gave them a data dump from our files they don't have any automated systems to run it against."

"Damn!"

"Something else. I had a call from the Kuwaitis this morning. It looks like your friend's father, Mr. Al Subaie, is going to be back in town this week. Apparently their security people have developed some new information. Have you ever met this fellow, Alghanim? Thamir Alghanim?"

Logan's guard went up. He didn't want to lie to Breen, but he needed to be circumspect about how well he knew Thamir.

"I met him a few weeks ago when Mr. Al Subaie asked me to help him out. I picked him up at the airport and we had him over to the house for dinner that night." Logan shrugged. "He seemed all right. Didn't have much to say."

Breen gave Logan a thoughtful look. "If Khorasani is working for the Iranians, the Kuwaitis might be able to develop some information."

"What do you mean?"

Breen pulled some notes out of a folder on his desk. "I did a little research on the Al Subaies. They run Kuwait. Alghanim is Intel. I doubt if he would've shown up here right after Hamid was killed if we were talking about just some other Kuwaiti. This case is getting a lot of attention in his organization. I think the Al Subaies are leaning on him. They want answers, and they want them now."

Logan nodded his head in agreement. "It's their back yard, so they might be able to get some insights into Khorasani's whereabouts, particularly if he's working out of Iran. But that's not a given. He's all over the place — here, Iran, Madrid, and who knows where he was heading that day."

Breen stood up to signal that the meeting was over. "Let's stay in touch, Logan. We're going to get this bastard yet."

As Logan got up, he realized that something had been bothering him. The large-breasted ceramic mermaid ashtray that had been the centerpiece on Breen's desk was missing.

"What happened to your ashtray? That was a unique piece."

Breen gave Logan a mournful look and shook his head. "Would you believe my secretary came in one day last week and told me that I was a male chauvinist, and that my displaying that piece of art amounted to sexual harassment? The next morning when I came in it was gone. But I found this in my trash." He reached down and retrieved a bag of crushed ceramic pieces. "What's the world coming to?"

Logan grinned and shook hands. As he walked out of the station his cell phone vibrated. Getting into his car he glanced at the caller ID and saw that it was his sister, Millie.

"Hey, Mills, how are you?"

"Fine, and how was your trip?"

"Good, except for that little episode in Madrid with Khorasani. I don't think I've ever been that frustrated in my entire life."

"I'll bet. Hey, I wanted to let you know that Nayef is going to be in town for a couple of days this week. It's business, but he made a point of saying that he wanted to see you."

"Yeah. I just got out of a meeting with Detective Breen, and he mentioned that Nayef had been in touch with them. I wonder if they've dug up anything on Khorasani?"

"He didn't mention anything. He's coming over to our place for drinks Friday. Can you make it, say seven o'clock?"

"I'll be there. Anyone else coming?"

"Ryan's going to be out of town for a couple of days, taking depositions. He has to go to Springfield to do them because the witnesses are in federal custody there and the bureau doesn't want to move them. I don't think he'll be back until late Friday. Why don't you bring Zahir?"

"I'll see if she's free. I know she'd like to see Nayef."

"Plus, she knows so much about that part of the world. She just cuts right to the chase." Logan could sense the admiration in Millie's voice. She and Zahir had become close over the past year.

On Friday, Logan and Zahir got to Millie's Stillman Street loft just after seven o'clock. Before their wedding, Millie and Ryan had decided to keep Millie's condo and break the lease on Ryan's Beacon Hill apartment. Their North End address offered a painless commute for both of them. Ryan's Government Service Center offices were just down the street from historic Faneuil Hall and Millie's offices at Huber, Steele and O'Reilly were in the nearby Sears Crescent building at the corner of Cornhill and Court Streets.

Millie greeted them at the door. As they walked in, Logan could see Nayef in the living room, staring out at the expansive view of the Zakim Bridge. He turned towards them and Logan was startled by how much the Kuwaiti billionaire had aged. Naturally slim in stature, his face was drawn, almost haggard. Despite his smile and warm greeting there was a melancholy air about him.

"Logan, Zahir, so nice to see you both."

Zahir clasped his hands in hers and searched his face. "How are you doing, Nayef? How is your family holding up?"

"It's still very hard. My wife is struggling to understand everything. It's only been a month since..." His voice caught and he looked away. Struggling to regain his composure, he looked back at them. "I have some news."

Logan gave him a questioning look as he led Nayef over to the leather sofa and sat down. Zahir followed Millie into the kitchen and helped her arrange a small tray of hors d'oeuvres.

"He seems so sad," she whispered to Millie.

"I know. I can't imagine what he's going through."

They searched each other's faces with empathy. Both had been traumatized by Cooper's death over a year ago. One, the older sister, the other his lover.

Meanwhile, in the living room, Logan listened as Nayef began speaking.

"Thamir's people have been in touch with Khorasani's uncle."

Logan stared at him in surprise. "How was he able to do that?"

"I didn't ask for all the details, but despite the damage done to our Iranian program after Simon's treachery, it seems that we still have some capabilities there.

"Thamir activated one of their assets, and tasked him to find out what he could about the uncle. The uncle is Farid

Khorasani. He remained behind in Iran in the early '80s when the rest of the family immigrated to the U.S. According to Thamir, Farid was opposed to the Shah's government. He was one of those protesting in the streets against government corruption, calling for the exiled clerics to come back and straighten things out."

"It sounds as though he was one of the true believers. If he was one of those pro-Khomeini conservatives, what's he doing talking to Thamir's people?"

"It seems that things haven't gone as well for Mr. Khorasani as he had hoped. He was rewarded with a job working on immigration issues, and since the regime trusted him, he became a sort of spotter for the Iranian Revolutionary Guard Corps, passing them leads, procuring foreign passports, that sort of thing. They like him where he is but his career is going nowhere. He's been stuck in the same job for ten years."

"Do you think he passed his nephew's name to them?"

"Ah, this is where it gets interesting." Nayef accepted a drink from Zahir as she and Millie came in with a tray.

"Farid initially said that he didn't know anything about that when asked, but in a follow-up meeting, Thamir's man offered him a generous incentive to tell all, and his story changed.

"He said that Nouri had shown up at his apartment about five years ago. He seemed restless and didn't know what he was going to do. After he'd been there for a couple of weeks, Farid introduced him to a Colonel Kashani in the Qods Force. Nouri disappeared shortly after that and Kashani never told him what had happened to him."

"Does it seem likely that Kashani recruited Nouri?" Millie passed a plate of mini-quiches around.

"Farid had heard rumors about a push within the Qods Force to recruit foreigners for an elite unit that would be working and traveling abroad. At first he didn't think that Nouri had the right kind of background, but later Farid became convinced that he was working for them."

"What changed his mind?" Zahir asked.

Nayef paused to take a sip of his drink. "The Qods Force has a quality control program for the alias passports they issue to their officers. They send them over randomly to Farid's office to see if any flags go up. The people there have all this data on foreign passports and they are the established experts in the government on these documents.

"About three years after his nephew had gone missing, Farid was stunned one day in his office to find himself looking at an American passport with Nouri's picture on it. Only it wasn't Nouri's name."

"An American passport? Did he remember the name?" Logan was fidgeting on the edge of his seat.

"Yes. He wrote it down. Claudio. Claudio Diez Perea."

"That's a Spanish name. In an American passport." Logan ran through the possibilities. U.S. passports were nearly impossible to fabricate. The paper, inks, biometrics and machine-readable technology required to duplicate a U.S. passport would take a very sophisticated forger. Were the Iranians capable of that level of sophistication?

"Has Thamir done anything with this?"

"Yes. We're proceeding with care, because we're uncertain how we are going to go forward. Thamir has a colleague, an ally from another service. Sometimes they help each other out. Thamir gave him a list of names, among which was buried the name of Claudio Diez Perea, so as to downplay our interest in him. Thamir asked this person to request name traces from the CIA and the Spanish National Intelligence Center."

"Have you heard back from them yet?" Logan could barely contain himself.

"Yes, and the results will surprise you. The CIA had no record of a U.S. citizen by the name of Claudio Diez Perea. However, there was a Spanish record of a U.S. citizen by that name, who had applied for and been granted Spanish citizenship about one year ago based upon his relationship to a deceased Spanish immigrant to the U.S.

"Even more interesting, the CIA reported that a Claudio Diez Perea of Spanish nationality traveled to Madrid from the U.S. earlier this month. He flew from Bradley International Airport to Toronto, and from Toronto to Madrid on the day that Hamid was killed. Claudio Diez Perea is Nouri Khorasani!"

Chapter 17

Nouri dodged a delivery truck as he crossed against traffic and entered Parque Los Chorros, a spacious city park located at the base of Avila Mountain in north Caracas. The enclosure comprised terraces, with steps leading 100 feet below to a system of tunnels and bridges. Ancient trees and tropical vegetation fed by mountain springs offered respite from the mid-day heat for *Caraqueños,* the city's querulous residents. Couples strolled hand in hand, oblivious to the surveillance team following a man not far ahead.

Nouri signaled Azar to follow him as he fell in about a hundred feet behind the surveillants. Colonel Samadi had set up this exercise to give Azar some practical experience observing a live surveillance team in action. Samadi had arranged for the local Qods Force station chief to contact his counterparts in SEBIN, Venezuela's Intelligence service. The information the Qods officer was to pass along was that he had received word from Tehran that an Israeli Intelligence officer had entered the country to meet with Jewish dissidents. Samadi had then dispatched a Qods Force officer, posing as an Israeli, to Caracas where he planned to run through several pre-planned surveillance detection routes.

The Venezuelans were pretty good. The tricky part for Nouri and Azar was not to expose themselves to the surveillance team. They had been able to blend in well thus far, and since all of the exercises were on foot, and they already knew the routes the role player would take, they could position themselves to see the team in action without exposing themselves.

Azar had initially found it difficult to follow the surveillance team's movements. It was a twelve-person unit supported by two cars and a motorbike. They created a loose cordon around the target, trailing from behind, paralleling him on both side streets and leapfrogging ahead when they anticipated his direction. The cars were used to move the team members around to lessen their exposure to the target. They did a good job of rotating people around to make it difficult for him. To complicate things they went through multiple clothing changes and in some cases had used disguises to alter their appearance.

Nouri and Azar exited the park and walked southeast to Avenida El Rosario where there was a coffee shop. Nouri waited until she had caught up with him.

"Let's take a break in here. We don't want them to spot us. Our friend is going to be making a stop soon, so we should be able to catch up with them in about thirty minutes if we take a cab."

"I think I'm beginning to get a feel for it." Azar pulled her hair back into a knot and secured it with an elastic band. They ordered coffee and sat back in their booth.

Nouri studied the woman across from him. For someone in her late thirties, she was very attractive — firm breasts, long dark hair, and a dancer's figure. There was a melancholy air about her, though. Samadi had told him that she had lost her father and husband within months of each other the year before. She had accepted her father's death as nature taking its course, but her husband's violent demise had thrown her into a deep depression from which she had emerged only six months ago.

Azar had been resolute, telling Samadi that she no longer had anything to live for and wanting to strike back at the people who had robbed her of her lifelong love. Nouri felt she was aptly named as Azar meant "fire maiden" in Persian.

"Watching this surveillance team makes me wonder if I'll ever feel 100 percent certain about my own surveillance status," she confessed. "When they move the surveillants around in cars, especially when they're walking towards you wearing something completely different, it throws you off."

"It's true, if they have a big enough team and the resources, they can make it very complicated. But that's where you have to be creative in designing your route. You want to force them to expose themselves. You can do this by covering a lot of territory, changing your mode of transportation, making them follow you into places where they're afraid to lose you. Techniques like that."

"I know. It just seems so hard." Azar looked dejected but then brightened. "I know I can do it. I'm observant. And one thing I've figured out is that it pays not to have any preconceptions about what surveillance looks like. It may be that young man in the leather jacket or that street person sitting in the doorway."

"What are the main things you need to figure out to know if you're under surveillance?" Nouri studied her face.

"You have to see the person more than once."

"That's true. But it's more complicated than that. There have to be repeated sightings over time and distance and change in direction. I mean, if you see someone in here and they're walking around, they go to the bathroom, go outside to get a newspaper and come back, that's not surveillance, even though you saw them multiple times.

"That's why when you devise your surveillance detection run, it should be several hours long and should take you into different parts of the city. Also, it shouldn't be too predictable, like going in a straight line or to places you normally go. You have to change direction, in order to force surveillance to change direction, but your movement has to make sense too. You can't just randomly walk around."

He looked at his watch and saw that they had been in the coffee shop for thirty minutes. "We should get going." He signaled to the waiter, and after they had paid the bill, they walked outside and caught a cab on the street.

Nouri gave the driver an address just south of the Altamira Metro Station. Skirting the Parque del Este, the driver turned south onto Avenida Luis Roche, pulling over 200 feet from the metro station. Nouri pulled out a wad of Bolivars and peeled off twenty, about five dollars.

Getting out of the cab, they walked to within 100 feet of the station and positioned themselves to see their colleague come out. They were surprised a few minutes later when he exited the station to see two of the surveillants confront him. They began questioning him, one on either side. He withdrew his wallet from his back pocket and seemed to be showing some form of identification to the two men.

"This isn't good. The surveillance team must be getting upset because he's jerking them around. They've figured out he's doing a surveillance detection run. And in their minds, they think he's an Israeli Intel officer, so they're not screwing around." Nouri stared intently as the scene in front of them unfolded.

"What should we do?"

"There's not much we can do right now. The Venezuelans hate the Israelis almost as much as we do. At least if you listen to what their president says that's how it seems. Our friend there has a good cover story, and his documentation is backed up. Worst case scenario, they haul him in for questioning and then let him off with a warning.

"We should get out of here. We need to get in touch with Samadi, so he knows what's going on." Nouri consulted a map of the city. "Let's go this way," he said, pointing west.

They walked to the Chacao Metro Station and took Line 1 to Plaza Venezuela where they transferred to a line in the direction of El Valle.

Nouri had found a short-term rental apartment in El Valle for them to work out of. He had outfitted one of the rooms with mats so that he and Azar could carry on their martial arts training while in Caracas. She was athletic. She had told him that she had been into horseback riding when she was younger, and had been able to keep it up despite conservative attitudes about the role of women in Iranian society.

They changed into their workout gear and began sparring. An hour later, drenched from their exertions, they sat on the mats to catch their breath. After they had recovered, Nouri went into another room and came back holding a boot knife.

"Have you done any work with close-in combat using knives?"

Azar shook her head.

"We'll spend some time on the basics and go on from there. The first thing you have to do is find a weapon you're comfortable with. I have all my knives custom made. You have to find a designer who can make a knife that fits your hand like a glove. It's like getting a dress made. The measurements have to be perfect."

Nouri held up the knife for her to see. "These edges on the handle are called quillons. They keep your hand snug in the grip and prevent it from slipping down onto the blade.

"Once you get your knife you should spend a lot of time getting familiar with it. You need to have a good feeling for its weight, balance and shape. These all affect how it feels in your hand and how you'll do when you have to use it."

"How do you know what kind of knife works best? It seems as though there are hundreds of designs to choose from."

"That's a good question. By its very nature, knife fighting is a close combat activity. Our situation is different from a military environment where they're not really concerned about concealing the weapon. We have to be stealthy, so that alone will make a difference in what kind of knife you choose.

"I usually have a couple of blades on me. One like this one that can be concealed around your ankle." He demonstrated where he would wear it and then walked back into the other room, returning with a stiletto in his hand. "Something like this stiletto gives you a completely different range of options."

He handed the blade to Azar. She handled it gingerly, testing its sharpness against her thumb, emitting a surprised cry when it drew blood. She handed the knife back to Nouri and sucked on her injured thumb to stop the bleeding.

"You have to treat them with respect. Today we'll spend some time talking about grips. Over the years many different kinds of grips have been used, but you can break them down into three basic types – the forward grip, reverse grip, and special grips."

"Which one do you use?"

"It depends on the knife and the situation. Generally I like to use a hammer grip. It's a kind of forward grip and is probably the most common one." He demonstrated the position to Azar, fingers wrapped around the bottom of the grip, with the thumb and forefinger coming into contact. He assumed a defensive stance, with the knife angled up and his wrist locked.

"With this grip you can maintain some distance from the target, but still achieve a good slashing range of motion. The downside is that with your arm extended this way, your opponent has a better chance of trapping your hand.

"The other thing is that it's difficult to keep your wrist in a locked forward position. If your hand gets tired and you tend to hold it like this," he demonstrated a more relaxed punching type position, "then you leave yourself open to the knife being pushed back into your body."

He then demonstrated the saber and Filipino forward grips, highlighting the pluses and minuses of each. He had Azar stand next to him and modeled each grip for her, each time adjusting her hand on the knife to achieve the desired position. They spent forty-five minutes alternating between hammer, saber and Filipino grips until Azar felt comfortable with each one.

They hadn't had anything to eat since breakfast, and it was already after three o'clock. After showering and changing back into their street clothes, Azar suggested that they try out an *arepera*, one of the local restaurants found all over Caracas specializing in this traditional fare. Made from a savory corn flour bread, *arepas* can be stuffed with a choice of fillings.

They found an *arepera* several blocks from the apartment, went in and seated themselves at a Formica-covered table. Despite the off-hour, the restaurant was humming with activity. The pungent smells coming from the kitchen made Nouri's mouth water as he realized how hungry he was. After perusing the menu they both selected the *reina pepiada*, or gorgeous queen, an arepa stuffed with shredded chicken, avocado, and chopped spring onions slathered in mayonnaise. They both ordered a side of red beans and Nouri asked for a *Polar*, a draft pale lager beer. Azar raised an eyebrow but didn't say anything. She ordered a *merengada*, a milkshake made from fresh papaya.

After their food came they were quiet as they tucked into their meals. The *arepas* were as advertised, flavorful and stuffed with fresh ingredients. Nouri washed down the last morsel with a swig of beer and then burped appreciatively.

"Something else we need to start working on is our cover for being here. We can get by for a few months saying that we are looking for business opportunities, but at some point we need to come up with a concrete idea. I know Samadi and the others like Venezuela, because if there is a flap, it shouldn't be a big deal here. The administration is aligned with Iran. But I can't think of a worse place to try and operate."

"What do you mean?"

"The country is dysfunctional. The PSUV, the United Socialist Party of Venezuela, controls everything, so there's no real economic freedom. They nationalized most of the heavy industry, especially the oil industry and are generally anti-free-market.

"The good thing is that there is no minimum capital requirement for foreigners to start a business here, but it can take awhile to get the approvals we'll need."

"How long?"

"Over three months. I think for our purposes, we can do something like what I have set up in Spain. It's a consulting business that doesn't require a big office, goods or employees. We can even fabricate our cash flow profile using bogus foreign clients to make it look like we're doing real business. All the Venezuelans care about is getting tax revenue from us, and Tehran won't mind funding that just to give us the capability of operating out of here.

"Whatever we come up with needs to be good enough to keep us under the radar, and give us the flexibility to travel. From what Colonel Samadi said, Europe is heating up and we may get shut out of there."

"I don't care where we are. I want to find…" Her voice quivered but then hardened. "I want to find the people who killed my husband."

"And when you do?"

Her voice was steady and her gaze unflinching. "Kill them!"

Chapter 18

Logan, Norm Stoddard and Bruce Wellington waited in their rental car just down the street from the apartment building in Burgos, Spain, where Nouri Khorasani, masquerading as Claudio Diez Perea, was alleged to be living. It had been a whirlwind ten days since Nayef had dropped the bombshell in Boston.

At that meeting Nayef had asked Logan to help him find Khorasani. He didn't want to take this information to INTERPOL or the Boston PD out of concern that Kuwait's role in the Bandar Deylam operation would be divulged.

Right after his meeting with his Kuwaiti friend, Logan had reached out to the two former Navy SEALS who had been on the Bandar Deylam raid with him. Nayef had been able to give them Khorasani's precise location in Spain because of information obtained from Khorasani's uncle. Both Stoddard and Wellington were available and when Logan briefed them on what had happened to Hamid, they said they wanted in. They had been close to the little Kuwaiti while training on Failaka Island and had been in action with him in Bandar Deylam. He had considered bringing along Alicia for her Spanish language skills, but decided it wouldn't be necessary given how widely English was spoken in Spain.

The Kuwaiti Intel Service's liaison in Madrid was their local contact. He had met them in Burgos three days before, having driven down from Madrid with all of the gear Logan had requested. Weapons, surveillance gear, and maps made up most of it. In addition the Kuwaitis had rented two vehicles, hotel rooms and a separate apartment where they planned to take Khorasani for questioning. All of the procurements had been done through a cut-out to avoid any linkage between Kuwait and Logan's team.

"Where the hell is this guy?" Stoddard yawned and peered through the front windshield in the direction of Khorasani's apartment.

"Damned if I know. He must still be traveling. I spotted him in Madrid about three weeks ago. I wonder if he got spooked when he saw me? He made eye contact with me but didn't act as though he recognized me."

"Maybe he figured it out later," Wellington chimed in.

"We can't do this much longer. We're heating up the neighborhood." Logan was disappointed. He'd been pumped up at the thought of getting his hands on the Qods Force killer.

They had done the best they could to lower their profile. The problem was that Khorasani lived on San Juan, a residential street in a center city neighborhood, with few places for outsiders to blend in. Logan had decided to set up initially on the apartment in the mornings and late afternoons, when Khorasani could be expected to be going to and coming from work. He had rotated the two cars and their location on San Juan, but thus far they had come up empty-handed. Khorasani was either holed up in his apartment or was out of town.

"All right. Let's make a pretext call to the apartment. We won't say anything but if anyone picks up, we won't be going in."

Logan pulled one of the cell phones the Kuwaitis had given him out of a bag and keyed in Khorasani's home phone number. They all held their breath as the phone rang. It eventually went to voicemail, and they breathed again.

Looking at his watch, Logan saw that it was seven-thirty. "Let's grab a bite to eat and come back later. It'll be better if it's quieter on the street when we go in."

At eleven-thirty Logan eased their rental car into a parking spot opposite the apartment with a view to the entrance.

"OK. Radios on TAC. We'll do a comms check when we get into the building. Bruce, let us know if you see anybody going in. We don't know if Khorasani is living by himself, if he's got a girlfriend, nothing. Obviously if you spot him that'll be huge. We'll take him down as soon as he gets into the apartment. It'll be dicey getting him out of there though and into our safe site."

They had not been inside the building, although Stoddard had approached the front entrance and, using a blank key coated with dye, had inserted it into the lock to obtain the pattern of the locking apparatus. Back in the car Stoddard had used a file to shape the key to fit into the lock. It had taken three attempts over two days to get it right. Once inside they planned to bypass the elevators and take the stairs to Khorasani's fourth floor apartment, where they would pick the lock.

Logan and Stoddard slipped out of their vehicle and crossed the street. In thirty seconds they were standing before the building's main entrance. As Stoddard reached for the door, a young couple walked through the lobby, but before reaching the entrance, turned left down a hallway. Logan was tense as Stoddard inserted the key and wriggled it in the lock. It turned and they went inside. There was no concierge and, except for the couple who had just walked through, the entryway was empty.

There were two elevators immediately in front of them, but they ignored those and chose the dimly lit stairwell to the right. Their footsteps echoed as they took the stairs two at a time to the fourth floor. Logan and Stoddard found Khorasani's apartment midway down the carpeted hallway on the left side. There was the sound of music playing from the adjoining apartment. They paused outside Khorasani's door and listened intently for any sound from within.

Satisfied that no one was home, Stoddard withdrew a lock-picking set from his bag. He inserted a tension wrench into the lock cylinder and then selected a pin, which he inserted into the lock. With deft touch he located each of the pins inside and set them to the open position. After all five were set, he applied additional torque and turned the lock.

There was no sign of an alarm system, but they moved through the apartment quickly to clear it and to make certain that it was not alarmed. Satisfied that no one was home, and there was no alarm, they breathed more easily.

Withdrawing his radio, Logan whispered into it. "Base, this is Alpha 1. Radio check."

"Alpha 1, this is Base. Read you loud and clear. How you me?"

"Loud and clear, Base. We're in."

"Roger that."

Logan set the radio on a coffee table and he and Stoddard began a methodical search of the apartment. Two hours later they had inspected virtually every inch of the space but had found nothing of interest.

"The guy's living a double life, Norm. Unless he's got some other place that he works out of, there has to be some point where those two lives come together. I don't get it."

"Maybe we missed something. He might have some kind of concealment device in here. Something in the furniture or walls."

Forty-five minutes later they found it. Logan had tapped his way around the apartment and was working his way around the wooden floors when he detected a distinctly hollow sound in a section of flooring in the bedroom.

"Norm, come listen to this."

"It's definitely hollow." Stoddard got down on all fours and examined the space. It took him an additional fifteen minutes to figure out how the concealment opened. "Bingo!" The door flipped up on a spring action hinge to reveal the cavity below.

The radio crackled and Wellington's voice came through. "I've got a single male, late thirties, medium build, entering the building, over."

"Does he look like Khorasani?" Logan tensed up at the prospect of engaging the Qods Force killer.

"I don't think so. I can't be sure, but this guy looks heavier than the one in the picture."

Logan's mind raced. "Let's set up in the other room just in case it's him." They took up prearranged positions in the living room and waited. Ten minutes later there was no sign of Khorasani, so they returned to the bedroom.

Logan reached into the cavity and withdrew a bundle of euros, three handguns and what appeared to be an assortment of keys to safe deposit boxes.

"Interesting. I wonder where these safe deposit boxes are and what he's got stashed in them."

"Who knows? Weapons? Other identities? He's being very careful, even here in his own apartment. This cache doesn't give us much."

Logan frowned. He reached back down into the cavity and ran his hand all around. His fingers touched something flat, which he grasped and withdrew from the concealment. In his hand was an envelope that had been left lying flat on the floor of the concealment. Opening it he withdrew a passport, national identity card, credit cards and other pocket litter in the name of Claudio Diez Perea. Thumbing through the passport Logan saw the entry stamps for Hartford International Airport that corresponded with Khorasani's recent travel to the U.S.

One item that stood out from the others was a laminated Costa Rican national identity card in the name of one Claudio Frontera. The face on the card was that of Nouri Khorasani.

"Well, well, well. What do we have here? Looks like Mr. Khorasani just gave us something we might be able to use."

"You think he's traveling on this Costa Rican ID now?" Stoddard studied the face on the foreign ID card.

"Hard to say. Maybe he's traveling on a passport in this name and left the ID card here. We've got some work to do. Let's photograph all this stuff. The Kuwaitis might be able to develop additional info from the credit cards and passport. I don't know what kind of resources they have, but they ought to be able to build a travel and spending profile on the Perea identity."

They spent the next half-hour photographing everything in the concealment. Logan was using a Canon EOS 7 D SLR camera capable of taking still and video shots. At

eighteen megapixels, the clarity of the photos was unbeliev-
able. After they had photographed everything they put it all
back in the order they had removed it and closed the trap
door. If Khorasani did come back to his apartment before
they found him, they didn't want to tip him off that they
were on to him.

After they had closed up the concealment, they vide-
otaped the interior of the apartment. Logan looked at his
watch. They had been inside for close to four hours. Way
more than he had expected. It was going on four o'clock.
Yawning, he did an inventory of everything in his bag. He
and Stoddard edged over to the front door and listened for
sounds of anyone in the hallway outside. It was silent. They
closed the door, reset the pins in the lock, and walked out
into the night.

Chapter 19

Logan listened intently to Thamir Alghanim's readout from the Burgos operation. They were sitting in Thamir's Hyatt Regency Hotel suite in Boston. Two weeks had passed since Logan, Stoddard and Wellington had traveled to Spain to hunt down the elusive Qods Force operative, Nouri Khorasani. In the interim, Thamir's people, working with the CIA and Spanish authorities, had developed some interesting data that Thamir was now sharing.

As in an earlier approach to the CIA, Thamir's organization had not divulged to the agency that the individuals they were investigating had anything to do with Hamid Al Subaie's murder. Rather, the names they asked them to trace were raised in the context of a broader counterterrorism investigation Kuwait was undertaking.

Thamir was explaining some of the methodology the government employed to develop its analysis.

"Customs Border Patrol uses something called the Passenger Name Record, or PNR, program to pull together disparate data in order to analyze travel patterns. CIA's Counterterrorism Center and some of the other centers working on transnational issues have access to the PNR data."

"What does this PNR data actually give you?" Logan leaned forward in his chair.

"It's basically all the information that a traveler uses with an airline when they book their travel. Items like their itinerary, contact information, and credit card or other payment information.

"After 9/11, CBP was able to get electronic access to this data. They could get the PNR from all the airlines using online reservation systems. And most importantly it wasn't

152

just for domestic flights but for any airline operating international flights to and from the U.S."

"How do they actually use the data?"

"CBP has something called an Automated Tracking System, where they input the PNR data and then use trend analysis and pattern-based rules to identify suspicious travel behavior.

"For instance, they can pinpoint the actual point of origin for any traveler and any stops they make along the way. They can also identify suspicious reservations or payment methods such as cash transactions, one-way tickets and last-minute purchases."

"I've heard some of this before. Do you remember that guy, Faisal Shahzad, who tried to blow up a car bomb in Times Square in New York City?" Logan shifted in his seat.

"That was in 2010, I believe."

"Right. So, if I remember correctly, CBP originally targeted this guy based on his PNR, after he had gone to Pakistan to receive terrorist training. They didn't have anything conclusive early on, so he was released. But later on, the FBI was digging into his background information and used the PNR to identify him as he was trying to leave the country. He ended up confessing to everything," Logan said.

"So how does all this come into play with Khorasani?"

"I thought you would never ask." Thamir bared his teeth in a grim smile. "When we were over there the agency complained about new protocols for data sharing with the European Union nations. In the past these exchanges were routine, but now the EU Parliament, which has about seven hundred members, votes on these data sharing agreements with a thumbs up or down vote."

"Are we having problems with the Europeans?"

"The CIA seems to feel that the overarching issue in information sharing with them is their concern over protecting the privacy rights of the individual. That means they're being less forthcoming with individuals' personal data. Although most of these countries have seen the benefit of information sharing, particularly in the area of transnational crime – human trafficking, drug and weapons smuggling – left-leaning constituents in these countries are forcing everybody to overhaul their information sharing protocols.

"Still there was some very interesting information to come out of our query, which adds to what we got on Khorasani earlier. First, his Claudio Diez Perea persona is not all that old. It's been in existence for maybe three years. As we found out before, he'd used a false U.S. passport, identifying himself as the grandson of a deceased Spanish national who had immigrated to the U.S.

"Naturally, the Spanish authorities had not gone back to validate the original U.S. passport, so Khorasani was able to pull off this charade. It seems he used the Perea persona to enroll in the university at Salamanca, and set up a consulting business in Burgos. CIA is continuing to do transactional analysis on Perea's spending patterns. So far it seems that except for his most recent trip to the U.S., almost all of his travel has been in Europe."

"That's interesting. I wonder why the Qods Force took the risk of sending him on a mission in his own back yard?" Logan stood up to stretch. "Hey, all this talking's making me thirsty. Do you want some water or anything?"

"Help yourself. I'm fine."

Logan got up and opened the small fridge beneath the mini-bar where he found a bottle of water. He returned to his seat and took a long swig. "You were saying?"

"We went in separately to the Spanish with the Costa Rican identity. I knew that if we gave that to CIA and they saw that Khorasani was traveling in another alias identity, they would put him on a watchlist and maybe even go after him themselves. This is personal. Nayef wants us to take care of it."

"What makes you think the agency won't take the Perea file to the Spanish?"

"Third party rule. They should come to us first if they want to make it available to the Spanish. That doesn't mean that they will, though." Thamir paused before continuing. "It seems our friend, Mr. Khorasani, has made his first mistake."

Logan fidgeted in his seat. Thamir could be circumspect to the point of distraction. "What?"

"It appears that one Claudio Frontera of Costa Rican nationality flew out of Madrid Barajas Airport on the same day that you spotted Khorasani in Terminal 1."

"Bingo! Do they know where he was going?"

Thamir paused before responding. "He was on a direct flight to Caracas, Venezuela."

Logan felt a jolt of adrenaline as Thamir uttered these words. Maybe this was the break they needed. It was the first direct link they had to a name and a travel destination for the slippery Qods Force assassin.

"But it gets even more interesting. It turns out that the Qods Force is either more arrogant or sloppier than we thought."

"How so?"

"We know that intelligence services often meet their deep cover officers in third countries to minimize exposure and unnecessary risk to their operations. On a hunch, one of our analysts was able to get hold of the flight manifests for direct flights from Tehran to Caracas for the week that Khorasani traveled. There were a fair number of travelers, but two names stood out."

Logan held his breath.

"Tahmouress Samadi and Azar Ghabel."

He breathed again. Hamid had mentioned Samadi from the time he had infiltrated Bandar Deylam with a foreign fighter group. Samadi was the chief of operations at the base. And Azar Ghabel must be related to the base commander, Colonel Barzin Ghabel, the one he and Hamid had killed.

"From the identifying information on her passport, it's almost certain that Azar Ghabel is Colonel Ghabel's widow. And of course you remember Samadi's name coming up when you first debriefed Hamid after he went into Iran with that foreign fighter group."

Logan let out a low whistle. "That is really interesting. What's the Qods Force doing in Caracas? And, what's Azar Ghabel doing with the Qods Force?"

"That's what we'd like you to find out, Logan." There was a glint in Thamir's eyes. "Nayef and I have complete confidence in your ability to do this. Would you go? Take a small team to Venezuela and find out what the Iranians are up to?"

Logan nodded his assent. "I need to talk to Zahir to make sure she's all right with it. I also have to call around to see if some of the guys from the Bandar Deylam Op are available. I'm also going to need a Spanish interpreter, but I think I have that covered." He smiled to himself as he thought of the look on Alicia Gomez's face when she found out she was going to Venezuela.

"What's the time frame?"

"The sooner the better."

"We won't need a very big footprint. If Stoddard and Wellington are both still available, I'll just take them, and my secretary as our interpreter. What kind of support can you give us?"

"Just give me a list of what you need. Our man in Caracas, Zed, is very good. He'll take care of local procurements for you and we can ship in weapons and the like in the diplomatic pouch. We still have your alias Canadian passports. Are you comfortable traveling on those?"

"I think so. They're pretty clean. The only entry and exit stamps are in and out of several countries in Europe. Maybe we can fly to Caracas via Mexico. Do you have anyone there that can handle the passports for us?"

"That won't be a problem. We'll have one of our officers at our Embassy in Mexico insert the Mexican entry stamps into your Canadian passports. You'll have to stagger your departures over a day or two. As for the exit stamp, I think you can just tell the immigration officer that you lost the paper that goes with it. The Mexicans are so disorganized that it shouldn't ring any bells."

"Do you see any problem with my secretary, Alicia, traveling on her U.S. passport?

"That should be fine. She doesn't have your kind of profile, right?"

"No, she's basically been in California for most of her life. Her brother, John Gomez, was the guy who got killed in London last year."

Thamir gave a sympathetic nod but didn't say anything. He consulted his calendar and did the mental arithmetic.

"We need to move on this soon. I don't know how long Khorasani and the others are going to be in Caracas, but the longer we wait, the greater the chance that they'll finish their business down there and return home. They may already be gone for all we know. I can have everything prepositioned for you in three days. Can you move that fast?"

"It shouldn't be a problem. I'll need contact instructions for your men in Mexico and Caracas. Also anything you have on where the Iranians are staying in Caracas and passport photos of Samadi and Azar Ghabel would be helpful."

"We have all that from the information the Spanish gave us."

"Let me make a list of all the things we'll need."

Logan grabbed a notepad and wrote down a list of surveillance gear the team would need — personal weapons, Tasers, encrypted radios, cellphones, still cameras, video cameras, flashlights, binoculars, and audio equipment.

He stood up and handed the list to Thamir. "We'll also need a couple of vehicles and a safehouse where we can meet."

"We'll take care of everything."

"We'll get this done, Thamir. You can tell Nayef that I promise him that." They shook hands and Logan left.

After a short drive through mid-afternoon traffic, he pulled into his parking space at Fan Pier. Walking towards the concierge desk in his office complex, he caught sight of Miguel standing next to an attractive Hispanic woman holding a wriggling infant in her arms.

"You must be Paula," Logan said. Peering down at the baby he smiled at the memory of holding Cooper in his arms the first time. "And this must be Dennis."

Miguel looked as if he would burst from pride.

"Mamita, this is Mr. Alexander."

Paula gave Logan a shy smile in greeting as she continued to wrestle with the wiggling baby.

"May I hold him?"

Paula gave Miguel a questioning look and when he nodded she handed the baby to Logan.

"Dennis Martinez Colon, huh? Are you going to be a
baseball player?"

The baby stared into Logan's eyes, gave a mighty yawn
and then began to squawk. Logan handed him back to his
mother and the future Red Sox prospect promptly fell asleep
in her arms.

"Thank you for the flowers, Mr. Alexander. It was very
thoughtful of you."

"No, we're very happy for you. My wife and I just had a
baby a few months ago, and we know it's an exciting time."
He chatted with the happy couple for a few more minutes
and then continued upstairs to his office.

Alicia was on the phone when he arrived. "Thank you
for calling, Mr. Johnson. I'll have him give you a call when
he gets in." She wrote down the phone number and hung
up.

"Hi. That was Nick Johnson from Sperry/Johnson
Maritime. They're looking for a maritime consultant to
work with them on a Navy project they have coming up in
a few months."

"Did he give you any specifics?"

"No. He said that he was just putting out feelers to see if
you would be available."

"All right. I'll give him a call. Oh, by the way. Do you
have a passport?"

"Yes. Why?" She gave him a quizzical look.

"How would you feel about taking a little trip down to
Venezuela early next week with me and couple of my buddies from the Bandar Deylam operation?"

Alicia's eyes got big. "You found him, didn't you? This
is about that guy that killed your friend."

Logan had to hand it to her. Alicia had a lot on the ball.
He gave her a rundown on his meeting with Thamir.

"What is it you need me for?"

"Translating for us. Helping us to get around the city. If we actually get our hands on Khorasani, I won't need you when we interrogate him because he's a native English speaker."

Alicia looked doubtful, but nodded her agreement. "Anything I can do."

They decided that Alicia would fly directly from the U.S. to Caracas, to separate her travel from that of Logan and the others. Since she wouldn't be traveling on an alias passport, there was no need for her to jump through hoops to conceal her identity. They talked for a few more minutes after which Logan decided that he needed to talk to Zahir.

Thirty minutes later he let himself into the apartment. Zahir was working at her desk. She put her finger to her lips, indicating that Cooper was down for a nap. Logan bent down to kiss her. "Want a glass of wine?"

She looked at her watch. "It's already six o'clock. How'd it get so late?

Logan pulled a Pinot Noir out of the wine rack and rummaged around for a corkscrew. Zahir followed him into the kitchen.

"I saw Thamir today."

"Oh. How'd that go?"

"He thinks he knows where Khorasani is, or at least where he was going when I spotted him in Madrid."

"Where's that?"

"Caracas."

"Caracas!"

"Yeah. That was my reaction too. And it gets even more interesting." He told her about the Iranians traveling to Caracas and Khorasani's use of a Costa Rican alias.

"Nayef wants me to go down and look for him."

"What did you tell him?"

"I told Thamir that I needed to clear it with you but that I thought you would be supportive."

Zahir looked pensive as she took a glass of wine from Logan and perched on a kitchen stool.

"Would you go by yourself?"

"No. I was thinking of taking Stoddard and Wellington with me. Also, Alicia for her Spanish."

"How long do you think you'd be gone?"

"I don't know. Three, four days. A week at the most."

"You need to do this, don't you?"

"I just keep thinking back to that night in Bandar Deylam when Ghabel was about to kill us. If Hamid hadn't been there, we might not have made it out of there. I feel like I owe it to Nayef."

Zahir reached up to stroke his cheek. He caught her hand and brought it to his lips.

"If you don't want me to go just say so."

"How could I say no? You would never forgive me." She stood and wrapped her arms around him, burying her face in his chest.

"Just promise that you'll come back to me, Logan Alexander."

He massaged her shoulders, kissing the top of her head, a faraway look in his eyes.

"I promise," he whispered.

Chapter 20

The drug dealer slinked along a decrepit row of tin and cardboard huts in impoverished Barrio Nuevo Tacagua, on the west side of Caracas. Here the hopeless and destitute residents eked out an existence that could rightly be described as hell on earth. Perched on a treacherous hillside, the slum existed at the mercy of torrential rains threatening to wash it into the unwelcoming valley below.

Nouri and Azar had been trailing the unsuspecting criminal for two hours, surreptitiously observing him making his rounds. It was three o'clock in the morning and there was still some activity in the rutted lanes, but the city was finally settling down for a fitful rest.

Nouri had randomly selected the thug for Azar's first kill. She had been intense in her preparation in recent days and it was time to test her ability to take it to the next level. He didn't doubt her commitment, or her talent, but for some, the actual act of taking another's life was too overwhelming. She needed to be tested. What better way than this?

The man was in his mid-thirties, swarthy, with greasy, unkempt hair and a light beard. He was wearing faded blue jeans and a burgundy tee-shirt emblazoned with the symbol for La Vinotinto, the nickname for Venezuela's national football team. Nouri had chosen the target because he was dangerous. Azar would not be sent after children or old women. No, her targets would be men, men who would fight back. He had to know if she had it in her to confront this man.

She was walking about 200 feet ahead. Dressed in jeans and a short-sleeved blouse, Azar blended in well. She looked like any other Venezuelan woman on the street. They had rehearsed her approach to the target several times.

"If he's a drug dealer, all I need to do is approach him to buy amphetamines."

"Do you think you can handle that in Spanish?" Azar had studied some Spanish while in Tehran in preparation for her assignment to Venezuela, and it had improved significantly over the last three weeks as she made a point of using it every day with shopkeepers, taxi drivers and the like.

"I think so. It's not perfect, but I'm comfortable with it."

Ahead, their target had rounded a corner, forcing Azar to cross the street in order to close the gap between them. As she rounded the corner, Nouri continued straight ahead so that he could keep an eye on the two of them without arousing the target's suspicions.

As he looked back over his shoulder he was surprised to see that the man had reversed himself and was walking towards Azar. He stopped a few feet from her, his head tilted back with his arms akimbo, seemingly challenging her. Nouri was too far away to hear their exchange, but sensed that something had gone wrong. Perhaps the tough had spotted them trailing him.

Azar took a step forward, gesturing with her arm and speaking to him. Nouri edged closer to get a better view of the exchange. He was committed to letting Azar see it through, but at the same time he was mindful of the fact that she was untested and that putting her up against a hardened street thug was a risky proposition at best. He didn't want to, but if things got out of control, he would step in to help her.

The drug dealer took a half step towards Azar, putting Nouri on edge. He stopped just short of her and reached into a shoulder bag that he was carrying to withdraw a small plastic baggie, which he held out to her. Nouri guessed that it was the amphetamines she was bargaining for, and he breathed more easily.

But as Azar reached for the bag, he grasped her wrist and wrenched her towards him. Twisting her arm, he tried to throw her to the ground, and appeared surprised when she resisted. He raised his arm to strike her and she delivered a well-aimed kick to his groin.

He went down immediately, writhing on the street as Azar circled behind him. Bending, she withdrew a knife from her boot and knelt beside her tormenter. Grasping his hair in one hand, she yanked his head back, pausing to stare into his terrified eyes before slicing deep into his throat.

Nouri could tell from the vigorous motion of the knife that Azar had sliced through the jugular and the carotid artery. The windpipe and larynx were most certainly severed. Their victim would be dead in minutes, his life-blood draining into the already filthy gutter.

Azar wiped the blade on the man's tee shirt, stood, and furtively looked around. She nudged the motionless body with her boot and, spotting Nouri, walked over to where he was standing. She was breathing deeply and there was a dull look in her eyes.

"Let's keep moving before someone spots us." Nouri took her by the arm and they walked south out of the barrio before catching a roving taxi to take them back into center city. They were quiet on the ride back into town and soon Azar's breathing returned to normal.

After making certain that they weren't being followed the two returned to the El Valle apartment. Azar was wordless as she walked into the bathroom, stripped and stepped into the shower. Nouri could tell from the steam seeping out from under the door that she had turned the hot water on full force. She emerged twenty minutes later and walked into her room, closing the door behind her.

Nouri went to his own room and climbed into bed. He tended not to over-analyze what he was doing. He thought back to his first kill and tried to summon up those feelings but found that he had become inured to any feeling whatsoever. He was a ruthless killing machine. He wondered about Azar.

Hours later he was awakened by an almost imperceptible sound. Reaching for the knife beneath his pillow he tensed as he readied himself to spring into action, but saw that it was only Azar. She was standing naked beside his bed looking at him.

"What?"

She held her finger to her lips, and pulling the sheets back slipped in next to him. Nouri's earlier appraisal of her was reinforced. As her firm breasts brushed across his chest her lips hungrily sought out his, the tip of her tongue exploring his. She reached for him and finding him ready, offered herself, guiding him into her moistness with one hand.

Ghabel had been a lucky man, Nouri reflected several minutes later, as Azar climaxed. She was aptly named. She was a fire maiden. He had met few women who made love with the passion and reckless abandon he had just experienced.

When their breathing returned to normal and he slid down next to her, she turned away, and as he reached for her, she slipped out of the bed. She turned and bent down to kiss him softly on the lips before stealing out of the room and closing the door behind her.

Nouri lay back in bed, his hands behind his head, and pondered what had just happened. It was unprofessional of him to have given in to Azar's desire. He did not want to become emotionally involved with the woman. Such emotions had no place in his world. On the other hand, if it was just sex, why not? He was a man. She was a woman. They both had physical needs. He fell into a deep sleep.

The next morning he awoke with a start. Glancing at his watch he was startled to see that it was already nine o'clock. Rubbing the sleep from his eyes, he rose from the bed and looked into the living room. Azar was doing stretches on the mats. She smiled a greeting, but said nothing about last night.

After dressing, Nouri sat down across from her.

"I'd like to go over everything from last night. How you thought it went. What we could have done differently. How you felt."

Azar thought for a moment before replying. "He knew we had been following him, at least from the time that we entered the barrio. I think we stood out."

"How do you know that?"

"From what he said when I approached him. He asked me why I was following him. I told him that I was looking for drugs, and I thought at first that he believed me, but when he grabbed my arm, I wasn't sure. I thought he was going to…" Her voice trailed off.

"To what?" Nouri looked at her with a raised eyebrow.

Azar drew her self up and returned his stare. "To rape me. But then the training just kicked in. I don't think he was expecting me to fight back, so he left himself completely wide open. Once I took him down, then I knew that I had him."

"Remember what I told you when we were practicing knife fighting moves? Very often in a knife fight people end up on the ground. That's not a good thing. In this case, your opponent outweighed you by probably seventy-five pounds. If he had managed to pin you, it could have been very dangerous."

"Why the emphasis on the knife? It seems that we could reduce these close-in risks by just shooting them."

"That part's true. In many ways it's a more complicated scenario. Using a rifle is nothing like a knife attack. We're usually out there on our own, without inside support. That makes it hard to transport weapons, particularly when you're crossing international borders.

"Did you ever see that George Clooney movie, *The American*?"

"No. Why?" Azar rose from her position on the floor and went into the kitchen to heat water for tea.

"It's about an American assassin in Europe. Clooney plays the lead character, and for most of the film he is in a small village in Italy, Abruzzo, I think. Apparently, Clooney is supposed to be an expert gunsmith, and he is tasked to manufacture a special sniper rifle for a female assassin that he has never met.

"Anyway, he spends days, maybe weeks, cultivating relationships with all of these people who will get him the materiel and tools that he needs to build this weapon in his rented apartment."

When the water was ready, Azar made two cups of dark tea and brought them to the table. She sat down opposite Nouri and took a sip from the steaming mug.

"Careful, it's very hot. So, what happens to him?"

"In the end he's killed. But the point I wanted to make is that it's completely unrealistic that someone could show up in a small town like that and do what he was doing without arousing suspicions. Oh, there was this one priest who I think questioned his activities, but he had his own problems, a bastard son running around the village.

"If anything, our job is going to get more complicated. Still, I understand that we have certain capabilities in the U.S. and that they can support us there without exposing us."

"Give me an example."

"All right. Let's imagine that we have a target in Chicago. We fly into O'Hare with nothing incriminating on our person. The only thing would be our laptop, which has our covert communications. Once we're there we will receive a message directing us to where they've hidden a key to a supply cache. It might be for a locker at a gym, or a train station or even outside. Inside the cache will be our weapons, operational funds, and the target package."

"Isn't it risky for them to just leave this cache in public?"

"They'll use an agent to pull it all together and put it in place. It's someone who the police would have no reason to suspect. Someone who is under the radar. You and I will never meet this person. They don't know who we are.

"How did you feel about actually killing this guy?" he asked. "I noticed you seemed to pause just before you did it."

"It was easier than I thought it would be, maybe because he was scum, and at that point I was feeling defensive because he had attacked me. I paused because I wanted to look into his eyes and feel his fear. He was whimpering, begging me for his life. There was a look of terror in his eyes when he saw the knife and realized what I was about to do. It wasn't that hard." She shrugged.

"Good." Nouri concealed the admiration he felt for her handling of the assassination. Azar was one cold bitch.

"Let's get to work."

Chapter 21

Logan watched with amusement the looks of fascination on the faces of the Mexicans listening to Mariachi Divina, an all female mariachi band from Los Angeles performing in Mexico City's Plaza Garibaldi. He, Stoddard and Wellington had arrived earlier in the afternoon on an Avianca Airlines flight out of San Antonio.

After walking around the Zona Rosa, Mexico City's entertainment district, the three of them had wandered through Alameda Park, up Calle Republica de Honduras, passing the opulent Palacio de Bellas Artes, before meandering over to the square.

Famed for its mariachi music, roving bands of every stripe and color crowded the plaza, creating a cacophony of sound as they vied for gigs with tourists and locals. They would play one song, their entire repertoire, or even pile into their cars and do a party gig at their *patron's* venue on a moment's notice. Their glittering costumes, leather cowboy boots and broad-brimmed sombreros were a stark contrast to Boston's buttoned-down sensibility, Logan reflected.

Known as Plaza Santa Cecilia before 1910, the square was renamed during the Mexican Revolution after Lt. Colonel José Garibaldi, who had thrown his support behind Francisco Madero, the wealthy Mexican statesman who overthrew strongman Porfirio Díaz and later became Mexico's thirty-third president.

Logan's group was killing time until seven o'clock when they were supposed to meet Thamir's man to exchange passports. The meeting place was on the terrace of La Cata, a bar and restaurant on the top floor of the Museum of Tequila and Mezcal.

"Will you look at that view? Mariachi bands as far as you can see. It's a wonder they make any money." Logan took an appreciative sip of mezcal, and gazed out over the plaza.

"Most of them are probably just moonlighting. They must have day jobs." Stoddard grunted as he swigged his tequila and examined the empty glass in front of him.

"I can't really taste the difference between tequila and mezcal," Wellington grumbled.

"Didn't you listen to anything our guide said?" Logan shook his head. They had just finished a guided tour of the museum in which their guide had traced the origins of the fiery Mexican liquor.

"He was too busy checking out her ass," Stoddard jibed. "I'll bet he didn't hear a word she said."

Wellington became defensive. "Sure I did. Let's see… all right. The liquors both come from the agave plant — *maguey*, the natives called it. But after the Spanish came in they started using European distilling methods and the drink evolved into two different spirits. And tequila is mostly made in Jalisco and comes from a variety of the agave plant; I think she said blue agave."

He lifted his glass and squinted at it. "Oh yeah — she said mezcal's the one with the worm or scorpion in the bottle, mostly made in Oaxaca. They use the heart of the agave plant and pretty much cook it up the same way they did hundreds of years ago."

"Not bad, Brucie. Your brain was still working even though your eyes were glued to that chick's ass."

"Hey, what can I say. I'm a multi-tasker." Wellington grinned. "But I still can't taste the difference."

Their banter was interrupted by the appearance of a forty-something Middle Eastern male approaching their table.

"Mr. Alexander?"

"Yes?"

"Hello. I'm Wahid. I work for Thamir." He waved off Logan's offer of tequila and signaled to the waiter to bring him a soft drink. They made room for him at the table and after their server had departed, he withdrew an envelope from inside his jacket and handed it to Logan.

"These are your passports and airline tickets. We've inserted entry stamps into all three of them. You shouldn't have a problem departing customs and immigration. We do this for our officers transiting Mexico in alias all the time. So far we haven't had a problem."

Logan peered into the envelope and thumbed through the passports and tickets to make certain everyone's was there. The Kuwaitis had also included pocket litter in their alias names as well. Rummaging through the documents he found three alias Visa credit cards.

"This is new. I didn't know that we were going to have credit cards too. What's that all about?"

"Our experience is that it's best not to carry around a lot of cash in Venezuela. Caracas has one of the highest violent crime rates in the world. You should carry a throwaway wallet with a small amount of cash in it in case you're robbed. But keep your other valuables in an inside pocket." He patted his jacket to emphasize the point.

"Are these credit cards backstopped?"

"Yes. Thamir has contacts in a couple of the big banks. They don't ask questions. We give them the information, work up a fake personal credit history and put a credit limit of $20,000 on each card. You just need to call in and activate the cards and establish your own PIN."

Wahid collected their U.S. passports and other true name identifying information.

"This will be in my safe at the embassy. I don't expect to be going anywhere in the next week or two, but I'll give you contact information for my secretary in case I have to travel unexpectedly."

They worked out a rudimentary commo plan and Wahid gave them contact instructions for their meeting with his colleague in Caracas.

"Zed will be expecting your call tomorrow morning." Wahid stood up and they shook hands all around. "Good luck."

The three of them had separate flights out of Mexico City International Airport. Logan was catching a one a.m. Aero Mexico flight that was scheduled to arrive Caracas at about seven o'clock. He did the math. Caracas was an hour and a half ahead of Mexico City. About four and a half hours flying time.

They split up after agreeing to meet in Logan's hotel room in Caracas the following morning.

Later, at the airport, Logan remained outwardly calm but inwardly anxious as the immigration officer examined his passport.

"Where's your exit form?" he inquired.

"I'm sorry. I seem to have lost it." He held up his hands in a helpless gesture. The officer complained under his breath and continued to search through his database looking for the entry. He picked up Logan's passport and eyeballed the entry stamp, but then set the passport aside.

"When did you say you entered the country?"

"Just yesterday. It must have fallen out of my passport."

Logan decided to take a calculated risk.

"Is there somewhere that I can pay the Mexican government for causing all this trouble?"

The officer glared at him over his glasses. Logan fidgeted, thinking that he might have miscalculated, but was relieved when he smiled broadly.

"Yes, I'm authorized to receive payments right there." He glanced furtively around and then pretended to search his computer for the correct figure. "That will be 200 pesos," he said with a smug look on his face.

Corrupt bastard, Logan thought. He slid the pesos across the counter and watched them disappear into an open cash drawer.

The official cleared his throat. "You should be more careful with your paperwork the next time," he admonished. Stamping the passport with a resounding thump, he handed it to Logan and nodded that he was free to pass through.

The flight was only half-full, so after they had reached cruising altitude, Logan settled back into his seat, stretching his long legs, and dozed. He was awakened an hour later by the sound of shouting a couple of rows behind him.

Turning in his seat he saw a beefy, florid-faced male passenger screaming at one of the flight attendants. She was trying to push a drinks cart down the aisle but he had stuck his foot out in an attempt to stop her. He was roaring and grabbing at the bottles on the cart, while the attendant tried to move out of his reach.

Without warning the man grabbed the woman's wrist and pulled her nearer, leering at her as he slurred his words. She cried for help, but the other passengers cringed, paralyzed by the drama unfolding before them.

Logan shrugged off his torpor and leapt from his seat. He reached the struggling flight attendant in two strides.

"Let her go!"

The drunk glared at him, pulling the woman closer while cursing loudly. He snarled and shouted back.

"Gringo!"

Without missing a beat, Logan cold-cocked the bully and caught the flight attendant in his arms as the man's grip loosened. She was shaking and whimpering from the assault.

Everyone began talking at once. The door to the cockpit opened and the co-pilot hurried down the aisle.

"What's going on here?" He gave Logan a wary look.

The flight attendant had recovered from her shock and answered the co-pilot in rapid-fire Spanish, gesturing towards the unconscious drunk and tossing her head in anger.

After checking his pulse, the co-pilot pulled two heavy-duty, plastic cuff restraints from his jacket pocket and affixed them to the man's wrists, securing them to the arm-rests on the seat. He then directed the passenger sitting next to the troublemaker to change seats.

Turning to Logan he gave him a grateful look.

"Thank you for stepping in. She might have been injured or worse. Who knows what this fool would have done if no one had stepped in to help her? Are you all right?"

Logan examined his scraped knuckles. "It's nothing. I think I'm going to feel better than him when he wakes up."

He inclined his head towards the drunk, whose thunderous snores resonated throughout the cabin.

"We have already radioed ahead and asked for police assistance planeside. It's illegal to interfere with crew members performing their duties." He turned and strode back to the cockpit.

Thirty minutes later Logan could hear the culprit reviving two rows behind him. When he realized that he was restrained, the offender began to yell in Spanish. Logan turned in his seat and gave him a menacing look, making the troublemaker immediately fall silent.

The remainder of the journey was uneventful. When their plane landed in Caracas a few hours later, the pilot taxied over to the gate, and announced that everyone should remain in their seats until the *Policia* had boarded the plane to take the rabble-rouser into custody.

After what seemed an interminable delay, the hatch swung open and two stern-faced plainclothes officers appeared, conversing briefly with the flight attendant before walking down the aisle to where the subdued drunk was restrained. They asked him several questions; his muted replies stood in stark contrast to his earlier obnoxious behavior.

Moments later the two officers cut the restraints holding the man down, handcuffed him and hustled him off the plane. Logan held his breath as they passed by his seat, expecting that they would want to question him for his role in suppressing their prisoner. His alias passport and cover story were rock solid, but he preferred not to draw attention to himself, especially with the police. The police continued past him, and he breathed a sigh of relief.

Sometimes you just have to do the right thing, regardless of the risks, he reasoned. It was so typical, though, that none of these passengers had stepped up to help. People were too afraid or apathetic to do the right thing. He shook his head in dismay as he waited his turn to disembark.

He became melancholy as he reminisced about a former SEAL buddy who had been on United Flight 93 on 9/11 when Al Qaeda hijackers commandeered the aircraft. The flight had crashed into a field in Pennsylvania while passengers stormed the cabin. His buddy had led the passenger assault on the cabin when they realized they'd been hijacked.

After exiting customs and immigration he followed signs for ground transportation, and was soon ensconced in the back seat of a recent model SUV taxi. The ride into the city was uneventful. The black Ford Explorer exited Simón Bolívar Airport and picked up the highway in the shadow of the coastal mountains. They were racing through a narrow valley and in the distance he could see Caracas at the foot of Mount Ávila, a behemoth, part of the Venezuelan Coastal Range rising to almost 9,000 feet above sea level.

Forty minutes later, his driver pulled up in front of the Tamanaco Caracas, an Intercontinental hotel located in the Las Mercedes neighborhood. Logan paid the driver 300 *Bolívares fuertes,* about fifty dollars, collected his suitcase and walked inside.

"Good morning, sir. How may I help you?"

"Yes. Campbell, checking in please."

The wisp of a girl manning the check-in counter found his name.

"Mr. Logan Campbell?

Logan acknowledged his alias identity.

"I requested early check-in. Will that be possible?"

"Let me just check. Yes, your room is ready. Do you need help with your bag?"

"No, thank you. I'm fine."

Logan walked across the colorful lobby and rode the elevator up to the eighth floor. Once inside the room he pulled the curtain back and saw that the hotel was situated amidst tropical gardens with a view of the mountains. He stood there for a moment gazing out at the city, before releasing the curtain.

"You're out there somewhere Mr. Khorasani, Perea, Frontera, whoever the fuck you are. You better watch your back, because we're coming for you!"

Chapter 22

Pedro Martínez looked on as Logan, Stoddard and Wellington listened to Alicia translate what he had just said into English. The five of them were sitting in a scantily appointed safehouse that Zed, Thamir's man in Caracas, had rented for their use.

Zed had turned out to be a gold mine, not only procuring everything on Logan's list, but also arranging an introduction to this long-time asset the Kuwaitis had been running in the Venezuelan capital.

"Pedro was a rising star in the Caracas Police Force," Zed had told them, before introducing the retired cop. "But in 2006 President Chavez created the National Commission on Police Reform to shake things up. After a lot of talk, he decided to consolidate all the different police agencies into one federal police force.

"Once it was created, the Federal Police focused on getting more resources and training for themselves, creating a stronger bureaucracy within the force and putting more emphasis on human rights. Most of that was done in 2009 and they renamed themselves the Bolivarian National Police."

"Was this just about creating greater efficiencies or was there something else going on? You know, police brutality?" Logan asked.

"Worse. Extrajudicial killings, primarily," Zed grimaced. "One case got a lot of attention. The Ortega family in Aragua State. Six family members were killed by the police between 2004 and 2010. In each case the security forces suspected the family member of criminal behavior, and summarily executed them."

"Was Martínez involved in any of the killings?"

"Not directly. He was a precinct captain at the time, and

two of the men under his command were indicted. The way Pedro tells it, there were two members of the commission who had it out for him.

"By then he could see the writing on the wall. The commission wanted to make a statement, and this was their chance to clean house, so he was forced out. He wasn't accused of anything but they told him that if he went quietly he could keep his full pension."

"So how did you get to know him?" Logan looked at the Kuwaiti Intel officer.

"I met Pedro at a diplomatic reception when I first got here. It was right before he retired, and we stayed in touch after that. Then, he started his own security company, and I recruited him. He has about a dozen ex-cops working for him who do private investigative work – background checks, surveillance, wiretaps, phone-taps, and security, that sort of thing.

"He's well connected around town. If anybody can find this Costa Rican you're looking for, he can."

At that point in the conversation Martínez had arrived and Zed introduced him around. Zed left after the introductions, instructing Martínez to do whatever he could do for his friends.

Logan was not sure what Thamir had told Zed about their manhunt. The story he planned to use with Martínez was that Claudio Frontera had committed economic crimes in Canada and that as bounty hunters they had been hired by a wealthy businessman to track him down for prosecution in Toronto.

Logan spread out pictures of Khorasani, Azar Ghabel and Tahmouress Samadi on the table. Following Logan's instructions, Alicia provided Martínez the true names for Ghabel and Samadi, and the Claudio Frontera alias for Khorasani.

"Do you know what their relationship is?" Martínez looked pointedly at Logan.

Logan thought about the question before responding. Truth be told he wasn't exactly sure, although the facts were pointing to a Qods Force connection between all three of them.

"At this point, we're not sure."

Alicia had pulled additional details from all three immigration forms, including the names of the hotels where they were staying, and she gave this information to Martínez.

He scanned the documents and then turned his attention to Alicia, speaking in measured sentences.

"Mr. Martínez says that it will be easy for him to find out if Samadi is staying at the Gran Meliá. He doesn't recognize the other two hotels Ghabel and Frontera put on their forms."

"I'll bet they don't even exist," Logan said. "Typical tactic if you're trying to cover your tracks."

Alicia continued. "One other thing. He emphasized that they all entered Venezuela over three weeks ago. He doubts they're still here because most foreigners entering the country on business stay for less than a week. And tourists don't spend any time in Caracas.

"He said he has contacts in immigration, so he'll be able to find out if they've already left or, if they're still here, where they are."

Martínez looked up from the paper he was reading and spoke in rapid-fire Spanish.

"Mr. Campbell, I'll need twenty-four hours before I can give you an initial report. I'll send one of my men over to the Gran Meliá this afternoon to speak with the staff, and I'll personally talk to my contacts in the immigration service. We'll look into the other two hotels, but I'm pretty sure they don't exist. Shall we meet here again tomorrow afternoon, say three o'clock?"

Alicia continued to translate. When she had finished, Martínez rose, shook hands all around and then left to begin tracking down the trio.

"What do you think of this guy?" Stoddard asked Logan.

"Hard to say after just meeting him. Zed appears to trust him, and his instincts seem pretty good. I find it hard to believe that he didn't know about those killings, though.

If you're in charge you damn well better know what's going on with the guys under your command."

"You think they just covered it up to avoid a messy trial?" Wellington looked back and forth between Logan and Stoddard.

"Could be. Maybe he has family connections and was able to derail the investigation." Logan stood up and stretched.

"Anybody hungry? Why don't we take the two cars and split up? We might as well begin our area-fam while we're out there. I don't see much sense getting back together until we meet with the captain tomorrow, unless something urgent comes up. Let me think. We're meeting him at three o'clock, so let's plan to get back together at noon. That way we'll have time to compare notes. Who knows? Maybe we'll develop some new leads for Martínez by then."

Logan sat back down, pulled out a map of Caracas and began to divvy up the city into two sectors. He and Alicia would take the area bounded by Mount Ávila to the north, the Catuche River to the south, Francisco Fajarda Highway to the west and Metropolitan University to the east. That left Stoddard and Wellington with everything south of the river.

"Be careful out there and keep your eyes open, people. The metro area has over three million people, so I think it's unlikely we'll run into these guys. That shouldn't be an issue for you two anyway," he said, looking up at Stoddard and Wellington. "Khorasani's never set eyes on either of you.

"He's had at least two opportunities to see me, though. Once in Boston, when he knifed Hamid, and at the airport in Madrid. He didn't give any sign of recognition, but who knows? If he's thought about it, he just might put two and two together. I think to play it safe I'm going to wear a light disguise out on the street. I had Zed pick these up for me." He pulled a mustache and a wig out of a cloth bag on the floor.

Logan went into the bathroom and came out a minute later wearing the get-up. "What do you think?"

"Wow," Alicia said. "It really changes your appearance. I'd have to look twice to know it's you, and we work together every day."

Logan fiddled with the wig. "You know, half the battle is being comfortable wearing this stuff. If you think everybody sees through your disguise, you'll get nervous, and people will pick up on that. You need to act natural. All right. Let's get it done!"

The next afternoon the four of them re-convened back at the safehouse. It was noon and they were having an animated discussion over sandwiches that Logan and Alicia had picked up from a street vendor.

"How'd it go out there, guys?" Logan bit into his *pepito* sandwich, marinated beef on a hoagie roll with avocado relish and salsa.

"Man, these Venezuelan drivers are crazy. Everybody's driving 100 mph, ignoring lights, weaving in and out of traffic. It felt like I was training for the Daytona 500." Wellington shook his head.

"Tell them about the clowns." Stoddard started laughing.

"Clowns?" Logan looked puzzled.

"Yeah, I would say, in at least three intersections we saw these clowns out, directing traffic. They had on these baggy clown outfits. Their faces were all painted and they were wearing white gloves. It's almost like they were making fun of the drivers."

"We didn't see any, but I remember reading about them when I found out we were coming here," Alicia exclaimed. The mayor was looking for a way to get traffic under control and he decided to put something like 120 mimes out on the street to embarrass the reckless drivers. The mimes weren't really supposed to get aggressive or talk to the drivers, but they would gesture for them to slow down or put on their seat belts. Supposedly, the mayor of Bogotá, Colombia, tried it a couple of years ago and their accident rate went way down."

"They need to do something." Stoddard wiped his mouth with the back of his hand. I mean, hell, they don't even need all that violent crime down here. Just get the mimes off the street and they'll all kill each other in traffic accidents!"

The team spent the next two hours comparing notes on the city. At three o'clock there was a loud knock on the door, and Wellington got up to let Martínez in.

The former police captain sauntered into the room, wearing what appeared to be a perpetual frown on his face. He was toting a worn canvas briefcase, and after greeting everyone, took the empty chair at the table and began to rummage through his files. Extracting several folders, he set them on the table and looked expectantly in Alicia's direction.

"I have some information for you."

Logan and the others leaned in as Alicia translated.

"Mr. Samadi arrived in Caracas on September 26, on a direct flight from Tehran. He registered at the Gran Meliá on that same day and checked out five days later." He flipped through several papers and found a copy of Samadi's passenger card. "He exited the country on October 1st."

"Is that all we have?" Logan felt frustrated.

Martínez gave him a patient look. "No, Mr. Campbell." He pulled several more papers from a folder and waved them in his left hand.

"I seems that Mr. Samadi was very busy when he was here."

"What do you mean?"

"He was having business meetings or a conference in his suite. What's strange is that on the 27th, seven people showed up for a group meeting in the morning, and later on in the afternoon they all left the room one by one at roughly fifteen-minute intervals."

"How'd you find that out?" Logan asked.

"By coincidence there was a hotel maintenance crew painting the hallway on his floor. They observed the comings and goings of these people and thought it was unusual. Our source at the hotel pulled the feed from the lobby and floor video cameras for the 27th and the crew identified the people from the photographs as the ones who were in his room."

"Do we know who they are?" Logan was hunched forward in anticipation.

"Only the two from the photos you gave me — Azar Ghabel and Claudio Frontera, but Ghabel wasn't at the group meeting. She showed up the next day when Frontera was there with Samadi, just the two of them. Someone from housekeeping saw her go into the room." Martínez withdrew a pack of cigarettes from his breast pocket and lit one, inhaling deeply. He offered the pack around, but there were no takers.

"From the Gran Meliá's registry we know that no one other than Samadi was staying there, but over the next three days the others all came back for one-on-one sessions with him."

Wellington had a puzzled look on his face. "What the hell's going on?"

"I'm not sure but I've got an idea." Logan turned his head slightly and spoke out of the side of his mouth. "We'll talk about it later."

Wellington nodded, and turned his attention back to the detective.

Martinez continued. "None of the others have been back since their one-on-one meetings, except for Frontera."

Logan rifled through the still photos from the video feed, closely examining the faces. Only Ghabel and Khorasani stood out. The others were all unknown.

"Any chance of finding out who these other people are?" He waved the photos in his hand.

"Without a name or some idea of where they were staying, I would say next to impossible. I could pass the photos to my immigration contact." Martínez shrugged his shoulders, emphasizing the futility of such a course of action.

He cleared his throat, and pulled an additional folder out of his briefcase. "Speaking of my immigration contact, I did have some success with the Frontera and Ghabel files."

Logan looked up in anticipation. Maybe this was the break they needed.

"Neither Ms. Ghabel nor Mr. Frontera has left the country. In fact, they seem to have taken up temporary residence in an apartment in the El Valle part of the city. It was rented in Mr. Frontera's name at the beginning of October."

Logan felt his pulse quicken. "You mean they're here now?"

"I have not sent anyone out to check the apartment, so, no, I can't confirm that they're here, but it seems to be a reasonable assumption."

"How'd you find out about the apartment?"

"A foreigner is required to show their passport in order to rent a property in Caracas, and that information is relayed to the immigration police." Martínez gave Logan the address of the El Valle rental.

"That neighborhood is in the southern part of the city. The nearest metro station is Los Jardines." Martínez stubbed out his cigarette, and then closed his briefcase.

"That's all I have for now. Is there anything else you need from me?"

Logan and the others exchanged glances. Logan was first to speak.

"You've been a big help, Captain. I think we have enough to get us started. If anything else comes up, we'll have Zed get in touch."

"All right. Good luck then." He shook hands all around and departed.

When the door had closed behind him, Wellington turned to Logan and asked, "What do you think the Iranians are up to?"

"It's clear that Samadi is playing some kind of a role with Unit 400. We know he's Qods Force, and Unit 400 is a Qods Force element, so it seems reasonable to conclude that he has some kind of Unit 400 connection. We don't know what it is." Logan frowned, his mouth a tight line, and then continued.

"We know Khorasani is Unit 400, based on the uncle's information, so it's possible the other people meeting with Samadi were Unit 400 too. I think it was a meeting of the assassins. I think Unit 400 is planning their next move!"

Chapter 23

Nouri exited Line 1 at the Miranda subway station in Parque del Este. It was Saturday morning. He glanced at his runner's watch, and was surprised to see that it was only seven-thirty. He hadn't slept well last night, tossing and turning until deciding to get out of bed for a run in the park. He was looking for a change of scene; dodging cars in the pollution-filled concrete jungle around El Valle was getting on his nerves, not to mention destroying his lungs.

Entering the park, he stopped to stretch next to a worn soccer field where two rugby teams were practicing. He knew something about rugby because it had been a popular sport at his Boston high school. He'd been to a few Boston Rugby Football Club matches over the years. Once he'd even gone to the Boston 7's with his father and brother, Armeen, where BRFC qualified for the national championship tournament.

These players before him were setting up a scrum, a maneuver that puts the ball into play after a penalty. The teams were crouched down in three opposing rows, arms interlocked. When they were set, the referee tossed the ball into the tunnel created between the first two rows, and the players began kicking at the ball in an effort to hook it backward so that the number eight players could scoop it up and run with it.

While the number eights hovered around the fringes looking for an opening, the two hookers vied for possession as the rest of the scrum, a mass of sweaty jerseys and tangled limbs, pushed and shoved, panting and shouting encouragement to their teammates.

Nouri watched for a couple of minutes before setting off down the path. Although he was in good shape, and it was a sunny day, with cool temperatures, he was soon wiping the sweat from his brow. He set a brisk, six-minute pace. At four miles he began to feel the burn; he turned on the afterburners for the last two miles before running a cool-down lap around the planetarium.

Breathing heavily, he stopped at a dripping water fountain. On a nearby bulletin board he noticed a colorful Nike poster advertising a "We Run Caracas" 10 K race slated to take place in early November. Reading further, he was surprised to learn that the race had attracted over 12,000 runners the previous year and nearly 400,000 worldwide.

He was almost fast enough to tie the winning women's time of thirty-five minutes, but the men's time of thirty minutes and twenty seconds was almost six minutes faster than his best 10 K. As he boarded the subway for El Valle he thought that he might try running in the event if he was still in Caracas in November.

When he got back to the apartment, there was a note from Azar saying that she had gone out to pick up the knife she was having custom-made at a small knife shop in town. The place was in central Caracas on a nondescript side street behind the military academy.

He and Azar had wandered into the cluttered workshop owned by Don Alberto Cruz, a wiry *Caraqueño* with leathery skin and hands bearing the scars of a thousand nicks. Don Alberto was eighty if he was a day old. His lined face had remained expressionless as Nouri explained what they wanted.

"She's looking for a fixed blade, with Damascus steel, maybe a titanium handle," Nouri had elaborated.

"I can make the entire handle out of a single block of titanium. Also, for the blade I have something in mind. Take a look at this stainless raindrop Damascus." Don Alberto opened a cupboard and pulled out samples of the titanium and stainless steel.

Azar fingered the block of titanium. "How long will it take?"

"I can take your measurements now if you decide. I should have it ready for you in two weeks. Do you want a thumb rest?"

"Yes, I think so." She looked at Nouri who nodded in affirmation.

"How much will it weigh?"

"Just under seven ounces. The blade will be three-point-eight inches, and the entire knife, in the open position, will be slightly longer than eight inches."

"How much do you charge for a knife like this?"

The grizzled knife-maker pulled a pencil out of his shirt pocket, grabbed a notepad, and began scribbling figures on it. After several minutes he looked up from his calculations. "It will be 2,500 Bolivars." He scratched his chin. "That's about 400 dollars."

Azar nodded her assent.

While Don Alberto was busy measuring her hand, Nouri walked around the shop. It smelled of oil and steel. There was a drill press, and various saws and drills against one wall. A small forge took up half of another wall. One cabinet contained steel stock in sheets, blocks and tubes while another was jammed with knife guards, spacers, pommels and hinges. A worktable was equipped with vises on both ends while a variety of tools littered the tabletop.

"How long have you been making custom knives, Don Alberto?"

The old man scratched his head. "Since I was twelve years old. Almost seventy years," he cackled. "Longer than both of your ages combined! My father was a craftsman, and his father before him. We've been doing business in Caracas for over one hundred years, but at this location for only sixty." He chortled at his own joke.

Azar had gone back to the shop by herself last week, for a final fitting. She had been pleased with Don Alberto's craftsmanship, and was looking forward to the day her knife would be finished.

Nouri stripped off his running clothes and stepped into the shower. Removing a loofah from a plastic hook, he scrubbed his body in a vigorous, circular motion, relishing the feel of the sponge's scabrous surface against his skin. He luxuriated in the scalding water as it penetrated his sore muscles and then gasped under the icy stream as he turned the cold faucet on full blast.

As he was toweling off he heard the door to the apartment open and Azar call out, "Nouri, I'm back. Are you here?"

"In the bathroom. I'll be out in a minute."

When he was dressed, Nouri walked into the living room, where he found Azar seated on the sofa, examining her new weapon. She handed it to him as he sat down next to her.

"What do you think?"

He examined every inch of the knife, testing the grip and the sharpness of the blade on a sheet of paper.

"He did a great job on this. How's it feel?"

"It's strange but it almost feels like an extension of my hand. Almost as if it belongs there," she marveled.

"That's the work of a real craftsman. But remember, it'll only be as good as you are. Initially when you're home sitting around, you should hold onto it to develop good balance and muscle memory. You know that it's about eight inches long, but you need to feel that so that it's second nature. You must be confident about what it can and can't do."

He handed the weapon back to Azar.

"What else are we going to do today?" She held the knife loosely, rolling it back and forth across the palm of her hand as she tested its weight.

"Let me check to see if Colonel Samadi has sent us approval to go ahead and set up our cover company. If Tehran is all right with the concept, we can get started with the paperwork on our end."

"What do we need to do?"

"It's mostly bureaucratic stuff, nothing we can't handle. I've already gone through this once before when I set up my company in Spain. I don't think it'll be that different here. We have to file the company name, legalize all the company documents, open a bank account, notify local newspapers, and register with the tax authorities. Each of these steps builds on the other, so you can't do them all at once. We should be legal in about three months."

Nouri opened his laptop and saw from a subtle color change in the logo for his operating system, that there was a message from Tehran on the covert side of his system. The modified logo and attendant software was a genius invention by a Japanese cell phone manufacturer whose male customers needed a means to hide their infidelities from suspicious wives. With the display, these modern day Lotharios were able to run covert communications programs on their cell phones, concealing their girlfriends' messages from their wives' prying eyes.

Qods Force covert communications specialists had recently borrowed the innovation from the Japanese and now included this feature when they designed communication systems for newly deployed field operatives. It was helpful because it did away with unnecessary logons to check for messages.

Nouri's covert communications setup did not allow him to correspond with any other field office, only Tehran, but it did allow for two-way communications to and from Unit 400's operational desk.

With practiced skill, he entered the password that took him to a covert software program, and from memory entered a series of bold keystrokes that revealed a folder containing the encrypted clandestine message. Once he had accessed the message he entered another ten-digit code from memory that instructed the decryption software to begin deciphering the message. The computer hummed for thirty seconds, and then the clear text message was displayed on the screen.

It was from Colonel Samadi.

"Comrade,

"Greetings! We received your message dated October 10 and are pleased with the progress you're making. Just this week I personally briefed General Salehi on your mission and he expressed satisfaction with your progress. He has authorized you to take the next steps to set up your cover business there.

"We are also pleased with the advances Azar is making in her training. You are proving to be a good teacher and her performance has exceeded our expectations. Her handling of the 'test' with the drug dealer was particularly impressive.

"Keep us informed of your progress with the cover company. We may need to use it sooner than expected.

"However, I must bring up one note of security concern. You may know that your uncle was doing some work for the Qods Force having to do with his job in the immigration department. We recently decided to formalize our relationship with him. Part of that process involves a background check and polygraph exam. There were some inconsistencies in your uncle's results having to do with possible indiscretions involving your cover identity."

Nouri chewed his lip and thought about the implications. If his Spanish persona was compromised, all the hard work he'd done over the last two years would be for naught. What the hell had the old man done? He read on.

"It seems that through gross negligence on our unit's administrative side, your uncle may have had access to your Spanish identity. From what we have been able to find out, this exposure was accidental.

"We have a quality control program with one of the units in the immigration department. We give them random samples of our forged documents mixed in with authentic documents to see if they can spot the forgeries. Unfortunately your uncle was working in that office the day that your alias US passport was sent over for testing and he obviously recognized your picture.

"We are taking all precautions to make certain that there is no danger to you. But for now, you are not to use your Spanish identity until we give you the green light.

"Sincerely,

"Tahmouress Samadi

"Colonel, Islamic Revolutionary Guard Corps"

"Damn!" Nouri slammed his hand on the table.

Azar jumped at his sudden outburst. "Is there something wrong?"

"There may be a compromise of my Spanish identity. It's not certain, but Samadi says that security is looking into it."

"How did this happen?" Azar had a puzzled look on her face.

Nouri gave her the gist of Samadi's note and sat there for a moment, grim faced.

"I hope for the old man's sake that he didn't say anything to anyone." Nouri was ruthless, but he was conscious of a twinge of concern gnawing at his gut for his father's brother. His uncle had taken him in without question when he'd shown up on his doorstep five years ago. He'd hate to see him get hurt, even if he had been indiscreet.

"If they suspect that he's talked about this with anyone, they'll punish him. At a minimum he'll lose his job, but it could be worse. I'm sorry."

"He better cooperate or he'll end up in Evin Prison. Those bastards are tough. Part of my training a few years ago involved a hostile interrogation. It was there, in the prison. Only the superintendent knew who I was. All the guards and interrogators thought that I was a dissident that had been brought in for questioning."

"What did they do to you?"

"The prison is north of Tehran, at the foot of the Alborz Mountains. They drove me there in a sedan. I remember thinking how beautiful the mountains looked. Suddenly, we were there, and when we entered the gates I was blindfolded. I could feel myself being led down some stairs to an underground level. We walked down a long straight hallway and then turned into what must have been a small room. The guards tied me to a chair and then left me alone."

"How long were you there?"

"It felt like I sat there for two or three hours. I thought I was alone, but I could feel someone watching me. Later two men came in and began the interrogation. I kept telling them I didn't know what they were talking about. They didn't waste any time getting physical, slapping me in the face with the backs of their hands and then taking off my shoes and socks and beating my feet with a cable. I think at one point I must have passed out. When I woke up I had pissed myself and thrown up all over. The blindfold was off and I could see that my feet were bloody and swollen."

Azar's hands were up to her mouth and she cringed as she spoke. "How long did this go on for?"

"I lost track of time. Maybe three days. I almost passed out from pain again when they made me walk from the interrogation room to a cell. I was in there by myself. Someone would come by and leave water and a little food twice a day. There was no toilet. Just a bucket."

"What was the point?"

"There's always the possibility of being captured by the enemy. I think Tehran would rather see us dead than in enemy hands. But, if we are taken alive, they want to give us some techniques for holding out." He shrugged his shoulders. "Everyone has limits. Eventually they'll find yours."

Nouri's eyes had dulled as he recounted his ordeal. Then they cleared and he stared into Azar's eyes. "Or they'll kill you trying."

Chapter 24

"Any questions?" Logan searched Stoddard and Wellington's faces. It was eleven o'clock Saturday night, and the three of them were gathered in the safehouse, bunched around a map of Caracas.

"All we're doing tonight is a recon of El Valle. I want to see what kind of neighborhood it is, identify any hotspots around there and check out Khorasani's apartment building."

"What are the chances we'll spot him out there tonight?" Wellington traced the route from the safehouse to the apartment on the map with his finger.

"I don't know. I've got a lot of questions. Like, is he staying there, or is he just working out of there? How about Ghabel? Is she there? Or the others who went to the meeting at the Gran Melia? Maybe they're all working out of there." Logan was vexed by the possibilities.

"We'll figure it out once we get out there. Hopefully we won't stick out too much tonight." Stoddard looked away from the map. "This place never shuts down. I got up to take a leak at four o'clock this morning and all I could hear was people outside still partying."

"I don't think they even get started until after ten. I walked by an open-air bar last night in Plaza de Castellana." Wellington jabbed a finger at the Altamira section on the map. "Over in here. It was called something like Él León. There must have been 150 kids out there dancing and partying in the street."

"We'll just have to deal with it. Caracas reminds me of New York City. It just never shuts down. Tonight we'll split up so we don't draw as much attention to ourselves. That should help. Just keep a low profile out there. All right, let's do a final equipment check, and then we should be good to go." Logan went through his knapsack, systematically checking off everything.

The other two followed suit, each of them checking their gear – cell phones, encrypted radios, maps, binoculars, writing materials, weapons, and extra ammo. All three were armed with Glock 30S .45 Auto pistols. The subcompact handgun was lightweight — just over twenty ounces unloaded. It came with a standard magazine of ten rounds. Each of them carried two additional magazines of ammo.

Besides the Glock, Logan was carrying a collapsible spring whip flexible baton. It was only seven inches long closed, but could be extended to seventeen inches with a flick of the wrist. The final item on his checklist was the tactical knife that he wore in an ankle holster.

"OK, men. Let's get it done."

The three of them departed the safehouse together. Logan had decided not to bring Alicia along on this casing run. Surprisingly, she was the only one to come down with a mild case of Montezuma's revenge, and was resting at their hotel.

He reached the black Jeep Grand Cherokee and slid into the driver's seat. Wellington and Stoddard continued walking up to the next intersection and took a left in the direction of the nearest subway station. As Logan pulled into traffic he marveled at the number of American-brand cars on the street. Zed had told him that General Motors had been operating a manufacturing plant in Venezuela non-stop since 1948. It showed. By far the most popular car on the streets was the Chevy Aveo, followed by the Ford Fiesta.

He drove the route to El Valle from memory, taking a few extra turns along the way to make certain no one was tailing him. He didn't expect to have company, but Logan had learned long ago never to take anything for granted. When you started getting too comfortable, that's when the bad guys scored.

They'd been keeping a low profile on this trip. Besides, their Canadian passports probably counted for something.

Nobody cared what the Canadians did. Canada and Venezuela had enjoyed uninterrupted diplomatic ties going back to the late '40s, when that GM plant had opened for business. So, it was probably a safe bet to assume that the federal police weren't interested in them, and wouldn't bother putting scant surveillance resources on their tail.

But there were other unknowns that could have tipped off the police, starting with Zed. Sure, he was Thamir's man in Caracas, and he seemed professional, but that and two bucks would buy you a cup of coffee at Starbucks. Maybe the federal police were onto Zed, and Logan and his team would get ensnared in that net because they'd been seen with him. Or how about the operational asset Zed had used to lease the safehouse? Was he reporting to the police?

And then there was the matter of Pedro Martínez. He'd been helpful thus far, but Logan didn't buy Zed's story that Martínez hadn't known about his underlings' participation in the extrajudicial killings. That smacked of cover-up, pure and simple. If he was lying about that, what else was he lying about? Could he be trusted?

Logan swerved slightly to the right as a full-throated Indian Chief motorcycle loaded with chrome pulled even with him. The youthful cyclist was wearing leathers and had his head turned to the side in order to talk to the striking blonde sitting behind him, arms wrapped securely around his waist. He caught Logan admiring the bike and winked. Twisting the throttle he gunned it forward and sped through a traffic light. That kid must have money, Logan reflected. In the States a bike like that would easily go for $30K.

Turning his attention back to the road, he realized that he was fast approaching Khorasani's neighborhood. Two blocks east of the apartment building he turned off the main thoroughfare onto a narrow side street. He immediately regretted it because traffic had come to a standstill. A moment later it began crawling forward. Craning his neck he saw that there had been a collision up ahead on the opposite side of the street. Oncoming cars were attempting to inch around the two stalled vehicles, one of which was a taxi.

As he eased past the fender bender, Logan was startled to see Nouri Khorasani sitting in the back seat of the taxi next to an attractive woman who resembled the photo of Azar Ghabel. They were in heated conversation with the taxi driver and appeared unaware of their surroundings. Logan's mind raced as he averted his face and crept past the accident scene. Despite his light disguise he was worried that if Khorasani spotted him he might be recognized. He breathed a sigh of relief as traffic began to thin and he was able to distance himself from the accident scene.

Pulling over five minutes later, Logan dug his radio out of the knapsack. The Motorola XTN was a ruggedized model that operated on six channels. They were transmitting on channel 6. To make certain no one could intercept their communications in the clear, they were using digitized squelch, a privacy add-on feature. He checked to make sure he was on the right channel and began to talk.

"Bravo 1, Charlie 1, this is Alpha 1. Do you read me? Over." There was some static and then Stoddard came through.

"Alpha 1, this is Bravo 1. Read you loud and clear. How you me? Over."

"Loud and clear, Bravo 1. Over."

"Alpha 1, this is Charlie 1. You're coming in a little broken up. I'm between two buildings right now. Let me move to see if it's any better. Over."

A moment later, the radio crackled and Wellington's voice came through, better, but with some static.

"You're still coming in a little broken up, Charlie 1."

"All right. I'll keep moving but maybe it's just this unit. Over."

"Listen up. I just spotted Khorasani and Ghabel on the street. Repeat, Khorasani and Ghabel on the street. Over."

There was a moment of stunned silence as Stoddard and Wellington digested the news. Stoddard spoke up.

"Holy shit! They're still here. What's the game plan? Over."

"This is Alpha 1. We'll stick with our plan for tonight. No improvising. We need to get a good sense of this neighborhood and figure out how it's going to go down. We'll re-group in the morning. Over."

"This is Charlie 1. You think there's any chance this SOB is going to be on the move anytime soon? Over."

"I don't know. Remember our friend told us Khorasani put a three-month deposit on the apartment. He's only been in there for three weeks, so it seems reasonable that he'll stay put for a while. There are a lot of unknowns. Do either of you have eyes on the door to the apartment building?"

"I do," Wellington said. "Wait a minute. I think I see them. Yeah, that's them. They just went into the building."

"OK, here's what we're going to do. I'm coming back your way. I'm going to try and park on the street so I can keep an eye on the front entrance. When I give you the word, you two break off and continue with your casing.

"I'm going to have Alicia call Martínez to see if he can get a two-man surveillance detail out here all night, so we can get some shuteye. We're going to need everything we've got when this goes down tomorrow. Over and out."

Five minutes later he was in place, parked half a block down the street opposite Khorasani's building. He called Alicia and explained what he needed. After what seemed like an interminable wait his phone rang.

"OK. I talked to him. He said that he could have a husband-and-wife team in place in two hours. So, around one-thirty. He's going to meet them to make clear what you want and show them pictures of Khorasani and Ghabel. He'll rotate another team in at seven-thirty and keep moving them around on six-hour shifts until you tell him to stop.

"I told him what you said. That Khorasani was probably armed and dangerous. You want both of them followed if they leave the apartment, but they need to be discreet. Martínez will stay in the loop and he'll call me if anything changes."

"All right. Thanks, Alicia. How you feeling?"

"Better. I took some Motrin."

"Get some rest. But stay near your phone. Unless something goes down tonight we're going to meet at eight-thirty tomorrow morning."

"All right. I'll call you if I hear anything."

Logan settled in for the wait. Just before one-thirty a dark four-door sedan eased into a parking space fifty feet in front of him. He could tell from the silhouettes that a man and woman were in the car. His phone vibrated and he could see that there was a new text message from Alicia.

"They're in place."

"Roger that." After he hit the send button, Logan started the Jeep and pulled out of his parking space. Traffic was lighter than before, but there were still people on the street, spilling out of bars and clubs. As he drove back to the hotel, his mind was on one thing. Getting Khorasani.

After breakfast the next morning the four of them met at the safehouse. There had been no calls during the night. Martínez had phoned Alicia at seven o'clock with a status report.

Stoddard was describing his observations of the El Valle neighborhood. "The only hot spots I saw were a police sub-station six blocks north of Khorasani's apartment, a Banesco Bank branch office on Khorasani's street, three blocks away, and a maternity hospital about a half a mile from his place."

"The neighborhood was really busy, even at two-thirty when I called it quits," Wellington spoke up. "It's a mixed neighborhood – apartment buildings, offices and lots of retail shops, bars and clubs. Many of the shops had posted hours. It looks like they take a two-hour siesta from around one to three in the afternoon."

"Banesco closes at three-thirty." Stoddard looked at his notes. "They have cameras trained on the ATM, and I understand they have armed guards outside the banks during business hours.

"Anything unusual going on, local holidays or closures that we should factor in?" Logan twirled a pencil between two fingers as he digested the new information.

"We're lucky we just missed the 12th. You know that's Columbus Day — or what used to be called that — and in a lot of places people have the day off, so that means more people in the street." Alicia took a sip of water and continued. "In Venezuela they changed the name to Day of the Race, meaning the Hispanic race, and later, when Chavez came into power they renamed it the Day of Indigenous Resistance. A few years ago they tore down this big statue in downtown Caracas honoring Columbus."

"What's that all about? I don't get it." Wellington looked puzzled.

"Think about it. From their perspective, Columbus was part of the first wave of white men to exploit the locals, not someone to be honored."

"I guess."

"OK, let's pay attention. You guys with me? Here's what I'm thinking. "It'd be nice if we had a little more to go on, but we don't. A lot's going to depend on the surveillance team." Logan tapped the pencil against his hand.

"Once Khorasani and Ghabel come out and clear the area, we'll go into the apartment building. We'll set up in the apartment and wait for them to return. That way we'll avoid a scene on the street and we won't be knocking down doors and freaking out the neighbors.

"Once we're in, we'll get the lay of the land, figure out our best set-ups and then wait till they return. We'll use the Tasers to take them out. Once they're down we'll tranquilize them and get them ready to move." He chewed on the end of his pencil as he paused.

"What then?" Stoddard asked.

"We'll get them into the Jeep and drive them back here. Our goal is to find out what Unit 400 is up to. I don't care what it takes. We'll get what we can out of them, but we won't have a lot of time. I don't know how often they check in with their handlers or what kind of plan they have in place if they miss a contact."

"What are you going to do when you're done questioning them?" Alicia had been pretty quiet up until now.

"I wouldn't lose a lot of sleep just wasting Khorasani," Logan muttered, "but we can't do that." He grimaced. "There's a private airport about twenty miles southwest of Caracas, Aeropuerto Caracas. Zed told me that Martinez has customs and immigration in his back pocket." He rubbed his thumb and forefinger together.

"Anyway, the Kuwaitis are arranging for a corporate jet to fly the four of us and Khorasani into Key Largo. They'll meet us there with our U.S. passports, and pull some diplomatic mumbo-jumbo to get Khorasani into the U.S. We'll give the Boston PD a tipper that Khorasani's waiting to be picked up at a Motel 6 near Key Largo. After that it's in law enforcement's hands."

Everybody nodded slowly as they evaluated the specifics of the plan.

"What about Azar?" Alicia questioned. "You didn't mention her."

"I don't see the point of bringing her to the States. She hasn't committed any crimes there. Zed will keep her locked up until after we let him know that the police have Khorasani. He'll turn her loose on the street. Keep her under surveillance to see if she contacts anyone."

They rehearsed the plan for the rest of the day, taking a short break for lunch. There was only one call from Martínez, advising that Khorasani and Ghabel had gone out at eleven o'clock and returned at four-thirty.

By six-thirty they had loaded all of their gear into the two vehicles and set out for the El Valle neighborhood. They had only been in place for thirty minutes when Khorasani and Ghabel emerged from the apartment building. Logan noted that Khorasani was carrying a backpack and Ghabel had a handbag in her hand. They jumped into a passing taxi and nosed into traffic.

After waiting ten minutes, Logan, Stoddard and Wellington walked towards the front entrance of the building. Alicia remained behind to maintain contact with the surveillance team and act as an extra set of eyes on the street.

As they approached the entrance to the building, a matronly woman with a yapping Cairn terrier, struggled to maintain her balance as the dog wrapped its leash around her legs. Wellington caught her as she tripped and almost fell. She was flustered but grateful, and said nothing as the three men eased past her into the empty foyer.

They took the stairs to the fifth floor and found Khorasani's apartment just past the stairway. The dimly lit hallway was empty. They listened outside the door for several seconds. It was quiet. With Logan and Stoddard standing guard, Wellington set to work on the door with his lock picks. The lock was stubborn, but five minutes later it clicked open.

The trio edged into the darkened apartment, weapons drawn, searching for signs of activity. After clearing each of the rooms and making certain that there were no alarms, they set about preparing their welcoming party.

The apartment consisted of a sparsely furnished living room strewn with mats, two bedrooms, a bathroom, a small dining area and a galley kitchen. There was a countertop with stools separating the kitchen from the eating area.

As he searched the two bedrooms, Logan realized that there wasn't much there. Ghabel's room had mostly clothing and Khorasani's room was virtually empty. A gnawing doubt began to eat at him. Khorasani had been seen staying here. That was certain. Maybe he just didn't need much to get by. He'd hoped to find a laptop or some clues that would reveal what the Qods Force killer was up to.

Once they had finished casing the apartment, Logan and Stoddard took up positions behind the kitchen counter, while Wellington crouched behind the front door. They settled in, not knowing how long they might have to wait. After about two hours crouched behind the counter, Logan's bum leg began to cramp up. As he stretched it out to get some relief, his radio crackled.

"Alpha 1, this is Delta 1. I have Ghabel getting out of a taxi in front of the building. Over."

"Delta 1, this is Alpha 1. Say again. Is Khorasani with Ghabel? Over."

"That's negative, Alpha 1. Ghabel is alone. She's entering the building now. Over."

"Fuck. Where the hell is Khorasani?" Logan's mind raced as he thought through the possibilities. They'd have to take Ghabel now, and deal with Khorasani later.

She came through the door a few minutes later, turning the lights on as she entered the apartment. Wellington pressed against the wall as the door swung open, and Ghabel paused, as though she had heard something. She dropped her keys on the floor, and as she bent down to get them, Wellington reached for her.

She surprised him, whipping a knife out of an ankle holster and coming right at him. Wellington took her down with a sweep kick, but she rolled and came up panting, squaring off against him. That's when Logan hit her with the Taser.

She heard him moving behind her and dodged as he pulled the trigger. He had been aiming for her rib cage, but as she crouched to turn, the two metal probes lodged in her neck. She gasped and her eyes got big. The knife dropped from her hand and her body writhed as she slumped to the floor. Then she was still.

Logan bent over her and felt for a pulse. Her breathing was shallow and she remained unconscious although her limbs continued to jerk in uncontrollable spasms. He ran his hands lightly over her body searching for other weapons but found none. He stared down at her without remorse. So this was Barzan Ghabel's widow. What the hell was she up to?

"Let's get her into the bedroom." He and Stoddard lifted the woman up and carried her out of the living room into her bedroom. She was light but her body was a dead weight. They cuffed her to the bed and gagged her. Still, she showed no sign of awakening.

"You think she's all right?" Wellington stood at the bedroom door looking at the inert form slumped on the bed.

"She got a minimal jolt, but unfortunately it hit her in the neck. Most people feel pain and momentary paralysis. Let's keep an eye on her."

After policing the living room they resumed waiting for Khorasani to show up, periodically checking in on Ghabel, who thus far had showed no signs of reviving. At eleven o'clock Alicia's voice came over the radio.

"Alpha 1, this is Delta 1. Over."

Logan's pulse quickened. This was it. "Delta 1. Read you loud and clear. Do you have Khorasani?"

"That's a negative, Alpha 1. I just had a call from Martínez. It seems Khorasani gave the surveillance team the slip. But Pedro's friend from immigration just got in touch with him. It seems that Claudio Frontera boarded a plane for Mexico City shortly after eight o'clock."

Chapter 25

Nouri boarded his Conviasa Airlines flight at eight-fifteen. The Venezuelan state airline had begun operations in 2005, almost a decade after its predecessor, Viasa,
was privatized and sold off to the Spanish transnational,
Iberia. Iberia hadn't made any money on the Viasa routes
and eventually shut down all of its operations worldwide.

Nouri looked around the plane as he walked to his
window seat. Conviasa was leasing these Boeing 767s with
profits generated from Petroleos de Venezuela S.A., the
country's state-owned petroleum company. Not bad, he
thought, as he ran his hands over the like-new leather seats.
Ten million bucks in start-up money and you too can have
a national airline.

As he took his seat he reviewed in his mind the message
he had received that morning from Colonel Samadi that had
provoked this unexpected trip. Tehran had received intelligence that a prominent Israeli author by the name of Simon
ben Reznik, would be attending a conference on the history
of Mexican *Conversos,* those Crypto-Jews that the Spanish
had forced to convert to Catholicism during the Inquisition.

Ben Reznik had been a thorn in Tehran's side ever since a
series of articles he had written condemning the Republic's
treatment of Jews was published in *Yedioth Aronoth*, Israel's
most widely-circulated daily, and then picked up by the international press.

It's true that Jews hadn't fared so well in Iran post-1979,
Nouri snickered. Before the Shah was forced out, the Jewish
population there had numbered almost 100,000, most living
in big cities like Tehran, Esfahan and Kerman.

But in recent years that number had dwindled to less
than 10,000. Most of those who had left the country did so

out of fear they would be prosecuted for their religious beliefs. Ben Reznik had meticulously documented over a dozen high-profile cases of prominent Jewish leaders in Iran tried by Islamic Revolutionary Tribunals and sentenced to death for being Zionist agents.

Ben Reznik's exposé gave the impetus for a U.N. Human Rights Council hearing on religious tolerance in Iran, which had embarrassed the regime and led to a call for sanctions from the international body.

According to Samadi's message, General Salehi had called him the day before with explicit instructions to unleash Nouri on the unsuspecting ben Reznik. The reclusive author seldom traveled outside of Israel and the Qods Force commander wanted to strike back at him while the iron was hot.

Salehi was also eager to test Unit 400's nascent capability to conduct covert operations from their new base in Venezuela. Nouri and Azar had made rapid progress in the last three weeks and the general had told Samadi that he felt comfortable advancing their operational timetable. Part of what Nouri would be doing over the next few days, besides taking care of the ben Reznik business, would be to document his observations on border controls, determine his surveillance status and test the viability of operating in Mexico.

Four hours later his plane touched down at Mexico City's Benito Juarez International Airport. Nouri cleared customs without incident, and made his way to the men's room in the baggage claim area of Terminal 2. His contact was a Mexico City-based Qods Force officer under commercial cover, who was to pass him a bag with the gear he needed to conduct the operation.

When Nouri entered the men's room his contact was washing his hands at the sink closest to the door. There was a nondescript brown messenger bag sitting on the floor beside him. When Nouri whispered the verbal parole, the man inclined his head slightly towards the bag and strode out of the room. Nouri picked it up, walked over to one of the empty stalls and shut the door behind him.

The stall looked as though it hadn't been cleaned in days. There was no toilet seat and there were no supplies in any of the dispensers. Nouri set his own bag down and then rifled through the one he had just acquired. There was a bulging manila envelope, a bundle of pesos, neoprene gloves and a vial with a small quantity of the lethal toxin, dimethylmercury.

Nouri knew from his training that the poison was one of the most toxic in the world. It had killed a prominent American chemistry professor at Dartmouth College in the mid-1990s when she accidentally spilled several drops of it on her latex glove while working in the lab. It was readily absorbed through the glove into her body, but went undetected for months. By the time symptoms presented themselves it was too late to save her. Five months after the accidental exposure she began to develop serious neurological signs and eventually fell into a coma. It was a horrible, prolonged death. Just what Tehran had in mind for ben Reznik.

Nouri left the men's room and walked out of the baggage claim area towards the far end of the terminal where he found a booth marked "Taxi." The clerk manning the desk was wearing a bright yellow jacket emblazoned with the words *Taxi Autorizado,* which meant Authorized Taxi.

"What zone are you going to, sir?"

"Polanco." Polanco was home to one of the largest Jewish communities in Mexico City. The synagogue hosting the conference was in Polanco, as was the hotel where ben Reznik was staying.

The clerk studied a tariff sheet on the wall beside him and looked up. "That will be 300 pesos, sir."

Nouri paid the fare, took his ticket and walked outside to where the Yellow Cab Aéopuerto taxis were lining up.

The ride into the city took forty minutes. Nouri marveled at the expansive gardens in the heart of the city. "What's the name of this park?"

"Chapultepec. The Aztecs called it Grasshopper Hill. It's the biggest park in the city. There are museums, a castle and even two lakes!"

They continued north on Avenida Chapultepec, before turning onto Edgar Allen Poe. The Polanco Hotel was located at number eight. Its worn façade was in need of a facelift, but its spacious rooms and prime location overlooking Chapultepec Park more than made up for these shortcomings.

After checking in, Nouri unpacked his bag and sat down to study the targeting package Unit 400 had put together for him. It wasn't bad. There were photos of the writer, a bio sheet, information about the conference, ben Reznik's itinerary, hotel information, city maps and a security assessment. As he mulled over the material, a plan began to take shape in his mind. Ben Reznik was an avid swimmer who purportedly liked to begin his day with a thirty-minute swim. An hour later he left the hotel to walk around the neighborhood and to pick up several items that he would need tomorrow.

At six the next morning, Nouri left the hotel walking east on Paseo de la Reforma to the Hyatt Regency. He had cased the hotel the evening before, and had stolen a uniform from the hotel laundry. Slipping into a bathroom on the second floor, he changed into the maintenance crew disguise. After stowing a bag holding his own clothes behind a stack of boxes, he took the stairs to the third floor and walked into the fitness center. The clerk at the front desk gave him a passing glance when he said that he was there to check the dehumidifying system and air quality in the facility.

Walking into the pool area, he scanned the deck. No one was there. For a moment he wondered if he was too late. The fitness center was open from five o'clock in the morning until ten at night. No way ben Reznik would have been working out at five, he reasoned. Nouri looked at his watch. He was concerned about being in the center for too long. Even though the Hyatt was a huge hotel, with close to 800 rooms, and undoubtedly had a large staff, he didn't want to press his luck. Someone might notice that he didn't have a hotel ID.

A moment later he got lucky. Ben Reznik came through the fitness center doors and headed straight for the pool.

Nouri recognized him immediately. The sixty-five-year-old author was just under six feet tall, fit, and had a full head of white hair. He deposited his towel and robe on a lounge chair, pulled on a pair of swimming goggles and then headed for the shallow end of the pool. He tested the water with his toe and then plunged in.

Nouri watched him swimming laps for a moment and then walked over to the utility room housing the dehydration system. Inside, he pulled on the neoprene gloves and with care, extracted the vial of dimethylmercury from his bag. He also pulled out the portable thermal hydrometer that he had purchased the day before. The device was capable of taking temperature, humidity and dew point readings simultaneously. He continued to monitor ben Reznik through the slatted utility room door. About thirty minutes later the writer exited the pool and began walking back to his lounge chair.

Nouri felt a rush of adrenaline. Now! He grasped the vial in one hand, carefully unsealing it and exposing the deadly liquid. Moving deliberately he left the maintenance area and began walking around the pool, taking readings with the hydrometer. His path would take him behind ben Reznik's chair, where the writer, after toweling off, had sat down to read.

As Nouri neared the chair, he could see approaching from the opposite direction a corpulent hotel security guard waddling towards him. The man was waving a radio in one hand and as he approached, Nouri tensed, but the guard continued walking with only a passing nod.

As he drew even with ben Reznik's chair Nouri casually splashed the contents of the vial onto the unsuspecting writer's head and continued walking. He held his breath as he moved away, but as expected, the writer's mound of wet hair absorbed the liquid, and his victim gave no sign that anything was amiss.

Nouri continued out of the fitness center and back down to the second floor. He changed back into his own clothing and walked out of the hotel.

As he hurried back to the Polanco, Nouri thought about the surprise that was in store for ben Reznik. In four months his speech would begin to slur and the physically active Jew would find that his balance was a little bit off. He would be concerned, of course, and would schedule an appointment with his doctor. There they would soon figure out that these neurological symptoms were the result of mercury intoxication.

Further tests would reveal that his blood mercury levels were at 6,000 micrograms per liter, nearly 100 times the toxic threshold. Urine tests would also show that his urine mercury content was off the charts. His doctors would recommend aggressive chelation therapy to remove the heavy metals from his body. They would be determined, administering the chelating agent, dimercaprol, in painful intramuscular injections.

These in turn would likely produce serious side effects such as nephrotoxicity, which can lead to renal failure, and hypertension. And just as ben Reznik and his medical team were grappling with these mysteries, he would slip into a coma, from which he would never recover. His brain would cease to function and although his body might hang on for weeks, even months, his death sentence was irrevocable.

Nouri reached his hotel and before going up to his room searched for the incinerator room in the basement. He threw the messenger bag with his disguise, the targeting package, gloves and the empty vial into the furnace and watched the flames consume it all.

Back in his room he checked his computer to see if there were any messages from Tehran. He also needed to send them a report of his successful attack on the Jew. There was a message from Colonel Samadi waiting for him.

"Comrade,

"By now you will have reached Mexico City and may have even concluded your assignment here. We are eager to hear of your success.

"But we have an urgent development you need to know about. Something serious has happened in Caracas in your absence, and we are concerned that our operation there has been compromised.

"Azar was attacked and has been hospitalized at the Centro Médico de Caracas. She's in a coma, although her vital statistics and brain function appear normal. When she was found at the apartment she had two puncture wounds in her neck, which we believe were made by a Taser."

Damn, Nouri thought as the shock of what had happened began to hit him. Azar in a coma in the hospital! He continued reading with a feeling of dread.

"We are trying to piece together what happened. There was an anonymous call to the hospital at around eleven p.m. on the night that you flew to Mexico City. The caller was female and she said that there had been an accident and that a woman was injured.

"When the ambulance arrived, they found her lying on the bed in her room. No one was there with her. She was transported to the hospital and they began looking for her next of kin. The hospital contacted the landlord of the apartment and he gave them your name."

"Of course, when the hospital contacted the Costa Rican Embassy, they had no record of your passport being issued, and so the hospital contacted the National Police who went to the apartment to investigate. They discovered Azar's passport there amongst her things and contacted our Embassy in Caracas."

Nouri looked up from the computer, his face tense. His Costa Rican persona had been exposed and was now blown. He sighed in exasperation and turned back to the computer screen.

"By pure coincidence our station chief in Caracas is under consular cover, and he called me on the secure line to tell me what had happened after he visited the hospital and spoke with the police.

"Obviously our Embassy has denied any knowledge of Claudio Frontera or of the Iranian citizen in that apartment. That said, if Azar's condition remains stable and she is able to be moved, we will attempt to have her medically transported back to Iran.

"Meanwhile, you are in danger. If the police think to check with the airlines, they may discover that you are in Mexico City and contact the authorities there. I want you to keep a low profile for the next day or two. We are going to have a support asset rent a hotel room in a clean alias. You will be contacted this morning and you should be prepared to move immediately. Meanwhile we are going to courier a new identity to you and give you additional instructions.

"We will have to abandon our current plans for Caracas given this development. Our station chief in Caracas will continue to apprise us of any developments in the National Police investigation. We must find out if this was simply criminal activity or if there is something more sinister at play.

"Stay well.

"Tahmouress Samadi

"Colonel, IRGC"

Nouri composed a message to Unit 400's operational desk, attention Colonel Samadi, acknowledging the latter's warning and briefly outlining his successful execution of the ben Reznik operation.

After hitting the send button, he shut down the computer and walked over to the window gazing out over the spacious gardens of the park. As he idly stared into the distance his mind was whirling. He had doubts that the attack on Azar was a random act of violence. No, there was more to this than met the eye. He packed his bag and left the room. After paying his bill he paid another visit to the basement incinerator room, watching as Claudio Frontera's passport was consumed in the flames.

Chapter 26

Interesting, Logan mused as he drummed his fingers on the coffee table. He and Nayef Al Subaie were sitting in Millie's apartment discussing Logan's trip to Venezuela. Nayef was in the U.S. for a week, attending a Telecommunications Products Expo at the Boston Convention and Exhibition Center. Logan had picked him up at the main Summer Street entrance for the short ride to the North End, and on the ride over Nayef had told him that Kuwait had decided to bring the Boston PD fully on board with their investigation.

Nayef's face was drawn and he looked as though he had aged ten years in the month since Logan, Millie and Zahir had last seen him. He took an appreciative sip of the aged single malt scotch Millie had poured him and settled back into his chair.

"It seems that Khorasani's been able to stay just one step ahead of us. Here, your chance encounter with him in Spain, and now this, disappearing under our very noses in Venezuela." He looked pointedly at Logan.

Logan shrugged his shoulders. "I keep second-guessing myself about not nailing him when we saw him on the street that night. But it was the right decision. We didn't have a solid plan at that point, and there were just too many unknown variables. Sure, if our only goal was to take him out, that would be one thing, but we were trying to take him alive so we could question him." Logan shook his head in frustration.

"And you weren't able to get anything out of the woman? Ghabel's wife?"

"More bad luck. She went after Wellington with a knife in the apartment." He pulled Azar's blade out of his pocket and passed it to Nayef. "Pretty nice. Looks like she had it custom-made." Nayef examined the knife and handed it back to him without comment.

"It wasn't a great outcome. Nine times out of ten a Taser shot will hit one of the major muscle groups, and neutralize the target for several minutes. The Taser has these two hooks that shoot out, and if they did hit a major nerve in her neck…" His voice trailed off. "That kind of head trauma can put you in the hurt locker.

"We were there at the apartment for another two hours waiting for Khorasani to come back when we got word that he'd flown to Mexico City. Ghabel was still unconscious. That's definitely not normal. She stopped having muscle spasms, but her breathing was shallow and there was no sign she was going to come out of it.

"That's when I had Alicia call 171. That's like our 911. We took her restraints and the gag off, left the door unlocked and waited in the car a block from the apartment.

"Once the ambulance showed up we cleared out. We met with Zed one more time to wrap everything up. I just got back two days ago."

"Thamir had a message from Zed this morning. He had Martínez make some inquiries after you left. It seems the Qods Force station chief in Caracas has gotten involved. He's been talking to the police and is trying to get Ghabel back to Iran on an emergency medical flight. She's still in a coma, but they're determined to get her back as soon as possible," Nayef said.

"They're probably afraid that if she comes out of it the police will question her and she'll say something out of school. Hell, she may even have amnesia."

"Zed will keep his ears open for any developments in her situation. He also has Martínez questioning his police contacts to see if there's anything new on Khorasani. We know the Costa Ricans reported the passport fraud to the National Police. I'm sure that as soon as the Iranians found out that Khorasani's Costa Rican identity was compromised, they warned him to keep a low profile and to definitely stay out of Venezuela.

"Thamir relayed a report to the Spanish, INTERPOL, CIA and the Boston PD this morning outlining everything we have developed over the last month."

Logan raised an eyebrow, and waited for Nayef to continue.

"We took particular pains to conceal your involvement in this, Logan. Your identity will be protected. You and the others." He paused. "You know how much I respect you, Logan. And I know how much you cared for Hamid." His voice choked up and he fought to regain his composure.

Logan felt a surge of anger, not at the Kuwaitis for moving the investigation fully into official channels, but at himself, for failing to nail Khorasani when he had the chance.

"What now?"

Nayef looked at him thoughtfully.

"Each of these organizations will pursue this within their own jurisdiction." Nayef's face hardened. "For my part, I will not rest until Hamid's murderer is found! But there remains the larger question of what Unit 400 is up to. My hope is that the intelligence agencies will continue their investigation and discover the answer to that question."

Millie came into the room and asked Nayef if he would like to stay for dinner.

"Thanks, Millie, but I'm meeting one of my clients for dinner tonight. As you know, most of these business deals don't happen at the expo, but over drinks and dinner."

Logan offered to give him a ride but Nayef declined. After he had left, Logan sprawled on the sofa with his head back staring at the ceiling. Millie refreshed his drink and sat down opposite him, feet curled up under her.

"It's too bad you were traveling last weekend."

"Yeah, I really wanted to be there. How are Mom and Dad doing?"

"You know. They're about the same. Still struggling to make sense of it all. I think they're seeing Father Pat. He said the mass." She swirled the wine around in her glass, watching it splash from one side to the other.

Millie, Ryan and Zahir had all gone up to Montpelier the weekend before to commemorate the one-year anniversary of Cooper's death. There had been a memorial mass at St. Augustine's Catholic Church, and their parents had hosted a reception for family and close friends at their country club.

"Father Pat said hi."

Logan smiled as he imagined the gregarious priest. His round face always smiling as he dispensed his wisdom and care, qualities that had endeared him to generations of parishioners at St. Augustine's.

For Logan, his brother's death remained a raw wound, chafing his heart. It had been bad enough for him to lose his brother, but Zahir had been in Iraq with Cooper when the IED attack had changed their lives forever. And then, to make matters worse, while he and Zahir were cataloging everything they had taken from the Qods Force base in Bandar Deylam last year, Zahir had discovered the DVD recording that the killers had made of the ambush in Iraq.

He and Zahir had watched it together in that corrugated warehouse on Failaka Island. He remembered holding her as sobs wracked her body. Later, back at the compound where they had been staying they drowned their grief in two bottles of Madeira and then comforted each other, making love until they were exhausted.

Logan stirred his scotch with his finger and thought back to the other night. After they had put the baby down, Zahir had talked about the weekend in Montpelier and how all the old wounds had opened up again. It wasn't cathartic, as she'd hoped it would be, but gut-wrenching, leaving her emotionally shattered.

He had held her until her sobs subsided, stroking her hair and kissing her face. And somehow her hurt had been transformed into desire, and they had come together, tasting, feeling, needing one another. Later, hearts hammering, they had lain side by side, holding hands, whispering their love for one another until at last they fell into a restless sleep.

"Logan?"

He stirred from his reverie and gave Millie a sheepish grin. "I must be tired from all the travel," he said.

Millie's phone rang. "Hi. No, Nayef has dinner with a client.

"It's Ryan," she mouthed.

"No, I don't think he's going to make it. He looks pretty beat." She listened for a minute. "Let me ask him."

She covered the mouthpiece of the phone. "I said you're too tired to do dinner tonight, but he wants to know if you and Zahir want to come over this weekend. Or we could go out."

"That'd be great. Let me check with Zahir, but I'm sure she'd be up for it."

Logan stood and took his glass into the kitchen. Returning to the living room he bent over and kissed Millie on the top of her head.

"Gotta go."

She blew him a kiss as he walked to the door. "Call me."

As Logan let himself out, he was aware of a growing sense of anger over the direction the hunt for Khorasani had taken. He should probably feel relieved that the Kuwaitis no longer were looking to him to catch Hamid's killer. But instead, angst and a growing sense of foreboding began to gnaw at him. He was certain that he had not seen the last of Mr. Khorasani.

The next morning Logan was eager to get to work. Alicia had beaten him to the office, and as he hurried through the door he saw that she was making notations in his calendar and had a half-dozen Post-it notes pasted neatly on his desk.

"Hey, how was your weekend?" Logan asked, before glancing at his appointment book, where she had penciled in a couple of tentative meetings.

"It was pretty laid back. I just did some laundry and food shopping. How about you?"

Logan told her about his meeting with Nayef. "I feel like I let him down."

"You shouldn't feel that way. You did more than most people would've."

"Yeah. Well, we'll see. Anything urgent going on?"

"Gordon Willoughby would like you to give him a call. And that detective left a message."

"Breen?"

"Yes. Detective Breen. He said he has some news he wants to share with you." Alicia raised her eyebrows. "You think he knows you've been involved?"

"I don't think so. Nayef was clear on that. They would've covered our tracks somehow. He probably told Breen that their Intel people had developed whatever it is that they gave them. Something like that."

Logan walked into his office, pausing as usual for a quick view of Boston Harbor. From his vantage point he could see a group of high school students on the Harborwalk in front of the Moakley Federal Courthouse making stone rubbings. They were clustered in front of a big medallion depicting the history of Boston and the dozen or so islands stretching across the harbor.

A tall ship with sails aloft caught his eye. It was the *USS Constitution*, Old Ironsides, taking a spin from its mooring in Charlestown. Logan marveled as the forty-four-gun frigate's sails fluttered in the wind. It was an impressive sight. The oldest surviving U.S. naval vessel still in active service, it was one of six frigates commissioned by President George Washington in 1794. And still going strong. Logan gave the ship a salute and then turned to his desk. He punched in Peter Breen's number and waited.

"Breen."

"Hey, Peter. Logan Alexander."

"Logan! Thanks for getting back to me. It's been what? Two weeks since we last talked?"

"Yeah, right after my Spain trip. What's up?"

"There have been some developments from the Kuwaitis."

"Oh?" Logan kept his voice noncommittal.

"Uh huh. It seems Mr. Khorasani's trying to rack up some frequent flier miles."

"What do you mean?"

215

"The Kuwaitis, or their friends, tracked Khorasani to Caracas in late September. Apparently they have somebody down there that was able to look into it. They think he's connected to this group calling themselves Unit 400, an Iranian terrorist outfit. Ever hear of it?"

"They were in the news a couple of years ago. Unit 400 tried to take out the Saudi ambassador here in the U.S. They used some Mexican drug cartel low-life to carry out the attack. I read somewhere that they're mainly assassins modeled after this radical Shia sect called the Hashashin. I mean, we're talking 11th century."

"Well, according to this report I got from the Kuwaitis, Unit 400's trying to recruit foreigners for special ops."

"We've seen that movie before. Remember that British guy? The shoe bomber?"

"Yeah. Richard Reid. Al Qaeda recruited him to blow up that flight and he almost pulled it off, but he was acting suspicious and a passenger called for help."

"So, how does this all relate to Khorasani?"

"It seems Mr. Khorasani has been operating incognito. In fact, he changes his identity faster than a New York minute!"

"How so?"

Breen went on to explain what he knew about Khorasani's Spanish and Costa Rican identities.

"The Kuwaitis believe he's in Mexico now on that Costa Rican identity."

Logan could hear Breen shuffling papers on his desk as he searched for something.

"Here it is. Claudio Frontera."

"What's he doing in Mexico?"

"We don't know, but based on this report we've put out an APB and notified the Federal Police in Mexico City. INTERPOL has an office down there, but I don't trust their asses."

"Why not?"

"They're all in bed with the drug cartels. A few years ago the head of INTERPOL in Mexico was arrested for leaking information to them.

"But getting back to Khorasani, I'm not sure he's in Mexico to carry out a hit. He may be. We haven't seen anything come over the wire that smells like a Unit 400 hit." Breen paused. No, I'm thinking of something more sinister."

"Like what?"

"I'm thinking the guy may have some unfinished business here. I'm thinking he's just using Mexico as a gateway into the U.S.!"

Chapter 27

Nouri Khorasani strolled into Mexico City's Northern Bus Terminal. After locating the Omnibus de México desk he handed the clerk the 1,010-peso fare and then sauntered down to platform 5, where passengers were already boarding the luxurious long-distance bus. The twelve-hour trip to Matamoros would give him time to think about everything that had happened over the last week. Matamoros, in the state of Tamaulipas, was just across the Rio Grande from Brownsville, Texas.

It had been four days since he had received the message from Colonel Samadi prompting him to destroy his Claudio Frontera identity and go on the lam. The Qods Force station in Mexico City had put him up in a modest, nondescript hotel in the Zona Rosa, or Pink Zone, west of the historic downtown district.

The Zona Rosa was more like a faded rose than the once prestigious residential area where Mexico City's elites, bohemians and well-heeled foreigners gathered in trendy bars, restaurants and art galleries. Little of that was apparent today as gay bars, fast food restaurants and clubs catering to the prostitution and gambling trade, gave evidence to the area's declining fortunes.

Nouri had kept a low profile while he was waiting. He was impatient to resolve his passport dilemma, seething because of the bureaucratic delay. Finally, he had received a message directing him to a meeting in San Ángel, a colonial era residential neighborhood south of the city center.

He had met his contact at the Iglesia San Jacinto, situated on Plaza San Jacinto, famous for its Saturday bazaar attracting tourists from all over. But that morning it had been quiet. He and his contact had met in a pew at the rear of the

218

church, where they blended in with tourists and worshipers admiring the church's 16th century baroque altar.

The meeting had lasted for no more than five minutes.

"There is an ops note from Tehran, and your papers," the man had said. "We have heard from our police informants that the immigration police are looking for a Costa Rican by the name of Claudio Frontera." He had looked pointedly at Nouri. "Tehran wants confirmation that you have disposed of the incriminating documents."

"Yes, I destroyed them when I found out that they were compromised."

"Details?"

"I threw them into an incinerator and waited until only ashes remained. They will not be a problem."

They talked for a couple more minutes and then split up.

"Good luck," his companion had said, but Nouri was already in the aisle moving out of the church and into the street. He walked to the La Bombilla metro station and took line 3 back into the city center, before returning to his hotel.

The note from Samadi had been cryptic, but clear.

"Comrade,

"We know from police informants that both your Costa Rican and Spanish identities have been linked and that intelligence services and INTERPOL are now investigating. It's unsafe for you to return to Venezuela or Spain."

Damn. His life had just gotten a lot more complicated.

"We are providing you with a new Belgian identity. The passport is one of several that we stole from a diplomatic pouch in Nigeria. It is a bona fide Belgian passport, not a fake. We know the Belgian authorities are working on a national immigration database they call Braingate, for tracking forgeries and such, but it is months from coming on line. You will be able to travel securely on this passport.

"We believe that your cover should remain similar to that of your Spanish identity. You will present yourself as an Internet security consultant. This is where your true skills and expertise lie.

"You are to travel by land to the U.S. and then wait for orders."

Nouri had been shocked that they were sending him back to the U.S. so soon, but as he read the rest of Samadi's note he had to agree that it was bold, and if it worked he would be certain to receive accolades from the Supreme Leader.

Nouri thumbed the Belgian passport open to the photo of himself. The face was familiar but the name was not. David Foster. He closed the passport and rubbed his hands over its burgundy cover. Emblazoned on the front were the Belgian coat of arms and the words "European Union" and "Passport" in French, German, and Dutch.

Nouri concentrated on memorizing the pertinent identifying information in the passport. In his mind he was already framing the cover story he would use if questioned by immigration authorities when leaving Mexico and entering the U.S. He wasn't concerned. He had been living a double life for so long that lying was second nature to him.

An hour later he was at Mexico City's North Bus Terminal. He boarded his bus and settled into the plush leather seat as it pulled out of the terminal heading north. Their route would take them west to San Luis Potosí, the famous mining capital situated on the Mexican Plateau. They would ride the Sierra Madre Oriental, and then turn north towards Monterrey before descending to the Gulf Coast plain and Matamoros, nestled along the Gulf of Mexico.

Nouri stared idly out the window. The coastal route might have been more scenic, but driving conditions were reputed to be less than ideal. There were fewer highways along the east coast, and the smaller local roads were more dangerous as gangs roamed them, preying upon unwary travelers. These criminals were aided by *topes,* the gigantic Mexican speed bumps that forced drivers to a screeching halt, making it child's play for the highway robbers to attack their victims. Even the Green Angels, the ubiquitous fleet of trucks that patrolled Mexico's highways and byways helping stranded travelers, were not a deterrent.

The conductor had come by with a selection of newspapers and Nouri was now absorbed in a copy of the *Reforma*, a Mexico City daily. On page two there was an article about the Crypto-Jews conference in Mexico City. Prominently displayed at the bottom of the article was a photo of noted Israeli author Simon ben Reznik. Nouri felt no remorse for his recent actions as he stared dispassionately at the picture. Ben Reznik's fate had been sealed when he decided to go after the Republic. He had made his bed, and now he would pay the price.

At San Luis Potosí they stopped for lunch at Rincón Huastecas, a restaurant specializing in Huasteca Indian fare. Nouri sat by himself and ordered a tamale wrapped in banana leaves, a side dish of red beans and a Negra Modelo beer to wash it down.

The meal had made him sleepy and after they reboarded the bus he dozed off and on. By late afternoon as they descended from the Sierra Madre to the coastal plain, Nouri felt refreshed and eager for the challenges ahead.

He had researched the border checkpoints into the U.S. and was surprised to discover that Matamoros had four bridges crossing the Rio Grande into Brownsville. That was the most of any Mexican city along the 2,000-mile border. Gateway International Bridge was the most heavily traveled and was the one he would try. It had thousands of pedestrian crossings daily.

He overheard a couple on the bus talking about Customs and Border Protection's new Ready Lane kiosk checkpoint system, designed to help the CBP officers identify pedestrians using fake documents. Under the new procedure, travelers were required to scan their documents at the kiosk before reaching the CBP agents, giving CBP valuable time to run checks so they could determine if the documents were legitimate. Nouri wasn't worried about the new procedure, given what Colonel Samadi had told him about the Belgian passport. He expected to sail through immigration without incident.

As he walked up to the kiosk, Nouri slid his passport face down through the scanner. A moment later he approached the CBP window, where one officer was seated and another was standing by his side looking over his shoulder.

"Mr. Foster, what brings you to the United States?"

"Tourism."

"How long have you been in Mexico?"

"A week."

The officer questioning him carefully scrutinized the passport picture and then looked up at him.

"What did you do in Mexico?"

"I wanted to see Mexico City and some of the country but I didn't think it would be safe to drive by myself, so I took the bus."

"Where in Belgium are you from?"

"Brussels."

"Oh, what part?"

"St. Gilles, near the Gare du Midi."

"Ah. My wife and I were in Etterbeek last summer for vacation. We had a small apartment near the Parc du Cinquantunaire. It was beautiful."

Nouri smiled. Inside his mind was racing. Sometimes these immigration officers would try to disarm you with small talk while someone in another room was doing a background check. He hoped Samadi had been right about the Belgians and their fucking Braingate system. Otherwise he was hosed.

His attention shifted back to the counter as he heard his passport being stamped.

"Welcome to the United States, Mr. Foster."

Chapter 28

Logan felt a surge of nostalgia as he watched Admiral Bucky Chesterton's change of command ceremony aboard the *USS Harry S. Truman* at U.S. Fleet Forces Command. Gordon Willoughby and Seaman First Class Cyle Hockaday were grinning broadly as the Chief of Naval Operations congratulated the new fleet commander.

The three of them were at Naval Station Norfolk in Hampton Roads, Virginia, for Mark V acceptance trials. Coincidentally, Admiral Chesterton, who had just been transferred from Portsmouth Naval Station, was aware of their presence on base and had extended an invitation to his ceremony.

As Logan immersed himself in the pageantry, he realized how much he missed the time-honored rituals of the Navy. Standing before Old Glory in their impeccable full dress whites with swords and medals, the three admirals, outgoing and incoming commanders alongside the Chief of Naval Operations, struck a pose as timeless as the service itself.

All hands had been called to quarters fifteen minutes earlier and stood at attention as the honor guard escorted the brass up to the platform where the "Star Spangled Banner" was played by the Navy band, evoking emotions of tradition and patriotism in the hearts of all present.

The ceremony was short and precise. A Navy chaplain offered an invocation and the outgoing commander, Vice-Admiral Robert Keller, read his orders of detachment to the officers and crew.

"I am ready to be relieved," he announced, as he stood back from the podium.

Admiral Chesterton stepped forward to read his orders to command. When he had finished he extended a salute to Admiral Keller and then proclaimed, "I relieve you, sir." Turning to face the crew he advised, "Standing orders will remain in effect until otherwise notified." He spoke briefly and then the chaplain offered a benediction.

Logan and the others offered both officers congratulations and mingled briefly with the other guests attending the reception. When they left they stepped outside into a flawless fall day. They descended the Nimitz-class supercarrier's gangway to the pier. Looking up at the Lone Warrior, as her crew fondly called her, Logan marveled at the ship's self-sufficiency. Powered by two Westinghouse nuclear reactors, the carrier could travel 3 million miles before refueling.

As they walked down the pier towards their rental car, Logan thought back to what he knew of Norfolk. The Naval base had a storied past, that was certain. Originally authorized by Congress at the onset of World War I, Norfolk had supported both seaplane and submarine operations during the war. With a contingent of over 34,000 sailors by 1918, the Hampton Roads facility continued to grow in strategic importance over the years.

In the lead-up to World War II, Naval Station Norfolk was denoted the home of the Atlantic Fleet, a position it holds to this very day under the name, Fleet Forces Command. The command was humongous, Logan thought as they drove onto the base earlier in the day. In addition to hosting the largest contingent of naval personnel in the world, Norfolk was also home to a significant number of Army, Air Force, Marine and Coast Guard personnel who augmented the fleet's impressive joint capabilities.

"How many ships do you think are based out of here, Gordon?"

"I heard they've got something like seventy-five. Everything from missile frigates to aircraft carriers. They've got almost twice as many aircraft based here too. It's a busy place.

"What do you say we get over to the Gateway and check in?"

Logan chuckled. The Navy Gateway Inn and Suites had listed its address as Longitude 36.9483998835059 by Latitude 76.3166570663452. That translated into Gilbert Street in downtown Norfolk in layman's language.

After they stowed their gear in their quarters, the three of them returned to the base, where they had a 14:00 hours meeting with personnel from the U.S. Navy Board of Inspection and Survey. Two members of the board would participate in the three-day acceptance trials for the Mark V. In addition to conducting steering and handling checks, they were planning to scrub all of the major systems onboard: propulsion engineering, ship controls, combat, communications, radar and navigation.

Logan had immersed himself in the Mark V project almost immediately upon his return from Caracas. Despite his disappointment that Nouri Khorasani was still out there, he was in a sense relieved that the Kuwaitis had decided to bring the CIA and law enforcement on board with their investigation. Their combined capabilities would make it difficult for the Unit 400 assassin to continue operating. He would begin to feel the noose tightening. Every time he moved he would leave a footprint, and maybe, just maybe, he would make a mistake.

The two officers from the Board of Inspection and Survey were waiting for them. Lt. Calvin Holcomb and Commander Cynthia Stewart were both on rotation from sea duty to the board.

"This isn't my first rodeo," Stewart pronounced. "I've been doing this now for two years. "Lt. Holcomb just checked in this week, and this'll be his first survey."

"Have you had much experience with the Mark V's, Commander?" Logan looked around the sterile conference room.

"Not really. We get a little bit of everything coming through here. The last inspection I worked on was for the *USNS Montford Point*."

Logan gave her a quizzical look. "I'm not familiar with that ship. What is it?"

"It's an MLP. A mobile landing platform. It's the first in its class."

"What's their mission?"

"They're designed to use new float-on, float-off technology to move equipment and personnel from one vessel to another. What they do is partially submerge the deck to accomplish this."

"Now that's interesting," Willoughby acknowledged. "How deep do they submerge them?"

"Oh, to about the height of a dock. The ship's configured with mooring fenders on the sides so that cargo ships can tie up and transfer their load. Very impressive," she said.

"The other unique thing about the *Montford Point* and the other ships in this class is that you can also reconfigure their decks, depending upon the particular mission. They're pretty versatile."

After Lt. Holcomb offered them coffee, they settled into their seats. Holcomb turned on an overhead projector and began running through a set of slides detailing the results of recent Mark V builder's trials. The University of Maine, Maine Marine Manufacturing, and an East Boothbay boatbuilding firm had carried out the trials.

"As you know, the main thing the Navy has asked this group to do is improve the Mark V's seakeeping." Holcomb didn't need to add that seakeeping is a measure of how well a watercraft is able to deal with a variety of sea conditions when underway for these experienced sailors.

"The university put up some numbers measuring seakeeping performance criteria that the boys at Little Creek and Patuxent River have had a hard time replicating. We're not saying they didn't get it right, but at this point we are seeing some disparity in the outcomes."

"Are these results based upon actual trials on board the Mark V or are they based on physical models?"

Holcomb consulted a sheaf of papers in a binder on the desk in front of him. "It looks like it's a combination of computer modeling and physical models. They haven't actually had it out on the water."

"Working in the lab will only get you so far. At some point you have to get beyond the modeling and get wet. I wonder if the university has a seakeeping basin at their testing facility? That's the only way to do proper hydrodynamic testing."

"I think it was their Advanced Structures and Composites Department that was handling the testing on structural hybrid composites."

"You mean the idea behind a Kevlar composite for the hull, sir?" Hockaday asked.

Holcomb looked his way. "Yes. Their expertise is in composite materials manufacturing science, resin infusion, polymer/interface science, and some other areas that don't directly relate to the Mark V. They're running some cutting edge programs and partner with the private sector and the government on things like new product development and testing.

"I don't know for certain, but my guess would be that they don't have a seakeeping basin up there. They have the Darling Marine Center, but that's more for marine biology than engineering."

The five of them spent the next four hours looking at data from the builder's trials and discussing the schedule over the next couple of days. Logan was not particularly concerned about the Mark V's other systems. The craft had been battle tested time and time again, and for the most part performed superbly. It was the rigid hull, and the twenty-five-percent injury rate that had earned the boat the moniker "The Jackhammer" that left him doubting its long-term viability for special operations.

Logan knew the Navy was already thinking beyond the Mark V to the next generation craft. There had been rumors that the Sealion, a SEAL insertion, observation, and neutralization craft being designed by the Navy's Surface Warfare Center in Maryland, was a leading candidate.

"We've been asked to evaluate the Sealion as well," Commander Stewart announced. "In fact, we've got one down at the pier undergoing testing.

"Sealion has some significant differences. It's eleven feet shorter than the Mark V, making it possible to transport on a C-17."

The C-17 Globemaster was a more versatile delivery system than the more cumbersome C-5 Galaxy that was required to transport the Mark V.

"Like the Mark V, the Sealion also has an all-aluminum rigid hull, although in tests, it hasn't had the same vibration issues," Stewart said.

"One big unknown is what weapons system would be deployed on Sealion. Right now the higher ups are billing it as a high-speed, low-signature technology demonstrator, so they haven't bothered to arm it. Based on my reading of her specs, I'd say the Sealion could pretty much handle everything that's on the Mark V."

With that they wrapped it up for the day. Holcomb and Stewart begged off when Logan and the others invited them to dinner. After leaving the base they decided to check out the nearby town of Newport News. After dinner at a local crab shack that Holcomb had recommended, Logan, Willoughby and Hockaday were sipping beers in the Funny Bone Comedy Club. They had spotted it as they strolled down Main Street in historic Hilton Village tucked in next door to the Peninsula Community Theatre just down the street from the Main Street Library. After a full afternoon of technical discussions they were ready to unwind.

It was amateur night and Hockaday, much to Logan and Willoughby's surprise, volunteered to lead off the evening with a couple of jokes. The beers had loosened him up, and he was feeling no pain.

He paused nervously in front of the crowd and then gathered his courage.

"So, did you hear about the blind man who walked into the bar with his seeing-eye dog?" Someone in the audience groaned.

Hockaday looked in that direction but then continued. "Instead of ordering a beer, he walks over to the middle of the room, picks up his dog by the chain and begins to swing him around in a circle over his head.

"No one can believe it. They all just stare at him except for this one lady. She's a dog lover and so she runs up to him and starts screaming at the top of her lungs.

"'What the hell do you think you're doing? You can't treat a dog like that!'

"The blind man turns toward the lady and says, 'Oh, sorry, I'm just having a look around.'"

The joke drew a smattering of titters from the crowd.

"Or how about this transcript of a conversation between a U.S. Navy warship and the Coast Guard?"

"'This is the U.S. Coast Guard. We request that you divert your course fifteen degrees to the north, to avoid collision.'

"'This is the U.S. Navy. I recommend that you divert *your* course fifteen degrees to the north, to avoid collision.'"

"'That's a negative, U.S. Navy. You'll have to divert fifteen degrees to the north to avoid collision.'

"'I'll have you know that this is the captain of a U.S. Naval warship. I repeat, divert your course!'

"'That's a negative, U.S. Navy. I repeat again, you must divert *your* course!'

"'This is one of the largest destroyers in the U.S. Navy fleet. Two missile frigates and a tender also accompany us. I demand that you change your course fifteen degrees to the north, or you will bear responsibility for any countermeasures that I must take!'

"'U.S. Navy, this is West Quoddy Head Lighthouse. Your call!'"

There was a smattering of applause as Hockaday returned to his seat.

"Damn, Hockaday. I didn't know you were that funny." Willoughby clapped him on the back and ordered a round of beers as another aspiring comedian got up to try out his material.

They closed the joint down at eleven-thirty and decided to call it a night. They were going to be busy over the next two days.

When they reported in early the next morning the propulsion systems checks were already underway. They went pretty much as Logan had expected. There were no issues with those or any of the other major systems tests on the Mark V over the next two days.

Late on their last day at Norfolk Logan was talking to a Hull Division engineer by the name of Calvin who worked in the Field Engineering Design Division. They were standing on one of the fourteen piers on base next to a Sealion craft moored next to the modified Mark V.

"You know historically steel ships didn't have their hulls tested other than at the time of fabrication or when they were in drydock. But with all the off-shore drilling going on in the private sector, the Navy took a chapter from those folks who were doing underwater nondestructive testing on their rigs."

Calvin withdrew a tin of chew and placed a wad in his cheek. He offered it to Logan, who declined. "Well, we got the Ship Structure Committee to agree to take a look at this practice and after we experimented with it we found that it had practical applications for our testing purposes."

"How are you currently doing your nondestructive testing?" Logan thumped the Sealion's hull.

"When they're in drydock we'll do visual inspections, radiography, ultrasonics, magnetic particle and liquid penetrant tests. All these can be done underwater as well, except for the liquid penetrant." He scratched his chest.

"Now, underwater's a whole different ball of wax in terms of procedure. Typically you'll have a diver or divers in dry suits. They have to clean the hull surface so they'll use tools like water jets, needle guns or grinders to prepare the surface for inspection. Here, take a look at this." He pulled several underwater photo shots of the Sealion's hull from a folder he was carrying.

"Here are some before and after shots of this one. You can see how clean the crew got it for testing."

Logan examined the photos. Calvin was right. There was no comparison to the before and after shots. "So once you get it clean, what tests do you perform?"

"Take a look at this." He pulled out a chart showing degradation of radiographic sensitivity on the vessel's hull.

"We used commercially available ultrasonic inspection gear which we kept topside on the Sealion. Our diver took a probe down below. He was equipped with a camera on his helmet so the technician on the surface could steer him to the right places to inspect."

Logan whistled. Pretty impressive. "So being able to do these underwater tests is more efficient. I mean, you don't have to pull these babies out and put them in drydock to do this."

"That's the idea."

"So what did you find out?"

"We're going to have to do additional testing. There are some shortcomings with the ultrasonics."

"Like what?"

"An ideal test assumes a flat surface to scan with the probe. But there may be corrosion pits on the surface of the hull and this affects the way the beam is directed. It may weaken the beam and give you a false reading. That's what we think happened. Now you know the hulls on these boats are all aluminum, right?"

Logan nodded.

Calvin walked down the pier to where the Mark V was anchored. "This modified hull has a Kevlar exterior. The interior is made up of layers of carbon fiber and a foam core. It's actually supposed to be fifty percent stronger than the original copy." He patted the hull affectionately.

"We're working up a test protocol for the modified hull. But the real test will be when we put this baby into the inventory and put it through its paces."

"So it's already a done deal?" Logan turned towards the chubby engineer.

"Yep. They're calling her Mako, after the shark. The Mark V 1. Saw the order myself this morning."

Logan whistled softly. "So the Mako is already approved for action. Wait till Gordon hears about this!"

Chapter 29

Nouri Khorasani edged the Chrysler 300 rental into a parking space in front of La Hacienda Apartments on Las Palmas Drive. He had crossed over into Brownsville four days before, and was getting restless as he waited for orders from Tehran.

He gathered up his shopping bags and let himself into the apartment. He was in dire need of a new wardrobe since virtually everything he owned remained in his apartment in Burgos. Or more than likely in some police lab in Madrid, he reflected. So much for Claudio Diez Perea. It had been a good life while it lasted. The shopping tip from his waitress at the Tex Mex BBQ joint had been a good one. The drive to the Rio Grande Valley Outlets in Mercedes hadn't taken that long and there was a big selection.

Nouri poured himself a drink and sat down in the living room. He wondered what this chain of events meant for him long-term. From his perspective, Tehran should be thinking about putting him on ice for a few weeks, a month or even longer. But he was just a low-level cadre in this war. If Colonel Samadi wanted to send him right back into battle, it wasn't his job to question the wisdom of his decision. He would do whatever was asked of him. Unit 400 had given him a new lease on life, and he was a good foot soldier.

He kept turning over the events of the past several weeks in his mind, trying to figure out how the police could have tracked him to Caracas. He bristled as he reasoned that the most likely link was his uncle. If he had been indiscreet, that in all likelihood had led the authorities to his apartment in Burgos.

The Spanish police were not that good, though. They had to be working with somebody else. Who had his uncle been talking to? Foreign Intel? Probably the damn CIA. If they'd torn his apartment apart they would have found his hidden cache. And then it dawned on him. Damn! His Costa Rican identity card. That was the link they had needed to tie the Spaniard, Claudio Diez Perea, to Costa Rican Claudio Frontera!

Nouri held his head in despair. That slip-up had led whoever "they" were to Caracas, the attack on Azar at the El Valle apartment, and the compromise of their whole Venezuela operation. And that's why he was sitting in this fucking apartment in Brownsville. He was screwed. He shivered as he realized that they must have been there in the apartment waiting to ambush him.

He hadn't known it at the time, but the Mexico City operation had given him a reprieve. If he had gone down in Caracas, he'd probably be sitting in some fucking CIA interrogation cell in Gitmo.

His mind cleared and he felt renewed resolve. Despite the screw-ups there had been a clean break between Claudio Frontera and David Foster. Nouri ticked off the events of the past week, feeling confident that he had successfully made the transition from Costa Rican businessman to Belgian tourist.

He had eased into the David Foster identity, keeping a low profile over the last few days. But he needed an outlet for all the tension that had been building in him as he realized how close he had come to losing everything.

It was late in the afternoon when Nouri decided to drive through the university district in search of some action. Sex was his antidote for tension.

The University of Texas and Texas Southmost College, once combined but now separate institutions, had campuses in Brownsville, so he decided to check them out first.

Nouri parked near the University of Texas, observing with surprise that many of its buildings reminded him of an old U.S. Army outpost. He found out later that many of them dated back to the 1840s, around the time of the Mexican-American War. There must be some interesting stories behind those walls, he thought as he strolled around the campus.

Walking east on East 11th Street, Nouri spotted the Mean-Eyed Cat, a bar housed in a Spanish-style one-story building with faded white stucco front and a dull orange Mexican tile roof. Pushing inside he stepped into another world. It was a real Tejano dive. The floor was covered in sawdust. Grimy faux wood paneling lined the wall behind the bar and black spray-painted designs on the other walls rounded out the décor.

A jukebox on one wall delivered a steady stream of favorites by Tejano mega-star Selena. Behind the jukebox was a poster of the Latin beauty titled the Queen of Tejano Music.

Nouri stood before the poster of the deceased singer. He had gone out with a girl in high school who had been obsessed with the Latina phenomena. His own tastes had run more towards Alice Cooper, but he had to admit that Selena's flowing chestnut hair, framing a seductive, yet innocent face, was a turn-on.

He thought back to how distraught his girlfriend had been when she'd heard the news that Selena had been murdered. The president of her fan club had shot her, just barely into her twenties. The world had gone into mourning and President Bush had even declared April 16, Selena's birthday, as Selena Day in Texas. What a waste, he thought.

"She was really beautiful."

A Latin beauty in her own right had come up behind him while he was admiring the poster. She leaned nonchalantly against the jukebox as she scrolled through the selections. She chose three Selena songs and dropped a dollar's worth of quarters into the machine.

Nouri eyed the young woman as "Como La Flor," Selena's signature song, filled the room. Several couples left their tables and began an impromptu *cumbia*, swaying to the pulsating rhythm of the song. Knowing something about the singer from his former girlfriend's interest, on an impulse he decided to play it up.

"She was from around here, right?" Nouri eyed the young woman, who had her hands on her hips and, with eyes closed and lips slightly parted, was mouthing the words to the song as she swayed to the beat.

"Not Brownsville. Closer to Houston. A small town called Lake Jackson. What's your name? I haven't seen you in here before."

"David. David Foster. I just got in a couple of days ago."

"Where you from?" She turned to face him and her face could not mask her attraction.

"Belgium."

Nouri appraised the woman standing next to him. She was in her late twenties, slim with small, round breasts and dark hair framing an angular yet decidedly soft, vulnerable face.

"So they listen to Selena in Belgium?"

"She was international. I remember when she was planning her Crossover Tour in 1995. She was supposed to do some concerts in Europe, but then she was killed. Did you see her movie? The one Jennifer Lopez did?"

"Selena Forever?"

"Yeah." Nouri decided to give it a shot. If it didn't work out at least they had the Selena thing to talk about. "Can I buy you a drink?"

The girl appraised him briefly and then flashed a smile. "Why not? My name's Martina."

They sat at the bar, and Nouri ordered a wine cooler for the girl and a draft beer for himself. The sallow-faced bartender wore a pencil-thin mustache and had slick black hair combed over to the side. He gave Nouri a wary look and then turned his attention to Martina.

"What's up?" There was an almost imperceptible tilt of the head in Nouri's direction.

Martina shrugged, and lifted her chin in a defiant gesture.

He sighed and turned to fill their drink order.

"My brother, Carlos" she confided. "He's very protective."

Carlos wiped the bar with a cloth, deposited two coasters in front of them and served their drinks. He fixed his gaze on Nouri for a moment without saying anything, and then walked away to serve another customer.

"Brothers can be like that."

"Carlos more than others. He's been looking after me ever since..." Martina's voice caught, but then she continued. "Ever since our parents were killed in a crash when I was in middle school."

"I'm sorry."

"No, it was many years ago." She clasped her drink in her hands. "My father was a baseball player. He played in the Mexican League."

"Is that like the Majors?"

"No, it's the Minors. Triple A. He played for the Broncos de Reynosa. Shortstop. Anyway, he and my mom were driving back from a home game late at night and a drunk driver hit their car. They were both killed instantly." Her hands gripped the wine glass.

"His big dream was to play in the Major Leagues here in the U.S., but he never got called up. His biggest moment was in 1969, when the Broncos defeated the Sultanes de Monterrey in the championship game. There." Martina pointed to a yellowing newspaper clipping behind the cash register.

Titled "Broncos Shock Sultanes," the clipping went on to describe an epic contest at Adolfo Lopez Mateos Stadium in 1969.

"Monterrey has the biggest stadium in the league. I think it seats 25,000 but the Broncos' stadium can only handle 7,000. Everyone said it was such a big deal for them to win at home that night. That was ten years before I was even born." Martina's voice trailed off as she reminisced.

As she stared off, Nouri turned his attention to the two hookers working the bar a few feet from where they were seated. They were both plump, overly made-up with big hair. These working girls were wearing gaudy polyester dresses cut mid-thigh, nylons long past their useful life, and scuffed black high heels. Fake costume jewelry rounded

out their get-up. One of the women had her hand on a customer's thigh, rubbing it as she persuaded him to buy her
a drink.

Nouri never paid for sex. He was easy on the eyes and he
knew it. Women were naturally attracted to him and readily
fell for his charms. However, once they sensed his indiffer-
ence and felt that dangerous edge rippling beneath the surface, they invariably had the opposite reaction. They were
repulsed, and couldn't wait to get away from him. Usually
he managed to get them into bed sometime between that
period of infatuation and the onset of revulsion.

The other slut was nibbling on her customer's ear. She
had a coquettish look on her face as she massaged his shoulders and pressed up against him. The object of her affec-
tions seemed oblivious to her charms. He was in a heated
discussion with the man seated next to him about the merits
of showing one of his heifers at next spring's Rio Grande
Valley Livestock Show.

"David, you want to get out of here?"

Shifting his attention from the drama unfolding beside
him, Nouri saw Martina observing him with a slight pout on
her lips. She raised an eyebrow to accentuate her question.

"Sure. Where to?"

"For a ride."

Nouri paid their bill. Carlos seemed about to say something to him but thought better of it. He thrust the change
at Nouri and turned away from them as they walked outside. They walked the short distance to Nouri's car where
Martina gave him directions to Texas 48 East in the direction
of South Padre Island.

Nouri relaxed as they drove away from the city. He
wasn't sure what she had in mind, but found himself tingling in anticipation. Forty-five minutes later they entered
the park. There was about an hour of daylight left and Nouri
could see vast tidal flats stretching out before him and to the
south, sand beaches and then, dunes.

It was a weekday, and at this hour the beach was deserted. They locked the car and walked down to the beach,

pulling off their shoes and socks as they walked parallel to the tidal flats.

"Padre Island is a barrier island. All that out there that you can see is the Gulf of Mexico. This shoreline goes all the way from Closed Beach to the Mansfield Channel." When they reached the seclusion of the dunes about three hundred yards away, Martina dropped her shoes and socks, turned and challenged him, "Race you!"

She began to pull off her clothing, hesitating momentarily before running down to the water's edge. She paused briefly, where the waves crashed into the shore, testing the water before plunging in.

Nouri watched as her lissome body disappeared into the waves. His heart raced as he shed his clothes and raced into the water. He had always been under the impression that Latina girls were ultra-conservative and had been wondering how he was going to score. But this one seemed completely uninhibited.

Turning back towards the shore she ducked her head into the spray and emerged five feet in front of him, water streaming over her, hair clinging to her face. As she paddled up to him she straightened and then wrapped herself around his waist, clinging to him as he rocked in waist-high water. She was evenly tanned, almost a cinnamon hue, and Nouri bent to take the bud of a nipple in his mouth and tease it with his tongue.

She groaned and held him tight. Her tongue flicked in his ear and Nouri felt himself harden. They stood like that for several minutes, waves buffeting them, and then he slid into her, allowing the waves to rock them back and forth. It was as though Mother Nature was having an orgasm and they were caught up in its embrace. Wave after wave buffeted them as they climaxed, leaving them gasping. Nouri released her and they floated there side by side on their backs until they had recovered. And then they did it again.

Later, after they had dressed, they strolled back to the car. It was dusk and they were each lost in their own thoughts as Nouri navigated through what passed for Brownsville's rush hour. He wondered if saying goodbye would be awkward, but, as it turned out, it wasn't.

Martina gave him directions to a modest ranch in a development off of Clubhouse Drive. As he pulled up she leaned over and kissed him lightly on the lips. "I'm at the bar some afternoons, if you're going to be in town for a while." She gave him an impish look. "I wouldn't say no if you want to go for a ride again." And with that she was gone.

Nouri watched her as she let herself into the house and then pulled away. He was relieved that she hadn't been possessive. He doubted that he would see her again. He expected to be out of Brownsville before long.

He didn't have long to wait. There was a message from Colonel Samadi waiting for him when he got back to the apartment. He read it twice and then looked off in the distance. Rising from the couch he walked into the bedroom and began to pack. No sense hanging around. It was going to be a long drive to Boston.

Chapter 30

Nouri merged onto US 91 North just south of Victoria. Texas was a big frigging state, he complained to himself as he hit the cruise control. He looked at the clock illuminated on the dashboard; it was just after midnight. He calculated that at this rate it would take him just over thirty-three hours straight driving time to Boston.

The temptation was to open the Chrysler up and let it rip but the last thing he needed was to be pulled over for speeding. No, he was going to stay below the radar. Sixty-five to seventy mph might not be sexy but it sure as hell beat a brush with law enforcement.

It hadn't taken him long to pack the car and leave Brownsville in his rear view mirror. He toyed with the notion of driving straight through, but he didn't want to get to Boston all sleep deprived and edgy. He'd pace himself. Two, three days at most.

His mind wandered to Azar. Samadi's message hadn't said anything about her. It was just bad luck that she had walked into that ambush alone. At least if there had been two of them they could have made it a contest. He wondered how many attackers there had been. One? Two? Possibly more.

From what he'd observed over the past month, Azar was one tough broad. No way she went down without a fight. The way she had taken out that drug dealer – her first kill. She'd been stone cold.

He tried to envision her lying there comatose in the Caracas hospital. With no next of kin to look after her, he wasn't optimistic about the kind of medical attention she'd get.

He'd read somewhere that Venezuela was desperate for qualified medical personnel. The government counted on Cuba to send qualified doctors, nurses and technicians to the petroleum behemoth to meet its health care needs. Their Doctors for Oil program had unleashed a backlash amongst *Cubanos* because of the medical shortfall the deal had spawned on the communist island. Aging revolutionaries like Fidel could get the care they needed, but it was the everyday people, the *campesinos,* who had no access to basic medical treatment.

Nouri yawned. There was a lot of truck traffic, even at this hour. He took the exit toward Beaumont East and then merged onto I-10. He wanted to get through Houston before daylight and calculated that he had another three hours to the Louisiana border. He turned the radio on and fixed his eyes on the road ahead.

Three and a half hours later he crossed the Louisiana state line. It was three-thirty in the morning. His ears perked up as a public service announcement for Acadia Parish Sheriff's Office came on the radio.

"The Acadia Parish Sheriff's office is investigating the theft of a bass boat that was abandoned on I-10 east of Crowley. It is believed that the boat was stolen while the owner went for a spare tire for the trailer. The boat is a 2008 Skeeter ZX 190 and was last seen Monday evening at around ten-thirty p.m.

"If you have any information regarding the whereabouts of this missing boat, please contact the tip line at 752-TIPS. All callers will remain anonymous and the owner is offering a $500 reward for the safe return of his boat."

Nouri clucked his tongue. Damn if crime wasn't alive and well right here in Acadia Parish. Still, he needed to pay attention. The last thing he wanted right now was for some nosy hick sheriff to go after his out-of-state plate. He decided to call it a night.

He exited onto Route 35 South in search of a place to bed down. His GPS showed a Best Western on North Polk Street.

The yawning Cajun receptionist barely acknowledged him as he checked in.

"You're in room 216, Mr. Foster. That'll be $77 plus tax."

Nouri was amused by the bold plaque on the wall behind the front desk. It was inscribed "Rayne, Louisiana – Frog Capital of the World."

"What's with the frogs?" he asked.

The old-timer gave him a disdainful look from behind smudged bifocals, but then perked up. "You're not from around these parts, are you?"

"No. I'm from Europe."

"That distinction, Frog Capital, goes back a long ways. Eighteen-hundreds, I'd guess. Back in the day, Rayne had this famous chef named Donat Pucheau who started selling his bullfrogs to Cajun restaurants in New Orleans. Well, these French fellers got wind of it and they set up an export business, shipping our frogs all over the country and even to France.

"Yep, the Weill brothers made Rayne and frogs synonymous." He scratched behind his ear, and then handed Nouri the room key.

"Are you going to be around tomorrow, Mr. Foster?"

"No, I'll be leaving mid-morning. Just passing through."

"If you have time, go on down to the historic district. There's a whole bunch of murals down there done by local artists. Mighty rare if I say so myself."

"Let me guess. There's a frog theme to this?"

"Oh, yes. There's frogs painted on everything. Trees, walls, buildings. Too bad you won't be here next month. We have our annual Frog Festival in November."

"Frog Festival?" Nouri couldn't believe his ears, but the old duffer had suddenly become animated.

"Yep. We got frog jumping and a frog derby. There's a carnival for the kids, and all kinds of things. Hell, one year we even had Percy Sledge down here giving us some soul." He started humming the R&B classic "When a Man Loves a Woman."

Nouri thanked the old coot for the information but rebuffed his offer to carry his bag. Five minutes later he was in his room. As soon as his head hit the pillow he was asleep.

He awoke at nine o'clock, groggy but somewhat re-freshed. After a hot shower he was feeling better but de-cided to skip breakfast and instead take a late lunch break on the road.

The monotony of driving gave him time to plan for his Boston arrival. He ticked off the names on the highway signs as he followed the interstate east and then north – Lafayette, Hattiesburg, Hammond, Gadsden, Chattanooga and Knoxville.

He'd stopped in Moselle, Mississippi, at one-thirty for lunch. His GPS guided him to a catfish camp where he tried the local fare – farm-raised catfish with a creamy crawfish sauce. It was rich but he was ravenous and so he scarfed it down.

As he looked around the restaurant he realized that something had been gnawing at him and then he realized what it was. Fully one-quarter of the people seated around him were obese. He didn't mean just a little bit overweight, but huge. He pushed the rest of his lunch away as he looked around. All that fried food clogging up their arteries. No wonder Mississippi had come in first in the country in a na-tionwide poll on obesity. I mean, we're talking doublewides, he calculated.

He was on the road again by two-thirty. He drove until ten o'clock when he spotted a sign for Waynesboro, Virginia. After he had checked into the Holiday Inn Express, he rode the elevator up to the third floor and walked down the hall to his room.

He shed his clothes and tumbled into bed. He was phys-ically tired but his mind was razor sharp. He ticked through his checklist of details for tomorrow. He wanted to be on the road early, but not too early. Thankfully, he didn't have to drive into Boston itself. He was headed for Bridgewater, a university town thirty miles south of the city. He calculated that he had about 600 miles to cover, ten hours at the most. When sleep finally came it enveloped him.

The trip to Bridgewater the following day was unevent-ful except for a near accident on the New Jersey Turnpike.

A tractor-trailer jack-knifed in the lane to his right as he was passing on the left. He sensed the situation developing and had the presence of mind and quick reactions to gun the V-6 and speed past the rig before it started rolling across the median strip, coming to rest just short of west-bound traffic.

Nouri eased back into the right lane and checked his rear view mirror. The wreck was receding from his view, but from what he had seen, it would take a miracle for the driver to have survived.

He stopped in Providence to eat and scout out a location to stash his car. He decided on the Airport Valet on Post Road about a half mile from the airport. After locking the vehicle he took the shuttle to the departure area and took a cab to the Emerald Square Mall in North Attleboro. He cruised the mall before calling another cab to drive the final stretch to Bridgewater.

It was ten o'clock when his cab took exit 6A off of I-95 onto I-495 south in the direction of Cape Cod. After about fifteen minutes the cab turned onto MA-24 North towards Boston and minutes later merged onto East Pleasant Street. Nouri directed the driver to drop him off at the Campus Plaza Shopping Center, even though it was getting late and in all likelihood nothing would be open.

He began walking north on Broad Street. Moments later he passed the entrance to the Portuguese Holy Ghost Society and turned into the parking lot, walking with purpose towards a wooded area west of the property. He planned to hunker down in the woods until midnight. His target was a single-family house on Ball Avenue 400 feet south of his current location. The house backed onto the woods, and would allow a stealthy approach.

Nouri settled on the ground, his back up against the trunk of a giant maple tree, facing the target. His mind was racing as he went over the plan. He had a fairly good idea of what to expect, but he had not seen a layout of the property, so it could be touch and go. It was quiet now, except for the occasional bark of a dog, and the wind rustling the few remaining leaves clinging to the otherwise bare branches.

Traffic on Broad Street had died down, except for the occasional sound of tires humming on pavement and the flash of headlights.

He awoke with a start. Checking his watch he saw that it was already one o'clock. He must have dozed off. He stood up, stretched and then, cat-like, began moving towards Ball Avenue.

Minutes later he was at the rear of the property. He waited there in the dark for fifteen minutes, searching for signs of life. There were no exterior lights on, but he could see a dim, bluish hue emanating from a room at the front of the house. Other than that it was quiet. He held his breath as he hurried across the open space of the back yard and up to the rear door. He had been worried about motion sensor lights but there were none.

It only took him five minutes to crack the lock. It was a single-cylinder deadbolt. He held his breath as the cylinder turned and he opened the door. He'd calculated that there would be no alarm system and he had been right. He knew that there would be no dog.

He found himself in a mudroom off the kitchen. Moving soundlessly into the hallway he edged closer to the source of light. It was a television and the figure reclining before it was motionless. Creeping up behind the chair he paused and looked down with no feeling. As he edged around the chair for a better position, a floorboard creaked and the figure in the chair fidgeted.

Nouri positioned himself in front of his target, and the man's eyes flashed open. A look of confusion and then recognition set in as his mouth opened.

Nouri launched a blow to the man's temple, fist clenched and hips swiveling like a golfer's to generate the most power. The man's head snapped back and he blacked out. He lay there, slumped to one side.

Moving without haste, Nouri removed the plastic ties he had purchased from his bag and cuffed his victim's hands and feet together and then, grunting, lugged him up the stairs, checking two rooms before finding the master bedroom. He deposited the man on the bed and secured him so that he could not get up.

Moments later, as he was rummaging through the closet, Nouri heard a groaning sound come from the bed. Sticking his head out he waited until the man's eyes opened. His victim struggled to get out of the bed but then must have realized that he had been immobilized. Swiveling his head, he caught sight of Nouri, who had walked from the closet to the side of the bed.

Nouri had something in his hand, and as the man struggled to focus, Nouri held it up for him to see.

"I think I look good in blue, don't you?" In his hand was a Boston Police Department uniform.

"Nouri!"

"Armeen."

Chapter 31

The weather had turned. Logan looked at the Weather Channel app on his smart phone and noted that it had dropped to thirty-five degrees overnight and was supposed to rain all day. He'd have to scratch his run with Ryan. They'd established a Saturday morning ritual of running in different parts of the city. It had been his turn to design the route for today. He'd scouted out the Emerald Necklace, a smattering of parks around the city taking them along the Riverway Footpath to Jamaica Pond, a loop around the Arnold Arboretum and back to the Fenway T stop.

Normally a little rain and cold wouldn't bother him, but ever since his knee injury, he was cautious about running on slippery surfaces. It just wasn't worth taking the risk that he would fall.

Cooper was still sleeping and Zahir was breathing softly next to him. She must have sensed him looking at her because her eyes fluttered open and she sat up.

"What?" She reached up to touch his cheek.

"I love you. I was just thinking how lucky I am." He caught her hand and brought it to his lips. "I'll put the coffee on. It's raining so I'm going to cancel my run with Ryan. He'll probably think I'm a wuss."

"He knows you can't run in the rain. Why don't you ask them if they want to do something today? If it's going to be like this all day we could go over to the Sackler. Their photo exhibit on the Pahlavi family begins Monday, but I can get us in today."

"Is that the one you donated some of your family pictures to?"

"Loaned. Yes."

Zahir's mother was Mohammad Reza Shah Pahlavi's niece. The Shah had died in 1980, just before Zahir was born. He was the last in a dynasty that had spanned only fifty-five years. His father, Reza Shah, had deposed Ahmad Shah Qajar, ending the 140-year reign of the Qajars in 1925. And he himself had been deposed by the Islamic cleric Ayatollah Ruholla Khomeini in 1979.

Logan got up to put the coffee on and Zahir trailed after him, pulling on a cotton robe to ward off the chill.

"Have you seen much of what they're exhibiting?"

"Some." She yawned and stretched to reach two mugs in the cupboard. "You know while you were in Spain, I had a long talk with my mother and got her to speak with the Sackler's lead for the exhibit, Spencer Pearson. They had a good conversation on the phone and he decided to send a curator down to see if they could use anything she had.

"It turns out to have been worth the effort. Her mother, my grandmother, was a real packrat and something of an amateur historian. She had hundreds of family photos that have never been seen by the public. Some of them I don't ever remember seeing."

"How far back do they go?"

"I think she had some from before Reza Shah became Shah."

The coffee pot beeped and Zahir poured them two cups. They moved into the living room and sat down, feet propped up on the coffee table. Zahir had a faraway look on her face.

"I hope people enjoy the exhibit. So much of the media attention on Iranian history nowadays focuses on the post-1979 revolution era. Khomeini and the strict Islamists. I just don't know if things will ever be normal there again." She sighed, looking off in the distance.

Logan gave her a hug. She rested her head on his shoulder for a moment but then jumped up when Cooper's cries erupted over the baby monitor.

While Zahir was changing Cooper's diaper, Logan called Ryan to cancel their run and to see if he and Millie were interested in going to the Sackler.

"What time are you thinking of going?" Ryan asked.

"I think Zahir said that they open at ten o'clock today. We should have Cooper ready in an hour, so do you just want to meet over there at ten?"

"That's fine. The Sackler's still on Broadway, right?"

"Yeah, 485. I know they've been renovating the museum property on Quincy Street but I don't think that impacted the Sackler."

Later that morning, the Alexanders joined Millie and Ryan at the museum. Zahir had phoned Spencer Pearson, who had arranged passes for the four of them. He met them at the entrance to the exhibit.

"Zahir, so nice to see you again. Thanks again for introducing me to your mother. She was a gold mine, especially with some of these earlier photos of Reza Shah."

Zahir introduced Logan, Millie and Ryan. Looking over Spencer's shoulder she could see the exhibit was nearing completion.

Stepping into the gallery was like being transported back to another era. Early photos of a young Reza Pahlavi showed him in his birthplace, the village of Alalsht in northeast Iran. In his youth, when he was still known as Reza Khan, the future Shah went to live with an uncle in Tehran after his father unexpectedly passed away. Photos from that period showed a slender, serious, dark-haired young man. Later he moved in with a family friend who was an officer in the Persian military.

Reza must have been influenced by his surroundings, enlisting in the Cossacks at the early age of sixteen. He became a gunnery sergeant in the Iranian Army, and eventually rose to the rank of brigadier general. In the 1920s, right after the Russian Revolution, he was promoted to general, where he made a name for himself as a result of his heroics on the battlefield.

After the revolution, the British attacked the Bolsheviks from inside Iran's border, forcing them to retaliate by annexing some of Iran's northern territory. The Red Army enlisted Kurds, Azerbaijanis and Armenians to throw their support behind them and the situation began to deteriorate all over Iran.

At that time Reza was Commander of the Iranian Army and Minister of War. He spent the next two years fighting those people who were trying to destroy Iran. By 1923, when things had settled down, he came back to Tehran and was named Prime Minister. Two years later the Majilis crowned him Shah.

A great number of the photos in the exhibit were new to Zahir, especially the earlier ones of her great-grand-uncle. The exhibit was arranged in chronological order and as they neared the very end she came upon a more recent family photo.

"Do you recognize everyone?" Logan asked coming up beside her. Cooper squirmed in his front pack and clutched at Zahir's hair, tugging on a strand.

"Pretty much." She scanned the picture and then stopped on the right- hand side. "Look! There's Mom!"

Logan peered at the photo. "She looks pregnant."

Zahir looked again and gasped. There was a very young child holding her mother's hand. And Mrs. Parandeh was definitely pregnant. "This picture must have been taken when she was pregnant with me!"

They all crowded around.

"That must have been right after my grand-uncle left Iran." Zahir seemed transfixed by the photograph. "Mom told me that he was here in the States for medical treatment in 1979, but just for a few months. The U.S. wouldn't let him stay, because his presence here created so much tension with Khomeini. Some say that's what got the students all fired up. Taking over the Embassy and holding all of our diplomats hostage."

As they walked towards the museum exit, Zahir poked her head into Pearson's office to thank him again for their passes and then rejoined everyone outside the Sackler. Later, over lunch, the conversation turned to developments in Hamid's murder investigation. Logan hadn't spoken with Millie or Ryan about his Caracas trip so he filled them in on his close encounter with the Unit 400 killer.

"We were right there. Two of the guys that went into Iran with me last year were there too. We actually saw Khorasani on the street, not far from this apartment he was renting. He was in a taxi with Ghabel's widow, Azar Ghabel."

"What are they doing in Venezuela? I mean, that's a long way from Spain." Millie offered to hold Cooper so that Zahir could eat her lunch.

"It's hard to say. I'm thinking that the Qods Force pulled him out of Spain because it was getting too hot. Who knows? Maybe they found out we'd been in his apartment. The timing is just too suspicious. Or it could be they're just branching out? Setting up an operational base in Caracas," he said.

"If their mission is to target U.S. and Israeli interests, they could do that from Venezuela and minimize any blowback because the Venezuelans would just look the other way."

Millie and Ryan were whispering to each other, and Logan had a feeling they'd heard enough about Venezuela for now. Millie handed Cooper off to Ryan, who bounced him on his knee and looked expectantly at his wife.

"We have an announcement to make." She gave her brother and Zahir a shy look. "Ryan and I are expecting."

Logan was about to take a bite out of his sandwich but put it back down on his plate. He looked back and forth between his sister and Ryan.

"When?"

"July."

They all started talking at once as Zahir leapt up from her seat to give Millie a hug. Logan reached over to clasp Ryan's hand as he grinned at his little sister.

"That's fantastic news, Mills. Congratulations."

Cooper swiveled his head around and reached for Logan. As he took the baby from Ryan's hands he couldn't stop beaming.

"Hear that, big guy? You're going to be a cousin."

Cooper's eyes got big, as though he understood what Logan had said, and then he turned to look out towards the window next to their table. Logan followed his gaze and his heart stopped momentarily. Nouri Khorasani stood outside the window looking in at them.

He was about to hand Cooper to Zahir when he caught himself and realized that it was Police Officer Armeen Khorasani who held his gaze. He acknowledged the BPD rookie, who in turn gave him a wave of recognition and turned away.

Ryan and Millie were transfixed, following Khorasani's receding back as he walked down the sidewalk. Millie exhaled.

"That guy gives me the creeps. I know it's wrong. It's not his fault his brother's a killer. But he looks just like him. How could two brothers be so different?"

Ryan rubbed the knuckles on his right hand. "I was about ready to deck the bastard after what happened at Hamid's apartment."

Logan grinned at his brother-in-law as the tension subsided. "Easy, big boy. Even if he is just a rookie for the BPD, he could probably eat you for lunch."

"Hey!" Ryan protested as they all started laughing.

Logan's cell phone rang. Looking at the caller ID he saw that it was from Detective Breen.

Getting up from the table, he mouthed Breen's name and took the call in a hallway leading to the kitchen and restrooms.

"Hey, Peter, how've you been?"

"Good. It's been awhile since we talked. We just had an interesting development and I wanted to fill you in."

"What's going on?"

"Remember, last time we talked, we had found out that Khorasani had traveled to Caracas and Mexico City on a fake Costa Rican identity, right?

"Yeah. Did the Mexicans come through for you?"

"No. Not the Mexicans. The CIA."

"What!" Logan's ears pricked at the mention of the agency.

"Yeah. Those guys are good. It seems that a couple of weeks ago the station in Brussels got a call from their

Belgian State Security counterparts about the theft of a batch of Belgian tourist passports from a diplomatic pouch.

"Anyway, the Belgians had done their own internal investigation and figured out that it was probably the Iranians who pulled it off."

Logan's pulse quickened. "When did they tell CIA about this?"

"Just last week. But here's where it gets interesting. Some bright analyst got the numbers of all those passports just the other day and put them on a watchlist. One of them just came up yesterday."

"Let me guess. Mexico City."

"No. Worse yet. Brownsville, Texas. Khorasani crossed from Matamoros, Mexico, into Brownsville four days ago. They faxed us the photo page of the passport. No question. It's Khorasani. He's traveling under the alias David Foster. We've got an APB out and the passport's been watchlisted. He'll have an easier time sticking a wet noodle up a tiger's ass than moving around without our knowing it."

"How did he get through Brownsville if he was watchlisted?"

"Lucky timing. If he'd made the border crossing a couple of days later we would have nailed him. He wasn't in the system until after he had already entered the country. Once the data was entered it flagged his arrival."

Logan and Breen talked for a couple more minutes. After he hung up he made his way back to his table. Breen's revelation that Nouri Khorasani was back in the U.S. was troubling. What the hell was the Qods Force killer up to?

Chapter 32

"It's true, isn't it? You're the one who killed Hamid Al Subaie."

Armeen Khorasani had spat out the accusation earlier this morning as he stared with contempt at his twin brother. He was still trussed up like some common thief, lying in his own bedroom, head throbbing from the blow that Nouri had dealt him. That sucker punch the night before had cleaned his clock.

Looking out the bedroom window he could tell from the lengthening shadows that it was afternoon. His head ached, making it difficult to focus on the events of the night before. He remembered falling asleep in front of the TV and the next thing he knew he had sensed an intruder in the house. He'd started to get up to investigate and that's when the lights had gone out.

When he'd come to, he thought he was hallucinating. The brother who had vanished without a word five years ago had attacked him in his own home, hog-tied him and was there rummaging through his closet. Nouri had remained tight-lipped when Armeen had tried to question him and by mid-morning he had donned one of the starched blue police uniforms from the closet, taken his wallet and police revolver from the bureau and left the house.

Armeen had heard the car pull out of the garage. He'd struggled to free himself, but the restraints were cinched tight. He'd fallen into a restless sleep and throughout the morning had repeatedly awakened only to doze off again.

Now, hours later, Nouri was back, standing beside the bed. Craning his head to one side Armeen could see from the alarm clock on his night table that it was five-thirty in the afternoon.

He looked back at his brother. "What happened to you, Nouri? Where the fuck have you been for the last five years? What are you doing here?"

"Living large, Armeen. Living large." Nouri yawned, sat down on the edge of the bed and stared down at his brother. He had wondered how he would feel when this moment came. It didn't really surprise him that he felt very little. Residual anger was the thought that came to mind. For him, Armeen posed an immediate problem he had to solve. Not an insurmountable one, but a problem nonetheless.

"I want you to listen very carefully, Armeen. I have some unfinished business to take care of. I expect it'll take a couple of days. No more than three. Unfortunately for you, you'll have to remain here, tied up for the duration. When I leave I'll let someone know where you are."

"You can't get away with this. People will be looking for me."

"Your precinct captain's secretary was very understanding when I called to report the unexpected demise of our dearly beloved grandfather. She gave me three days of bereavement leave. No one will be looking for you."

Armeen struggled against his bonds. "Why are you here? Everyone's looking for you. The department, Homeland Security, INTERPOL, CIA. You can't get away with this."

Nouri stood up and gave him a playful punch on the shoulder. "Your problem, Armeen, is that you never had any imagination. Of course they'll be looking for me. But they won't be looking for you, will they?"

He went down to the kitchen and rummaged through the refrigerator where he found a six-pack of Sam Adams Octoberfest. It took him a little longer to find a bottle opener. He missed the local microbrew; American craft beers weren't easy to find in Spain. He popped the top and took a long swig, savoring the rich malty flavor.

With a bottle in one hand and the six-pack in the other, he wandered into the living room, plunked himself down in an easy chair and powered up his laptop. He was expecting another message from Colonel Samadi. The one he had received earlier in the day had taken him by surprise. It was an update on the Qods Force investigation into the Bandar Deylam attack.

Tehran had been working the Bandar Deylam case at a feverish pitch ever since their source in Kuwaiti intelligence had informed them that Hamid Al Subaie was the Kuwaiti Intel officer who had infiltrated the IED training camp weeks before it was destroyed. The one where Azar's husband, Colonel Ghabel, had subsequently been killed.

In the wake of the Bandar Deylam attack, every Qods Force officer abroad had been put on notice to hunt down the perpetrators. The Qods Force chief in Kuwait City, Major Esfahani, had been particularly diligent. Since he'd arrived there three years ago, very little that went on escaped his attention. It was just a matter of good instincts, some sleuthing and a little bit of luck that he had come up with the name Logan Alexander.

His spotter at Kuwait International Airport had seen the foreigner met by the car service the Kuwaiti Intelligence and Security Service routinely used to shuttle foreign visitors around the city. He had slipped the driver some *baksheesh* when he saw him later in the day to tell him where he had dropped the man off.

After that it was a simple matter to grease the palms of the clerk at the JW Marriott and learn the name of the traveler, which he passed on that night in his report to Major Esfahani. Additional details included a description of Alexander, noting his athletic build and military bearing. He concluded his write-up by advising that Alexander had been entertained in a private dining room at the Crowne Plaza Hotel that same evening by billionaire tycoon Nayef Al Subaie. Interestingly, Al Subaie's uncle Ali, and Thamir Alghanim, the director of operations for Kuwait's Intelligence and Security Service, had also been in attendance.

Major Esfahani had dutifully filed his report, and it had lain gathering dust on someone's desk at Qods Force headquarters until much later an analyst had linked the names Logan Alexander and Logan Campbell.

That connection was made almost a year later after two Qods Force assets in Venezuela working on a unilateral surveillance team told their case officer that they had been tasked to surveil an Iranian target. Their handler, a Qods Force captain known to them as *Zhubin*, meaning short spear, because, frankly, he had a puny dick, became suspicious and tasked them to find out who was behind it. They had followed up and had learned from their boss, former Caracas Police Force captain, Pedro Martinez, that a Canadian by the name of Logan Campbell had commissioned the surveillance.

This report had set off alarm bells in Tehran and led to an all-out effort to figure out why a Canadian named Logan Campbell was interested in Nouri Khorasani. It took a week, but employing a new software program that the Qods Force had stolen from the Russians, Tehran had used transactional analysis to link Logan Alexander's travel with that of Logan Campbell, who had traveled from Europe to Kuwait weeks before the attack on Bandar Deylam. The passport pictures told them everything they needed to know. Logan Alexander and Logan Campbell were one and the same.

The pictures also satisfied a doubt that had been nagging at him for some time. The guy outside Macello and the one at the airport in Madrid were also same. Logan Alexander. And how strange was it for him to run into him in Cambridge today. He'd seen the reaction on Alexander's face. But then Alexander had been sucked in by the fiction that he was Armeen, and had waved.

Nouri opened up the message and began to read.

"Greetings. You have done well, but drastic measures must be taken if you are to succeed. We have just learned that the Belgians have watchlisted the numbers from the stolen passports with international law enforcement and intelligence organizations. Although we have no definitive proof, it is likely that your David Foster persona has been compromised."

Nouri massaged his temples. This couldn't be happening again. Three identities gone in a poof within the last six weeks. What did Tehran have in store for him now? He turned his attention back to Samadi's note.

"The consensus here is that your ability to assume your twin brother's persona offers a unique opportunity for us to get close to the serpent and cut off its head. Of course, certain sacrifices must be made, but we are confident that you will manage this as you have every other operation you have undertaken. We have every confidence in you.

"Azar has returned home. Our chief in Caracas got her onto a special medical flight and she is now resting at Shiraz Central Hospital. Her mother lives nearby and is looking after her. She remains in a coma, but she is young and the prognosis for her recovery is favorable."

Samadi went on to provide the location of an emergency meeting site near Boston where he would be picked up if all hell broke loose and they had to get him out of the US.

"The Republic is counting on you."

Nouri knew what he had to do. As he rose from the chair he had a flashback to his childhood. He and Armeen were walking home from middle school and a gang of boys was taunting him over something he had said earlier in the day. They were pelting him with snowballs, and one had caught him on the side of the head. He had begun to run, but he slipped on the ice and fell. As he looked back at the boys he could see that Armeen had joined them and was throwing snowballs too. They were running toward him.

Nouri crept up the stairs. He paused outside of Armeen's bedroom. It was quiet inside. Only the sound of Armeen's raspy breathing punctuated by an occasional snore broke the silence. Nouri moved to the side of the bed and looked down at his brother. It was eerie, almost as if he were gazing down at himself. He stood there for a moment and then reached for a pillow. This would be quick.

Armeen's eyes flicked open and went wide with recognition and then fear. Then the pillow came down, and a hundred thousand million nerve cells began to flash a code red warning to millions of brain connectors that something was very wrong.

Nouri broke into a sweat as he forced the pillow down onto his brother's face. The fierce struggle went on for several minutes, with Armeen struggling against the restraints, arching his back and thrashing. And then it was finished.

Nouri looked down at his brother with no emotion on his face. He was breathing deeply from the exertion. He reached for Armeen's wrist and felt for a pulse. It was limp and warm, but there was no sign of life. Armeen was dead. Nouri examined the body to see if the restraints had left any bruising. The ankles and wrists were slightly chafed, but not noticeably so. It was critical for the rest of his plan to succeed that Armeen's death appear to be accidental.

Nouri was surprised to see that it was already six-thirty. He removed the restraints and stripped the body. He knew that he had several hours before rigor mortis began to set in but the sooner he got this done the better off he would be.

After he had dressed the corpse in David Foster's clothing he placed Foster's Belgian passport and wallet in Armeen's pockets. Anything that would link back to Nouri Khorasani or David Foster would have to go.

Nouri waited until it was dark and then hefted Armeen's body, dragging it down the stairs, through the house and out into the garage. He reached up to turn on the light and struggled as he placed the body into the trunk of the car.

Returning to the house, he searched for any evidence that Nouri Khorasani or David Foster had been there. The only remaining link was his laptop, and its complex software made it virtually impossible for anyone without the right sequence of passwords to break into the covert communications program.

Returning downstairs, Nouri pressed the garage door opener just outside the kitchen door and cringed at the racket the door made as it yawned open. The clatter reverberated through the night. He paused behind the car, holding his breath as he looked out towards the street, but all was quiet.

Sliding into the driver's seat he started the engine and backed out of the garage, turning left on Crapo Street and then south on North Broad. He followed the route he had taken the night before, staying on I-95 until he saw the signs for North Attleboro. Exiting the highway he drove for several minutes and then parked the car in a dark residential neighborhood. From there he caught a cab near the Emerald Square Mall to the airport valet parking lot on Post Road, where he had left the rental car.

After retrieving the rental, Nouri re-traced his route back to North Attleboro. Glancing at the dashboard clock he was surprised to see that it was already ten-thirty. He searched for signs of life in the neighborhood, but all was quiet. He eased the Buick up behind Armeen's car and turned off the lights.

Rigor mortis was beginning to set in. Nouri wrestled his brother's body out of the trunk, nearly dropping it in his haste. He lost no time making the transfer into the Buick's trunk. There could be no explaining what he was doing if someone were to come along and question him. Armeen didn't look drunk or ill. He looked dead. Nouri breathed easier once he had deposited the body inside and closed the lid.

He had scouted a location on a satellite picture from Google Earth that was not too far from North Attleboro. Getting onto State Route 44, Nouri navigated the sedan east to where Route 44 dumped into Plymouth. From there he turned north on Route 3 and after a couple of miles merged onto Route 3-A, taking him into the affluent Boston suburb of Duxbury.

He almost missed his turn onto Alden, which would take him over to St. George and Powder Point Avenue. His destination was Powder Point Bridge, which spanned the Back River and led over to Duxbury Beach Park. The bridge had once held the distinction in the *Guinness Book of World Records* of being the oldest and longest wooden bridge in the world.

Nouri drove onto the trestle. He had decided to go no more than 100 yards because it was essential to his plan's success that he disappear from the scene before anyone

260

discovered what had happened. This part would be tricky. He checked his rear view mirror one more time, and saw that all was quiet. He found his target on the bridge and rammed the vehicle into the wooden slats to the point where the car was barely stable.

He tested the car's stability as he opened the door and stepped out onto the road. Hurrying to the rear he kept an eye out for traffic as he eased the body out of the trunk. Lugging the dead weight to the front of the car, Nouri panted as he struggled to prop the body up in the driver's seat, and buckle the seatbelt.

Slamming the door, he strode back to the rear of the vehicle and began pushing. He grunted as he dug his shoulder into it, but the car remained immobile.

"Damn," he cursed as it dawned on him that he'd forgotten to release the emergency brake. He returned to the driver's side and eased off the brake. He had to leap backwards as the vehicle began to slide sideways, and then, as it gathered momentum, tilted and plunged into the dark water below.

There was a whoosh as water sprayed against the night. He watched as the car bobbled and then began to sink.

"Goodnight, Armeen. Goodnight, Nouri. Goodnight, David." He chuckled to himself as he turned away from his handiwork and began jogging back across the bridge. He had work to do.

Chapter 33

"The Old Man kept at his court such boys of twelve years old as seemed to him destined to become courageous men. When the Old Man sent them into the garden in groups of four, ten or twenty, he gave them hashish to drink. They slept for three days, then they were carried sleeping into the garden where he had them awakened.

"When these young men woke, and found themselves in the garden with all these marvelous things, they truly believed themselves to be in paradise. And these damsels were always with them in songs and great entertainments; they received everything they asked for, so that they would never have left that garden of their own will.

"And when the Old Man wished to kill someone, he would take him and say: 'Go and do this thing. I do this because I want to make you return to paradise.' And the assassins go and perform the deed willingly."

Logan closed *The Travels of Marco Polo* and set the book down beside him. He sipped his scotch on the rocks and stared off into space. He had picked up the book written by the famous Venetian explorer and merchant because it contained one of the first western accounts of the Persian Hashashin. He thought that it might give him some early insights into what made these guys tick.

Marco Polo had traveled throughout much of Asia from his home in Venice in the 13th century. In fact he, his father, Niccolò, and uncle Maffeo had spent many years in the service of the renowned Mongol ruler, Genghis Khan's grandson, Kublai Khan, who in his own right had become the powerful emperor of Cathay, latter day China.

Marco Polo had passed through Persia on his way to Cathay in 1271 and then had an opportunity to return there decades later in service to Kublai Khan. Towards the end of his time in the emperor's court, he was asked to accompany Kublai Khan's daughter, Princess Cocachin, to Persia where she was to marry the Persian monarch.

In 1291 Marco Polo set forth from Canton on the southern tip of present-day China, and began an arduous two-year voyage which would take the princess's fleet of fourteen ships west across the South China Sea, across the Indian Ocean, and north into the Arabian Sea where they would finally enter the Gulf of Oman, gateway to the Persian Gulf.

Their two-year voyage would take them through Sumatra, Sri Lanka and India. Logan knew there was some controversy about if and when Marco Polo had actually traveled to Alamut but he wasn't bothered by it. These events had taken place over seven hundred years ago.

Zahir came into the room and sat down opposite him.

"I just put Cooper down. I think he's out for the night. What are you reading?"

Logan picked up the book and handed it to her. "*The Travels of Marco Polo*. I just thought if I went back to Unit 400's roots, maybe I'd get some insights into what makes them tick. Why they do what they do."

Zahir thumbed through the book to the chapter on Marco Polo's trip to Alamut. She paused and looked up at him.

"Did you know you can find interactive maps on Google where you can re-trace the routes of famous explorers? They're set up with their routes, and famous sites along the way. You can even put it into three-dimensional mode and walk around old forts or historical sites just like the original explorers did."

"Let's check it out." Logan jumped up from his seat and walked over to the computer. He logged onto the My Reading Mapped website and entered "The Travels of Marco Polo." A series of interactive maps appeared. He read through them and saw that there were some interesting posts by different users of the website who had researched the various routes based upon Marco Polo's original text, but had drawn different conclusions about the accuracy of what he had written.

He looked up at Zahir. "You know, there are questions about these early reports. I mean, look at what Marco Polo wrote about giving hashish to the boys to drink. According to research, the Old Man was opposed to using hashish based upon his strict interpretation of the Koran's teachings. So it seems unlikely that he would have used any narcotic substances. If what Marco Polo wrote is true, that the boys were drugged, then the Old Man must not have known about it or he was a hypocrite.

"And some historians made the assumption that the word *Hashashin* comes from the word hashish and that it translates into the modern word 'assassin.' In reality, it comes from the name Hassan. It means the followers of Hassan. Hassan I Sabbah was the Ismaili Lord of Alamut. He was the Old Man."

Logan got up and walked over to the window. As he looked out at the night lights he spoke. "This is really just a roundabout way of trying to get into Nouri Khorasani's head. Do you remember when Iran was at war with Iraq, and the Iranians used child suicide bombers?"

Zahir went over to where he was standing and wrapped her arms around his waist, hugging him from behind. "Yes. They joined the Basij, which was a militia force. I remember that they used to wear these little gold keys on chains around their necks so that they would be able to open the gates of heaven when they died. One of my college professors estimated that 95,000 Iranian child soldiers were killed in the Iran-Iraq War."

Logan gasped at the size of the number. "I wonder if Khorasani was brainwashed. What's his little gold key? I can't think of anything that Iran could promise him that would make him take the path he's on. Was the U.S. so bad? Did his family reject him? Was he such a misfit that he found no redeeming value in calling himself an American? Is being a Unit 400 killer so attractive?" Logan shook his head in frustration.

"You know a lot of people have been looking at the whole issue of self-radicalizing jihadists. NYPD probably has the best-known program of any police department in the country. They set up an intelligence unit there after 9/11 to get a better handle on these threats, and that's one of the issues they've explored."

Logan turned to face Zahir and put his arms around her waist. He inhaled her scent and nuzzled her hair. "All of these guys seem to be searching for an ideology they can identify with. I know that there are jihadist recruiters looking for recruits in the mosques, on the Internet, and even on the Hajj. They prey on these people.

"Once they make that connection there's often a rapid shift in ideology. These new recruits tend to embrace these radical ideas. Then they end up on a path taking them towards some kind of lethal action."

"Another big motivator for these guys is this prevailing sense of injustice," Zahir said. "They themselves may not even be victims of any wrongdoing, but they make the case for social injustice or they personalize it by demonizing actions the West has allegedly taken against Muslims in places like Iraq and Afghanistan."

"Sort of a solidarity with the Muslim brothers?" Logan asked.

Zahir nodded in agreement. "Something like that."

Logan grew more serious. "I'm concerned about what Khorasani's up to. Simon's betrayal of Hamid to the Qods Force, Hamid's warning about Unit 400 just before Khorasani murdered him, and now all this activity from Khorasani in Spain and Venezuela and back here again has me worried. We need to find him before he does more harm."

Logan paused and then looked into Zahir's eyes. "I want you and Cooper to visit your mom and dad for a few days, maybe a week."

She started to protest, but Logan held up his hand. "I'm serious, sweetheart. We know this guy is serious and he's dangerous. I've never been big on sitting around waiting for something to happen. If he's back in the States because he has unfinished business, it has to be with us, or at least me. Simon must have somehow given me away to the Iranians too. I can't risk you and Cooper getting hurt."

Zahir gave him a plaintive look but didn't protest. She would fiercely protect Cooper from any danger, and she recognized that leaving Boston for a few days was probably the safest way of doing that.

"I can get someone to sub for me, so that shouldn't be a problem." She reached for his hand. "But, what about you? What if Khorasani comes looking for you?"

"I've already reached out to Norm Stoddard and Bruce Wellington. They get in tomorrow afternoon. If Nouri Khorasani comes to Boston looking for some action he's going to find it. It won't just be the three of us looking for him. He's pissed off a whole lot of people." Logan's mouth set in a tight line as he looked into Zahir's eyes.

"We're going to finish this. It ends here!"

Chapter 34

Logan had half an hour to kill between Zahir's departure for Washington and Stoddard and Wellington's arrival. He felt a sense of relief when she and Cooper boarded the Delta Shuttle. He would miss them, but he would never forgive himself if something were to happen to them with Khorasani on the loose.

She had held him tight before gathering her things and walking away. Turning once to gaze at him before going through security, she had placed her fingertips to her lips and blown him a kiss. Then she had done the same for Cooper. Logan smiled and waved, blowing a kiss back. The empty feeling he felt overpowered him, but it was fleeting. He couldn't afford to wallow in self-pity with so much to be done.

Stoddard's and Wellington's flights were scheduled to arrive within twenty minutes of each other. Stoddard's flight out of Harrisburg International had been on time but Wellington had texted him that his truck had blown a water pump on the way to Oklahoma City, where he was scheduled to fly out of Will Rogers World Airport. He had missed his flight but had managed to get on one leaving an hour later.

Will Rogers. Logan thought back to a childhood trip out west when he had first heard of the famous Sooner. Born into a Cherokee Nation family in the late 1800s, he had become a figure larger than life and become one of the most beloved folk heroes of all time. His claim that he had "never met a man he didn't like" touched a chord with people from all walks of life.

He had never met Nouri Khorasani, though. Logan scowled as he pictured the cold, expressionless face of the

Qods Force killer. Looking up from his reflections, he spotted Stoddard striding through baggage claim.

"Hey, Norm! Over here."

Norm saw him and waved.

Logan stuck his hand out and smiled. "Thanks for coming on such short notice."

Stoddard set his bag down and gripped Logan's hand. "I thought we'd seen the last of that little freak in Caracas. Now you're telling me he's here?"

"We don't know for sure that he's back in Boston, yet. But he definitely made it across the border from Matamoros less than a week ago. He's out there somewhere."

Logan filled Stoddard in on Wellington's delay and truck woes as they walked away from baggage claim. "There's a sports bar before you go through security upstairs. Want to grab a beer while we wait?"

"Sure, why not?"

The bar had an impressive selection of beers on tap. Stoddard ordered a Harpoon India Pale Ale and Logan asked for a Magic Hat. While waiting for their beers to arrive, Logan updated Stoddard on the most recent developments.

"Boston PD has an APB out on Khorasani. And so does the CIA, INTERPOL, the Spanish, the Mexicans. Fuck, everybody. Anyway, the lead detective on the case here is Peter Breen. He's been good about keeping me in the loop. I talked to him this morning. He said they missed Khorasani crossing the border by just a few days, because he's using a stolen Belgian passport that wasn't in the system when he entered the U.S. He's traveling under the alias David Foster, but the photo on the passport is Khorasani's.

"When the Belgians told CIA this week about a batch of tourist passports that had been stolen, they put the passport numbers onto their watchlist and got an immediate hit. They sent a FLASH message through the system warning everyone that someone had used one of the stolen passports. When Boston PD got a copy of the photo scan from Homeland Security, they ID'd Khorasani."

"Is he just hunkered down somewhere? With everybody looking for him you'd think he'd come up on someone's radar."

"Peter's pretty sure he's coming this way. Apparently he rented a car from Hertz in Brownsville, a Chrysler 300. And it looks like he stayed in a short-term rental apartment in Brownsville for several days."

"What the hell's he up to?"

"My guess is he was waiting for marching orders from his bosses. If the Iranians are plotting something, they probably had to adjust their timetable. Scramble around and get him out of Mexico. Anyway, he's being careful. The authorities have been able to track credit card purchases at a couple of hotels – one in Rayne, Louisiana, and another in Waynesboro, Virginia. He had to show ID in both those places when he checked in.

"He's also used a couple of ATMs, but it seems like his gas purchases must have been with cash. The trail goes cold after Waynesboro."

Logan's phone beeped. It was a text message from Wellington.

"Just landed."

Logan texted him back. "Meet you in baggage claim."

"That's Brucie. He just got in."

Ten minutes after they returned to baggage claim they saw him pushing through the crowd. He looked worn out from his travels.

"Sorry, guys," he said as he pulled up in front of them. "It may be time to get rid of that damn truck."

"What's your ride, Brucie?" Stoddard had asked the question because he knew Wellington loved talking about his truck.

"It's a 1949 Ford F-3."

"Ford made the F series seventy-five years ago?"

"Don't knock it. It's a damn good truck. It's got a 239-cubic-inch V-8. A hundred horsepower. I paid $1,500 for it, rebuilt the engine, did a little bit of body work."

"Sounds like you should of rebuilt the water pump." Norm grinned at his buddy.

Bruce glared back at him. "That's not funny."

"All right, you two." Logan grabbed Wellington's bag. "You guys are staying with me, if that suits you. Zahir and the baby are at her parents' house for a few days, so there's plenty of space."

It was a quick ride from the airport to Logan and Zahir's Porter Street condo.

Wellington let out a low whistle as the elevator opened up into the two-story penthouse. "Nice digs." He walked over to the floor to ceiling windows and looked out over the city.

After Logan had showed them their rooms, he grabbed some beers from the fridge and ushered them into the living room.

"The way I see it, the Qods Force is on some kind of vendetta. We have a pretty good idea from what the Kuwaitis have told us that there was a mole in their organization who tipped the Iranians to Hamid's identity, and in all likelihood mine as well."

"How'd he do that? We went over there on Canadian passports and used aliases." Stoddard had a puzzled frown on his face.

"The first time I went over there to pitch the Iran operation to Thamir and Nayef's uncle, I was in true name. I thought I was being pretty circumspect, but the Iranians must have had the place wired. Someone at the airport must have ID'd me and then reported it to the Iranians."

"They can't follow every foreigner that comes into Kuwait City."

"That's true. But when I thought back on it I remembered that the Kuwaitis picked me up at the airport. The car didn't have official plates, but it might've been a car service they regularly use. If so, it would be pretty simple for the Iranians to track where I was dropped off and figure out the rest of it.

"I'm not sure," he added. "This is just speculation, but I have a theory about what happened. After our operation in Caracas, I'm sure the Iranians started asking questions. If you think about it, the only Venezuelan we dealt with personally was Martínez. I had my doubts about him from the beginning."

"The police captain? It could be him or someone on his surveillance team."

"Right. Either way. So somebody tells the Iranians about the surveillance and they put two and two together. We'll probably never know."

Stoddard rubbed his chin. "We don't know what their capabilities are, but let's just say what you said is true. When that report went back to Tehran they probably started an investigation. If they had any way of accessing photos of Logan Alexander and Logan Campbell, game over."

Logan's mouth was set in a tight line. He jumped up from the sofa and began pacing around the room.

"Easy, Logan. It's not like you're going to have to pull a Salman Rushdie or anything," Wellington joked.

"That's not funny, Brucie. The Iranians are like pit bulls when they go after someone."

Wellington's reference to the famous British author of *The Satanic Verses* was not humorous. There had been a lot of controversy in Muslim circles after Rushdie's book was published in 1988 because they believed that his depiction of the prophet Muhammad was disrespectful.

Emotions had escalated in 1989, and Rushdie was forced into hiding when then Iranian Supreme Leader, Ayatollah Khomeini, issued a *fatwa* ordering the writer's execution. The price on his head had surpassed $3 million by the late 1990s and Rushdie was still in semi-seclusion somewhere in New York City almost twenty years later.

Logan's phone rang. "Hello?"

"Logan? Peter Breen here."

Logan covered the mouthpiece. "It's Detective Breen," he said.

"Hey, Peter. How's it going?"

"Good. Look, there's been a fast-breaking development overnight."

"What's going on?"

"Looks like our man Khorasani's dead."

"What! What happened?"

Breen went on to explain that a couple of early morning joggers had been running across the Powder Point Bridge in Duxbury, when they came across a torn-up section of bridge. They had stopped to check it out and had spotted a vehicle in the water.

"Don't tell me it was Khorasani?"

"We got the Coast Guard and some police divers out there right after the call came in. It's pretty shallow right under the bridge. That's where Duxbury Bay and the Back River come together. There's a channel in there. I'd say no deeper than eight feet.

"Anyway, they pulled him out of the water. He was still strapped in his seat, although the window on the driver's side had shattered. Had the David Foster passport in his jacket. They've taken the body over to the morgue and have contacted his next of kin, the parents. They're on their way over now. It's a pretty grisly look, though. There were a couple of sand tiger sharks feeding on the body when the salvage crew showed up."

"You're sure it was his rental car?"

"We've got a salvage boat down there as we speak, trying to get it out of the water. Initial ID is a 2013 Chrysler 300 four-door sedan. That matches the description of the Hertz car he was driving. We should have it up for the forensics people to go over by this afternoon."

Logan and Breen talked for a couple more minutes. After he'd hung up Logan turned to Stoddard and Wellington.

"Did you get much of that?"

"Bits and pieces. Sounds like they found Khorasani's rental car."

"More than that." Logan relayed his conversation with Detective Breen. "Khorasani's parents are on their way over to ID the body."

"Looks like you're not going to be needing us after all."

"I can't believe that bastard's dead." Logan went into the kitchen and rummaged around the pantry until he found a bag of chips and some salsa. He grabbed three more beers from the fridge and returned to the living room.

As the three friends sat talking about this latest development Logan's phone rang again. Looking at the caller ID he was surprised to see that it was Detective Breen.

"Hello?"

"Logan? Breen again. You're not going to believe this. We just had Khorasani's parents in to ID the body. It was the usual — lots of tears and grief. But then a strange thing happened. Mrs. Khorasani got this bizarre look on her face and said that she didn't think it was Nouri. That it was Armeen!"

"What!"

"Yep. The twins are identical, but apparently twins are rarely completely identical. She said Armeen's right ear was slightly lower on his head than his left. Nouri's were both the same. Based on that description this corpse would be Armeen, not Nouri."

"Can't you ID him through his fingerprints? Those aren't identical, are they?"

"We could, but the sharks beat us to it. We can't get a fingerprint off this body. I'm sending a unit over to Armeen's house right now. That should clear this up."

"They need to be careful, Peter. Khorasani is dangerous. He must be desperate if he did this to his brother, just so he could move around without attracting attention."

When he had hung up he had a grim look on his face. "Things just got a lot more interesting. It looks like Nouri Khorasani may still be out there. We need to find him before he hurts anyone else."

Chapter 35

"I don't like the way this is playing out." It was ten-thirty at night and Logan had just gotten off the phone with Peter Breen. He, Stoddard and Wellington were sitting in the kitchen polishing off their beers and planning their next move.

"Khorasani's parents are adamant that it was Armeen in the car, not Nouri. That's based on just a minute difference in his ears. But even more ominous is the fact that Armeen called his precinct captain the other day with a story about his grandfather dying."

"Let me guess. There is no grandfather." Wellington had a dubious look on his face.

"Oh, there's a grandfather all right. Problem is he's on a cruise to the Bahamas, and didn't know that he was dead."

"So what are you thinking?" Stoddard drained his beer and belched appreciatively.

"I'm thinking this bastard snuck into town, took out his brother so he could assume his identity and then came up with this dead grandfather scenario so that no one would be looking for him for a few days.

"Breen said it's routine to give bereavement leave when a family member dies. No one would think to check into it. Khorasani talked to the precinct captain's secretary when he called in. She's the one who took the call. She didn't notice anything unusual when she talked to him. Of course, she hadn't had that much contact with Armeen. He was a rookie officer and it wasn't like he was spending a lot of time hobnobbing with the front office."

Logan drummed his fingers on the countertop. "I think it's pretty obvious that Armeen is the corpse down in the morgue and Nouri is the one who's out there. We don't know who his target is for certain, but I'm pretty sure I'm at the top of his list.

"We don't know where he is. He's probably holed up somewhere plotting his next move. What we do know is that he's ruthless. Look at the way he murdered Hamid, and his own brother, for God's sake.

"What makes him dangerous, though, is that he seems to have bought into the assassin's creed. His own life doesn't mean anything to him. He'll give it up in an instant for the cause."

"So what do you want to do?" Wellington's face looked impassive, but Logan knew that the Oklahoman's mind was churning.

"I don't like the idea of just sitting around waiting for this bastard to come after us. We need to get going. We don't know what he knows, but just from public records the Iranians probably could have figured out my office address."

"How about your apartment?" Stoddard asked.

"I don't think so. It's in Zahir's name, and I don't think there's any way they could have figured that out. I think some kind of attack aimed at the office is the most likely scenario, although, I don't think we can rule out the possibility of a random public attack either. I mean, take the Macello Restaurant as a case in point."

"He'd have to know something about your patterns or have your phone bugged. I think we need to focus on your office."

Logan walked into the study and returned a minute later with a map of the Fan Pier development and surrounding area. He also had a detailed floor plan for his office building at One Marina Park Drive. The three of them pored over the materials until Stoddard and Wellington were comfortable with the layout. Morning would come soon enough.

* * *

Nouri hurried through the dark streets of Duxbury. He glanced at his watch and saw that it was already four o'clock. The adrenaline rush he had felt when his rental car had plunged over the side of the bridge had subsided. He had to get to Bridgewater before daybreak. He was uncertain how much time his diversion would buy him. A day, maybe two at the most?

If Boston PD was up to its usual standards, they'd do forensics on the body and might even figure out that it was Armeen and not he who had died on Powder Point Bridge. But he knew from his reading on the subject that cases involving identical twins had posed a significant problem for criminologists, particularly when there were no eyewitnesses to the crime or when there were no distinctive markings on either twin's body, like tattoos, to differentiate the criminal from the innocent sibling.

Fingerprints might be a giveaway, he reasoned. He'd thought about doing something with Armeen's prints but that would have been too obvious. No, he would let the Boston PD conduct its investigation, and meanwhile he would hide in plain sight as he carried out the final stage of his plan.

He'd already decided that it was too risky to stay in Armeen's house any longer, though. Nosy neighbors or police investigating the accident in Duxbury might trip him up. He'd dump Armeen's car in the garage, pick up everything that he'd assembled there to carry out the rest of his mission, and then take public transportation into the city. The MBTA had a station on the university campus not too far from where Armeen lived.

Before going into the city he would stage his operation from the safehouse he'd found two days ago. He'd taken the studio apartment in Quincy, paying cash for the short-term rental. The Newbury Avenue address was on the rail line into Boston, making it easy for him to move about. He had selected the large, nondescript brick building with multiple entrances because he was unlikely to attract attention coming and going and because the on-site manager had agreed to do a cash deal, no questions asked.

Day was breaking as he pulled into Armeen's driveway. He parked the car in the garage and entered the house. He decided to shower before packing his bag and catching the train. His body ached and the lack of sleep was beginning to take its toll. He needed to remain sharp.

Thirty minutes later he was dressed in casual clothes, compliments of Armeen. In his bag he had placed a complete Boston PD uniform – tunic, trousers, cap, shoes and utility belt. He'd also packed Armeen's handcuffs, nightstick and the standard issue Glock 17 semiautomatic pistol. He had noted with approval that Armeen used thirty-three-round high-capacity magazines. There were several of these and extra cases of shells in the gun safe. He added those to the bag.

When he was finished he locked the door and walked to the MBTA stop. There was a train scheduled for a few minutes after seven. At this hour there were a number of commuters milling around the station, sipping their Starbucks coffees, their noses in newspapers. Nouri tensed when he saw two transit police officers walking down the platform, but they were immersed in conversation and did not give him a second glance.

The train arrived on time and Nouri boarded, choosing a seat near the middle of the car. The thirty-minute ride to Quincy passed quickly and without incident. It was only a two-minute walk from the East Squantum Street and Newbury Avenue Station to his hideaway.

There was no one in the elevator or in the fifth floor hallway when he entered the building. He set his bag down outside the apartment and jiggled the key in the lock. Walking inside he switched on a light and looked around with approval. This was going to work out really well.

Nouri unpacked his bag and laid everything out on the bed. He was methodical in his actions, but inside he was beginning to feel that sense of anticipation that invariably enveloped him at the beginning of a mission.

He dressed with attention to detail. Strapping on the utility belt, he adjusted the nightstick and pistol on his hips and then surveyed himself in the mirror. Staring back at him was one of Boston's finest.

Nouri sat down and went over his targeting package one more time. The familiar face of Logan Alexander stared back at him from the profile that Tehran had forwarded two days ago.

I'm not sure what your game is, Mr. Alexander, he thought with an ominous look on his face, but you're going down. He adjusted his hat, smoothed his blouse and gave himself one final going over before picking up his bag and leaving the apartment.

* * *

Nouri transferred to the Silver Line at South Station. As he hurried through the Great Room, he blended in with the morning commuter crowd. There was a time when South Station had been the largest and one of the busiest train stations in the world. It still retained an affluent air dating back to when it was first constructed in the 19th century.

He only had to wait a couple of minutes for his train. He boarded but remained standing as he was only going one stop. Getting out at Courthouse Station, Nouri began the short walk to Fan Pier. It was seven-forty-five.

* * *

Alicia had arrived at Alexander Maritime early. Logan's project on the Mark V had wrapped up sooner than he had expected because of the Navy's decision to put the Mark V 1, the Mako, into their inventory ahead of schedule. They weren't really dropping the Mark V completely, but for all intents and purposes they were moving forward with the modified vessel.

Later in the week Logan would be bidding on a new project with Sperry/Johnson Maritime. As the primary contractors they had a multi-million-dollar contract with the Navy to develop a new design for submarine hatches, the type used by divers when they are locked out and isolated before leaving a submerged sub. The steel hatches that had been in use for decades were prone to corrosion, so the Navy was looking to replace them with composite based enclosures.

Alicia was working at her desk when she noticed a Boston PD patrolman coming through the front entrance.

"May I help you?"

"Yes, I'm Officer Shannon. I'm looking for Mr. Alexander."

"He isn't in yet, but I expect him momentarily. Is there anything I can help you with?"

"It has to do with the department's investigation into the murder of his friend, Hamid Al Subaie. We believe the murder suspect is on the loose in the area, and Mr. Alexander's safety may be in jeopardy. I've been sent over to provide security here until the suspect has been apprehended or we feel that he no longer presents a threat."

Alicia's hand went up to her mouth. "Oh, my God. Do you think he's going to come here? Mr. Alexander should be here any minute. Let me call him on his cell to let him know that you're here. Please make yourself comfortable."

As she reached for the phone, Alicia looked up and found herself staring into the barrel of Patrolman Shannon's pistol.

"Put the phone down," he ordered.

"But —"

"I mean it. Now. Do what I say and you won't get hurt."

Shannon's polite demeanor had changed. His tone was cold as he waved the gun in front of her.

Alicia's face drained of all color. She carefully replaced the phone in its cradle and looked at the menacing figure before her.

"What is this? What do you want?"

"This doesn't concern you. Just do what I tell you and you won't get hurt."

*   *   *

Logan walked into the office a few minutes later. Alicia must have arrived early because the door to the suite was unlocked, but she wasn't at her desk. Then he remembered that she had planned to come in early to work on the Sperry/Johnson Maritime proposal. Maybe she'd stepped out for a minute to make a coffee run.

As he entered his office he was surprised to see Alicia sitting at his desk. She had a terrified look on her face.

"What?"

"Ah, Mr. Alexander."

Startled, Logan looked to his right and saw a Boston PD officer standing with a Glock pistol trained on him.

"What's this all about? Who are you?"

"Officer Shannon," Alicia blurted out. "He said he was here to provide security for the office because they believe Nouri Khorasani may be looking for you."

"No, I think it's safe to say that Mr. Khorasani has found you, Mr. Alexander." As Shannon uttered these words he reached up and peeled a rubber mask off of his face to reveal the features of the Qods Force killer.

Alicia gasped when she recognized Nouri from the photos she had studied during the Caracas operation. The mask he had been wearing was so lifelike that she hadn't realized he was wearing a disguise.

"What do you want, Khorasani?" Logan's voice was steely and his mind was racing as he considered their predicament.

"We have some unfinished business, Mr. Alexander. You didn't really think you could just waltz into Iran, blow up a bunch of shit and get away with it, did you?

"And then you had the nerve to take your story to the press. Did you think we'd just sit back and take it on the chin without any kind of response? America's been sticking it to us for decades, ever since your puppet the Shah got forced out. We'll see who gets the last laugh this time. Your buddy Hamid was the first to pay the price and you're next."

"You're not going to get away with this, Nouri. The police know all about Armeen. You'll never get out of here. Turn yourself in."

Nouri uttered a mirthless laugh. "You've got it wrong. You're the one who's not getting out of here. When I'm finished with you, I'm walking out that door."

"What happened to you, Nouri? Do you hate this country so much?"

"Shut up!" The hatred in his voice was palpable. As he took aim with the Glock, the closet door to his left swung open and Norm Stoddard barged out.

"Drop it," he ordered.

Stoddard didn't have a clear shot because Alicia was in his line of fire. He pulled back behind the door as the Qods Force assassin unleashed a volley in his direction.

Nouri grabbed Alicia with his free hand and pulled her close. Logan had dropped down to the floor and rolled behind a sofa opposite the desk. Nouri began firing rounds into the sofa, staccato bursts shattering the quiet. Stoddard had dropped to one knee and taken cover behind the door frame.

Nouri inserted a fresh magazine clip in one fluid motion and fanned his pistol from left to right.

Alicia let out a shriek as Nouri clenched her tighter to him. "Shut up, bitch," he shouted.

He continued to alternate firing rounds into the sofa and in the direction of where he had seen Norm Stoddard. He wasn't too worried. The struggling woman in his grasp was beginning to get on his nerves though so he pulled her closer to him, reasoning that his two opponents would hold fire lest they injure her.

"Shut the fuck up," he hissed in her ear. "I swear to God, if you don't settle down I'm going to put a bullet in your ear."

Alicia whimpered but struggled to control her fears.

Nouri was beginning to worry that all this noise would alert people in neighboring offices. It was just a matter of time before someone called it in.

Clutching Alicia to him he called out. "Come out now, Alexander. Your friend too. Throw out your weapons by the count of three or I'll shoot her!

"One, two…"

Nouri saw a slight movement in the ceiling to his left and instinctively ducked as the blast of a round whizzed past him and shattered the window behind him. Taking aim he fired at the ceiling tile that had moved and was rewarded with a howl from above.

As he took aim on the spot, he unconsciously loosened his grip on Alicia, who turned and drove a pair of scissors into his thigh.

Nouri gasped in pain, and backhanded Alicia in the face, knocking her down. As he prepared to put a round into her head, Wellington fired another shot from the ceiling, this time catching Nouri in the shoulder, spinning him around.

The Glock flew out of his hand, sliding along the floor past the desk. He dove for it but it was beyond his reach. Grasping for Alicia, he pulled her limp body to him and scrambled to his feet. Counting, he figured there were three shooters in the room.

"It's over, Nouri. Come out with your hands in plain sight and you won't be hurt. Give us the girl. Now!"

Nouri backed up, grasping Alicia's inert form close to his body. His shoulder throbbed, and his head was killing him. His eyes began to blur and he realized that he had lost quite a bit of blood. He couldn't risk passing out.

"It's not over, Alexander. It will never be over until you die." He pushed Alicia away from him, and as a hail of gunshots thudded into his body, he turned and dove out of the shattered glass window into the abyss.

Logan rushed over to where Alicia lay, curled up on the floor. Luckily she had not been hit in the hail of gunfire. He looked up as he heard groaning from the ceiling and saw Wellington's face grimacing in pain.

"Bastard almost got lucky. He got me in my right hand. I had to switch hands to shoot. Never was a very good leftie." He grimaced as he clambered out of his hiding place in the ceiling.

Stoddard walked over to the window and looked out. "I can't believe that freak went out the window."

Logan turned away from Alicia and looked out. He could barely make out the crumpled figure lying on the ground sixteen floors below. A crowd had begun to gather, and the sound of emergency vehicles wafted up through the shattered glass.

Alicia was beginning to revive, and Logan helped her to her feet and then led her over to the sofa where she sat in shock. He pulled out his cell phone and made three calls. The first was a 911 call requesting an ambulance for Wellington and Alicia.

The second was to Peter Breen. "Peter? Logan Alexander here." Logan gave the detective a brief rundown on the events of the last hour. As he was talking, he looked out towards the entrance and could see Manuel, framing the doorway. The young concierge had a troubled look on his face as he surveyed the wreckage.

"Whoa, Mr. A. You all right?

Logan held up his hand to signal that he would be with him as soon as he got off the phone.

"We heard the calls come in, Logan. When I heard the address my first thought was this was Khorasani. I've got three squad cars and a SWAT team responding even as we speak. Did anybody get hurt?"

"One of my buddies who was visiting got caught in the crossfire. And my secretary's pretty shaken up. Khorasani had his hands on her and was threatening to kill her. Khorasani's the only fatality." They talked for a couple of minutes and then hung up.

Miguel walked over to where Logan was sitting. "Man, Mr. A. This is unreal. Who was this guy?"

Logan gave him the *Reader's Digest* version of events and asked him to get somebody up to clean up the mess after the police had done their forensics work.

The rest of the morning flew by as EMT personnel tended to Alicia and Wellington, and Boston PD personnel worked the crime scene and took statements.

Before sitting down with them Logan called Zahir. "It's over, sweetheart. Khorasani's dead." He filled her in on the events of the morning.

"Oh, Logan." Her voice was strained as the realization of how close Logan had come to being killed hit her. "I'm coming home as soon as I can."

Logan didn't argue with her. He was smiling at the thought of seeing Zahir and Cooper as he set the phone down.

Chapter 36

A week had flown by since the showdown at Fan Pier. Logan looked around the apartment where family and friends had gathered for a muted celebratory dinner to mark the occasion.

Nayef had risen to propose a toast. His beautiful wife, Nisreen, was seated beside him. Her soft face still bore the lines of grief so cruelly etched there by Nouri Khorasani, but she looked up as her husband spoke.

"Logan, our family, indeed our country, owes you a debt of gratitude that we will never be able to repay. You assumed tremendous personal risk when you took on this problem to the point that you and your own family's lives were in danger.

"While nothing will bring back Hamid..." Nayef's voice caught as he spoke his son's name, but then gathered strength as he continued, "we can take consolation in the fact that he led a purposeful life dedicated to the security of Kuwait. Nisreen and I are very proud of what he did. We are pleased to announce tonight that we have reached out to Harvard University and are endowing a chair at the university. It will be named in his honor. The Hamid Al Subaie Chair for Counterterrorism Studies."

Logan and the others clapped as Nayef took his seat. Logan stole a look at Zahir, who had a sliver of a smile on her face as she returned his gaze. He felt a surge of emotion as he shared the moment with her.

He looked away and was surprised to see Millie and Ryan in animated discussion. Millie put down her napkin and catching Logan's eye, inclined her head to one side. She rose from the table and walked into the living room.

Logan followed her there and caught up with her by the floor-to-ceiling windows looking out over the city.

"What was that all about?"

"Ryan and I had a visit at home this morning from someone who said he was from the Department of Defense. He was asking a bunch of questions about you, Logan. He told us not to say anything to you about it but I told Ryan I was going to anyway. That's what we were arguing about."

"Could have to do with my security clearances. I'm bidding on a classified DOD project."

"I didn't get the feeling it was about that. They were asking about past international travel and your foreign contacts. They specifically asked about the Kuwaitis."

Logan raised an eyebrow in surprise. Maybe Breen had talked to them.

"Obviously I didn't lie. I told them about my work with Kuwait and that you had met Nayef through me. I knew they could track your travel to Kuwait, so I told him that you had gone there a year ago, and I assumed it had something to do with the Al Subaies, although I didn't know anything else." She looked worried. "Do you think you're in trouble?"

"I don't know. The Feds may have stumbled across something with all the attention the Khorasani case has been getting. I guess I'll just have to wait and see."

After their guests had left, Logan mentioned his conversation with Millie to Zahir.

"Are you worried?" she asked.

"No, we didn't break any U.S. laws, but if the Feds found out about our involvement and didn't like it, they could make it hard for me to work on federal contracts. I don't know if they would go so far as to take away my security clearance." Logan scrunched up his face as he puzzled through the question, but then dismissed it and filed it away.

The next several weeks flew by as Logan immersed himself in the details of the Sperry/Johnson contract. He had put the whole DOD issue behind him until one morning in November when he arrived at work and found a muscular middle-aged man waiting in the outer office.

He rose when Logan walked in and introduced himself as William Channing Jr. from Washington.

Logan assessed Channing with a practiced eye. The smooth demeanor and Brooks Brothers suit did little to conceal the confident air of authority exuding from the man, whose muscles rippled beneath his suit. His handshake was crushing and his eyes were unblinking as he followed Logan into his office.

"Alicia, please hold all calls until Mr. Channing and I have finished our business." He turned to the visitor. Would you like a coffee or something else to drink?"

"No, thank you, Mr. Alexander. I'm fine."

When Logan closed the door, the government man pulled a heavy file from his briefcase and held it briefly on his lap as he fixed a steady gaze on Logan. He waited for just a moment before beginning.

"You've been quite busy, Mr. Alexander."

"I'm not sure what you mean." Logan's mind raced as he tried to figure out what Channing's angle was. Was he here to bust him? Lecture him? Well, he'd have to work for it. Logan Alexander wasn't one to roll over for anybody.

Channing set the bulky file down delicately before Logan, nodding his head in approbation. "You'll find it all in here, I believe."

Logan gave him a wary look and opened the folder. Twenty minutes later he looked up. "Who put this together?"

"Oh, there are bits and pieces from all over the place, but it was really a team of counterterrorism analysts at CIA that figured out what you pulled off. Very impressive." Channing went on to give a detailed account of how agency analysts had pulled together all source data to reach the conclusion that former Navy SEAL Logan Alexander had been the driving force behind the attack on Iran's IED facility at Bandar Deylam almost a year ago.

Channing sat back in his seat and sized up the former SEAL.

Inwardly Logan squirmed under Channing's scrutiny. If the government was here to make an example of him over the attack on Bandar Deylam, why this charade? Was Channing some sadistic bastard who liked to watch his victims squirm?

Logan felt mounting anger. He didn't have anything to apologize for. He knew that he'd done the right thing. Something the government wasn't up to tackling.

He set his mouth and gave Channing a defiant stare. "So what happens now? Is the government going to pull my clearances?"

Channing looked confused, but then smiled. "Ah, you misunderstand my intentions, Mr. Alexander. I'm sorry if I haven't made myself clear. You see, we quite admire what you did in Bandar Deylam, and everything since then. In fact, I believe it's a model for how we might take care of some nasty problems that we've been having elsewhere.

"No, Mr. Alexander, I'm not here to revoke your security clearance. Quite the contrary. I'm here to seek your assistance and offer collaboration."

Pulling another folder from his briefcase he placed it on Logan's desk.

"You see, we've been having this little problem with China." His eyes gleamed and his mouth was set in a firm line as he probed deep into Logan's eyes. Then he stood and strolled out of the room, calling back over his shoulder, "We'll be in touch, Mr. Alexander. We'll be in touch."

THE END

CPSIA information can be obtained at www.ICGtesting.com
Printed in the USA
LVOW13s0216301013

359077LV00002B/2/P